Praise for Louise Dean and *Becoming Strangers*
Winner of the Betty Trask Prize 2004

'I didn't know whether to laugh or cry. In the end, I was so uplifted,
I did both'
Julie Myerson

'Both page-turning and heartbreaking, one of the books of the year'
Independent

'Dean has a deliciously lucid and seemingly effortless style, as well as
the gift of being able to write about each character from the inside.
An exceptionally enjoyable book'
Daily Mail

'The best book in its genre that I have read in a long time'
Jenni Murray, *Woman's Hour*

'Both heartbreaking and thrilling. Dean deserves a huge readership'
The Times

'All her characters are perfectly conceived, their inner dialogues spot
on, her observations so sharp they make you wince'
Time Out

'It's quite hard to put into words the special qualities of this novel,
although you feel these at once when you begin to read it. A very
accomplished piece of writing'
Helen Dunmore

Also by Louise Dean

Becoming Strangers

This Human Season

LOUISE DEAN

Scribner

First published in Great Britain by Scribner, 2005
This paperback edition published by Scribner, 2006
An imprint of Simon and Schuster UK Ltd
A CBS COMPANY

3 5 7 9 10 8 6 4 2

Simon and Schuster UK Ltd
Africa house
64–78 Kingsway
London WC2B 6AH

www.simonsays.co.uk

Simon & Schuster Australia
Sydney

A CIP catalogue record for this book is available from the British Library

ISBN: 0–7432–4002–2
EAN: 9780743240024

Typeset by M Rules
Printed and bound in Great Britain by
Cox & Wyman Ltd, Reading, Berks

For my own boys Jules and Cassien and
for my daughter Elsa Rose.

'Therein is the whole business of man's life; to seek out and save in his soul that which is perishing.'

Tolstoy: The Gospel in Brief – Luke 19:9

November and December
1979

1

When the soldiers came the time before, the father went off with them. He had the same name as his son, so he went in his place. After a few days he was released. Their son was far away by then, down south.

This time the son was in prison and they didn't want the father. So what could the father do, except stand in the front room, in his underpants, hands in the sagging pockets of his cardigan, watching the soldiers moving back and forth between the front and back doors of his home.

He was trying to think of something to say. His children and his wife were sat about in their nightclothes; they weren't looking at him.

'Yous think you know it all,' was what he'd told them up at Castlereagh, the interrogation centre, when they'd come to realize their mistake. The first day they'd had him hands against the wall, legs apart and when his knees weakened they'd shouted at him or kicked him. He'd not had anything he could tell them. Nor had he defied them. For two days they'd stopped him from sleeping, told him to sweep the hallway and when he'd sat down, they'd emptied out the bucket again and gone kicking the dust, cigarette butts, apple cores, and empty bleach bottles down along the corridor. Then they'd handed him back the broom. They let him go first thing on the third morning.

He'd got off lightly, he knew it, when he stepped outside, turned his collar up and set off, the sky all of one colour, a licked pale grey. It was a damp morning to come home on, and no one was about. He'd had to wait for the dinnertime session for the telling.

His son, Sean, had been inside Long Kesh for a month now. These men knew that. They were there because of the boy, because of where they lived, because they had another son and because they were Catholic.

There was a stack of rifles on the living room floor. 'Don't you be touching those,' he said to his children in a low voice with a light whistle in it, the air from the open front door catching on his back teeth. 'They leave them there on purpose to see what the kids know.'

From upstairs came the sound of a door being forced, once, twice, and through. His wife shook her head.

'It's true,' said her husband. 'They do.'

The electric light was impotent, the daylight had taken over and so his wife got up to switch it off and pull back the curtains that gave on to their scrap of back garden – some grass, bare patches, a washing line with a pair of pants on it, legs sewn to hold pegs. To the right-hand side of the line, within the creosote armpit of a shed, was a gap that went through to the next street. The last time, she'd had a go at the soldiers when they came in, she'd jumped up to stall them, to make sure her son got away through that gap. She'd kept them then at the front door, offered them her husband herself. 'If it's Sean you're after, well here he is.' And sure enough they looked at the man in his jumper and Y-fronts and agreed he'd do. She, herself, had had him by one of his sleeves, shaking it.

'Who gave you permission to come in my house?' she said now.

'We've got all the permission we need,' said one, loafing by the sideboard, looking at her ornaments.

'You've got the guns is all.'

'We're not the only ones. Show us where you keep yours and we'll be away.'

'Liam, show the man your water pistol.'

Upstairs, they were crow-barring the floorboards, emptying drawers and cupboards. There wasn't a house in Ballymurphy that hadn't been pulled apart by the British Army. The soldier at the sideboard was going through those drawers, taking out chequebooks and bills, newspaper cuttings and photos. He left the drawers open, looked again, then picked up a black rubber bullet that was on the top shelf. It was about three inches long and an inch wide.

'Souvenir?' he asked her.

'Is it one of yours?' she asked. 'One just like that was fired into the face of my neighbour's boy. Fifteen years old. His mother's only son and now he can't even feed himself.' One of the soldier's boots came through the ceiling into the living room and a shower of brown dust came shooting down. 'Jesus, Joseph and Mary! And what if this was your own mother's home?'

'My mother didn't raise a terrorist,' said the soldier by the door to the hallway, leaning back, looking casual. He was tall, his back was straight, his eyes blue. He was in his twenties, smart in his uniform, his beret poised. There was a light white powder in the air. When her husband made to go into the kitchen, the soldier told him to sit down.

Those who'd been upstairs came clattering down the narrow stairway, one after the other until most of them were in the front room, filling it entirely, with two more in the hall. A shorter man stood in the doorway with his hands up above his head holding on to the frame.

'Clear, Sarge,' he said to the soldier at the sideboard.

This man, their sergeant, took a last look around the living room, taking in the vases and knick-knacks on the sideboard and mantelpiece, a small pale blue Madonna, a large conch sea shell, a few dark-coloured glass vases with gilt lettering, place names, a maple-leaf shaped piece of wood with 'Canada' carved on to it.

'You've got a nice home, Mrs,' he said. 'One of the cleanest I've been in anyway. Any chance of a cup of tea for the lads?'

'Go fuck yourselves,' she said.

Her younger son stood up beside her, the shoulders of his small frame rose and fell; with his mouth open, he was like a baby bird wanting to be fed.

'Starting him off young, are you?' said the sergeant. 'That's what you call infantry, that is.' He threw a look at the handsome soldier.

Kathleen pointed towards the door.

'Out, yous!'

They were in no rush. The sergeant took another look around, clapped his hands together, strolled across to the stairwell and gave the order. His men started to move themselves, gather the guns. The last one out was the handsome soldier, who looked up at the framed poster of the Proclamation of the Irish Republic on his way and tutted. He tipped the barrel of his rifle at the wife, touching her very lightly at her throat, where her dressing gown crossed. 'I bet you were one of them who used to be nice to us, once.'

Her cheeks flushed, Kathleen went to the front door to close it after them. She saw that the porch light had been smashed in. 'Ach for God's sake!' she called out, and started to shove the jarred door with fury and hurt.

'Harassment, that's all it is,' said her husband, coming up behind her, his voice growing as they watched the men going down the path and through the front gate. 'To keep us in our place . . .'

'And what are you going to do about it?' she said, turning to him.

He had a moment to look at her, her face backing into the new day-light, her neck stretching, a space between utterances, and he said nothing, paused between difficult things.

And then she was moving. 'Go up and get yourselves dressed,' she yelled at the children. 'Can't any of you do anything without me telling you?'

'Why did they come round here, Mummy?' said Aine, a brown enve-lope and a pen in her hands; she'd been sitting drawing pictures while the soldiers were there.

'Will you up and get yourself dressed, Aine, please. Don't make me say it again.'

'They'll be back again soon enough anyway.'

Upstairs, her brother, Liam, was taking two empty jam jars out from under his bed. 'You've to go in one, and I'll go in the other,' he told his sister.

'I can fill them both,' said the girl, 'I'm bursting now.'

'Just do the one.'

She went off towards the bathroom. Then she was back. 'What's it for, Liam?'

'For when the Brits come along by the side window, down the alley-way,' he said, pushing the cardboard box back under his bed.

Hearing her daughter fumbling with the bathroom lock the mother called up the stairs. 'For God's sake. No one's coming in to watch you peeing, Aine. We've got a television.'

The father was standing near the kitchen with his hands out, dripping water, shaking them just a little, waiting for his wife to show him the dishcloth.

Kathleen was bent in front of the television, tending to it. In her thin nightdress, her body was long, spare curves. The drone of the TV made a sudden acceleration, jumping from hum to chatter. The picture filled the screen; the outside world sprang.

2

As dawn comes on, a man is in his car with his back to the night, hunched over his own warmth, driving towards the daylight. The countryside is unfolding as a series of surprises that are much the same, as it does in Northern Ireland. You can see neither ahead of you nor behind; at each hilltop the car rolls into a rural scene of grazing cows and farmhouses. Everywhere the grass is unbearably green, the brushwood of wintertime is auburn, the wet grey of the road surface is like dark silk. The moon is ahead of the man's car, low and translucent and beneath it the sky is a band of pink with clouds like long bruises.

John Dunn was on 'early unlock' and he needed to report into Her Majesty's Prison, The Maze, just before eight. When he left home in the dark, an hour earlier, he stalled at the traffic lights and a car with three men inside had moved out from behind him. As it passed by, the passenger window was wound down and a man shouted out at him, just some random abuse.

His heart beat hard as he watched the car move off; by the time he had gathered himself the light was red again.

'The moment you've put that uniform on, you are a target.' He'd done four weeks' training as a prison officer at the college, Millisle, where they'd impressed upon him the importance of presentation, discipline, punctuality. The instructing officer had come out on to the square when they arrived, seen them standing around with their bags and cases, ready for the four week training course and screamed at them to fall in; one fellow had said, 'Fuck this,' got back into his small brown Austin Marina

and gone. The car had made a screeching noise as it took to the coastal road and the rest of them had exchanged looks, laughed.

'You make sure you're smart at all times,' their training officer had said and instructed them to soap the creases of their trousers and to use hot teaspoons on their black boots. A few of them were like him, ex-soldiers, they were used to the taking-the-orders crap. The others were more like the man in the Marina.

At the Maze the week before, for a briefing session, he was told to forget everything he'd learnt at Millisle. 'This place is a cesspit,' the senior officer said.

The site of the prison, Long Kesh, was a desperate place, squat and dreary, a wide, flat area of land, contained by high-wire fencing, punctuated by watch-towers. In the staff car-park he drove across to the furthest corner, careful not to park in what might be someone else's spot.

With his feet churning progress on the gravel and the simple impetus of every step, he felt glad to be starting a new job that was well paid and he was pleased even with the feeling of the rain about to fall, ominous and close, like a wet towel around his neck.

The locker rooms were busy. Tin doors slamming, the growl of abuse and easy laughter. He changed into his uniform and went down through what was something like an abandoned fairground: lights, dogs, soldiers, jerry-built huts, mobile homes, caravans.

He had a long wait in the damp cold outside the tally lodge, queuing with his fellow officers. It was like being back in the army with all the chat, the name-calling, the jostling: the pecking order.

'Tally number 1022. Dunn, John, Sir, on the white sheet,' he said, presenting his pass at the window. The white sheet gave him his next two weeks of supervised duties, before he'd be allowed keys. He waited for his instructions; the British soldier of twenty-two years standing, and the new prison officer in Northern Ireland. He was evidently the former, with a not-quite-London accent and unfashionably short hair.

The duty officer was turning the pen in his mouth and breathing through his nose as he studied the lists. Dunn could smell that he had a cold, his breath was fruited, rank. He heard the anxiety of a prison officer behind him, saying loud enough, 'Please God I'm not on a fucking grille outside, let it be inside a block.'

After a moment, Dunn said to the man behind him. 'Where were you last week?'

'Ask yer girl,' the man replied, and behind him three or four men fell about laughing.

'That's what they call the prison catch-phrase,' the duty officer said. He was picking up granules of sugar from around three fruit pastilles on his open book, his fingertip wetted, making dirty marks on the page. He pushed back his cap, picked up his biro and rubbed his forehead with the blunt end then slapped his notes.

'There's your wee name now. You're on the get-rich-quick scheme, Mr Dunn.'

'I don't follow, Sir.'

'Working on the protest blocks.'

'Yes, that's right, Sir.'

'Aye. Well, Dunn, have I got the H block for you. Bolton's welfare programme! Nice people. Shame about the shit.'

John Dunn went off, pass in hand, his shoulders stiff, with the duty officer calling out after him, 'I see you've dressed for the occasion!'

He went behind the administration building, and took a long walk around the H block to which he'd been assigned. He had seen pictures of the H blocks on the news the night before; there was an item on the pace of their construction.

Ahead of him was the site for the last two; stacks of materials, dumpers, a single tree like a flag planted on the moon. Sealed off beyond the fence – like something from a different era, or the set of a film – were the nissen huts of Long Kesh's former RAF camp, active but quiet, the prison for terrorists captured before 1976.

John Dunn showed his pass and was admitted through two grilles into the front yard. Ahead of him was a single storey, office-type building, low and slit-eyed, with two arms reaching forwards.

Walking up to the block door, he looked left and right, at the prisoners' cell windows. The bars and spaces of the window were of equal width, a vertically striped space. He caught sight of a prisoner at his window. Dunn couldn't see the whole face, just as from the man's sideways movements he could tell that a person inside couldn't see a whole view. He saw the man's hand extend across the deep ledge, palm upwards, as if weighing the air. There was no glass to the window.

A step further and the smell of the place hit him. It was human excrement, a thick and knowing stench. It got stronger as he got closer and when the front door was opened, it was overpowering.

Dunn was let through two further grilles to enter 'the circle' – the rectangular administration area of the block, named after the rounded area of the Victorian model. The senior officer stood there with a row of five men in front of him. He was finishing up giving them their detail and there was a degree of teasing going on, for the senior officer was repeating himself with heavy emphasis, and the officers looked obliged to laugh again.

Dunn wasn't feeling humorous. The smell had taken him over completely and he could neither think, hear, nor talk. He was straight-faced, earnest to the point of grief-stricken when the senior officer greeted him.

'Well cheer up now, Mr Dunn,' said the big man, veined-cheeked, swollen-eyed, with a mouth that was merely a companion to his volatile moustache. 'I'm Senior Officer Campbell. I see you're an ex-army man like myself. I'll expect you to know what you're about. One rule here, watch yourself. The walls have ears so take care what you say when the Provies are about. Now get yourself a cup of something in the mess.'

Campbell opened the door to the officers' mess and nodded at the two officers sat at the table. 'This here is John Dunn, fellas. These two young men before you are Officer Higgins and Officer Harding. Better known as Shandy and Frig. I'll leave laughing boy with you then,' he said, going out. 'Mind you keep it down now, wouldn't want to wake Principal Officer.'

The one called Frig went back to reading aloud from the paper. '"... *screws can rest assured that they will remain targets and will continue to die while they implement the barbaric penal policies of the Northern Ireland office and the British government."* A statement from Sinn Fein. There you go Mr Dunn,' he said. 'Welcome aboard HMS Maze! First they built the *Titanic*, then they built the Maze.'

The man further away, Shandy, put down his knife and fork. There was egg down the handle of the knife and brown sauce in the corners of his mouth. He had soft shoulders and maudlin eyes and he sat back chewing at the new officer.

'You see, the fact is we're all in the same boat. Of course it's more what you call a sinking ship.' Frig offered Dunn his hand. He was slight with fair hair, thin at the front, long at the sides, with a Birmingham accent. His jacket was on the back of the chair. 'Anyway, I don't give a frig, me, that's how I got the name.'

Dunn still had the excrement very much in mind. He looked over at the frying pan on the ring, saw the burnt petticoat tail of the egg white around the sides of it. Shandy's jaw was moving, regular as a cement mixer, and even when he took a drink of his tea, it turned, folding the liquid in with the rest.

'Don't you listen to the wee man. He loves this job. He'd do it even if they didn't pay him.' He took an open-mouthed breath, his jaw askew, indicated a chair. 'You should grow your hair, Mr Dunn. What do they call you? John? Johnno? Welcome to the Maze,' he looked down at his plate, assessed it with dissatisfaction and lay down his cutlery.

'Did you have a long drive in then John?' asked Frig, a little nervy in his nonchalance.

'East Belfast.' Dunn said, sitting. The pair of them relaxed visibly.

'Ach well there now in that case,' Shandy's voice rolled forth like a welcome mat, 'you're one of us then, even if you are a Brit. Your man Frig here, he's neither fish nor fowl. He's a mercenary like, he's here for the beer money, no family, next to no friends, and he doesn't give a fuck about this place. He could be shovelling shit . . .'

'I do shovel shit,' said Frig, indicating the Wellington boots on his lower legs. 'Every bloody day.'

'Can you buy cigarettes round here?' asked Dunn. The table was white, the walls were a sickening gloss white, even the floor was white. There were no pictures or notices, the strip lighting glimmered.

'Have one,' said Frig, tossing one across. 'There's a machine in Clean Jim's, we'll be heading down there later. You get used to the smell of shit but it takes a few days. I don't even notice it now. It's like working on a farm or something. It's amazing what you get used to. Right Shandy mate?'

Dunn leant forward to receive the light Frig offered him. He took a drag of dirt and relief. 'Cheers.'

The door opened. A prisoner in overalls, an orderly, came in and picked up a couple of breakfast plates and took them to the sink.

'Aye and about fucking time,' said Shandy.

'About ye, gents, any news from the outside worth the having?'

'You'd already know it if there was,' said Shandy.

The orderly at the sink shrugged, rolled his sleeves up and stood back from the spluttering tap. He set about the washing up.

'Baxter's what you call an ODC, an ordinary decent criminal,' said Frig.

Baxter cast a glance behind him at the two mugs on the table. At the same time, he threw a look at the new prison officer. Then he moved almost imperceptibly, quickly, and took up the cups while they were talking. Dunn saw the tattoos on the back of his neck and over his forearms.

'He killed some bloke – a bar brawl, wasn't it?'

'He lived. Broken collarbone,' put in Baxter.

'He wasn't a Catholic, was he Bax? It wasn't because he was a Taig, was it now?' said Shandy.

'They tried to claim him, the loyalist block,' Frig explained. 'But Baxter's too ordinary and decent for sectarian hate, he'll have a go at anyone, never mind his religion or his skin colour. He's what you call open-minded. Make the man a cuppa, Bax, will you?'

'No need. I'll make it myself,' said Dunn, taking a drag and then laying the cigarette down in the ashtray.

Baxter moved to stand between Dunn and the kettle. He had a

regularity of features and a bonhomie that made him seem familiar. Dunn was tall, six-foot two. His own eyes, he knew, were unfriendly.

'How do you take it? Milk and sugar?'

'Thank you.'

'Well now that I come to think of it, soldier-boy,' Shandy went on, looking at Dunn but never losing sight of Frig. 'You with your squaddie haircut there, you might just take my spot on the hit list.' He laughed. 'I'll have to buy you a beer for that John Dunn.'

Baxter put the cup down in front of Dunn with care. Shandy removed something from his teeth that he wiped on to his trousers. 'Frig was it you on the bacon today?'

'Yup.'

'I might have bloody known, it was a quare stringy piece of shite. I'm doing the lads a dinner this week Mr Dunn. I make a fantastic spaghetti bolognese. We have a wee drink with it and a game of cards; it makes for a very pleasant evening.'

Shandy stood up and stretched himself, the keys at his trouser belt fell and swung. He looked out of the window across the yard. 'Ah, fuck,' he said. He checked his watch. 'We might as well get on with the unlock. Come on then, Dunn, that way you'll get a chance to meet our guests.'

Dunn looked down at the abandoned plate on the table, with its marks on it like it had been used for painting, saw Baxter put his thumb in the side of the red and move behind and away.

At the door, Shandy was hat on, jacket on, adjusting his waistband.

'Ready then?'

3

'I took three packets in the Kesh with me yesterday afternoon, gave them all out, and when I got out I hadn't even the one for myself to smoke.'

Kathleen gave Father Pearse a cup of tea and offered him a cigarette from her pack. He fumbled as he tried to take one. She took it out herself, lit it between her lips and handed it to him.

'We had the Brits in this morning. My first thought was to get Sean out the back door.'

Her living room was a mess. Where the plaster had come through and hit the floor, there was grey dust in the pile of the carpet, and the ceiling was still gaping, with bits falling every time one of them was walking upstairs. She closed the exercise book next to her; she'd been working backwards and forwards through their money problems when the priest called in.

'I haven't had a chance to get any fags today. Been up at the Royal.' The priest was shaking, cigarette ash falling into a fortunately-placed dustpan, settling on top of bits of white plaster.

'You're a bag of nerves, Father,' said Kathleen. She was thinking, '*His pay covers the rent at eight pound and leaves us forty-two pound for bills and food, which is just over ten pound a week and I can carry on doing part time at the butcher's but I might still have to take out a loan from the Ballymurphy Credit Union . . .*'

'No, I'm grand. I like my days up at the hospital. They all know me there now and I get a good dinner in the canteen at staff price.'

She placed the packet on the arm of the chair and tapped them.

'You keep them,' she said bravely. It was about two-thirds full.

The priest was sitting forward on the armchair, his round collar open, his tummy over the top of his trousers, his jacket creased. His fingertips bore dark brown stains. He removed a rolled up newspaper from behind him and smoothed it out on the armrest; it fell down on to the carpet, settling noiselessly.

The father shook his head, stuttering a little before coming to the point. 'Well now. When I was up the Kesh, Kathleen, ah, yesterday was it, well, you see now, I was giving confession to the boys and I saw your Sean.'

'Oh Jesus,' she said and sat down.

He put both hands out. 'He's all right, Kathleen, he's all right.'

'Lord have mercy. I've been praying for all I'm worth, Father.' She glanced at the Christ figure on her mantelpiece. It was propping up a small square photo of Sean standing next to his grandfather's Hillman. In fact, her prayers were short, angry, cheated, and they had been that way since two men came to their door one evening two years before, asking for Sean and not leaving their names.

'How is he? Is he bad? What was it like, Father?'

'He's in a cell with a nice fellow from Andersonstown who used to be a teacher, Gerard McIlvenny. He came to one or two of the ecumenical dos, wouldn't know a stick of gelignite from an altar candle! A nice lad. We all had a chat together like. Well you see there's not the space for what you call privacy.'

'Were you able to give Sean his confession?'

The father shifted on his seat. He put his forefinger and thumb up to the bridge of his nose underneath the frame of his glasses. 'To tell you the truth, I don't do it unless they bother me for it. I never feel it is for me to act as if I was better than them. It's an awful place, Kathleen. Every cell, filthy like, your feet stick to the floor and the smell knocks you for six. They've got a foam mattress each on the floor that gets smaller every time I see them, with them ripping a handful off every day to use for putting their shite on the walls. The smell! Words can't describe it. And the food is served to them on the damn floor.'

'Lord have mercy.'

'Aye.'

'And what about the boys in there, how are they, in themselves?'

Father Pearse took a sip of tea and looked at the mantelpiece, gesturing at the figurine. 'Half naked, thin like, with the blanket on you know. Long-haired most of them, beards on those that can grown them. They're all so young, Kathleen. And it's "Sorry Father for the smell and the mess." That's what you get from them. I always say to myself, if they can stick this for three years I can stick an afternoon. "Yous have no need to apologize to me, boys," I tell them. "It's the perfume of Christ himself I'm smelling." Well, they laugh at that, you see. You've got to make light of it.' He stubbed out his cigarette and took another one from the pack she had left by him.

Kathleen got up to give him the lighter.

'They're concerned for you on the outside, like. They ask after their families.'

'Well you tell him he's no need to worry for us. I'm down to a couple of mornings at the butcher's, but I'll get something else after Christmas and Sean is working at the Fiddlers near every day, drinking most of his wages, but we're getting food on the table so you can't complain. There's some that can't.'

'Well now he said to tell you he knows why he's there. He's very firm on that. He said to tell you not to worry they're looking out for each other. They've got their rosary beads and they know their Bible inside out. It's the only book they have to read.'

'Still I'd like him to be getting his confession.'

Father Pearse shook his head, exhaling brown smoke. He seemed to be absorbed by the pattern on the carpet, looking at it the way people look out of a window. 'God help me, Kathleen, sometimes I wish it was me with the gun.'

'I know, Father. I know. My Sean, he's all right, though?'

'Aye, aye, he's dead on, Kathleen. He'll manage. They all stick it, God knows how they do.'

There was the sound of the front door slurring against the doormat and Aine came in wearing a duffel coat.

'We're having a grown-ups chat the wee moment, Aine,' said her mother, nodding at the kitchen. 'There's a couple of biscuits in there for you, then pop off down to Una's will you and bring me back the iron her mummy's borrowed.'

The girl's hair had the netting of fine rain on it.

'What about ye, Father. Mummy, I couldn't find my pencils to take to school this morning. I was the only one as didn't do the nativity in colour.'

'Use your eyes to find them; they're better than mine so they are. Would you like to tell me what's the difference between me looking and you looking?'

'You know where they are, that's the difference.' The girl dropped her heavy coat on to the side of the banister and went upstairs.

'Would you like a biscuit, Father?'

'I ought to be away.'

Kathleen went to the kitchen and returned with custard creams on a plate. She placed them next to the cigarettes on the armchair, then leant down to pick a piece of plaster out of her sock; it was like a child's tooth.

Her son, Liam, came in, short of breath and told them that the Brits were out in the side alley. 'What about ye, Father. Is it chips for tea, Mummy?'

'No it's not, it's corned beef. You'll be keeping in then, Liam!'

'And how is young Liam doing?' asked the father, looking after him as the boy took to the stairs.

'Near the top of his class at St Thomas's. The Lord knows how. I can only think they're an ignorant lot in there. I'm always having to chase him round the Murph, if there's rioting going on you can be sure he's there.'

'Any news from your Mary?'

'No news is good news.'

Aine went past them into the kitchen and came out with a biscuit in each hand. 'You go straight to Una's, miss, and come right back. Get Mrs McCann to watch you back. What do you do if one of them soldiers speaks to you?'

'Ask where my pencils is gone?'

'You never, never speak to them. Mind you, Father, they took a Parker pen from this house one time, so they did. Off you go then, love.'

Kathleen stood at the door watching as the girl crossed over the street and went into her friend's home. She was wearing her older brother's football shirt over her jeans, it looked like a dress on her, she was so thin, with long dark-red hair that curled, like her mother's.

Opposite the house, a Brit was crouching at the side of Mrs Mulhern's, his gun across his lap. He looked over at Kathleen and she crossed her arms and closed the door, bumping into the stand with the phone on it. She picked up the receiver to listen for its heartbeat then put it back gently. 'It's a miracle the ambulances still come up here at all. They've got the army hiding out at Mrs Mulhern's. Do they think she's a volunteer now? Sure, there's no sense to any of it.'

The father gave a dry laugh, felt for his handkerchief. 'I sometimes feel like I've not a clue how to be a priest any more. Mrs Mulhern gave me a talking to the other day when I put my head in the door. She called me a rebel priest. This and that about not following the Church. They want the priests to come out against the 'Ra.'

The afternoon light flooded in through the back window. There was a small birthmark on Father Pearse's forehead that looked like a sickle. He looked lonely there in the living room, not a part of her family nor of anyone else's.

'You've got to stay a little bit apart, Father. In your line.'

'I'd have to be hard-hearted to do that. We live and breathe it, don't we? I can't help loving, no more can I help hating. That's the cross. Well now I meant to bring you comfort and I don't know if I have.'

'It's good to know that Sean's all right, Father.' She stood surveying the mess. 'Well as far as he can be. We'll all have to get used to it anyhow. There's no use sitting here doing nothing, waiting for news, worrying and fretting. You wait and do nothing thinking it won't be your son and then one day it is. Even if you just stop in and turn up the television it still comes right into your house. You're already involved, aren't you, just by living here; so you might as well try and do something about it all. That's what I think.'

She tried to get him to take the cigarettes. He refused them.

'Well thanks for stopping by with news of Sean, you know how much it means to me.' She swept up the mugs and took them out. He waited there for her to come back, but when he heard the edge of sobs and short breaths from the kitchen he let himself out.

The priest took the side path by the Moran house to cut across to another parishioner whose mother was dying of cancer. It seemed incredible to him that cancer could still happen here with so much else going on. Across the playing fields he saw a group of boys gathering stones for the evening's rioting. He trod unwittingly into some broken glass. Laying in the curved remnants of a jar were little pools of yellow liquid. 'Jesus Christ,' he said, shaking his shoe.

4

A handful of prison officers followed Shandy and Dunn into the circle to assemble. Principal Officer Bolton opened the door of his office and looked out at them as if they were guests arrived early. He was a tall, balding man with over-sized spectacles, his top half clad in a pale yellow, silk pyjama top and his bottom half in regulation trousers and socks. He had a newspaper under his arm and a pen behind his ear.

'Work detail, Sir,' said Campbell.

'Carry on,' said Bolton.

'Fella name of Dunn come in on the white sheet, Sir.'

Bolton nodded without much interest and went back into his office.

'Principal Officer Bolton will have a word with you in his office after unlock, Johnno.'

Baxter brushed past them to get to Campbell. 'Should I give the wing a quick going over before you go down it? They'll have slopped out by now.'

'Aye, save my shoes from going white. The piss ruins good shoe leather, Dunn.' Campbell assigned their duties, man by man, and dismissed them. Shandy went ahead, using his shoulders to lever the furniture of his jacket into the right place. Frig and Dunn followed him to the wings. The stench was such that Dunn swallowed, bit his lip, held his breath.

'You're wondering why you're here, Johnno,' said Frig, putting a hand on Dunn's shoulder as they waited to go into the airlock. 'Money, mate. Money. That's why we're here. I'm going to bugger off to the

Costa Brava with mine.' The first grille was locked again and they stood in the airlock while the second was being opened. 'But our friend Shandy he's a family man, he's going to buy one of those nice houses you pass coming down the A1, you know, all new brickwork, set up on a hill, with a tree and a field of its own. Are you a family man, Johnno?'

'No.'

Frig gave him a little push as the second grille was locked behind them and they were on the wing. 'You've got nothing to worry about then. Take a lungful of that. You can smell the countryside, Shandy.'

'"A" wing,' said Shandy, pointing left and then right. '"B" wing.'

They went left. A long hallway with a black floor and a white ceiling stretched before them, cell doors at two or three feet apart, each one white-grey with a shielded slit at eye level. The floor was sticky underfoot, grasping the soles of their shoes with the ferocity of wood glue. Before the cells, to the left, was the recreation room, to the right a light-blue bathroom with urinals, hand basins, showers and a bathroom; all of these pristine.

It was cold enough to see your own breath. After an initial warning cry that went up when the first grille was opened, the place was quiet, apart from a few low noises, the sound of cattle in stalls waiting out the winter.

The three of them went forwards, Shandy with the keys and Frig taking pantomime steps, finger to lips.

'Don't want to wake the sleeping beauties,' said Shandy. He had pulled his cap down across his brow. 'Ready?' he asked in a stage whisper, outside the first cell on the left, feeling for his keys, scrutinizing them, one hand tenderly on the door while he put the key in the lock.

Dunn nodded, motionless, expressionless as the door opened and Shandy filled the narrow open space. Dunn took a look inside. He had to be careful not to knock his head on the low doorframe. Inside the cell was empty apart from two men in their own shit. It was a small space, there was just room for two men to lie side by side on the floor. The temperature was that of the cold room of a butcher's.

The two prisoners looked like brothers. One got up, dirty-handed, levering himself, sinews and hair, bare apart from a thin grey blanket around his waist. A long strand of hair was caught in the corner of his mouth and he pulled it out and squinted at them, arms ready. The other prisoner was at the back of the cell by the window, holding his forearms in the weak light.

'Any requests?'

The prisoner nearest to them sucked in his cheeks, but otherwise he was still, apart from his eyes, which were working fast, going from one officer to the other. His cellmate had a blanket around his shoulders as well as his waist and he pulled it about him as he turned to watch the yard. The near one said something in low tones in Irish and the other replied with a single word. The light changed. The sun reared up at the prison window with a flash of light, then subsided, cowed and done.

'Don't speak Irish I'm afraid. All right lock them up. On to the next.' Frig swung the door back and Dunn saw that the tall man continued to look directly at him as the door was closing. Moving off, Dunn nearly tripped as the congealed urine tugged on one of his shoes.

In the next cell a boy was in the process of spreading shit on the wall with a small piece of sponge. His thickset cellmate started to laugh when the door was opened. Around the room were spread in brown the artefacts of the home, a fireplace, a picture above it, a pelmet over the window. The boy was adding curtains.

'Handy he had a touch of diarrhoea,' said Frig as they ducked out and closed the door again. 'Would you call that satin or gloss?'

Thus they went on to the end of the block with the prisoners alike in their appearance and disinterest. Only once did a prisoner begin to say something, but the sharp reproof of his cellmate made him reconsider.

'They look like Jesus Christ, I always think,' said Frig, with shy pride.

When they reached the second-to-last cell on the right, Frig nodded significantly at Dunn. 'O'Malley,' he said. 'OC.'

'I want to see the PO,' said the man, when the door opened. This was Kevin O'Malley, a full beard, bare torso, the officer commanding for the Republican prisoners there. He was big jawed, built like a builder, yet with the long hair they all had. He had eyes that looked like they'd got drink in them, and the set of his mouth was ugly, Dunn thought. He was the least imprisoned. His cellmate had two blankets around his shoulders and was looking down at the ground, apparently in concentration. This side of the block was the coldest; the wind seemed to whistle through the wire fences, build up speed across the tarmac and launch an assault on the open window spaces.

'Anything I can help you with 2350 O'Malley?'

'I want to see your principal officer.'

'Yeah, yeah, yeah.' Shandy got behind the door. 'Away and fuck. My family's been here for generations. It's our country too.'

With the grilles secured behind them, Shandy went over to Campbell who was seated at the desk in the circle, made a note in the book there and gave his verbal report. Campbell beckoned Dunn to follow him over to the PO's office. Just then, Bolton rounded the corner from the officers' toilets dabbing at his face with a towel. He was now fully dressed, though his jacket was open.

'All present and correct, Sir. One request from O'Malley to see you.'

'Aye, well there's no rush. See you get on with their breakfasts now, while I have a wee chat with Mr . . . what's your name?'

'He's Dunn, Sir.'

Probing his ears with the corner of the towel, Bolton invited Dunn into his office and shut the door. There was a camp-bed folded untidily by the back wall. Bolton offered Dunn a chair and remained standing, looking out the barred window.

'First impressions?'

'Smells like shit, Sir.' Dunn attempted an easy and dependable expression.

Bolton's taut face broke loose, he seemed pleased. 'Yes,' he laughed. 'Fair enough Mr Dunn. Look, I say just a few things to new men on my block, though you'll find each block is a law unto itself. I'm a man who joined the service because I believe a State has to be upheld. When I read the prison rule book I bought it lock, stock and barrel. It made sense to me. It is wise.' He stressed the word with an almost savoury pleasure. 'I don't have trouble here. Not from the men, not from the officers. Because I go by the book and I'm very careful. I know who I can trust with what. There are things we have to do we don't like very much. The mirror-searches for instance. We do them minimally. We go by the book but we do not go above and beyond. You do what you have to do because you're told to, not because you like to. Do you follow? Whatever you might hear about other blocks, whatever you might see on other blocks, you just remember that on my block we play it my way. Easy does it, Mr Dunn. I know there are some officers here who can be inclined to make it personal, or should I say political. As you probably know, it's all much the same here. Are you a political man, Dunn?'

'No Sir, I'm not.'

'Well, good for you. All I'll say to you,' he put his hands into his pockets, 'is not to get personally involved. Do the job and go home, do your time, if you like, because this is a prison for all of us in some ways, do your hours and go easy. Remember, the punishment is being here, we're not here to give it, merely to close the doors.' Bolton looked Dunn in the eyes and smiled and frowned at the same time. 'So, that's it. Any observations or thoughts on the conditions in the wings over there, beyond the smell?'

'Not really, Sir. Just here to do the job.'

'Aye, well, if you want my opinion, the whole thing is bloody disgraceful, it shouldn't have come about,' said Bolton, smile gone. 'But my job is to uphold whatever orders I'm given. We've got to believe they know what they're doing. In the long run.'

'Sir, can I ask, why are there no windows in the cells? It's bloody freezing down the wings.'

'They broke them when we started to clean the cells the summer of '77. The disinfectant was that bloody strong. One of them gave the order and they started breaking their furniture up to smash the windows through, to get air. They shouldn't have used a chemical like that but well, with the shite and piss everywhere . . . Last winter the temperatures fell to minus eleven because the pipes weren't working. We had heaters and we were cold. I don't know whether they could sleep at nights, I doubt it. So I went to see O'Malley to talk about the windows being put back in. He more or less laughed in my face, Dunn. It's a waste of time trying to help them, they won't have any dealings with us . . .' His voice tailed off and his eyes narrowed. He appeared to be looking at the chart on the wall opposite. 'They consider it a weakness.'

'"It is not those who can inflict the most, but those that can suffer the most who will conquer,"' said Dunn.

Bolton looked at him. 'Aye, as indeed Mr MacSwiney put it. These boys are good at suffering, it's a religion. Fuck Catholicism, fuck Republicanism, fuck Marxism, I think they're good at being oppressed, that's what I think. You know what happened to MacSwiney, Dunn?'

'He died on a hunger strike.'

'That's right.' Bolton reached into a fruit bowl on his desk and tossed what appeared to be a brown hairy egg at Dunn. 'Do you like kiwi fruit, Dunn?'

'I've never tried one,' he said.

'Eat it with a teaspoon, full of goodness. I try to eat one every day. The taste of far away places.' Bolton started to look at some papers on his desk.

Dunn brought the kiwi fruit to his nose. It didn't smell of anything.

'Send Baxter in will you. My day off tomorrow. About bloody time.' He looked up from his papers, caught Dunn's eyes for a second and gave a flicker of an uneasy smile, half apology, half guilt. Dunn closed the door behind him and stood leaning against it, his hands staying the handle, holding it down a moment before he let the locking mechanism click into its proper place.

5

Andersonstown Leisure Centre was all the talk; it had a big indoor pool. On Saturday Kathleen let Aine and Liam go down there with the two Purcell boys. Her husband was going off to work; Saturday dinnertime seemed to be a weekend-long shift. She saw how he ducked his head as walked underneath the hole in the ceiling, spilling more dust, grinding it under his bare feet. He made an attempt to embrace her in the kitchen and before she could fail to respond he started going on about 'normal wives, normal human beings'.

'No wonder I take a drop from time to time.' He was pacing about behind her, socks and shoes in hand. 'Living in the Arctic circle here.'

His breath was animal, like a dog's behind, she thought, his lips were thick and gluey. She chose his cheek if they kissed. In bed she avoided his mouth.

'You're stuck with me. So go drink yourself into an early grave.'

'Ah, fuck away with you!'

She threw a mug at the kitchen wall, looked at where it fell, heard him trying to slam the front door.

She was crouching, her hair a curtain over her face, using the dustpan and brush when her husband came back in a few minutes later, looking both bitter and remorseful. 'I've not come back to say I'm sorry, I just forgot my cigarettes,' he said, spotting the mug handle on one of her fingers. He sat to put his shoes and socks on. 'Sure, why don't you come up for a drink later, it'll cheer you up,' he said, going out the back door before she could answer.

*

'Mummy was late, love, that's why I'm a wee bit after three.' Collette Heaney put her head in the kitchen. She usually popped in on a Saturday afternoon. Her husband was in the Kesh, but he was in 'the Cages', the prisoner-of-war side, as he'd gone in before political status was revoked. Her son was the one shot in the face by a rubber bullet that summer. He'd been with the Purcell boys himself that day, they didn't tend to get involved like the other boys, they were a bit soft. A car had come down the street, crashed into the barricades and a man had got out and ran off just before the army arrived. In seconds there were soldiers jumping out the back of an armoured vehicle, shooting up the place. When the boy came home from hospital after a few weeks, they all went round to see him, and it was a wake that wasn't a wake, the boy on the settee, head in bandages, the mother fussing at him with rice pudding.

'We'll have a cup before we go down the road, if I can find one. I've fired that many of them at the wall.'

Collette leant against the back door. She wore smart little court shoes. 'I've not seen the new leisure centre yet.' She pronounced the word 'lee-shure'. 'We could go up the Green Briar one night. Would you like to go up? It would do you good. Does everyone a bit of good, a drink and a bit of chat,' she said, arranging her coat lapels and shirt collar.

'Och. I might as well stop in. Sean does the drinking for both of us and I get plenty of chat.'

'From someone else though, for a change. I get lonely, even though he's not bad company, Gerry. Well he's a good listener,' she gave a short dark laugh. 'There's only so many people I can talk to round here. If I don't talk about my Gerry they think I'm a heartless bitch and if I do you see people's faces go like you've just shown them your glass eye.'

'I know love.' Kathleen felt along the wet ridge behind the sink, in and out of the pan scrubbers and knick-knacks to find her watch. She was going to meet the kids when they came out of their swim. Collette had agreed to go with her.

'You won't come to the Green Briar,' said Collette, heading for the mirror in the hallway, her shoes bouncing on the carpet. 'You should though. They have some lovely music. People come from all around to hear it.'

'Go with Bernadette.'

'I'd not get a look in with Bernie Curran about.'

'Well now I know where I stand.'

'You know how she is.'

They went out, pulling their coats about them. There was rubble at the sides of the streets, and the fences were broken down or burnt. The semi-detached houses were small and white, each had three windows, two down, one up. They were huddled, with barely any front yard, on the narrow curving roadway. As you walked along the pavement, you had to step over debris and broken glass. One or two of the houses had Christmas decorations up already and Christmas trees in the window. Some of them had palm trees out the front, ragged things. Coconuts in Belfast! One or two of the houses had a car parked outside.

At the entrance to the housing estate there was a great mural on the side of one of the first houses, a portrait of one of the first Volunteers killed. Someone had been out the night before and painted on the wall the slogan, 'Republic of Ballymurphy'. The women nudged each other.

A man came towards them who worked part time up at The Fiddlers. With his hands in his pockets too, he nodded at them. Collette looked after him. 'He's got a cow of a wife, the poor man. It's desperate cold, it's going to snow if it keeps on like this.'

'No it won't. Rain is all we're good for and rain is all we'll get. It's got to get down below freezing for snow.'

'Well it's freezing fucking cold.'

'And that's what they said was it? Everywhere else they're saying, "With the temperature falling below freezing point, we foresee the possibility of snow," but here it's, "Good even'n to yous, it's fucking freezing cold, so it is, and what with the rubber bullets, mind you keep a hand on your bollocks."'

They were on the Whiterock road, with the cemetery ahead of them, topsy-turvy gravestones and memorials amongst long grass. As they came up the hill they could see down across Belfast, over the river and the factories, they could see little Divis Tower, orange like a Lego block to the left and the spire of St Peters. Down beyond was East Belfast and from where they stood the hills behind it seemed low, conceding to the general falling away of the land over the Irish Sea, towards England.

They were stopped at a road-block. A Saracen was parked across the street and there were two soldiers standing outside, one with a gun, the other ready to go through bags.

Collette handed over her bag. 'A hand grenade, a semi-automatic, some gelignite . . .' she reeled off. Kathleen offered hers. The soldier had his gloves off to unzip it. They bought the bags with the most zips, it gave a certain advantage.

'Bloody hell,' he said, going from the main compartment to the six small pockets on the front. She'd put a tampon in each one, and he went through them, giving nothing away, but she and Collette had a snigger and knew it would grow in the telling.

'All right ladies,' he said, flexing his knuckles and blowing his hands against the cold, 'on your way.'

They went off, arms linked now, down past the more groomed part of the cemetery. 'How's your Sean, love? Any news?'

'Father Pearse saw him last week. He's all right so far as I could make out. The Father's not himself though, it must get to you seeing them like that. Sean's not getting his confession. I know it's not the end of the world but I can't help thinking it would give him comfort. He's not like the other boys. He's always been one for the church. Quietly. You know boys that age don't let on much. I've got a visit with him on the twelfth. I tell you, I'm that desperate lonely without him in the house. We're two of a kind, me and Sean, he's the one of all of them who's the most like me. On the inside.'

She looked at Collette. Who was the luckier? What kind of bargains could be made? *Dear God, if only* . . . Kathleen flushed.

Their feet broke out into a fair tempo as the hill descended sharply on

'Did you hear about that other screw this week? The INLA are claiming it,' said Collette.

'Aye, a wages clerk or whatever they're putting out he was. What I say is them screws are soldiers just the same as the others walking about round here. Worse 'cause they're only doing it for the money. God knows what they think they're bringing on themselves! Them with their sticks on naked unarmed men! Sean's granddaddy was a prize fighter. He always used to say, "The one to watch is the one with nothing to lose." Sean's a lot like him, though he's not so ignorant.'

When they got to the Falls Road, they went to cross at the roundabout. Collette put her hand on Kathleen's forearm as a Saracen came speeding past. They stood still.

'There's a rumour, Kathleen, about the boys on the protest taking it further.'

Kathleen took a deep breath, moving off, her lungs filling with cold air, a foot dropping from the pavement on to the road; a sudden miss, the rest of your body unprepared, the mishap that shunts you from a near-dream to waking.

They walked a few yards in silence up towards Milltown cemetery. Kathleen put her hand out and a black cab swung in beside them.

'What about ye,' they said as they got in, nodding at the two other women on the far side. There was a young girl on a stool in the middle.

'Just as far as Andytown, thanks Jim.'

'Aye, all right love. News from your Patrick?' he asked Collette.

'Not much. Same as ever,' she said. She was on the pull-down spring seat, alongside him but facing the other way. Kathleen sat in front of her, chin on her palm, gazing across the scrap yard. Collette leant forward then appeared to change her mind, leant her head against the Perspex.

When they got up towards Andersonstown, the cab had to pull over because of the riots. Kathleen and Collette gave the driver their five pence each and got out quickly. A group of boys had waylaid a 'pig', as the armoured cars were known, by throwing beer barrels in its path so that, wedged, it was unable to advance or retreat. A troop of soldiers was coming down the street from Lenadoon and the teenage boys behind the pig were throwing stones at them. Behind the teenagers were groups of smaller boys crouching, holding bags and boxes of stones and a few others preparing petrol bombs.

Kathleen knew that the moment one of the petrol bombs was thrown, the soldiers would open up with the rubber bullets. She looked around. To the right side of the street, half hidden by a bus shelter, was a boy putting a long piece of rag into the neck of a milk bottle. Liam.

She saw her 13-year-old boy, his face a mask, with the smile that isn't a smile but a challenge, an affront upon which he depended. This face she'd seen already in the urgent tenor of his games; ready to kill. All the talk of the 'Ra and of guns and bombs, all the shouting in the back yard and in the street, immoderate and uncontrollable outside, noisy and messy inside, it was all a training they put themselves through, the boys. She saw him about to make a move, frowning like a footballer taking a goal, aware of the other boys looking at him, his jar aloft as a signal. She saw the boy next to him cupping his hands around a match, tending it for her Liam.

In a flash she was across the street and had him by an ear, dragging him backwards into a shop doorway, swearing.

'Where's your fucking sister?'

Collette called her name and Kathleen turned to see her and Aine standing in a shop doorway with Aine's hair, wet from the swimming pool, hanging like icicles, dripping. Kathleen hustled Liam across to them. Aine's cheeks were rough-skinned, red and chapped and Kathleen wondered why she hadn't seen before that they needed Vaseline on them. She looked into Aine's green eyes, and saw how the top lashes were black and long and the bottom lashes pale and short. Her own baby girl born in 1969, when the Troubles began.

'Come on, let's move.'

'I'm not going,' Liam said.

'Don't make me give you a good hiding in front of your pals and the Brits.' She pushed his back. 'Get walking.'

'I'll not be trusting you with Aine again,' she shouted, running them up the street as rubber bullets hit the road. They rounded a corner and stood together, catching their breath.

'Where were the bloody Purcell boys?'

'Them? They went off – the great girls.'

'Well they could have made sure yous were all right before they did.' It was a long walk back and no hope of a cab.

'The great useless sacks of shite. Fat lumps.' Kathleen was growing more upset as they walked. Suddenly she exploded in tears and anger and turned and smacked Liam around the head. 'I just can't live like this any more!'

Her boy assessed the impact of her blow, head on one side, eyes averted, saying nothing.

'Your own sister! You don't go and get her killed, d'you hear me? She's the only good one I've got. I might as well just about give up on you.'

And then his mother went on ahead with Aine.

'I'm joining the Fianna Cubs!' he shouted, watching his mother and sister going on at a fair pace, hand-in-hand, walking the same way, shoulders hunching, making much work for their rears.

'Jesus, Joseph and Mary,' said Collette, waiting alongside him. 'As if your going and dying is going to change anything, except for breaking your mother's heart.'

'She doesn't care about me. She only cares about him! About Sean!'

Kathleen turned around in the drizzle. She could see Liam as a little boy standing in the empty bath, soap in hand, rounded tummy sticking out and v-shaped mickey underneath, his eyes and mouth about to burst, looking for her to save him when his father was shouting. It was family life that made you the way you were, that made your kids the way they were and nothing was irreversible but there was a general direction. It was too hard to bear if you thought about it as a whole, you had to divide the awful task of raising children into days of trials and tempers, minutes of love, seconds of comprehension.

She redoubled her hold on Aine and they set forth with the purpose of the last hill in the light rain. She was thinking how she'd sat next to him

on the settee the night before and put her arm round him, stroked the
golden hairs on his forearm, felt how his shoulders were narrow like old
furniture, well turned but for smaller folk. She was sick of crying. She
couldn't keep crying. She'd have to use her brain and do something. For
all of them. She couldn't count on her husband.

Collette had stayed back with the boy but now she started to walk on
too. Only Liam stood still, rain-browed, watching the women going up
the hill, past the grey stone walls of the cemetery, against the weather.

6

He went to the duty officer's at five to clock off with the others covering their mouths, sharing some kind of a joke. He was sent straight back. Overtime was not optional.

He rejoined the evening stupor in the mess. Shandy was dozing, his feet up, and Frig was trawling through his newspaper, having read out everyone's horoscope. Shandy came to momentarily, considered whether to wake and hedged his bets with a single eye open, passing his tongue over his lips. Frig gave his paper a prod. 'I bloody love these problem pages. *"Dear Irma, My husband wants me to see a doctor because I don't have an orgasm. Is there something wrong with me?"* She's even put down her name and address. No phone number.'

'Not signed Mrs Higgins is it?' said Shandy, with a slow-burning grin.

'Nah,' said Frig, a thumb twiddling at a nostril, 'she always comes like clockwork your Marjorie. Digs her nails in.' He looked up, making sure he'd gauged their responses, each of them. Shandy caught a belch in the closed purse of his mouth.

'Christ, I bet you behave like a prince when you get home.'

John Dunn put his cigarette out. Shandy got up and ran a mug full of water, which he drank down in one.

Frig held up the front page with its black and white picture of Gilligan, the murdered prison officer, alongside his own head. 'Shot dead point blank through his windscreen on his way home. Twenty-five. That could have been me on that page there. He was three years younger than me and they had kids, but you get my drift lads. Makes you think doesn't it.'

'His wife will still be a young woman. My Marjorie's no spring chicken, and the kids are after this and that for school all the time. There's nothing for the widows when we go. They've conveniently forgotten that part. Aye, they pay us well while we're alive, the Brits, but they've done their sums, make no mistake.' Shandy looked up, drawing up before the rough ground of his thinking. 'The Brits don't have to live here. As long as it's not them getting killed, they don't care. But when it's over on the mainland now that's another story, so it is. By God, don't they go on about it then, one small bomb in Woolworth's and it's all over the papers, meanwhile us lot over here are lucky to see in a new day.'

Dunn checked his watch, thoughts undercover.

'You know what I'm saying's true. I'm right am I not, Mr Dunn?'

Everybody had to be right – outside the army. In the army you signed up and you did whatever you were told to do. But outside you couldn't just be following orders you had to be right as well. A soldier took a side because he had to and it was better to stand with those you knew you could trust if you had to stand with anyone, and you severed whatever vein or nerve there is that runs between your head and your hands. Bayoneting sacks of straw seemed funny at first when they were spotty seventeen-year-olds, limbering up in the cold air, getting shouted at it. *'Move it! Move it you sorry lot!'* There they were, late-autumn light, hands on hips, careful not to grin. *'Make no mistake boys, there's no better way to kill a man, you look him in the eyes, twist the blade, pull it back out with his guts on and you know he's dead. That's what we're here for. That's what we're paid to do.'*

Campbell walked in the mess early evening, heading for the coffee jar, giving his mug a good two spoonfulls, putting in milk and sugar before the hot water.

'Gilligan's funeral tomorrow, Mr Campbell.'

'Will PO cancel visits?' asked Shandy.

'Aye, prison rule. Nothing Mr Bolton can do about that. Take heart, lads. The streakers are getting a special breakfast from me tomorrow, three fifths of two thirds of fuck all. And I'll have a special wee surprise for the bastards as well. Right, now what's for my tea-time.'

Campbell shook the bread wrapper, pressed his palms upon the last thick crust that remained. Shandy handed him the crumb-strewn margarine tub and Campbell set to complaining that they were a bunch of animals.

Frig took it upon himself to skim the top off the margarine with a knife.

After the prisoners' tea was served and lockup done, Dunn was allowed off. It was about nine. Campbell got the front door guard to let him out. 'I've told the lads to come in early tomorrow. Want you in at five.'

'Five?'

'Have you got a problem with that, Dunn?'

Baxter was being let out with him. He had a pile of the PO's dirty washing under his arm. Dunn heard him swear. As they reached the next set of grilles and the officer inspected their passes and directed them their separate ways, Baxter looked at him in the acid glare of the night-time lighting. 'Fuel on the fire that is,' he said, 'it can only make things worse for you lot.'

Dunn watched him away, nursing his bundle, head down.

Driving out of the prison in the dark, he started to turn over the events of his first day in his head.

The image of his grandfather came to mind again, the old man down on one knee examining a piece of turf he'd dug. And him, standing on the day of his fifteenth birthday, just the other side of the garden gate, looking but not asked in. '*See you then.*' He went down King Street, saw the recruiting sergeant, then went back to his mother, one last time, for a signature.

When it came to the army, Dunn had nothing to lose and everything to give. He was a blank slate. It was the army that taught him to shave when there was nothing to shave. The other lads had personal possessions to be taken off them. Not him. One or two stuck photos on their lockers, their mothers, their girlfriends – it was fair game to laugh at the girlfriends, but they didn't like you laughing at the pictures of their mothers.

He went into the Royal Electric and Mechanical Engineers, the REME, because no one else did, became a storeman. In 1960 he became a lance corporal, then a corporal when he was in Cyprus and he didn't want to go any further. The men that stayed corporals were good blokes, reliable, neither too close, nor too far from the men themselves. They got the job done. He'd done twenty-two years in the army, a few months in military intelligence, begun a law degree and ditched it. He was thirty-nine now. It was a new start, but not from scratch.

He came into the city via the motorway. It ended abruptly presenting him with the choice of west or east. He felt a lurch of fear that was akin to excitement; fight or flight.

It was like a love affair that was bad for him, Belfast. A guilty secret. He had spent time in other countries with the army: Cyprus, Germany, Aden, but he'd stayed on in Belfast after his last tour of duty. Not because of Angie, because of Belfast. Because of what he'd seen and done here. Others left for the same reason. Many of the men he knew would never come back willingly. He couldn't leave.

By ten in the evening, Belfast was long into the night. He had noted the day before that at three forty-five in the afternoon it was twilight and at three forty-six exactly it was night-time. By four the night had taken over entirely and only the street lights made any sense of the moat of dark countryside in which the city of Belfast lay. The mountains, dense and heavy-browed to the west were to him like Ireland in waiting, Ireland at bay; they were disarmed only by the night that made all things even. The evening presided. For a good part of the day it was close at hand; the quiet settling in, settling down, the gloom, the waiting, the menace, the other person close by, the window showing nothing. This was his place, this evening kingdom. Not England.

He went there first of all in 1969, as a corporal but in civvies, driving around units, collecting and delivering stores. He took a sleeping bag wherever he went and slept where he ended the day. He got to know people everywhere. Catholics and Protestants. He did twenty-five thousand miles in four months. He fell in love with the place; the countryside that took your breath away. Up and over the brow of one hill, plunging down into a valley ready for the next, like a green roller-coaster. He found the people of the north hard but sentimental, with their savage bad feeling, their grievances, loyalties to die for. He'd had his dinner once with a Catholic family in Armagh, they'd joked about the chicken being poisoned.

He was back again in 1974, and they stuck him into screening. After a six week course in Ashford, he and a few others were at Glassmullin off the Falls playing 'Mutt and Jeff' with IRA men, and then he was back again in late '76. On that last tour he met Angie, which was handy, because he was staying.

He checked his mirror and his side mirrors, went the long way round and then drove down the road on which they lived and up on to the small driveway; room for one car, arse out over the pavement. They'd get another car at Christmas, so Angie could come and go without waiting on the buses, see her parents. They'd have to park it on the road. His pay was more than it was even a month ago when he was at Millisle and all the men talked about at lunchtimes was the money. The overtime, what they got extra for being on the 'dirt' blocks, how much it was for doing the cleaning, and how the union was going for a big pay rise, thirty per cent. With the murders, they were desperate for men. The 'conveyor belt' court system was shovelling men into the prisons like coal into a furnace. And now he was at the back end, closing the doors.

Angie wanted a house, she wanted children, she wanted to get married, she wanted to have a holiday abroad, she wanted to get out of Belfast. Her parents had had the farm in the family hundreds of years. Her dad wanted John to make a decent woman of his daughter before he got himself killed. But he didn't want to invest too much in the effort in case John was killed before the wedding. It was a fine line, meanly drawn. *'Will you offer John a drink for God's sake, Daddy!'* Angie wanted them to move to Lisburn. It was closer to the prison and her parents. It made sense. But it was a dead end for John Dunn. Her old man, every Sunday, all tolerance and temperance, the chastened suffering of another man in his house; gums chasing false teeth, suggestive of all the work that was going on inside of him, keeping the new man out.

She wasn't stupid, Angie, she was doing the accounts where she worked now. She read about a lot of things he'd never even think to read about. She talked about what she read but he just switched off for that, and let her talk, giving the minimum, a nod of agreement, a small expression of surprise or sympathetic disgust. It was the same with all her chat about her family.

They got along well. They had a lot of sex; they liked to have sex together, it was worth staying in for. They saved money. He didn't know whether he loved her. She was a nice girl, they laughed at the same things and she fancied him and he fancied her. Why make it more than that?

He didn't want her to leave him. He did not want her to leave him on his own. If he had to marry her to stop that happening he would.

The light was still on in the front room; it was after ten. He remembered seeing the TV advertisement for the prison service, the new officer saying '*I enjoy the comradeship of fellow officers and I can earn eighty pounds a week without overtime.*' A comic strip, it had a man telling his wife and child that there was job security and a pension, training on full pay and a free uniform.

Angie came to the door. 'All right love?'

'All right,' he said, giving her a kiss.

'Bloody hell, John, you stink.'

He was surprised. He had had a shower before he left and changed into civilian clothes. He pulled the armpits of his shirt to his nose one at a time, tenderly sniffing.

'You're exaggerating.'

'No, you smell terrible, John.' She was recoiling, her nose taut like an exclamation mark.

'Oh,' he said.

'Jesus. Get those clothes off you, you need to get in the bath and shower yourself down all over. Use plenty of soap.'

'Let me get in the door first, Angela.'

She looked outside the front door left and right, closed it behind him then followed him through to the kitchen.

'Have a cup of tea then.'

He shook his head. 'I'll have a Scotch.'

'You've had a bad day. Ach, John it's bound to give you a wee shock to the system so it is, all that carry on in there.'

'I don't think that was a bad day, Angie. I think it was more than likely a normal day in the Maze. It's like a bloody zoo in there. The smell. Jesus Christ you wouldn't believe it.'

'I would. Have your drink and get in the shower.' She went to the drinks cabinet in the front room and brought the bottle of whiskey into the kitchen with her, putting a good splash into a mug. He drank, sighed, then topped it up with a little more.

'Are you all set then?'

'Give us a minute, Angie. Come on.'

'Och, before I forget it, this came for you today, John, from England.' She picked up a letter from in front of the toaster and put it on the table.

'Oh yeah?' He got up to go to the fridge, stooping then ripping the door open with the bout of effort that was required. 'Can't see anything I fancy. I'm on bloody early tomorrow. Five a.m.'

'You're kidding me, John.'

'Nope.'

'Are they trying to break you in hard like?'

'Seems like you get a day off now and again from what the other lads were saying, they said figure on one Sunday or what-have-you every month. The good news is, you get one-and-a-half time on a Saturday and double-time on a Sunday, so on a weekend you can near double your week's pay.'

'We're never going to see each other.'

'Look, think about it, we can save the money, then we can buy a house. Get a new fridge and all. You play your cards right and you might be driving your own car after this Christmas. All right? It's not for ever. You'll be able to pop down and see your family whenever you want. If I'm working late you can always go down there for an evening, can't you?'

'Well I can always wait for your days off to go down and see them. But it will be handy for work, a car. You know, I still quite like you, John Dunn. I'm not ready never to see you again. Give me a kiss, you smelly git.' He kissed her perfunctorily on the mouth. 'Jesus, the smell. Listen they're getting rid of one of the reps' Datsuns so they might give us a good price. I'll ask if we can have a test drive maybe. You never know your luck, John Dunn, if we get a new car I might do something naughty to you in the front seat.'

John put his tea down and felt inside his pockets. He took out two pound notes and slapped them down. 'Can I get anything in advance?'

'Do you want a cheese bap?'

'Yeah, all right. Stick some Branston in with it.'

She took a knife from the cutlery drawer. John opened the fridge for her once more and passed over the small square of cheese. 'So now, what's that there letter about then?'

'It looks like it's from the insurance company. It'll all be yours one day.' He was ten years older than her.

'You're a thrifty old man, so you are.' She lopped off some cheese, sliced like tombstones fallen over, spooned sauce and pressed the bap down hard with her palm. 'Och I might as well go up and have my bath while you eat that. I've got to wash my hair. I can't wait on you if it's to dry at all.'

'Thanks love. Yeah, you go on up,' he told her, 'I'll have another drink first and finish the sandwich.' She bent her head for a kiss and he swallowed his mouthful grudgingly, saying irritably with cheese round his teeth, 'Go on, then.' He took a sip of Scotch, then caught her by the hand. 'Angie, did you ever hear of a fella named Baxter from round here?'

'There's a few Baxters.'

'He's an orderly in the prison.'

'Not Bobby Baxter as was a male nurse?'

'No. A male nurse?'

'Aye. Took them stitches out my knee. Nice lad.'

Angie went off to have her bath and he sat a while in the dark, thinking. He could hear the repetitive hollow clink of the jug against the side of the bath.

When he'd finished the sandwich, he put the plate in the sink and took his glass into the front room. 'Nothing good comes in letters,' he thought, index finger jerking bluntly through the envelope's seal.

'Mark,' he said, looking at the bottom of the unfolded page, and he pressed the inside of his palm to his left eye.

The letter was short. When he'd read it through twice, he put it on the arm of the chair and went to the drinks cabinet for his packet of Panatela cigarillos. Then, turning off the light and checking the front door was locked, John went back into the kitchen with the letter and glass. He took matches from the small bowl on the table, a saucer from the draining board and lit his cigarillo, looking outside across their small bit of paving and grass, with the clapped out circular washing line, its arms lowered, a lonely tea-towel stuck to the mast. Beyond that the kitchen light couldn't reach, and there was darkness apart from a downstairs light here and an upstairs light there. The back of their house faced the backs of the terraced houses on the next street, all built to the same scheme.

He picked up the letter and read it again. Ash fell on to the linoleum floor. His hands were shaking. He looked through the back window again and merging with his reflection was an upstairs light in a house opposite.

It was extinguished.

Against the dark, he saw himself wholly.

'Nineteen.'

7

Over her first cigarette of the day, Kathleen said to her husband. 'You're not working the night. If I can get my arse over to Clonard to pray for your two sons, then you can stop at home and explain to Liam why he shouldn't be following his brother into Long Kesh. He needs to think about his schooling more than going rioting.'

'Give my head peace,' he moaned, his toes curling. Sean had a bad taste in his mouth; he was standing in the kitchen like a dog chewing bile and grass.

'Would you take a look at yourself?' she said. 'Jesus.'

'The boys were in last night buying me drinks on account of the old days.'

'Aye, and there was a fella came in here, looked like Roger Moore, begging me for to go away with him.' She washed her cup out and went to call for Aine and Liam. 'I can't leave yous here because I can't trust yous, so hurry up and get down here, we're going up the Clonard. After that your daddy's going to spend the afternoon with you.'

She heard Sean in the kitchen delivering a lengthy fart. 'Oh Christ, I'm not well.'

Clonard monastery was a long way along the Falls, past the Royal Victoria Hospital. Although Kathleen's family had always gone to St Peters which was closer, after Bombay Street was burnt out people had gathered in Clonard and she felt a loyalty to it. She hated Corpus Christi, the great brutish modern church in Ballymurphy. There it stood, unscathed, while all around it Ballymurphy was reduced to rubble on a regular basis and she just couldn't stand to see it, nor its priests who apart from Father Pearse were trying to pretend none of it was going on. And now Father Pearse was going more and more to Clonard to help out Father Fitzgerald. They were more Republican-minded up there, more a part of the community.

She loved the look of the place. It was like something out of medieval Europe, with its triple portal doorway, a huge Rose window above and then two octagonal towers that reached up to the sky in fine, twisting finials that were like a lady's fingers outstretched.

The usual crowd of older men and women were hurrying inside, hands in pockets.

Inside, the church was a red granite that looked like pink-speckled marble and your eyes went naturally to a round golden mosaic of the ascension of Christ. His arms were open and beside him were angels and birds. Mary was at his side praying for all she was worth.

The priests came in. Father Fitzgerald and Father Pearse side by side. The altar boy came up swinging the incense too flippantly; he nearly hit the stairs with it. Underneath his robe were a pair of dirty running shoes with the laces undone. Father Fitzgerald took the incense from him and with little careful movements gave it to the Bible and then to the altar. The elderly man recited his words with all the enjoyment of a newly-ordained priest.

Her children went off to the separate glass-fronted side room.

Slack-bodied, heads bowed, the congregation stood together, the narrative of their own lives outside still rolling in their heads and then the choir struck up, trying to intervene.

Responding automatically to the chords of the organ's tune, they picked up the song, '*Morning has broken, like the first morning*.' After the hymn, they bowed their heads to say the Thanksgiving Prayer together. '*O Mother of Perpetual Help, with grateful hearts we join you . . .*'

The image of Our Lady of Perpetual Help was protected by a three-arched golden gateway, and the egg shape was illuminated like a golden fruit, an eternal womb. Mary's head was lowered to one side towards the baby and her arms encircled him. The priest read out the letters of thanks to Our Lady. *'Thank you for our three year old son who is so lovely and inno-cent and I pray he stays that way as long as possible, and thanks for our families that get on so well. I pray, Mary, that we can always keep it that way.'*

Kathleen lifted her head out of the field of folk. She looked up at the wooden depiction of Jesus, his long hair back behind his neck, a single cloth around his waist, draped over his forearm. There were centurions stand-ing about him. His face was solemn, already beyond the world, and she could see in his expression those words to come. *'Forgive them, Father . . .'*

Afterwards, set free, most of the congregation and the kids from the side room went out into the forecourt to share a yarn. A hard-core group of old timers chanted the rosary together, and a few others went to wait their turn for the confession boxes and Kathleen took her purse to the altar of Our Lady of Perpetual Help and doled out her small change. The clattering of coins sounded like a fruit machine on a win.

'Now, you must have something you need from Our Lady desperate bad.'

Sinking to their knees, side by side, Kathleen and her neighbour exchanged smiles.

'Margaret Coogan! Whatever are you doing down at the Clonard? How's your son Brendan getting along. I was just thinking about you the other day.' Kathleen had worked with Mrs Coogan at Gallaghers, rolling cigarettes, some ten years ago. Back then, Mrs Coogan was always on about her son going to university. He didn't. It was 1969 and he was eighteen. Kathleen had gone round to their house in the days after Bombay Street was burnt to borrow a travel bag. When she got there Margaret's son was packing the bag in a state of fury and excitement. Nowadays Brendan Coogan had a regular column in *An Phlobacht* that she made a point of reading when she could. She saw him from time to time on the Falls Road. He was striking, fierce looking, dark, like he'd come out the woods.

'Aye, dead on, thanks, Kathleen. He's coming round for his dinner today for the first time in months. Our boy James is getting married in the new year and Michelle is courting. What about your Mary? She must be married already. She was always such a lovely looking girl.'

'She's off over in England. Calls me every Sunday like. Shouldn't wonder if I don't hear from her this afternoon. As for my Sean, well, did you not know he's in the H blocks, on the blanket.'

The surface of Mrs Coogan's tongue was a matt pale yellow. 'He can't be more than fifteen!'

'He's nineteen! And my Liam's thirteen and going the same way.'

'Och God save us, Kathleen. What can you do? If it's in them, it's in them. You don't know what they're doing and you don't ask.' Mrs Coogan crossed herself and looked at the altar, shifting her knees to allow her raincoat to secede.

'That's great for you about James. I've no hope of my Sean getting married now. Sixteen years he's got inside. He'll be thirty-five when he comes out. No remission, even though they say he's a criminal. They have it every which way they like. It makes you sick.'

With Mrs Coogan's hand on Kathleen's forearm they walked up the side aisle towards the doors, past the confession boxes and the rosary-sayers. 'I just pray my Liam doesn't follow him in there. Like you say, it's as if the boys are drawn to it.'

'I'm a good Republican and I don't care who knows it but with some of them they're choosing a way of life. It's not what their fathers had is it; getting married, having weans, the church, this job or that, getting by. They don't want any of that, this lot now. No, if there wasn't this war they would have had to have invented one. That's what I think.'

'You're dead right, Margaret. Listen I'm that glad I've seen you because I've not yet been in to see Sean in the Kesh and I'm worried for him. Could you ask your Brendan to call in for a wee chat like? I know he sees the boys all the time. I won't keep him long.'

'Are you still up at Ballymurphy?'

'Aye. The Republic of Ballymurphy they're after calling it now.'

'When I see him later on I'll ask him to pop over, Kathleen.' They were standing outside in the glittering half-light that precedes a down-pour. Mrs Coogan was pulling her coat to, fumbling with buttons in haste. 'God love you, Kathleen, it's a lot for a mother to bear having a son in that place. And on the blanket as well.'

Kathleen found Aine and Liam with a group of other children kicking horse chestnuts at a car. They walked home together, the children going on at each other over something Liam had said to Aine's friend's sister and Kathleen in her own thoughts, pleased with her bit of luck running into Margaret Coogan. Everyone knew which way the wind was blowing, Brendan Coogan was standing for election as a Sinn Fein MP and he was also, most certainly, on the army council.

'Can we have an ice-cream, Mummy?'

An ice-cream van was speeding down the Falls, out of control, veering all over both sides of the road. It crashed into a low wall, its bumper up like a snarl, then two men in balaclavas hopped out and ran off down an alleyway. The chimes were playing 'Dixie Land'.

8

John Dunn only needed to tell himself the time he had to wake. He switched the light on in the spare room and glanced at his watch. Three-thirty. It was a depressing ability.

In his vest and underpants he sat up, picked up his socks from the floor and smelt them. He took a new pair from the cupboard on the landing and tried to get them on his feet, hopping in the low light. In the bathroom mirror, his face was disgruntled as he prepared his toothbrush with paste, then left it on its side before taking a leak. The urine was thick and golden, concentrate. He felt rough, robbed of sleep; meat hooks on the inside of his head.

By three forty-five he was on the road. The car was cold. He flexed his hands at the wheel, chose his breathing. Although there were few cars about he checked the mirrors every few minutes. At the Maze by four-thirty, Dunn changed into his uniform and recalled with a pang that he had forgotten his sandwiches. He'd wanted to avoid the canteen and the heavy drinking.

The fellow on the first grille into the block was a joke. 'You new boys, you're keen, worried they're going to get out are you?'

'That's right.'

'Did you forget to lock the doors?'

'Yup.'

In the mess he put the kettle on and wiped clean a coffee cup. Before the kettle boiled, Campbell walked in.

'Good man,' he said, clapping his hands.

Shortly after him followed two other men, who Campbell introduced. One was a small thin man with bleary eyes and a severely eczematic face – Rabbit they called him. The other was Skids, a larger fellow with a hooked nose who was a class officer – he had put in some six years in the service at Crumlin Road, prior to the Maze.

Shandy came in with his large round pink Tupperware box under his arm. Frig had a tartan scarf around his neck. He looked preoccupied, and sat with his head in his hands.

'Morning lads,' said Campbell, putting out five more mugs and doling instant coffee into each. There was a strong smell of Old Spice as he twirled around. He took the milk from the fridge, stuck his nose into the rim of the bottle and smelt it. He handed the mugs around. 'Well done yous for getting in at this ungodly hour. Brass-monkey weather. Right, get these down you, come on, look sharp. Now, prisoner 2350 O'Malley made it known to PO yesterday that them lads on A and B wings not getting any exercise was a breach of his 'rights'. The day we get to hear about Thomas Gilligan's murder, he asks about his rights to have a run round. So Mr Bolton asks me what I think, which is his way of leaving it to me to sort it out. I says, aye, not to worry, Sir, we'll give them their exercise. So, now you're all here lads, let's go and get them out.'

'Who's got to stand out there with them then?' ventured Frig.

'You lot and the night guards.'

'For how long?'

'Let's go,' said Campbell, taking the keys from his pocket. 'I want you to be a bastard of an alarm clock today, Shandy, come on lads, let's give them one unholy racket.'

The men followed Campbell down both A and B wings banging on the doors with their batons. 'Rise and shine!'

Two night officers came back up each wing unlocking the doors to the cells, throwing in a towel for each man.

Dunn was standing between cells, half-way down the corridor. He saw men blinking at the light, saw that they were afraid, saw in their faces that they thought anything was possible. He tried to adjust his mindset, considered his time in screening out at Glassmullin. Tin roofs, breeze blocks, cold. Four hours to break them. Taking turns at them, hooding them, head in a bucket, head out the window. Now he looked straight into a cell at two disorientated, half-naked filthy boys and held his breath against the smell.

Suddenly he recalled gagging in his uncle's cattle shed, yellow fizz coming through his nose, spewing on to the brickwork. Marching to the bus stop, his grandfather's words about him all the way, all the hostile truth of who he was, and then what he wouldn't say. Not just hatred in his eyes, something else in there, turning about, eating itself.

He was functioning mechanically, telling the prisoners to move themselves. He saw one man, naked, dropping his blanket and reaching for his towel, then standing up again, on his foam mattress, he saw the urine squeezing out from it as the man wavered.

The prisoners gathered outside their cells, pulling the towels they were given about them, looking at each other.

Campbell opened the grille that led to B wing exercise yard and told the officers to start getting the men through to the outside. It was cold enough in the wings, but when Campbell opened the exterior door a fierce chill came in. Dunn tucked his fingers in his palms and put his hands across his chest. Jostled, prodded and harangued, the prisoners went slowly outside and stood bare foot on the dirt and gravel of the yard.

'Right, now get on and exercise yourselves! ' yelled Campbell. He blew out his lips and shivered with a certain delight. 'Brrr.' He went back inside, closing the door firmly behind him.

The artificial light from one of the lighting towers seemed to hold them all still as if in a painting. Through the rays of the spotlights, Dunn saw the fine drizzle. The prisoners gathered together speaking in the prison Irish patois dubbed *Jailic*. They grouped around O'Malley who spoke, putting his hand on a back, here and there.

One or two prisoners stood apart. Dunn noticed a tall young lad whose hair was shorter than the others, a new arrival. He was arguing with his cellmate in English and Dunn could hear snatches of the conversation, he could hear the word 'fuck'.

Frig lit a cigarette and cursed as it went out, drooping in the rain. 'Always nice to watch the sun come up at the Maze.'

The other two officers stood at the far side, arms across their chests, moving on the spot.

Suddenly the young man broke away and walked over to Dunn, singling him out. 'What the fuck have I done to you?' His voice broke like an axel coming off wheels.

Dunn looked into the boy's eyes, black and white, in the sepia light of the near-dawn.

'Stand away from the officer,' snapped Shandy coming up behind. 'Take your exercise 2892 Moran.'

'I'm talking to your man, not to you,' Moran replied, his bare chest rising and falling. His shoulders were soft and white, reluctant to follow suit.

'It's not personal,' Dunn said levelly.

'How is this not personal? Here I am standing here and there's you standing there.'

'Your OC wants exercise, you've got it,' interrupted Shandy. 'Now stop your whining and get to it. I'm warning you.' He pointed a finger but the boy wouldn't look at him.

'You've nothing to say, have you?' said the boy, his eyes on Dunn's.

O'Malley came over.

'Come over with the group. There's no use in that, Sean.'

Dunn had been in many situations in the army and outside, armed and unarmed and physical threats he could deal with but when it came to moral arguments, he was incapacitate. The boy Moran followed O'Malley.

The prisoners gathered in a circle, hands on each other's shoulders, and O'Malley's voice, low and quiet at first spoke, then sang and as the words took on melody, he raised his head. He and the forty men seemed to take a single breath at once then launched the song:

> *'It seemed to watch above my head, in forum field and fane,*
> *Its angel voice sang round my bed – a Nation once again!'*

O'Malley went on to the next verse. When Dunn looked at his fellow officers he saw they were smoking, looking away.

'It'd better fucking count as fucking overtime,' Rabbit was saying, rubbing his brow such that white dust fell before his glasses like a snow dome. 'I clocked in at four-thirty, I'll be here until ten tonight. How many hours is that?'

> *'A Nation once again, a Nation once again*
> *And Ireland, long a province, be a Nation once again.'*

A night guard came across to join them. 'I've been up all night, now this. I'm fucked if I'm staying past eight. I'm fit to drop.'

'Seventeen and a half hours, it is. That's more than likely against the law.'

Shandy's cigarette was like a wand making a long curve in the air. The song finished. 'Here's the part I like.'

'*Tiocfaidh ar là*!'

'Yeah and ours will too.'

'When I get paid.'

'I'm frozen to the bone,' said Frig and he sloped off to lean against the block door.

Dunn had a sense of déjà-vu looking at the prisoners underneath a single spotlight. It was as if he was caught in the corner of a dream. The sick feeling of it came first, then half-sense, like a child meeting a wall in the dark, hands first. Nothing concrete emerged, no pictures, no story at all, and then it was gone.

Frig was banging with a fist on the door. 'All right in there are you Campbell? You tosser.'

9

Kathleen had got some minced beef from the butcher so they had a shepherd's pie with a jelly to follow. After dinner she got Sean to take the kids out with a football up on to the playing fields and she went along to watch them for a while. He was miserable about it, complaining about the cold and saying how their older brother used to be able to amuse himself, he wasn't always after his father for entertainment. Liam and Aine stood by looking aimless, resentful, insulted while he finished his cigarette.

When she got back in, Roisin Doherty, her neighbour, stopped by for a cup of tea and a smoke. She was working for some Jewish people, cleaning, up on the Antrim Road. There was plenty of work with them as they were always planning something: a party, one of their religious dos, big holidays, and they went to see their family in America every year, sometimes twice. 'They've got matching suitcases, and she's got one of them vanity boxes with bottles in.' They shook their heads, unsmiling, reproachful, lighting up.

The phone did not ring. Kathleen finished up cleaning the kitchen, tossed the dishcloth on to the oven and strode out to the telephone, picked up the receiver and called the number she had for Mary in London. One of Mary's Australian flatmates answered and asked Kathleen to repeat what she was saying. Finally she understood. 'Oh, May-ery!' she said. Kathleen wanted to say, well I'm the one who bloody named her so I should know what she's called, but then she lit a cigarette instead and waited for Mary to come to the phone. She could hear music in the background and whorls of laughter. It was a million miles from Belfast. Kathleen said she was calling to tell her she'd found the bottle she'd given to her brother Sean and she was going to drink it with Auntie Eileen but she wanted to know if it was all right with her before she did. It was fine. She told Mary she was going to see Sean on Wednesday the twelfth. Mary told her to give him her love. She told her she could give it herself when she came home for Christmas, that she'd try and arrange a visit for her or they could go together.

'I'm not coming back, Mum, I'm going off to Tim's parents in the Lake District.' Her accent had changed.

'Are you courting?'

'They call it "going out" here.'

'So you just "go out" do you?'

'Sort of.'

'Well, mind you don't stay in.'

'He's not a Catholic, Mum.'

'And what's that got to do with anything? Sure, you don't think we're a shower of bigots here, I hope. I don't give a tuppence what he is. You know what *you* are.'

'I'm happy here.'

'Are you now?'

'Yes I am.'

'Well now of course, that's wonderful, so it is, Mary. I'll let your brother know when I see him.'

'Look, I've got to go, we're off out just now. Please would you say hello to Aine and Liam and give them and Daddy a kiss for me. I've something to put in the post for you all for Christmas.'

Kathleen put the phone down and burst into tears. She went back to the kitchen. '*I'm happy here*'. She gathered up the dishcloth and cried into it, blowing her nose then throwing it on the floor.

There was a small knock at the door. No one she knew knocked. Kathleen went first to the looking glass in the hallway, wiped underneath her eyes and let the pins out of her hair. Hastily she put them in the pockets of her trousers. 'Just a minute,' she said. She opened the door. A man with a mass of blunt-cropped, dark hair was standing there, looking aggrieved.

'Oh Jesus. Brendan Coogan, what about ye? And me a right mess. Come on in.'

'My mother asked me to drop in and see you, about your son.'

She went to make a cup of tea for him and he came out with her to the kitchen.

'The word from the blocks is that your Sean is a great fella, Mrs Moran.'

She didn't know what to say. She looked at him, then fell to murmuring agreement and feigning undue annoyance with her kettle. He was a handsome man. She shook the kettle and checked the lead. He turned sideways to look out across the yard. He had on a jacket and jeans, his shirt was open at the neck.

She was thinking of what Bernie had said at the last co-operative meeting.

'*Anyone'd want their fella banged up for the chance to have that Brendan Coogan round comforting you,*' and she'd pursed her lips and stuck her chest out and made them all laugh. '*I'd call the peelers myself, tell 'em what time they could find the old man at home.*'

'*Och well we're not all margarin' legs now,*' Eilish Purcell said.

'Your Sean must have been in and out of there a few times.' Brendan was looking at the gap in the fence.

'He was on the run for over a year,' she said, forcing the backside of a tea-bag up against the side of mug with a spoon and tossing it in the bin, leaving a near-broth, dark and astringent, shrinking. The milk smelt fishy. 'The woman in the shop up top knew more about where he was than I did, I used to go up there to find out whether he was still alive.' Two flecks of white circling the rim; others were bound to bob up and join them – she handed him the mug. He took a good mouthful of it, all the while looking at her. She smiled.

'That's a good cup,' he said rather formally, like an inspector.

Her laughter rang false. They went into the front room, Kathleen rubbing her hands on the tops of her jeans and looking unduly aghast in the aftermath of her laughter. He placed the tea on the side table, sat down, then leant forward, rubbing his hands together. His fingers were short, as if the ends had been cut off them.

'My mother tells me you're worried about Sean.'

'Aye. I am. Well he went straight on to the blanket. He said he would. I might have known it. But you see, what worries me is the protest has been going on for three years and it's getting worse and worse.' She looked at her cigarette as she lit it.

'Well, we hope, we think, it's building momentum. As you know, we've got one of us elected from the National H Block Committee and we're getting some world interest.' He put his hands together as if in prayer, placing the fingertips at his chin. 'The European Court at Strasbourg described the conditions as inhumane, you probably heard that. We were hoping to get more out of the Pope's visit but there you go. The Church has its own agenda. We're getting a lot of outside opinion on our side but we've got to keep the pressure on the Brits, and the Northern Ireland Office, one way or another.'

'That lot in Strasbourg, I don't know why they stop at words. They should have torn a strip off them for being torturers,' she blew smoke aside. 'Sorry it's a mess in here. I had this place pulled apart again just the other day and we've not had the chance to fix it yet. Do you not smoke?'

'I gave it up.'

'Did you now? That's a funny thing to do,' she said, stubbing out her cigarette and exhaling, sending afloat the strands of hair over her face, 'round here.'

'Well, to me you see it's a part of the whole system, the fags. Imperialism, capitalism, exploitation. Small comforts in exchange for the big things; like justice. Fags, Coca-cola, a bag of nuts, a nice car. That's what they throw you, instead of giving you your rights. It's what they call a pay off.'

'Oh,' said Kathleen, looking at her cigarette. 'Shite.'

'Not many people think about it.'

'Aye. Well, I suppose I should think more about these things. What with Sean and all. I ought to get more political. I'll tell you something, I'm sick of sitting waiting for them to come round here and wreck the place whenever they feel like it.'

'A lot of people feel the same way.'

'I try not to get angry. You're in it, you're in the thick of it when you live round here. That's always been the truth. But it's no use just sitting here, letting them come and get my kids one at a time.'

She looked at the floor and she had a quick vision of herself lying on it with Brendan above her. The weight of him, his mouth, her fingertips against his chest, holding him off. She glanced at him to see if he'd seen her thoughts.

Brendan was sat right back in the chair, at home now, expansive. 'We're thinking we'll be bringing it to a head soon. It's not fair for the lads to go on like this. We feel the same way you do. You know what's going on with the screws, well that won't let up until we get somewhere with the five demands. Then O'Fiaich is going to meet with one or two of us and see the Brits in the new year. So you just keep your fingers crossed, Mrs Moran.'

'Call me Kathleen, I'm not a granny yet. And I'm not going to sit back and keep my fingers crossed.' She stubbed out her cigarette, squashing its tail down in the small enamelled blue square. *Genoa.* What can I do to help?'

When he smiled now he seemed to see her. 'Kathleen. Just do what you do anyway, what everyone does. Play your part. Support Sean.'

She pushed her hair back from her face and stood up to look for the other lighter. 'They're bound to take it out on them, for the prison officer murders . . .'

'Executions.'

'Aye, shootings, what-have-you, I always get the wrong word. But what I mean is, it's going to get worse in there before it gets better. Ach, Brendan, those lads in there shouldn't be fighting this war! They're in there because they've done their bit.'

Brendan stood up, he took the lighter from the far end of the mantelpiece and offered her a light. As she bent forwards the tip of her cigarette shook over the flame and she drew harshly and turned away from him, pushing her hair back again, looking out the back window.

'I'll be honest with you, Kathleen, I hope to Jesus it doesn't get worse in there. We're morally opposed to them fighting the war inside. That's why we're focusing on the screws on the outside, to get them to go easy.

But you know Kathleen, they're proud, they're in there because they believe in the struggle. You can't stop them from fighting back at the treatment they're getting.'

'Well I'm morally opposed to my son getting beaten senseless day in day out so I'd as soon throw my lot in with yous properly like and help you, however I can, if you'll have me. '

They were about the same height. His face was worn, rough-shaven, pale. In the gloom, she was all dark-red hair and angles, thin and uncertain.

'It's going to be all right, Kathleen.' He stood there, looking at her with warmth, amusement.

Lost for something to say, she took the ashtray to empty it in the bin and he came along into the kitchen behind her, with his cup, saying, 'You've a nice place here. I had an aunt moved into one of these after they were built and she lived here up until last year. Thirty years. Good houses these.'

Leaning over the bin, she was considering whether to lift the stub off with her fingertip and what was beyond his smile – then she heard the tap running and startled, let the ashtray go. It sank soft and snug amongst the tea-bags. She couldn't be bothered to recover it.

Over at the sink she tried to take the cup from his hands. 'No you don't,' she said. The water from the tap hit the side of the cup and sprayed outwards over both of them.

'Look at you now!'

Her dark brown shirt was splattered with water. She had drops of water about her face. She wiped them off with her sleeve.

'Well you can leave off washing your own cup in my house!'

'I'm a well brought-up lad,' he said, his hands reaching for the tea-towel.

'Are you now?' She went to take the dishcloth from him but he didn't let go.

'Well, more or less.'

'I'm a mess,' she looked down at her shirt and pulled it away from where it was clinging. He was still holding the tea-towel. *Donegal.*

The front door went and with a great deal of noise and dispute her family were home. He let the tea-cloth drop on to the kitchen counter.

10

At lunchtime in the mess, Dunn passed on Shandy's fruitcake.

'Christmas cake gone wrong, so it is. Made it myself. Nothing the matter with it, it's just a wee bit loose,' Shandy said, looking wounded and closing up the box. 'Aye, well we'll go off and get some grub and have a few drinks as well. We could use them.'

John Dunn and Frig had spent the morning in the mess, for the most part. Frig had been on the piss the night before and took some shuteye in the stores. There were wooden slatted-shelves in there that the men had rigged up with mattresses and blankets nailed up at the side of them like curtains. They called it the Orient Express; it was taken regularly by those travelling to a hangover. In thick black pen on the side of one 'bunk' someone had written, 'Peg-Leg wanked off here. March 3rd, 1979'.

The night guards did a split shift and they and the orderlies gave the prisoners their food while the officers on early unlock went off for their lunch. The officers on dirt blocks got an hour off for lunch plus thirty minutes showering time and twenty minutes walking time there and back. They took Dunn over to the canteen, rising to go at precisely two minutes before twelve-thirty.

'It's twelve-thirty from the block door,' said Shandy.

'We can do it in eight minutes depending on who's on the grilles. Gives you a total of an extra four minutes, which is roughly a quarter pint of beer or a shot of vodka.'

'You can't argue with that.'

'Or, for some people round here who I won't name, it's a sip of lemonade top.'

After a plate of sausages and champ they headed across to the sergeants' mess, which served spirits at lunchtime; a smoky den with prison officers in a hurry to get the drink down their necks.

'Shandy likes to buy them in wholesale,' said Frig. He handed Shandy a couple of quid and Dunn followed suit.

'That way we don't waste precious drinking time queuing. We've got it all worked out Johnno. Stick with us.' He bought them two pints and two vodka chasers apiece. They were stood near the dart board alley. There were no spare seats, the place was packed.

'And it's all right to drink that lot is it? Even when you're on the white sheet?'

'All right? Why do you think they have nine frigging bars in the place?' said Frig, lighting up.

'What the fuck else is there to do?' Shandy put his pint to his lips. 'Cheers. Your health.' He took half the glass in one draft and shook his head with his cheeks loose. 'Now I need a gasper. Jeez. What are these? Brummy Boy's best?'

'Buy your own then. He's tight as a nun's twat.'

Dunn stood smoking, staring across at the bar, watching a young lad new to the job, smart as himself, but much younger, getting the mickey taken by some of the others. He thought about his son, Mark Wilson. He thought about the letter; just the shortest of notes, to introduce himself.

He'd slept with the boy's mother, Carol, on just one occasion, in a single bed in a bed and breakfast on the coast. She used to call him at the barracks at Tidworth. They'd gone out to the cinema a few times. It was the late fifties. Those years of his life were spent with a permanent hard-on. He'd got her to agree to come away to Bournemouth. In the morning they'd been kissing on the bed and he'd finally persuaded her to let him inside her. There was a knock on the door and the landlady shouted in, 'Time to check out now please.' They'd been embarrassed. He saw there was a bit of blood on the bed when he put his trousers on. They had to hurry out. He'd felt bad. He didn't like to do things like that, to leave a mess behind him; those small wrong things added up, in a way, and over the years they got you down. He hadn't known what to say to Carol afterwards. She'd sat in the car on the way back to Andover with her hands on her lap and a little fixed look, as if viewing the scenery. She'd given him a smile when they said goodbye and when he looked back at her, in the driving mirror, he'd seen her real face. He could see it now, the way she looked.

'Hey, Johnno, listen to this. Have you heard about the ramps allowance?' said Frig.

Shandy was coughing and laughing. He wiped his mouth and took his vodka chaser down in one.

Frig went on in his slightly wheedling voice. 'See, if you've noticed, when you drive in you pass over twenty-five or thirty ramps. Now that takes it out of the suspension of your car so the union's got us a special compensation called the Ramps Allowance. You get a penny a ramp. Don't forget you probably do thirty in and thirty out, so that's what, Shandy mate?'

'Sixty pence a day, three pound sixty a week . . .'

'You're kidding,' said Dunn.

'Scout's honour.'

'Gospel truth.'

'The money they're paying people in here. I mean it's not like anyone's been properly trained or anything . . .' Dunn looked around: a group of men playing cards, another group following the words of a senior officer with intense enjoyment, the four-man deep crowd at the bar showing signs of edginess.

The three of them sat down quickly at a table that had just become vacant.

'Listen lads.' Dunn continued. 'All that carry on the other day, in the yard, it puts the wind up me.'

'How do you mean?'

'You see someone like your Mr Campbell . . . Well, look, when I was in the army, you had to do the job right, you couldn't be seen to get personal.'

'What are you saying?' Shandy sat forwards.

'I did more than twenty years in the army, with prisoners, terrorists and all that. All that big man stuff, all the aggro, it doesn't pay when it's prisoners you're dealing with, well not in my book. It just makes them stronger as a group. The thing is to divide them, to set them against each other.'

Frig was looking at Shandy and not at all at Dunn.

'I'll tell you straight Johnno, *mate*. Twenty years or not, you'd best be getting off your high horse real fast. When you get a smack in the face with one of them piss pots, you'll see red. When it's your missus they're telling you's going to be next for a bullet, you'll work things out fast. Is it going to be one of them or is it going to be one of us that takes the hiding? Like in the army, you fire the fucking gun so your pal next to you doesn't catch it. Am I right? If you don't fire it, you're both dead. They're murdering us on the outside. Why aren't they doing it in here? Because they can't. We don't play games, we keep them down, however we can. Simple as that. We run the place, your man Campbell, myself and one or two others. And we're under no illusions about what we're dealing with here, Mr Dunn.'

Shandy looked both contrite and annoyed that he'd had to spell things out. He paused, booze-blown eyes trembling like jelly, his feet planted either side of his chair, riding it. 'They're killers who're totally single-minded and cunning as fuck. Last week I'm walking one of them to visits and he says to me, 'New car then?' He'd only seen that my car keys had changed. Do you see what I'm saying? They don't miss a thing. We've got nine dead this year so far – nine prison officers. And you want to play Mr Nice Guy?' Shandy gave a dry, rattling laugh. 'Who do you think's organizing the killings, telling them who to go for next? Your man O'Malley that's who. Well he's one of them anyway. This place is IRA H-fucking-Q.'

'Is that right?'

'Are you scared? You should be.' He stared at Dunn, unfocused, belligerent. Evidently Dunn's expression conceded too little, so Shandy came forwards again, ready to pick up where he hadn't left off. 'We've got the top brass in here, Dunn. We need to send them a message. It's not just a case of locking doors here. We're fighting a war.' He downed the remainder of his beer, pointed out a prison officer, said something to Frig that Dunn failed to catch, then laughed a couple of times, lighting a cigarette and pulling an open-mouthed expression that Dunn knew belonged to a popular comedian.

'I'm not fighting a war. I'm earning wages.' Frig was biting the inside of his cheek.

'Then you're a fool,' said Shandy flatly. 'Who's going to get all your money when you cop it? You've got no one.'

Frig seemed to consider this with a flicker of comprehension before alighting on a more general fact.

'One way that they put it in here is that you're either an officers' man or a prisoners' man. And believe me pal, you don't want to be a prisoners' man.' He took a sip of his beer, checked on Shandy's face.

Dunn couldn't afford to stand alone. Isolated, he'd crack up. 'Another beer lads?'

'Aye, go on then.'

'Apologies fellas if I spoke out of turn,' said Dunn, when he got back from the bar. Settling the beers, Dunn took his seat and laid down a new pack of cigarettes on the table, offering them to the other two, who both took one. Frig supplied a communal light and their heads dipped into it quickly, careful not to touch, each head springing back from the noose.

'Who is a prisoners' man, then. Anyone?'

Shandy put a fingertip in his nose and withdrew it hooked. His hands disappeared under the table.

'That assistant governor fella – he's a prisoners' man. They're all the same that lot. University degrees and they're brainless. We take the crap then he comes by from time to time, currying favour with the streakers. They're spineless the lot of them but he's the worst. The shit that comes out of his mouth. Every other week he's down chatting with them. Then once a year he comes round to speak to us, for the annual report. "Don't think I like you because I'm talking to you," I says to him last year and I'll say the same this year. What's it we call him, Frig? Cunnilingus. It means eats pussy because he's got no dick. It's Greek, so it is, right Frig, them being the dirty fucks who started it.'

'Carl Lingard, his name is. The Greeks didn't start it.'

'No, it was your lot from Birmingham.'

'Yeah, that's right mate,' said Frig happily. With exaggeration he pretended to remove a hair from between his two front teeth; the invisible hair was apparently endless.

'That Lingus – he knows fuck all about what it's like here. Now you, you live here now, so do me a favour, put your hand up your arse and pull yourself together.'

'All right,' he said. 'Fair enough.'

Shandy stood up, each of his five glasses empty. Frig stood up beside him. They put their caps on. Sitting, Dunn looked up at them. With their foreheads obscured, a shadow over their faces, the outsized black uniforms with silver buttons, lapels and key chains, they looked like big, powerful, anonymous men. Even Frig. *Peter Pan*, thought Dunn. His thoughts were loose from the booze. He looked up at Shandy. *Widow Twanky*.

A few greetings were exchanged on their way out. When the three of them got to the bar door there was a small group gathered trying to get through at the same time, some banter and a lot of alcohol-fuelled competitive belching. One man trod on Dunn's foot but didn't appear to notice.

On his way into the toilets on the block that afternoon, there was an orderly knelt, washing the floor, his back to Dunn, a large bucket on wheels beside him. It wasn't Baxter. Dunn shifted on his feet, making it clear he was waiting. The man ignored him, Dunn said, careful as a tourist, 'Excuse me, can I just get past you there quickly? Got to take a leak.' The man looked up at him with hostility, a dark-haired man, hatred down the length of his nose. 'No you can't get past me *quickly*,' he said. Dunn was taken aback. Then all of a sudden the man stood up and waved Dunn through, his hand showing the wet shiny floor for Dunn to tread.

'I asked you nicely,' said Dunn, stopping right alongside him.

'And there's no problem. No problem at all.'

Dunn stood in the cubicle peeing, his back tense, hearing the soft swishing of the man's cloth in the background. He couldn't figure out why an orderly, a prisoner, should feel safe enough to speak to him like that. When he turned back round, the man was in the medic's room – the door was ajar, held back by the bucket.

Going off for his break at five, the officer that trod on his foot in the bar was asleep on the ground at his grille. Dunn had to rouse him to get him to let him through.

Back in the mess that evening, he made himself a coffee and accepted a piece of Shandy's cake.

'Good cake that is,' he said, popping a piece of torn glacé cherry in his mouth.

'I told you so.'

11

'It's too bloody cold now, so it is. We'll do it again in the summer.'

Noticing Coogan, Sean corrected his posture and stood the way he always stood when there was a man in the house, straight-backed and facing him as if wanting to see official papers. Brendan Coogan offered his hand. Sean looked at it.

'Brendan has come up from the Republican Press Centre to have a word about Sean,' said Kathleen. She was stood there in tight jeans and with her shirt wet. Her hair was only partly tied back. She saw her husband assess her first; then he took the man's hand.

'I knew your daddy. You take after him, so I hear. Sure wasn't I only with the boys last night and they were telling me how you were the young man to get the thing straightened out, you and that Tommy McEvoy.' He made to dismiss Kathleen. 'Some tea love, a biscuit for Brendan here.'

'I've had a cup thanks.'

'Now your father and I were in the same crowd back in the early sixties. We were both in what was to become the Stickies, but we were always Provies at heart, so we were.' Sean reached for the pack of cigarettes on the mantelpiece and offered one to Brendan. 'Even before they was invented! Take one,' he insisted. 'Go on with you!' he winked. 'They're American. Best in the world.'

'He came here to talk about your son,' said Kathleen.

'Sean? On the blanket, so he is. Give the man a cup of tea love. I knew he would. Chip off the block that way. He'd never have said a word but I knew he was in the Provies. Of course, I was caught in a difficult position when it came to the split you see. I had friends in the Stickies and in the Provies.'

Brendan appeared to submit to Sean's enthusiasm and sat down on the settee. He glanced over at Kathleen, kept his smile folded. Sean took the chair.

'Go on and make the tea, Liam,' said Kathleen, giving her son a shove towards the kitchen. He curved his back to suggest she'd hurt him.

'Well you remember how it was in '69? No guns and the IRA was "I ran away". Did you know a man name of Finbar McNamee? He was in it with me, right since after those shenanigans with the flag and Paisley, back in '64. We got no guns, I says to him. We've got to have guns. Even then I could see what it was coming to. I was in the Merchants, back and forth from Australia and New Zealand, making a fair bit of money on the side.' He winked heavily. 'Bought her mother a pair of canary birds one time. When I went round to see this one, they was laying in the cage, feet up. She'd never fed them.'

Aine had sat down on the carpet with her chin on her father's arm-chair seat. She shook her father's arm.

'Is it true?'

'We stopped in Genoa in '66 and I walks into a shop and says to a man, I want to buy a gun. He started speaking Italian, yabber, yabber, yabber, leads me to understand he wants to see my passport. I brought out a wee photo I had of me in my pocket and I shows that to him and pointed at it saying "that's me". He gave me the gun and it cost four pound so I says I'll have another seven. Lugers and 45s. I brought them back and took them down to my cousin in Omeath. You'll have heard of Shorty O'Hagan. Aine, will you let go of my arm if you don't mind. Of course it's true. It's all true.'

'No I've not heard of him. But there's always been men, like yourself, willing . . .'

Kathleen was standing shaking her head by the kitchen. When the kettle could be heard boiling and rattling the loose cutlery on the kitchen counter, she told Liam to turn it off. Two more tea-bags into the bin, thud, thud. *Genoa* sinking . . .

Liam came out with two mugs of tea, one for his sister, one for himself and his mother followed, gave Brendan Coogan the mug he'd drunk from just before, offering him the handle.

'That's what you call a clean cup,' he said, glancing at her chest. 'Do you always take a bath when you do the washing-up?'

'She, herself there, the wife, she was ever the good Republican.' Sean sat up as his wife came to him holding his mug by the handle and offering him the body of it. 'Aye, it's a Republican family in this house, no bones about it. Jesus shite that's awful hot Kathy! She won't say as much but she's as strong a Republican as anyone. When it came to the curfew, off she went with the other women, all with their prams loaded with bread and milk and what have you, singing, hundreds of them weren't there, and when she was going down Leeson Street they pulled the pram into a doorway, grabbed our Aine here out the pram, put guns in underneath her and sent the missus down to Divis with it loaded up. She didn't bat an eyelid.'

'Well and that was a cockup. Some was bringing guns out, some was taking them in.' She looked over at Coogan and made a face.

'I was sitting on guns? D'ye hear that, Liam? I was sitting on guns.'

'You more than likely pissed on them and rusted up the mechanisms.' Liam stood, hands on hips, chest out, waiting to be seen.

'Kathleen, get a drink for the man,' said Sean, edgy with all the interruptions.

'We've no drink in the house.'

Sean started to stutter, chicken-necked, bum sunk, 'Oh now, don't come that with me. You manage to find some for your fat-arse sister, but there's none for your man here.' He turned to Brendan, raising a finger and slowing the moment as if to allow the man an important insight into his life.

'I won't take a drink thanks,' said Brendan.

'Aye, well I never did myself when I was on an operation.'

Kathleen snorted and laughed, glanced in the mirror, glimpsed the lipstick lying below it. Her fingers rolled it, covered it, concealed it in the palm of her hand. She looked again at Brendan who smiled warmly, complicit.

'We goes back down to Omeath, me and Finbar at the end of '69. We was living in Ardoyne then. Finbar's sister lived on Bombay Street. Don't they say now the Orangies had more than a hundred-thousand guns! What did we have? One or two. What they did to defend St Comgall's that alone would have got medals . . .'

'I was there myself that night.'

'Were you? Were you there too? I knew it! I myself was there for the early part. Any chance of another cup, Kathy? More than twenty years and she still short changes me and never thinks to put in the sugar. Well, now Finbar and I takes his car and we goes to this cousin of mine and we get the floorboards up and get the stuff out. My cousin O'Hagan was the man himself in Omeath. He'd got a lot of hardware there and he says, sure you lads are suffering take what you need. There were two bags of gelignite . . .'

'Away!' Kathleen pointed to the stairs. Liam and Aine protested, then went. There were exaggeratedly heavy footfalls on the stairs and then the sly creaking noise as they tiptoed back down.

'I didn't like blowy ups you know. Not like you young boys. I say wait it's wet, and I opened it with a knife and it was weeping something awful so we decides to ditch it in the river. I says to him, be careful, go steady like. He says I'll take it as he knew my wife was pregnant then with our Aine and the kids were young; his were all grown up. It must have gone out to sea. I put the rest of the stuff in bags, revolvers, rifles even some hand grenades. He comes back and says to me put one in your pocket for yourself, so I did. I knew a thing or two about guns, so I had no problem with that. We drives up to the border and I says to Finbar, if he stops us we'll have to shoot him, so he's shiteing himself and the fella says – a customs officer, nice man – he says, Where've you fellas been? I says we've been doing our Christmas shopping but couldn't find a thing. All so dear. He says, I could have told you that myself, so I could. Mind, it was pitch black and we'd only been an hour or two over there. We drive back up the Dublin Road and then we can't get into bloody West Belfast for all the barricades with soldiers and RUC and what have you. We drives up Clonard and this fella comes up to me and says, Where are you coming from? and I says it's none of your business and he says, Open the boot. Just an ordinary lad, younger than us. No sense. We says open your gate and Finbar puts a gun to his head and he says, Sure, there's nothing wrong with yous.' Sean laughed and wiped his eyes with the back of his hands. 'Sure, there's nothing wrong with yous! He says. We were only bringing in an arsenal!'

'I'm sure half of it has a grain of truth to it,' said Kathleen.

'Don't listen to her. Now the reason I'm telling you this, Brendan, is historical. We were supposed to take it over to the Stickies. But I says to Finbar I've changed my mind, we need to use this stuff, not bury it. So we goes round to this man I knew was gone over to the Provisionals, Calhoun. You know him, he'll tell you the same story. My heart was with the Provisionals, you see. Even then. His mother came out and I says, send Mickey out I've got some stuff for him. He looks in the back of the car and I says, take what yous need. He took what he wanted and the rest I took round to the Stickies. Just a couple of rifles. See the Stickies didn't know their arses from their elbows when it came to guns.'

Brendan nodded, swallowed the last of the cup and rose. 'I'm away now.' Kathleen took his mug from him. 'Thanks for the tea,' he said.

'Well that's how the Provies were founded really because they could-n't have been doing anything without guns.' Sean was following him to the door. 'There's a history to it.' He touched Coogan on the shoulder and put his head next to his saying in low tones, 'This has always been a good Republican home and always will be. I'm still a fit man. Now Sean's away, they'll be taking their eyes off us a wee bit, what I'm saying is, it's a safe house, if you want to pass that on to the boys.'

'You've done your share, Mr Moran.'

'Can't do enough. My boy Sean. Same cloth as me. I knew when he got involved. I come in one day and hear, click, click, click and I knew what that sound was, I went upstairs and looked through the crack of his door, he's sitting on the bed, taking a gun to bits, putting it back together. I said to him, I know what you're about, watch yourself. He said to me, I'll die for a united Ireland, Daddy, I'll die for it.'

'That's a powerful feeling.' Brendan was looking down at his feet.

Sean looked pleased. 'Let me get you a bap to take with you. I'll bet you've not eaten your dinner.' He went back in the house calling for Kathleen.

'I have to be going.'

Kathleen came back to the front door saying, 'Let me ask him then.'

'No, I don't want anything, thanks.' Coogan dropped his voice to say to her, 'Thanks for the tea there. I hope I've been some help. I'll keep an eye out for your Sean, Kathleen.' Then in a louder voice, 'Thanks for the yarn, Mr Moran.'

'Good to see you. Look after yourself,' Sean called back, offering a wave and then hurtling up the stairs in pursuit of the sound of screaming and swearing and then his own screaming and swearing took over. 'FOR THE LOVE OF GOD, WE CAN'T HAVE FIVE MINUTES OF GROWN-UP CON-VERSATION WITHOUT THE PAIR OF YOUS . . .'

Kathleen stepped out after Brendan. It was chilly. She crossed her forearms under her breasts ready to watch him away, but he turned and faced her.

'Just a thought but Sheila McCann and her brother, across the way there, well I'm sure you know, they're very active in the Relatives Action Committee. You said you wanted to get more involved. Well, we're having a meeting there Wednesday night. Would you be interested in coming along, maybe helping out?'

She looked across the road at the McCanns' house. A cold wind whipped up through her porch way and sent her hair all over her face. When she had unhooked it from her ears, eyebrows and nose, pushed it back behind her ears, she opened her eyes and saw that he was waiting for her answer.

12

The Principal Officer in charge of visits was known as Jaws due to his many visible silver coloured fillings. He displayed them quickly, then rapped his knuckles on the desk. A handful of prison officers sat before him.

'When yous're bringing a con down here, in particular one of those on the protest don't talk with him. Not a word. Your Provies were trained in the cages, before we had this fine establishment. It was a university for terrorism and a holiday camp. Those days are gone. You bring the con down for his visit, and you expect the worst of him and you'll be right. When they're not in their cells they're a danger. I used to have to walk into the Nissen huts in the old place every morning to count heads, and every other morning I'd be given a right pasting. I got a seeing to one time that near put me in hospital. That's how we learnt what you call jail-craft. Three words. Stay on top.'

They were sitting in an overheated staff room on the visiting block after the usual lunch: meat and potatoes, pudding and custard. A couple of pints.

'The sort of thing I'm talking about lads is the way you handle them when they're not in their cell. You won't find it in any book, but you'll pick it up. We used to have them "running the gauntlet" when we moved them, we'd have them legging it between two rows of us to get to the van, and just to keep them on their toes like we'd egg them on with our batons. Your man, SO Dan Dare says to us, give it to them hard. Now when this one fellow, Taggart, gets through us, the van's full. So he has to run all the way *back* down the line and gets a good second helping. Jesus. Laugh. I tell yous. You'll hear some of the old crowd saying "you've the luck of Taggart"'

He was sat up on the desk, enjoying himself. *Perry Como*. Dunn could see him dedicating the next number to the ladies working at Armagh. '*Ma-gic Mo-ments . . .*'

Jaws put on his glasses and took a look at his clipboard. 'The point is, you keep them where you want them when they're not locked up. It's not all fun and games though. Where's Mr Dunn?'

'Here,' said Dunn raising his arm. Dunn had been detailed visits runner for the block that day.

'Smart as a carrot,' said Jaws, looking over his glasses for effect, making the others laugh again. 'You'll be accompanying me today Mr Dunn, learning the ropes. I take Mr Gilligan's and Mr Garvey's deaths personally. I knew Garvey. Nice a fella as you'd ever meet. If you're in the visiting room, you stand over the prisoner and his visitor and make sure they can't say a thing you don't like. If they do – visit over. You remember what's at stake here now. No talking to the visitors, or the prisoners, for Christ's sakes. Don't laugh. No listen, lads, listen up. Where's Dawson? Young Mr Dawson there, are you standing on a box, Dawson, you're the bloody Jolly Green Giant are you not? Listen! He was caught having a wee chitter chatter last week and he won't be doing it again. Says, *that fellow used to work with my daddy*. I know that if you don't know someone in here you must have led a very sheltered life, fellas, but remember what uniform yous're wearing. All right, now. I'm going to start with the appeal visit. We've got that Fenian lawyer Mr Bernard in today, on his "human rights" bullshit. Wouldn't want to keep him over long would we? Come on Officer Dunn.'

With his stature and gait, in his dark uniform, Jaws moved from side to side like a refuse bag on the march. Dunn followed him through the prison, grille after grille, until they came to Bolton's block. Jaws pulled in his chin as they were admitted via the main entrance to the block.

'The stink of it, Dunn, turns your stomach.'

'Must be hell.'

Jaws stopped in his tracks. 'Hell? Hell is after you're dead, Dunn. That's coming to us quicker than it is for them.' They were waiting at the circle for the class officer. 'You keep your feelings for your own, Dunn.'

The class officer came out of the mess, wiping his hands on a tea-towel. 'All right Jaws?'

Jaws went ahead of Dunn and shook his head. 'New boy feels sorry for the streakers.'

He was sickened. He had never put a foot wrong that way in the army. There was no personal point of view. There was agreement and silence and both meant agreement in any case. By being there, by wearing the uniform you were in agreement with it all. You were a fool if you put it on and you were not. You only had to take it off.

The class officer looked unimpressed. 'Oh aye,' he shook his head. 'Does he feel sorry for that lad Garvey as well?'

Jaws went off with the class officer, leaving Dunn alone.

He stood looking about him – at the viscose floor, the white reflective walls, the pale-green painted grilles glimmering under neon. His vision was on the blink in one eye, like a migraine coming. His thoughts struggled. His heart faltered. His chest went tight. He put a hand on the desk. *Even a baby knows how to find breath.*

He forced himself to exhale. He was worried someone would see him. He looked up and down, swallowed, blew out. He heard sudden laughter from the mess behind him, the refrain of a football chant. He glanced over at the grilles ahead that contained silence. Terrorists. Men and boys, all thinking their thoughts, killers on the quiet, minds like clocks that needed no winding. What were they remembering, what were they learning? Was killing educational? Perhaps briefly, as a generation is brief. The young sowed horror in their springtime with high hopes for the crop and it rotted down through a long summer. They harvested grief in the autumn of their lives. And did they believe, even as they held their grandchildren, that there would be an end to it all? After a hard winter killed what was left of them off, it came again, this human season, this springtime of hatred. The young went to it because it was in their nature. Could a father teach his son to go against his nature? Could a son learn such a thing from his father? He didn't know.

The click-clack of Jaws and his mate called him back to attention. He tried to grasp his thoughts again but it was too late, the feeling of brilliance, of naked understanding had gone and he felt his usual anxious boredom return and remembered what he'd said. He didn't want to be caught out. He'd never been caught out before. He'd always been able to close down all the parts of himself he didn't need. He'd got himself to the point where he could even forget about killing people.

Jaws put his paperwork down on the desk for the class officer to see.

'Legal Visit for O'Malley? Oh aye. Officer Owen give me a hand here.'

A young man came across, his hat over his eyes, as Dunn had seen Frig affect. 'Step down with me then, Jaws – and your new boy.'

The class officer went down the wing swinging his keys. He called out 'Legal Visit for 2350 O'Malley. Want the visit, O'Malley?'

'Aye,'

'You'll need to do the search O'Malley, and put on the uniform.'

'I'll wear it.'

'And submit to the search?'

The grille guard joined Officer Owen in cell twenty-six, with Dunn and Jaws waiting outside.

'Just squat will you, I'm not doing this for my enjoyment. Squat or by God there'll be no visit, O'Malley. I'm going to need a hand here, Harries, in your own time. Hold him.'

There were a few shouts from the other prisoners.

'Give us a hand in here, new boy?'

Dunn went into the cell. O'Malley was naked facing the far wall and Owen was pulling ineffectually on one of his arms. The grille guard was standing by with gloves on, looking nervous. O'Malley glanced behind at Dunn and looked him in the eyes.

'Squat!'

'For fuck's sake Dunn! Get him into a squat!'

Dunn placed his hands on O'Malley's shoulders and the man flexed his knees. In truth he had decided to concede. Dunn looked away. The grille guard crouched down. His fingers were rubber gloved but he simply shone the torch between O'Malley's legs.

'All right you, get the begs on,' said Owen quickly. 'Come on with you, you're losing your visiting time. Thank you Mr Dunn.'

Jaws flashed a smile at Dunn when he came out of the cell, absently, as if he'd just come off the same ride. 'Right . . .'. He stood scratching the back of his head under his cap. He looked at his fingernail, used his thumbnail to eject some white matter from it. 'What do you drink, Dunn?' he said, as if they were elsewhere.

'Beer.'

'I'll buy you a pint teatime, I always buy the new lads a drink.'

The prisoner emerged with trousers that were loose, and boots that were too small. O'Malley was storing the grievance, his chin was awry, but he moved forwards. Dunn and Jaws accompanied him in silence through all the grilles and gates, and then for a ten-minute walk around the cell block and over to the visiting block, where he was taken into a back room and given a rub-down body search. Dunn and Jaws waited outside. When he emerged, he stood looking straight ahead as if they weren't there, waiting. He was signed in at the back desk. 2350 O'Malley, appeal visit.

They took him to one of the first cubicles in the visiting block. Waiting there was a thin middle-aged man in a suit and tie, with unkempt hair. O'Malley stepped forwards and Dunn saw the vertebrae of his back roll with relief. He tucked his hair behind his ears. The lawyer rose with joy.

'Goo-od morning Kevin!'

Jaws stepped in, hands up. 'Right that's it, visit off! Not allowed to discuss the weather!' He indicated the back door with his arm outstretched. Dunn watched O'Malley, his mouth blown wide with incomprehension then it closed around what he already knew; closed tight around what he'd always known.

Jaws called out 'Lads!' to the officers up at the main desk and two of them came down and took each of O'Malley's arms.

The lawyer said, 'I don't know what that does for you. Does it make you feel like the big man?'

'I am the big man,' said Jaws.

The lawyer gave him a look of loathing, then gathered his papers, put his briefcase under his arm and slid out of the cubicle. He pushed past Dunn, his shoes resounding on the floor all the way out.

Back at the visits detail room, Jaws told the remaining officers the story. '"Not allowed to talk about the weather," I says, and that's it, out.'

'He's a bloody character,' said a ruddy-faced man whose laugh became a bronchial spasm.

'The book of the Maze according to Jaws, Chapter One,' said another.

Dunn looked at his watch. He had another five or six hours to go before he'd be home. It suddenly occurred to him that Angie fancied her boss. The way she talked about him. Always with that girlish laughter, always with a new nickname for him, a pet name. It would suit her all right, his long hours away from home, her working late.

They hadn't had sex in a little while. Maybe she didn't want him any more. He was worrying about things he'd never worried about before, when he was in the army.

13

Thought you were clever when you lit the fuse,
Tore down the House of Commons in your brand new shoes . . .

Top of the Pops was on the TV and the kids were jumping from the settee on to the floor, along to The Jam. Liam had the boomerang his dad had brought back from Australia off the sideboard and was using it as guitar, a drumstick, a microphone, shouting,

. . . left me standing like a guilty schoolboy!

When Kathleen came out of the kitchen, wiping her hands, her sister Eileen was taking her coat off and sitting down. 'Is it Paddy Reilly you're apeing, Liam?'

Kathleen went over to the TV and turned the sound down and before she could say her piece both Aine and Liam were lying before the TV with their heads propped on their elbows.

'It's not over yet.'

'After this you've to go up and get ready for bed so I can talk to your auntie.'

'It's too early.'

'We've a right to some grown-up time.'

'It's too early.'

'I'm that hungry Mummy.'

'How about a cup of tea?'

'Just yous get yourselves up there! You can do some reading. See that, it's all done now. Number one! No one'll remember any of that rubbish in the years to come. The time you took moaning you could have been watching. Go on with yous. And do your teeth.'

Eileen was her older sister, a large woman with fading red hair, the woman her husband Sean called 'fat arse'. She came round when he was out. She had four children herself.

'Shall we wet the tea?' said Kathleen, using their mother's expression. Eileen got up to go to the kitchen with her. She surveyed Kathleen's kitchen with short-sighted squinting exaggeration, going up close to the notes taped on the fridge door and inspecting them, then opening cupboards and looking in.

'Is it a biscuit you're after?'

'Have you not got a drop?'

'Now how could I keep a drop in the house with himself about?'

'How is the Chief of Staff?'

'It's with him going putting ideas into Liam's head that I'll be all the time on the bus to Long Kesh. Hold on a minute there now. What am I saying. I do have a bottle, I found it in our Sean's things. Mary brought it back for him when she went to Gran Canaria with Auntie Maureen, it's a cherry brandy. I hid it up. I called her on Sunday and she said we could have it.'

'Bless her, how is she?'

'"*I'm happy here*", that's what she tells me on the phone last Sunday. She's got a voice on her sounds like Princess Anne.'

'Ah . . .' said Eileen fondly. 'Get that bottle open will you!'

'And bloody Aine. I don't know what's wrong with her. Moan, moan, moan all the time. She's driving me round the bend. Here's the bottle. I put it under the sink with the cleaning stuff, no one in this house is going to find it in there. Have you seen the ceiling in the front room?'

'Looks nice. The drink. You could use it like a serving hatch for when you're bedridden. I hear you're in the Relatives Action Committee. Our Jim gave Sammy McCann a ride back from town today.'

'Am I shite. I'm going to go along and see if I can help out with the protest march or something that's all.' She took a small paring knife to the top of the bottle.

'Aye, well, just keep a wee eye on that Liam. He's been telling our Eammon how he's in the Fianna Cubs.'

Kathleen gave a short laugh and poured the cherry brandy into mugs. 'For fuck's sake. He's like his father that one.'

'Oh don't tar him with that brush! The poor wee soul. *Slàinte*.'

'*Slàinte*. Fuck me.'

'Fuck.'

'That's strong.'

Eileen told her sister how she'd come along on the bus and heard someone ask to stop at the Pound Loney. 'I said I'm awful glad to hear you say that mister. Remember our mummy once said to that fella in Donegal, it's not the Pound Loney where we live, it's Ross Street, all snooty like. We used to go up on to the Shankill playing all the while, back then. You kissed that boy and I told Mummy you'd kissed an Orangie and she gave *me* a clip round the ear. She used to stand on that front doorstep and watch the Proddies going past the house on a Sunday and say good morning to each and everyone, "They're off to their place of worship, so they are." I was thinking of it all as I came along tonight. I could just see your Sean at the top of our street, the great fool, waiting on you. And you going off with him. Who was the bigger fool, then?'

'He bought me a bar of chocolate.'

'For Christ's sakes, Kathleen.'

They lit cigarettes in unison.

'When I was coming back from St Catherine's he was standing at the top of our street, handing out leaflets, or was it collecting for something . . .'

'Collecting schoolgirls more like. It broke Daddy's heart. He thought you'd be going on with school.'

'Mummy was all for the boys though wasn't she? A proper Irish mother, so she was. "Daddy will you whistle for the boys, help them concentrate on their work," and him standing at the bottom of the stairs whistling for what was hours. Have a top up.'

'Christ that's a lovely wee drop. We're going to finish the bottle that way, Kathleen, go steady. Jesus don't spill any of it, you silly cow, look you've spilt a good mouthful there. Rub it in so it won't show. Here y'are, use my sleeve. That's it. It's already stained. God it's better than whiskey. I might have to stay the night.'

'Sure you'd be welcome. I'll put Sean on the couch. He was good looking back then, Sean, he had a look, like, well what did I know, but he dressed like a rocker, you know. He had a look that said kill . . .' Kathleen put her feet up beside her on the settee. 'Jesus, what does it feel like to be in love? I've forgotten.'

'Our poor daddy was all down at the mouth at the wedding.'

'Aye.' Kathleen blew the smoke into the air in rings. 'Aye.'

'Your man stands up and gives the speech of his life. "I feel a bit of a prick standing up here," he says. You should have known then.'

'It was too late then. Christ, I wish I could have a holiday and go to the Canaries or somewhere, drink this with someone else's fella. I wish I could get away. I'll be forty next year.'

'You're looking old.'

'I've still got my figure.'

'You ought to be taking up knitting.'

'Will you shut it.'

'You'll be going through the change next.' Eileen had her feet up on the couch and Kathleen sat holding the bottle with two hands. She looked up at the ceiling. 'I say, up there, could you pass us down another bottle if you please?' Then she poured some more of the red liquid into her own mug and her sister's.

'You ought to go on a coach trip. Get him to save his earnings.'

'Some chance! Well, I am off on a coach trip anyway.'

'You're off to the house in the country are you?'

'Wednesday the twelfth. Twenty days time. Half an hour, once a month, that's all you get.'

'Jim's sister's boy, Brian, he's on his second year on the blanket, God love him. She's up there every month, lives for them visits. Make sure you've got the tobacco. Margaret, she took a camera in.' Eileen pointed between her legs. 'Up herself.'

'She's had eight kids.'

'Aye, but not at the same time. There's muscles down there. Not that I use them. I wouldn't want to encourage him.'

'Don't you ever fancy someone else?'

'Ach for fuck's sake, of course I do, who doesn't?' She pointed at the Celtic cross on the sideboard. 'That was Mummy's. We got it in Derry.'

'She gave it till me before she died, so don't start with your shite about not getting anything.'

'There was a fella I met one time out in Donegal, he could have been my husband, Francis O'Hare. He wanted to court me, so he did. Well last summer, when we goes back there, I ran into that fella's sister, working in the bar. I says to her, did she know a man by the name of O'Hare, Francis, and she says that's my brother and he lives just down from here. Married ten years ago, with the three children. Rory and James and the oldest is a girl, name of Eileen. Well I says to her, give him my regards. What name shall I say, she asks, and I say, Eileen.'

'You've told me that tale a hundred times. Och well, they're all nice before you marry them. It's the kids it's for, marriage, the same way Christmas is.'

'Mind you, if you lost one of the kids and you'd ever so much as looked at another fella you'd be broken up wouldn't you? Remember poor Mrs Toner? Sitting in St Peters, holding that wee lad of hers, shot dead. In her arms. Like a rag doll. I'll never forget that. Poor woman. And you're so busy you're shouting at them or you're telling them off for being out of sight for ten minutes or you're staring at them and they're saying, *"What's wrong with you, why are you looking at me like that for?"*'

Kathleen passed her sister a cigarette. 'Have one of mine.'

'I've got my own.'

'Have one of mine.'

Kathleen raised herself and went to get another pack of cigarettes from the kitchen. She took one from on top of the cupboards and she laughed. Then she laughed again. She came back into the sitting room, smiling.

'There was this soldier when we were up in Ardoyne. He used to come in every morning for his cup of tea. Frank. He was the quiet type but he did say a couple of things to me I'll never forget.'

'Unlike your Sean.'

'He used to say, we're here to do a job. You can be a soldier and save lives, he used to say. They were all sleeping in that wee back garden. I made them cooked breakfasts. We used to have a sing song with them in the evenings. One day he's having his cup of tea and I'm at the sink and he says, Mrs Moran, do you ever wear your hair down?'

'What did you say?'

'I said I had to get the lunch on. It was about nine o'clock. Sean was working up at Rathcoole, for that tool company, he had to go off at six in the morning. I think I smelt the way things were going with the Brits. I used to say to that Frank, you'll feel different when you get shot at. We used to joke about it, you know, you did joke with them then didn't you. One day he's sitting at the table with his tea and he says to me, I've had an erection since you walked into this kitchen.'

Eileen put her mug down. 'Jesus. Jesus. Did he?'

'No wonder they're after calling you Frank, I thought.'

'So what happened then?'

'Sometimes it's hard to remember what it's like to be young.'

He had stood behind her at the sink and put his hands on her to turn her around. Then, he'd put his hands behind her head, his fingers in her hair and he'd kissed her, his lips taking over. His eyes were closed, but hers were open. He was nineteen. She'd put her arms around his back, a hand on either shoulder blade, and pulled him to her.

14

There was a commotion in the block. Dunn could see the backs of two offi-cers shuffling sideways as if they had a dead body between them.

'Go easy there. Easy, you're going too fast.'

'Careful! I don't want it all over me for fucks sake.'

'Back, back, steady man, go steady there, let's get it in the medic's office in one piece.' Shandy looked over his shoulder. 'All right, Johnno. PO's looking for you.'

'Open the door for us, Dunn,' shouted Campbell, red-faced as they came up against the door of the medic's room. They were moving the water urn.

'Electrics don't work in here,' said Frig from the mess door. 'No toast or tea.' He waved a piece of limp bread.

'This is my office,' said the medic lamely as the door slammed against the wall.

Bolton called over to Dunn. He was in his doorway in full uniform, his forehead looked polished.

'Step in here a moment Mr Dunn would you? Adjudications today. We'll only be doing them one more time this year. Soon be December. The season of goodwill. It's always a tricky time. Now you're just the kind of man I want on the block at the present.' He squinted across at the large calendar on his corkboard then smiled at Dunn.

'"Adjudications" Sir? I'm not familiar.'

Perching on his desk, Bolton explained the formality that removed normal prison privileges from protesting prisoners once every two weeks. Staff were required to go to every cell and order every prisoner to wash, shave, go to work and wear prison uniform at which point the prisoner replied either no or fuck off or both. Adjudication reports and charge sheets needed to be filled in. Then the PO informed the deputy governor who designated an assistant governor to come down to the block and go into every cell, read the charge and ask the prisoner if he had anything to say. Again, it was either no or fuck off or both.

'It's really a waste of time, but there we go, the rules are there to protect us.' He nodded towards the wing. 'Are you getting used to the smell, Mr Dunn?'

'Yes, I am. My girlfriend's not, though.'

'It's bloody obnoxious, truly it is. Oh by the way, Dunn, I need your phone number and address for the files, scribble it down while you're here will you?' He handed him a small black notebook with a blank page. Dunn felt in his pocket for a pen then took one from Bolton's desk and leant forward to write.

Campbell appeared in the doorway. Bolton went on where he'd left off. 'The prisoner is then awarded loss of remission, loss of pay, loss of all privileges such as letters and visits . . . what other privileges are there?' His tongue, large, beige and square appeared as he considered. The strip lighting above him was reflected across the lenses of his glasses. 'Letters, visits, ah yes, reading materials, none of that, there are some other things too. Can't recall.'

'Furniture . . .' offered Dunn, putting the pen down.

'They broke what they got given,' Campbell put in. 'Their choice. Just like the windows.'

'Ah yes,' said Bolton, looking wistful. 'Well that's just the place we're at. Normally, I don't think a light or a bed or a window would be considered a privilege.' He put the notebook inside a drawer, then went to get his jacket that was hanging on a peg on the wall. It was warm in his office; there were heaters under both windows. The windows had the same concrete bars as all the others, but with green and beige striped curtains at either side.

'I'm going to begin adjudications Sir, just to let you know. Thought Mr Dunn could join us.'

'All right Campbell. I'll walk down with you this morning.'

'It's not normal procedure, Sir, I usually manage the business on my own.'

'Well, today I'm coming with you.' Bolton took off his glasses.

Campbell looked injured, turned on his heel. The three of them headed off to the C and D wings. Campbell's shoes had been customized, as had many of the officers', with a small plate of steel in the sole. They made the sound of a snare drum.

Frig was waiting for them by the grille, the peak of his cap down like a visor as ever.

They stopped outside the first cell on their right. Bolton put two fingertips in Frig's way to stay him.

'This fella in here, 2111 Lavery, Mickey, he was in with the old man but I've had him put on his own for a while as he's a bit loopy. Might have to put him into another block. He went off the protest a couple of weeks ago; called for me to come down, at six in the morning, in tears. Then he came back last week, out of the blue. There was a lot of cheering on the wing, they like that you see.' He indicated that Frig proceed. 'He's not a well man,' he added in low, quiet tones as if they were going into a nocturnal habitat in a zoo.

Campbell spoke. 'Prisoner 2111 Lavery, you are to comply with prison rules and regulations which require you to wash, to shave, to wear the prison uniform, to work . . .'

Dunn saw the man's arm, badly scarred with burn marks. It looked like a leg of lamb. There was a pile of excrement in the corner of the cell, and some half-hearted markings on the walls. Lavery was cross-legged on his bit of mattress, the blanket about his shoulders, rocking slightly. His eyes were rheumy, his cheeks hollow. He stood up, letting the blanket fall open and spoke up with his eyes distant.

'We are not criminals. We are prisoners of war. These are our five just and right demands. One, the right not to wear prison uniform. Two, the right not to do prison work. Three, the right to associate freely with other prisoners. Four, the right to a weekly visit, to a letter and a parcel and the right to organize recreational and educational pursuits. Five,' he licked his dry lips and carried on, 'the full restoration of remission lost through protest. These are our five demands.'

All of a sudden, a resounding cheer filled both wings followed by a chorus of tin-pot banging. The prison officers were obliged to wait for the noise to subside. They flashed looks at each other. Bolton went to speak, but just then, from the cell next to Lavery's, there was shouting in Irish and then a din started up over at the next block.

Frig grinned surreptitiously with the unbidden glee of a child whose mother was kicking up a fuss in the grocer's.

'All right,' said Bolton squarely. '2111 Lavery. You have stated your position. The deputy governor will be round this afternoon to charge you. Close the cell door, Campbell. Well that was a new one on me, Mr Dunn.' Bolton put his back to Campbell who was agitating to put across his own view.

In the next cell, both prisoners were standing. One was before them and the other was at the window making hand signals across to the other block, writing in the air at great speed. While Campbell repeated his phrase regarding regulations, Dunn realized that the one at the window was in fact writing backwards, with agile finger strokes, pianist turned painter. Dunn couldn't follow what was being written.

The one facing them repeated, word for word, the statement that Lavery had made. 'We are not criminals. We are prisoners of war. These are our five just and right demands. One, the right not to wear prison uniform—'

'We can't allow this, Sir. It wouldn't happen on any other block, not even in the Cages would this be tolerated.' Campbell addressed himself to Bolton.

'It's like a bloody stage play,' said Frig, frowning now and looking earnestly from Campbell to Bolton.

As the man concluded, 'These are our five demands,' another cheer went up around the block and the one at the window made a thumbs-up signal. Shortly, like a distant echo, a cheer went up from the other block.

'We have to do the adjudications, Campbell.'

'I'm not going to listen to that load of old bull forty-something times, Sir.'

'Every dog has its day.' Bolton indicated the next cell.

Campbell strode down the hallway, his shoes drumming and he told the grille guard to let him out.

'Right. Let's continue,' said Bolton, unperturbed.

'Are we to carry on, Sir?' asked Frig, something like Oliver Twist.

'Aye, the full tragedy.'

They proceeded from cell to cell, with every prisoner reciting the five demands; some faltering, one or two slower than others, but all of them clearly well rehearsed.

'1760 McIlvenny.' Frig looked peeved and sorry for himself. It had been a long morning, the drama had passed.

'The communications officer. This will be his work, you can be sure,' said Bolton as they got to the cell next to O'Malley's.

But young Moran, the lad who had challenged Dunn in the yard was determined also to have his day. He was now doing a little dance, jigging on the spot, his fists clenched, like a boxer warming up as his cellmate McIlvenny performed the piece with word-slow pleasure.

'2892 Moran.' The boy Moran delivered the reply with comic intonation, in an English accent of Churchillian resonance. McIlvenny had his fist up underneath his nose and was laughing. From next door, O'Malley was droning, '*Nevv-ah in the field of human conflict . . . was so much . . . Owed . . . by so many . . . to so few*.'

Frig closed the door.

'These are our FIVE DEMANDS!'

O'Malley delivered his own piece in strident tones, and added, 'I think you'll have got the idea of what we're after by now. We thought we'd teach yous our demands, parrot fashion, so you could spread the word.'

When Bolton got back to his office, he closed the door and Dunn heard classical music playing. Campbell was in the mess, complaining broadly and bitterly and casting dark looks around as if they were all a party to his betrayal.

'And that great girl's blouse from admin's coming down here this afternoon, awarding the punishments, he'll probably ask them for a repeat performance.'

Frig looked up from his paper where he was doing an anagram. He went on in a public school accent, 'Our friend Carl Lingus, you mean. *Rather! Good show!* He'll think he's got himself a right load of Hamlets.'

'The day that lot gets cigars is the day I quit.'

Frig and Shandy exchanged looks. Shandy put down his tea and snorted like a horse. Frig bit his grin in half.

'What? What?' said Campbell.

In the afternoon, the assistant governor, Carl Lingard did indeed come to the block.

'The "five demands",' he said sternly, standing opposite Mr Bolton, his forearms clasped across his body. 'Yes, I can quite see it must have been a performance. Religious discipline in a way. Like saying the rosary. It's the psychology that interests me, Trevor.'

They were standing close enough to the mess to hear a loud raspberry being blown. At Bolton's nod, Dunn popped into the mess to indicate to Campbell that he should be more discreet.

'Bullshit. They're pouring bullets into us and he wants to play mind games. It's fucking real, isn't it! And what were Gilligan's five demands, or Garvey's? Or any of them? To have a normal life,' he was counting on his fingers. 'To have a drink now and again, to play with their kids, to see Christmas in. They didn't get them did they?'

'*I* shan't be asking them what their damned five demands are,' Lingard was saying, petulantly. 'I'm not interested. Where do I always go first when I come into the block, Mr Bolton? Trevor?'

'The mess, Sir.'

'The officers' mess, Mr Bolton, did you say? Well I think that gives a pretty good indication of where I stand, don't you?'

'Shall we complete the adjudication process, Sir?' asked Bolton.

Lingard went from cell to cell, gave the prisoners the same cursory greeting then hurried on with more or less the same speech.

'So I'm afraid it falls to me to award – funny word that, in the situation – nevertheless, this is what I'm bound to say, to award you fourteen days' lost remission, fourteen days' lost pay, the loss of visits and all other privileges.'

It was customary for him to ask the prisoner if he had any questions but after a chat with Mr Bolton concerning the morning's events he decided not to pose the question.

'Well, if you need to contact me on any matter, in confidence, there is a mechanic provided via Mr Bolton. A piece of paper, yes, you may write me a private letter.'

Lingard had never received such a letter. There was the same procedure for prison officers. He'd never had one from them either.

'Anything you need to communicate, use the process,' he said to the grille guard and to John Dunn as they passed back into the circle. Noticing that Dunn was new he cheered up and added, 'Can be tricky the first weeks. If you've problems with the prisoners or the prison officers, let me know. We want to know.'

Lingard made his report to Bolton in the office with the door closed and then, with Bolton shepherding him out of the block, tapped on the mess door and put his head in to say farewell. Campbell was on the circle. Skids, Rabbit and Frig were playing cards with Frig exclaiming 'you tossers' every time he unfolded his hand.

'How the devil you lads keep your spirits up I don't know. We all know that this is the hard job. Especially with, well, what's going on on the outside. Not to say we don't all run the risk, desk-bound or not. All the very best then, and cheerio, lads.'

Frig looked up and gave him a glancing nod. Skids grunted. Little man Rabbit, with his feet up on the table, raised an arse cheek and screwed his eyes up.

'No. Just can't muster one.'

Lingard's face fell. He walked towards the block door, indicated the locks to the guard there and said irritably, 'Come on get on with it. I've got work to do, you know.'

15

Cleaning the front room, Kathleen found two pound-notes under the small brass harp on the sideboard. Father Pearse had left them there for her when he came by that morning. And she'd gone on about the cost of Christmas, chewed the ear off the poor man and he went off without even a cup of tea, leaving her the money, half-hidden. She could use it. She'd give it back after Christmas. She took two purses out of her handbag. One was for people who came round asking for money and one was for going to the shops with. She closed the bag and put the money instead in a jar on top of the sideboard.

Kathleen's older brother William was a painter and decorator and he came round in the afternoon and fixed up the ceiling for her. He could only do a temporary job, to hide it from below. He'd put some wood down, and he was plastering over. He'd paint it the next week.

She made him a cup of tea every half hour or so.

'Do you want a bap?' she'd called out, spreading one with margarine.

'Aye, go on then,' he said, coming in to wash his hands off. He looked critically at the spin dryer, rubber hose chugging water into her sink. He'd got a friend worked in the Hoover factory and they were talking about the chance of getting some refurbished twin tubs.

'I like it. It works and I like the noise. It's a hard worker.'

He emptied the dregs of his cup into the sink. 'Bridget swears by the twin tub. Eileen's after one but seeing how you can't get the HP living in the Murph, you're first. I told her that. On this occasion.' He smiled, put the cup upside down on the draining board and kissed her on the brow. Then he took his bap in hand and tore off half of it with his teeth.

What with the ceiling broken, she'd decided to take the house to task and she'd boxed her son Sean's things and left them on top of Liam's bed to go through. Most of it was Manchester United souvenirs. When Liam came in from school she told him to go have a look.

'What about when they let them wear their own clothes again?'

'Them clothes'll stand the washing.'

She went to the jar with the father's notes in it and took one out. He looked surprised when she handed him the money. 'Get yourself a book or comics, something to read, something about somewhere along way away from here.'

'You shouldn't give up on the lads, Mummy, they'll get their status.'

'You sound just like your brother. Listen, Liam love, we've got to start using our heads in this house. I'm going to join the Relatives Action Committee. What do you think about that? Your mother might end up in politics, like Owen McCann's lot. Could you see me with a loud-speaker?'

'It's a loud-hailer.'

'Oh aye.'

He handed the money back to her. 'Keep it for our Sean.'

'I'll worry about Sean. You get yourself something to read. You need your education. Besides, you don't get much from me.' She kissed the top of his head, smelling dust and feeling fur.

Aine came in from playing over the road at the McCanns', two grey streaks on her face, tears long dried. Other things had happened since and now she had freshly grazed knees and was out of breath. She stood panting by her mother, who was cleaning the inside of the fridge, then went upstairs.

Kathleen gave them their dinners; egg and chips, some tinned fruit and condensed milk to follow and told them to get ready for bed. She was going over the road to Sheila McCann's for seven-thirty. Roisin was coming in to babysit for her. Kathleen wanted to watch the news before she went. She lit up a cigarette and sipped her cup of tea. All around

Belfast, mothers like her were watching. Their lives were ordered by the schedule of the news. A chance to relax with a cup and a fag, listening to the killings. You were bound to know someone.

Aine came down. 'Do you need me to bring anything up to Daddy?'

'He'll be fine.'

'What about a bap or something?'

'I'm watching the news the wee moment.'

'Shall I go up the road with it?'

'No. It's not safe. You know that.'

'He'll be hungry.'

'He'll help himself to a bag of nuts.'

'Someone's got to think of him.'

'Let's hope he finds someone.' Kathleen got up and turned the volume up on the telly.

Roisin came in a few minutes later and dropped herself down in the armchair. She'd come straight from the heat of her own television and fell to pointing at their TV with a cigarette in her hand.

'I can't have a fag in peace over there now, with himself always at the coughing.'

When they came to the latest screw funeral, she started up about her new job up on the Antrim Road.

'Screw funeral on the telly,' said Kathleen, down at the mouth, eyes fixed on the screen.

Roisin went on that it was like going to heaven going up there, 'Ach there's flowers in the gardens . . .'

'Right. What's that they're saying, I can't hear. Where was he from? Was it the Crum or the Kesh?'

'It's what you call elegant.'

'Jesus wept, all right Roisin, you've told me before.'

Kathleen got up and turned the set off.

'There's *Coronation Street* coming on! And your set needs five minutes to warm up. You'd better get it fired up or we'll miss the start. They've gone over to colour up on the Antrim Road so they have. And it comes up like that.' She clicked her fingers.

Kathleen went to the mirror over the mantelpiece and picked up the lipstick.

'There's her friend needs someone starting in the new year. They pay a pound an hour, so say you do three mornings a week, that's twelve pound a week. That's worth doing, Kathleen.'

'Aye, well Sheila McCann says you get more on the berew and taking the berew hits the English where it hurts. But you know you could say it's a pay-off, taking their dole money. You know, part of the system.'

'I tell you, Kathleen, you wouldn't know all this was going on when you get up there. It's like a holiday. Then you come back here, to the barricades, watch out for the bloody stones being fired at you, pray the smoke isn't coming from your street.'

'Aye well I'll be taking a break from the dead animals after Christmas, he's got no more work for me, O'Donnell. Tell your woman I'll take it.' Kathleen went back over her mouth with the reddish pink and made a small popping sound with her lips. Aine called it a fish-kiss.

'I wish I was a Jew. I said to her I might become one myself, just for the peace and quiet.'

'My mummy worked in a mill that was owned by Jews. When the boss saw the Prods out the front shouting and screaming that there were Taigs working in there, he took all the Catholics out the back over the train lines, got them out safely and then they closed up the factory.'

'There's barely any left you know. You'd best get round there as soon as you can after Christmas, Kathleen.'

Coming up the Whiterock towards Ballymurphy, it smelt of war. Roisin was right about that. A few times she'd had to lie down and take cover. Once when the two of them were coming up from the Falls, they'd had the devil of a time trying to talk two young girls into getting down on the ground. Shots were coming through St Thomas's, hitting the tarmac and bouncing. 'Them's my new Gloria Vanderbilts,' said one of the girls as they shoved her down. 'You ought to know you can't wear anything decent round here,' Roisin had said to her as they got up. 'They're fucked now,' said the girl bitterly, dusting herself down.

The lights were all on over at the McCanns' and she was pleased to have somewhere to get out to, even if it was just over the road. Eilish Purcell came out of her front door to shake out her tablecloth. 'What about you Kathleen? Going out?'

'Aye, I'm off to see my fancy man.'

Eilish looked unimpressed and went back inside.

Sheila McCann was every Republican's dream date. Thin and intense looking, with not only this cause but plenty of others up her sleeves. She was a socialist. She was a woman's libber. She'd leant Kathleen a book called *Our Bodies, Our Selves*. It went through sex, masturbation, lesbianism, violence, birth control and abortion. There was a picture of a naked woman with her legs apart, and another woman grinning up at her over a speculum with a sort of Rolf Harris smile. She gave it back to Sheila the following night, before Sean saw it. 'When he gets new equipment, I'll give him the new manual,' she'd said to her sister. She told her what was in the book; all about fulfilment and stuff. Sheila said that women shouldn't feel guilty about their sexual desires. You couldn't argue with it. It seemed so unimportant, though. Sheila had liberated women coming from all over the world and staying in her house, now her husband was inside the Kesh. Sharing the bed. When she told Sean about it, he set to swallowing like he did when he carved a roast. She said to him, 'It's a very mutual experience making love with a woman, so they say.' He'd got himself all worked up over it. 'It's all just a laugh to them, and him on the inside, cold and lonely, for his country, and her practising feminism!' She liked to wind him up, it was her only pleasure. 'Me and Eileen are thinking of burning our bras as well.' 'If your Eileen burns her bra she'll look like she's got herself three arses.' Kathleen would go on wearing a bra, but she couldn't be fucked with doing the ironing any more.

It was just Sheila, her brother Sammy and Brendan Coogan in the front room. The kids were in bed. Brendan was sitting on the floor in front of the electric fire, his knees up, his jacket tight over his arms, his hands clasped, in argument with the long gaunt brother who stood by the window.

She set herself over on the far side of the settee, near to him. His head was level with her knees. When she saw Sheila coming in with a mug for her, she got up slightly to take it back from her, smoothing her dress down. She caught Brendan's eyes. 'Thanks,' she said, keeping an eye on the level of the tea as she took it.

Coogan stood to take his tea. 'Sammy,' he said. 'We can't afford to separate the issues. There's just the one issue. Whether you like it not, the Kesh is another front in the war. We're outnumbered, outgunned, outlawed and we're still going to win. Why? *"By any means necessary."* You can't fight force with pamphlets. History is in favour of the people, Sammy, look at Cuba!'

Sammy was long-faced. One of his friends had been picked up the night before.

'I just keep saying to myself, some day we'll have our civil rights and a normal life back. That's the day I want to see.' He opened his tobacco tin and took out a small paper and started to roll.

'We won't have civil rights till we're in our own land. Till we've got one Ireland. You don't think they're just going to give them to us?'

'Brendan, I want to vote, I want to be able to get a job, get a house. That's what I want. But that's all I want. You don't see them down in the Free State putting themselves out to give us a hand. They're not bothered about being united with us lot. I'm an Irish Catholic discriminated against. You're a Socialist.'

'You can't separate the system from the symptoms. They're linked, it's an oppression, you can play with the details Sammy but the fact will remain. It has to be overthrown.'

Sammy shook his head, doubtful, worried. Not looking at Coogan, he licked the Rizla paper then spoke again. 'I want to stick with the rights issue. Through politics, through persuasion. That's why I'm standing. There's too many killed.'

'Too many killed to cave in now. Whatever you say, and saying things is a fine thing I'm sure, but you know – and I know – they'll be men to back you up, with force. But you stick to the talking if that makes you feel better.'

There was a silence, then Brendan slurped his tea, looking across at Sammy from under his brow. Kathleen crossed her legs. Brendan noticed her and looked at her, grim at first, then gradually allowed her a small smile, taking her on to his side.

'Well you're supposed to be here as Sinn Fein tonight, Brendan – the friendly face of Republicanism. We're all here to get the first Relatives Action Committee march together, we can agree on that, so let's get to business.' Sammy let two pale streams of smoke emerge from his nostrils, then, picking at the tobacco bits on his lower lip, he looked at Sheila who agreed in an arch, off-hand way.

'Aye, oh aye.' She addressed herself to Coogan, warmly. 'Well we're really glad you could spare the time to be honest, Brendan, we know you're desperate busy right now. But having you on board with this will give it that little bit more . . . what's the word?'

Brendan closed his eyes and nodded, indicating that she should carry on.

Sheila had some papers on her lap. There was the sound of a toilet flushing upstairs. She raised her eyes and called out, 'Close the door after you.' She looked worn out. 'Else it bangs away on the latch and I have to go up myself and close it. Right, now then, we're all agreed that we need to get behind a programme of marches, to really bring the feeling together, make it plain the support for the H blocks, for their rights. So we'll have the first one the Tuesday before Christmas and then another one in January. We'll start off in Dunville Park, we'll meet there around two o'clock. Does that sound all right for your lot, Brendan? Right. This is the map for it. I drew it myself, though it looks like Una did it.'

Brendan came and knelt on one knee before them. Sammy stood behind Sheila. Between them, they hashed out the details of the next march, talked about what to expect, rallying points, who was going to speak.

Kathleen saw how Coogan concentrated his understanding on what he was about to say next and she thought of her son Sean; the same slightly vain impatience. She saw too how his nose was straight as if it had been cut out of clay. To her, he was almost beautiful.

Sammy began to dispute the tenor of the slogans his sister was proposing. Coogan was in the armchair, on the edge of it. He suggested they worked out the details another time. They had the right idea, he'd leave the words to them. Kathleen offered to help Sheila.

'I didn't think you were into politics, Kathleen,' said Sheila.

'There's Sean to think of.'

Sheila said nothing.

They left just after eleven, with quiet goodbyes, checking about them before they stepped out. Coogan stopped and looked up towards Divis mountain then his head fell backwards and he stood, looking at the white stars in a sky of cool air moving. 'Look up there at all that space.' She did so.

'You can almost see the season moving down on us. Winter's coming to do away with a bad year so we can start again,' he said.

'Aye, well, if you can ever start again.'

'There'll be a new year. No one, not even the Brits, can stop it coming.' He was facing her with brilliant eyes.

'Good night, then.'

There was no light from her house. Crossing the street, she glanced up at the big white house on the hill, with one single window lit, then she looked back and saw the shape of Coogan at his car.

She had her boy Sean to think of, she had her children to worry over, she had grown up round here, she knew everyone, her family were close by, there was a war on, terrible things happened all the time and they were in the thick of it, and they managed to feed their kids and get them to school, and the days went fast and yet she was lonely, unbearably lonely.

That house up on Divis mountain sat high above Belfast, with its windows looking down, apart, unharried, outside of time, far from the day-long drone of helicopters, cars, sirens and buses. She looked at it day in day out. It was a judgement in a language she hadn't learnt.

She pushed her front door open. The drains in the kitchen were chucking up a smell, the house was stale with tobacco. She heard Sean clear his throat to let her know he was awake.

She should have said to Coogan, 'I'm sick of my life, take me with you.' But he couldn't. There was no one who could rescue her from what she loved.

16

Shandy and two men Dunn didn't know were playing cards. The air was thick with smoke, their jackets were on the back of their chairs. He knocked on the PO's door. Bolton emerged in pyjamas, his glasses on, a book in his hand, his thumb guarding the page.

'Yes Sir, just come off the white sheet and it's my first time on night duty. Not sure what's required.'

'Do you not play cards?'

'I didn't bring any money with me.'

'Well, I'm not going to lend you any. Good night.'

In the mess, Shandy put his pile of money under a cup and placed it precisely between two cracks in the laminate surface of the table then he pulled a hair from his head and placed it under the rim of the cup. He took Dunn over to A wing.

'No one in B wing. Being cleaned. Your man Dougal's on C and D wings. That's the shaggy-haired monster of a man in there with us playing poker.'

He unlocked the gate, locked it behind them, opened the next, locked that and they were standing in the wing. There was a plastic-seated chair.

'You park your arse there, Johnno. From ten until seven. Every hour, on the hour, you peg.' He followed Shandy to the end of the corridor where there was a simple red button. 'You press that, on the hour, every hour. That's pegging. That way they know you're awake. You're supposed to look in on the prisoners too,' he said, walking up to the slit in the cell door that was like the sight in a knight's helmet. 'I never do. They're not going anywhere. When it's me I bring in a transistor radio and an earpiece. That way I don't have to hear them going on.'

He looked through the grille towards the circle, swayed a little and put a hand on Dunn's shoulder. Standing underneath the single hanging bulb, Dunn smelt the booze on his breath; the tail end of drink deteriorating made Shandy look lovesick.

'Listen, Johnno, there aren't many of us who sit there the whole night through. What I do is to swap a bit with the fella on control room and whoever else is about. We carve up the evening between us, take turns to check on that lot, but mostly we play cards, watch a bit of telly, have a nap, and sometimes cook a bit of a dinner up. What you do is up to you and you're the new boy so you'll want to play by the rules.'

'What about the pegging?'

'They understand if it's not done right. They've got a very relaxed attitude to these blocks, Johnno. They're just glad it's not them working here. Anyway. I'll leave you to it. Night-night,' and he took the keys from his pocket and handed them to Dunn.

Dunn looked at his watch, five to ten. He'd start the pegging at ten. He sat down. He heard the sounds of the men shifting in their cells. He felt conspicuous to himself. Like the one time he'd seen his son. There he was in his car, windscreen wipers making two rounded triangles of vision one of them squawking, the other moaning, going at each other like Punch and Judy, *Curshtebong*, *curshtebong*, enough to give him a second of sight, enough to see the boy nip up and down, in and out of the alleyways and front paths of the semis on New Street. Then back to the milk float, ducking in, too tall for his costume, too tall for the Noddy milk float; too tall for his boy's face, a minute at the clipboard, easing along a few yards, and drawing to a halt again. Doing the job right.

That was two years ago now. He had driven away thinking that Mark Wilson probably was his son.

At ten p.m., Dunn went to the button. As he made back to his chair he heard the sudden whoosh and splish-splash of every man pouring out his pot through the keyholes. He stood still, with urine now seeping out from under the doors and running in pools, amassing around the soles of his shoes.

'What the fuck?'

There was no reply.

'Is this for my benefit?'

There was no reply, and then some comment. A final splash.

As he made his way back up the corridor, the bottoms of his wet trousers clung to his ankles. He heard footsteps and saw Shandy coming between the grilles with a pair of Wellington boots in his hand and a squeegee in the other.

'They've all gone and pissed at the same time, it's come underneath the doors. I'm soaked.'

Seeing the look on Dunn's face Shandy laughed. 'It's not a special welcome for you, they do it every night. Here take these.'

'It's bloody disgusting.'

'I should have given you this lot before. Put the boots on at any rate. We squeegee the piss back under the doors.'

'What every night?'

'Aye that's the game, Johnno, tit for tat. They build wee dams out of bread or what-have-you so sometimes you can't get it back in. Just push it down and out the back door. Whatever you do though, don't leave it lying about. We had a chap did that once. Cuts your eyes in the morning when you walk in, the urine does. Your man says to us, they slopped out twice, caught me short. In that cell there, the streaker says to me, at breakfast, first time he's ever spoken to me, it's not true we slopped out twice. See they don't want it lying around either. Mr Rabbit put something of his own making into that fella's sandwich box. He got the message. So to speak.' Shandy slapped him on the back as he went. 'So slop out like the good fella y'are!'

Holding on to the chair, Dunn took each shoe off and put on the boots, then he went up the corridor, pushing the squeegee. It smelt very strongly and he had a lump of phlegm in his throat and his eyes were stinging. As he mopped, he thought of Mr Rabbit and there came to mind a boy at school who gave him a hard time, calling him 'pikey', stuffing bogeys or scabs in his lunch, putting his shit in envelopes and hiding them inside Dunn's desk or satchel. Getting the others to give him a pounding on the way home. He'd joined the boy's gang. Been pleased to be in it.

He stopped. *Fall in, cop out.* He was half-way down the corridor and he could hear two men talking heatedly in Irish and then laughing together.

Frig had been talking that morning about a prison officer who'd had 'oral sex with a handgun'. 'What, he killed himself? Why?' Dunn had asked. Frig shrugged. He didn't know. It was obvious.

He checked his watch and pressed the peg when he got to the end. Eleven o'clock. He went back to the chair. They could not see him. He could not see them. The doors were locked. He decided to go back beyond the two grilles. It made no sense but that was what he decided to do. He'd need to open up the grilles every time he went to peg but so be it. He shuffled the chair back a yard or so. He could hear muted chat from the mess, the door was closed.

A hubbub arose from the wing, the moment they heard the grilles locked; they thought he'd gone, there was some talking then laughter. The noise grew until one voice overtook the others. O'Malley started off speaking in *Jailic* and there was a round of clapping as he mentioned the name of Sean Moran. Moran had just come off the boards. McIlvenny started up in faltering Irish and English.

Dunn put his head forward to listen. He checked behind him – the door to the mess was still closed.

McIlvenny was being encouraged to find the Irish words by shouts from other cells but for the most part he spoke in English. He was reading out a letter to them and assigning their duties by cell.

'Seamy and Seamy.'

'Aye.'

'You're on for writing to the television and journalists. Liam and Calum, the Free State politicians.'

'Aye.'

And so he continued, gathering assent from twenty-two cells, forty-three men. A few questions were asked in Irish concerning the content of the letter itself and if McIlvenny couldn't follow, O'Malley would put in a word in English. There was some comment made and O'Malley replied slowly in Irish and then in English, 'It is a combination of different assaults that wins a war.'

When McIlvenny closed some sporadic applause followed. Dunn noted that it was nearly twelve. He didn't move to peg.

'What else have yous for us tonight, Gerard?' O'Malley called out.

'Seany here's going to give us another song.'

There was a roar of laughter and banging of piss pots. One of them started singing in falsetto. *'Do you know the way to San José . . .'* and the laughter redoubled.

'Am I fuck,' said Sean Moran. 'Gerard here's going to give you a full account of his experience with women.'

There were too many cries at the same time; all were jumping at the easy set-up.

'All right, all right' said Gerard. 'Thanks for the vote of confidence lads; I've got two wee boys to prove I managed the job twice. Well, if Moran won't sing, will I do The Godfather?'

'I've got a song,' Moran called out. 'It's a Christy Moore!' There was clapping, and whistling, a lot of chatter and one person kept shouting the same thing over and over again in Irish, determined it would catch on. Then a single piss pot was banged loudly and won out after a time. McIlvenny demanded quiet, O'Malley shouted out an Irish response to the repetitive demand, and then they were mostly quiet.

'All right,' said Moran. 'Here we go then.'

'Go on,'

'Ready?'

'Get going, Seany.'

> *'As I roved out on a bright May morning*
> *To view the meadows and flowers gay*

> *Whom should I spy but my own true lover*
> *As she sat under yon willow tree.'*

When his voice took up the ballad it was thin and modest but as the words and meaning gathered momentum, so did his feeling for the song and his voice trembled with the timbre of another man's regret.

> *'Now at nights when I go to my bed of slumber*
> *The thoughts of my true love run in my mind*
> *When I turned around to embrace my darling*
> *Instead of gold sure it's brass I find.'*

> *'And I wish the Queen would call home her army*
> *From the West Indies, Amerikay and Spain*
> *And every man to his wedded woman*
> *In hopes that you and I will meet again.'*

There was a moment of silence.

'Good job, Sean!' called out the old man from the bottom cell and this was followed with various commendations and abuse.

It occurred to Dunn that Moran was the same age as his son Mark. He sang like a man on the threshold of belonging; quavering, faulty, tender, sincere.

Dunn had to do the peg and he opened the first grille and closed it, then opened the next. All about him the men fell quiet, waiting for him to be gone again. He stepped softly along the corridor in the Wellington boots, *thwock-thwock*, the wet-socked interloper.

After he closed the second grille once more, the voices started pitter-patter here and there, now in English, now in Irish. There was something ghastly about it; it was like listening to the voices of men who'd died together, trapped in the hull of a boat or in a building on fire, hundreds of years ago. He couldn't hear what was being said, just heard the shimmering sibilance of their voices. Even though he was warmly dressed, it was too cold to nod off. It was no wonder they talked into the night, the low voice next door comforting like a coal fire.

When he got up to do the one o'clock peg, he heard a man say, 'Snoring,' and there was a lull, but before he locked the grille, the noise had resumed.

17

If Kathleen had something to tell Sean, she sent Liam up to The Fiddlers with the news, sure he'd be the sooner back. Even so, he had to bide his time, to sit and wait, for his daddy was usually engaged in a lengthy story. When she sent him to tell his father that Sean had been lifted he'd waited close to an hour for the chance. Unlike Aine, Liam did not like to go up there, he got bored, he saw all the men as drunk and useless and long-winded too if they started talking to him and he preferred to sit on the stairs than have his head ruffled at the bar.

'He tells them about things he's done for the 'Ra, Mummy, and he sends me off with a bag of crisps.'

'Liam, think about how your brother was. Think about your Uncle Pleader, for God's sake. If your daddy was in the 'Ra he wouldn't be after talking about it all the time.'

'I know that.'

Liam popped his head back round the upstairs bar door every fifteen minutes or so. His father would frown and wave him off and so he'd go back to the steps, pulling at the little straw-like threads in the dirty red carpeting, then plaiting them, then chewing his fingernails, then going to sit in a corner of the bar unnoticed, listening in. Some of them were good stories even after a lot of telling. His dad talked about all the places he'd been, about mafia men making moves and how they trusted him because he smuggled them from country to country hid inside his chest of drawers for which he'd made a false front. How he'd run a con on the Bank of New Zealand in the fifties, made a fortune and lost it in a bet in

Sydney, and about bringing guns in. That evening he was telling them about moving more guns up from the Free State when there was none to be had in West Belfast and the Prods were killing them, burning them out of their homes, and the RUC and the Brits were firing on them too. 'There's wee Kipper Malone, fearless as you like, running up to Bombay Street with a revolver and all the women cheering him on, shouting, Shoot for Jesus' sake, shoot! And he turns to the ladies and says, There's no fucking bullets in it. Aye. Well I say, this won't do. Them's got thousands of guns and they're going to kill the lot of us. So I goes round to see one of the boys and I says fuck this come on, we'll take a trip over the border the night. And we did.'

His father had an audience of labouring men in no hurry to go home. His father was rarely angry, but he could not bear to be interrupted, he lived for the punch line. His face would sour to see his wife or Liam come in the pub; it meant the certain ruination of his grand finale. 'And what is it you's after me for now?'

'Mother of God,' he'd said when Liam told them that their Sean was up at Castlereagh. He said the same thing when Liam came up and told him that Sean was being charged with the murder of a police officer.

Sean and his friend had been driving a car bomb into the city in 1977 but the traffic had been heavy and they'd decided to turn back. They'd parked up round the waste ground at Beechmount, hopped out to make a phone call and the car went up. An RUC patrol had been passing and stopped to investigate the oddly parked car. One of them was killed. Sean went on the run for over a year. He came home at Christmas to see his mother and was lifted shortly afterwards.

Each time Liam went up there with the news about his brother, the landlord, Flinty, had poured his father a whiskey and sat him down at the bar, and one whiskey had followed another and Liam slipped away again after about an hour. His own Coca-cola lasted him about fifteen minutes, after which he was idle and bored. In an hour he reckoned on the same conversation going round at least once. 'He'll be going on the blanket, then, your Sean,' one of the men had said and his father had replied for the umpteenth time. 'Aye, if I know my own son.'

'Is our Sean putting his shite on the walls, Mummy?' he asked when he came home.

'They've nowhere else to put it.'

'Bloody hell.'

He came home without his father but not entirely empty-handed. 'Dad says he has to be working late, being a Saturday night.'

She gave a short laugh. 'There's your father, devotion to duty. Did you get the fags off him?'

'Aye.'

'Give them over then.'

She went upstairs with him and put the covers back over Aine. One of Aine's long arms was outstretched with the fingers curled as if she'd grasped some falling treasure. Kathleen uncurled the fingers, kissed the palm of her hand and put it alongside her daughter's sleeping body. Once it had been Sean and Mary sleeping in those beds. When he came out of the bathroom she made Liam kneel by his bed to say his rosary.

Then she went into the bathroom; she loved it there in that small room that smelt of soap. It was the only place she got a minute's peace for herself. She sat on the toilet and had a pee, looking ahead at the basin and the shelf above it. There was a mug with no handle for the toothbrushes. Sean's was in the cupboard above it and Mary had taken hers with her. There was her husband's, strands akimbo as if it had been jumped on, there was Aine's small pink brush, barely used under the arc of her father's, then there was her own, pale green – brown at the roots as her gums were often bleeding – and Liam's red toothbrush beside hers. When he was younger he used to enmesh his own toothbrush in hers and she used to marvel at the jealousy of his love.

Childhood was filled with secrets and rites, ways of making sense of the unreason, of feeling safe. She used to have this funny thing she did as a kid where she kept back a piece of bread from her dinner and got up in the middle of the night to sit on the toilet and eat it on her own. It was hard to abandon your own ways for what everyone else agreed on, but you did and being a Catholic made it easier, you learnt by rote. Her children had had to leave their childhood behind long before she did. With their disgruntled breakfast faces, they were surly and unco-operative, as if they'd been kidnapped.

When she stood up, she held the sink with both hands and looked into the mirror. The last man to tell her she was beautiful was her son, Sean. She watched the tears coming out, forwards not sideways, like water spilling over the basin.

'Sure I'll go and have a cigarette and cheer myself up.' She wiped her eyes on a flannel and went downstairs to the kitchen.

No sooner had she switched the kettle on than Liam appeared at the foot of the stairs. He was wearing Sean's football shirt, with a pair of pyjama bottoms.

'Mummy can I have a cup of tea with you?'

'Aye love, come on then, quiet though, don't wake your sister.'

He stood barefoot on the kitchen floor, un-sticking one foot and then the other. She handed him a cup of tea.

'There's no sugar, again,' she said.

'Can I have a cigarette?'

She put her own tea down with a heavy bang, causing the tea to slop out over the sides. 'For the love of God, Liam, we might be half a home, half a family, I might even be half a mother but you're not going to be smoking at thirteen!'

He gave her his saucy smile and sipped on his tea. She picked up her own cup and he put his down and took the tea-cloth to wipe where a ring of brown was on the counter top. He handed her the cigarettes and the matches.

'This place is still dirty and a whole day it took me to clean it.'

'I'll light it for you, Mummy.'

'I'm in training for my next career. Go on then. I used to think I'd be somebody one day, you know. Like our Mary does. God knows where she is and what she's doing. At least we know where our Sean is. Go on with you and have it then. What difference does it make?'

'It's only a cigarette, Mummy.'

The two of them sat, side by side, smoking, with their mugs of tea between their knees.

'Use the ashtray, Liam.'

'Oh, aye,' he went to reach it on the side table but the ash hit the carpet. His mother didn't see. He put his bare foot over it and pressed it in. Then he tapped the cigarette softly on the ashtray and took a long hard drag, followed by another.

'You can take a breath between puffs you know. You're not a condemned man.'

They looked at each other.

'He won't be gone for ever,' said Liam, po-faced.

She put her arm around him. 'Drink your tea, your father will be in soon and he'll kill me if he sees you smoking, so he will.'

He took another few drags and put the cigarette out, then took his cup into the kitchen, and stood there, just beyond the doorway, looking at her. She'd brought her long hair round to one side of her neck, and there she was, tea between her hands, knees curved, feet up on the settee.

'I love you, Mummy.'

'I know.'

'Just as much as Sean does.'

Why was his love so jealous? Did it come from her, from her side of the family or did it come from the way she was with him? Or was it her husband's fault, or the both of theirs? Her sons, and Mary, even Aine . . . they all loved hard, as if it might be taken away from them if they didn't. She was close to something, but outside of understanding, like being at a fair without any money.

He shifted his feet, exhaled unevenly.

'What is it Liam?'

'There are things I'd die for Mummy; for the people round here, for Ireland, for our family, for you, for Sean and the others.'

'Liam, you don't have to take it all on your shoulders, love. Liam, I want you to live, not to die.'

He looked embarrassed and disappointed. The kitchen light-bulb blew with a tinny splintering noise and he stood in the dark. 'The light's broke.'

'Don't worry about the light. Your daddy will fix it when he comes in. Or I will. Go to bed now, Liam, love.'

He rose and went. She knew that he stood at the bottom of the stairs watching her and she called out from the dark, 'Go on up now!' He stood his ground for a while then moved off.

'Is that what you think I want for you?' she said to herself. Her mind slowed to a halt, her brow fell, her cheeks went slack, and her mouth fell open, the spittle drying.

18

John Dunn had a piece of Angie's blue writing paper on the mess table and a biro poised above it. The door was ajar and he saw Baxter knock on the PO's door, tapping out a little rhythm. He didn't hear any reply and Baxter went inside. After a few minutes Bolton emerged with Baxter and instructed the guard on the grilles to wings A and B to let Baxter go down on his own.

The big-nosed fellow Skids looked up from his paper. 'What are you looking at?'

'Nothing. What's Bax doing going down the wing on his own?'

'Don't know. Cleaning. You should look at the tits on this girl . . .' This was the regular line of conversation with Skids. Dunn suspected he talked about it to flush others out, to find out whether he was alone in his condition. That and the relief from stewing in his own juices too long.

Dunn bent over the pale-blue piece of paper. *Dear Mark, I'm not much good at letters so I'll keep this short. Yes, I would like to meet you. You decide when. I suggest you come and stay a few days over here when you knock off University. I work difficult hours so don't expect to see too much of me, but it will be better than nothing. I live with my girlfriend Angela. I'm putting some money in this for your fare etc. Come when you like. Yours sincerely, John Dunn.*

He read it through. He put his hands on the table. He thought that he had ugly, hairy, knobbly hands, like ropes knotted.

'Nipples like saucers.'

Everyone there was out of whack. Booze in Shandy's case, women in

Skid's, power in Campbell's, and money in Frig's. They were all of them in there for one thing or another.

Baxter came in and tidied around the sink area.

'Your team's on a winning streak then, Baxter,' said Skids, jabbing at the paper. Baxter looked over his shoulder, squinting at the print.

'Bax supports Celtic, the fuck-up,' said Skids, eyebrows aristocratic with distaste. 'You'll be able to tell the streakers some good news.'

'I support whoever's winning. Wing-shift this afternoon.'

'You're joking me, pal. No one's mentioned it to me. Does your man know?'

'Campbell? Don't know.'

'How do you know?'

'PO told me.'

'Told *you*?'

'Aye.'

'What time is it? Campbell might not be back from lunch a while, he was popping over to the Swinging Tit today.'

Baxter took a cigarette from behind his ear. 'You big fellas will be all right between you, so you will,' he said, lighting up.

Skids got up quickly, leaving his jacket on his chair and walked out, ducking as he passed through the doorway. Dunn saw him knocking on the PO's door. When the door opened, he heard the laboured refrain of dramatic music. When it opened a second time to allow Skids back out, the music was turned off. There was the sound of Skid's steel-toed shoes across the corridor and then his hat was on the table.

'That's fucking rich that is. He didn't mention it this morning did he? When he did the detail. Nobody knows. I'd have got a few drinks inside of me if I'd known. Campbell might not be back in time. You've *no* idea what you're in for, Johnno. Even you with your army training. We could take a hiding if it's not done right. You need numbers going in hard. They don't give us guns like with your lot.'

Baxter came in again, giving a little between-the-teeth whistle that sounded like the shuffle of feet.

'What happens then with a wing-shift?'

'Nothing if you've got your man Campbell doing it. We've got to get close to forty streakers from A wing into D wing. We've got to check their arses when we move them. It's murder trying to get them to go along with it. We used to do it at the circle, over a table, bend them over and do the job but sometimes we take them into the cell twenty-six and we do it over a mirror. Depends. What with Garvey being killed and that, Mr Campbell would have wanted to express a certain point of view. All part of letting them know what's what. He'll be that fucking scunnered if he gets here and it's all done.' Skids proceeded to walk up and down the mess, smoking and wheeling about to look at the clock.

'Who does what?'

'Whatever Campbell tells you to do, you do. Frig does the torch, does the looking up their arses. Rabbit does the worst bit, the fingers.' He twiddled his fingers like a puppeteer warming up. 'I just drag them about, get them moving. When you're in the middle of it, you just do what you've go to do.' He started to pace again.

At three o'clock, Bolton had eight men assembled ready for the wing-shift. Skids shook his head at Dunn.

'A wing-shift is not a nice thing. But we need to get the cells cleaned so we have to move the prisoners. Nobody likes the mirror-search, least of all Shandy here.'

Shandy had been asked to come back early from lunch and he was morose. He was holding a thin pair of latex gloves. 'It's usually Rabbit that does it,' he said.

'Someone's got to do it,' said Rabbit, straightforward, blinking through his glasses, which were as ever finely dusted, as if with icing sugar.

Frig held the mirror. A square piece of glass embedded in a thick piece of latex foam. 'Fucking stargazer, that's me. Oy, how does it look from the back, Sir, shall I take a bit more off the sides?'

'No need for the torch today Officer Harding.' said Bolton. 'We are going to make the big bad wing-shift a thing of the past. Gently does it. If you can show me you're a good team, who can get things done without trouble then you'll be sound with me and I'll be doing my best to make sure there's some days for you.'

Skids stopped him. 'There's no riot squad on hand then?'

'Nope. No need.'

'Should we wait for Senior Officer Campbell?' put in Shandy.

'I'm the Principal Officer here, you follow my orders.' Bolton narrowed his eyes, looked at each of them, wished them good luck and made for his office. 'You know where I am.'

'Come on then you lot.' Shandy dragged himself ahead of them, shaking his head.

As the officers were being admitted to the wing, a cry in Irish went up. *'Bogadh sciatháin!'*

There was a small commotion at the circle behind them and Dunn saw that Campbell was striding towards them, leaving his cap on the desk.

'Thank fuck you're back, mate,' said Skids, waiting at the second grille. The others expressed agreement.

'Aye,' said Campbell, tight-lipped. 'I didn't know there was a wingshift on.' Dunn could smell the booze on him. He was looking at each of them one at a time, as if assessing their moral fibre, his chest rising and falling.

'Owen, you gather up the lads on break and get them here in riot gear as soon as.'

Then he moved ahead and tapped on the grille door and they were admitted; once through to the wing each man was limbering up on the balls of his feet.

'All right lads let's get those fucking filthy bastards out of here and into D wing. Ditch the mirror, Frig. We'll do the check right here on the table before we cart them over into D wing. Shandy, you can work with me on getting the streakers out. Don't want to waste your big hands on their wee arses. Let Rabbit do that. Johnno you can help him hold them. Skids, you get them over it and off it. Frig, you, Owen and Pitt and the others get them across to D wing.'

A shout went up. It sounded like a command, the urgency

comprehensible in any language. The officers looked round at each other.

'Let's fucking have them!'

Skids and Shandy went down to the end cell with armfuls of the thin, white towels. Campbell followed.

'Out!' he shouted.

Dunn stood back with Rabbit, Frig and the other blokes. Rabbit was putting on the latex gloves. Shandy threw his towels on to the ground. The prisoner would not come out; Campbell and Shandy went in to get him, a man with grey chest hair. Shouts came from the other cells, a clamour rising with many of the prisoners beating the doors or pipes.

'Drop the blanket!' Campbell shouted at the prisoner.

The old man was trying to remain seated. 'Not without a towel round me.'

Campbell put his hand on to the old man's head and grabbed a handful of hair. He pulled him forwards with such a force that the man let drop his blanket.

The cells went berserk, tin to brick, tin to brick, 'Bastards!'

Campbell pulled the naked man by his hair up towards the mirror, sweating and grinding his teeth.

'Forget the fucking towels, bring them out naked!'

While Campbell and the others went back for the next one, Frig told the first prisoner to squat over the mirror. The old man said no, he would not. Frig stood behind him, hands on his shoulders, kicked his legs apart. The prisoner's body was shaking. Skids and Owen grabbed him, bent him forwards over the table, shoving his head down towards the floor and Dunn was to hold him there while they pulled his legs further apart. Dunn stood holding the man's shoulders down, tensing to hold the weight that was being propelled forwards time and time again as the man resisted – wriggling, clenching, raising his head, then moving his face to try and bite – when the two officers grabbed a knee each and forced them up alongside his waist. The man let out a long wail.

'Oh mother of God, oh sweet Mary . . .'

'Fucking shut up and keep still,' said Rabbit, shifting in closer. 'Keep him still, Johnno. I can't see a thing.' He put his two thumbs between the man's arse cheeks and the man's head surged forwards and he let out a shout. Dunn braced, holding the man's head against his stomach.

Dunn felt bile rising the wrong way up the centre of his body creating a channel where there should be a void. In his mind he saw the midday grey of outside, smelt the earnest fragile sickness of the humdrum rain and longed to be in it, walking under his own steam, headed any which way. *I never liked school, I never liked football, I never liked the army.*

Then Rabbit was done. He brushed his red flaking brow with his forearm, stepping backwards. 'You take him now Skids. Put him against the wall. Bring the next.'

Skids got behind the naked man, lifting him bodily, his arms in a lock under the man's rib cage, almost wearing him across to the other wing. 'Dead weight,' he panted, pushing him up against the wall. 'Keep your face to the wall.'

One by one the prisoners were brought up. Campbell didn't wait for a refusal but grabbed each one by the hair and dragged them. Some of them tried to remain in a sitting position and the other guards weighed in to help Campbell. As they got them to the table, Campbell would assert his mastery, kneeing a prisoner from behind, delivering blows with his stick.

The grille opened and four or five more prison officers came down the wing with visored helmets, shields and batons and as soon as a cell door was open they went in with their sticks out, grabbing men.

Rabbit took a breather to bid the reinforcements a good evening. He relaxed into the task now, saying to the prisoner before him, 'Would you please bend over it, Sir? No? Right! Get the bastard lads.' With the man held down, and Rabbit's two fingers inside him, the others started to laugh, a slow laugh at first, then turning aside to give vent to their full-throated laughter. Pitt and Owen were keeping watch over the searched prisoners against the wall and those who turned to look got a blow.

Dunn could hear O'Malley shouting. All the time the din coming from the cells was building. It sounded like a full-scale riot. Bolton must surely be hearing the noise, but he did not come out of his office.

Campbell was angry, excited, out of breath. 'Get a fucking move on!' he screamed at Rabbit. He strode up and down the wing, stopping outside of O'Malley's cell.

'Who's the fucking OC now, eh? Who's the fucking King of the Wing now, you Fenian scumbag.'

Dunn had a prisoner's head between his hands. He looked up to see Campbell's face, a mixture of rage and joy.

The other men were shaking their heads and cracking up. Frig was smiling on the side of his face nearest them. Skids was standing back with his hands on his hips; whether it was a physical pain on his face, or just breathlessness, Dunn couldn't tell, but he looked awry.

There was some frustration from the surplus officers, those who were standing outside the cells or up with the prisoners, and they were calling out to those who were handling the prisoners, 'Come on, come on, you lot.'

'Bloody hell take all day!'

'Hey Rabbit, get your finger out, Rabbit!'

'Yeah get your finger out!'

The grille officer was standing behind his locked door, looking bitterly wise like an old soothsayer, muttering, 'This isn't working right.'

The block door guard had his fingertips on the first grille and was peering through.

Skids had one of the younger prisoners and was bringing him up the wing, baton in the small of his back. It was the artist. One or two of the prisoners against the wall tried to turn and say something to him and got blows to their shoulders. He leant across the table.

'In there then,' Skids said.

The prisoner's head went limp. Dunn had no need to hold it but he put his hands either side anyway.

Rabbit scowled as if he were preparing an animal. Dunn recalled Rabbit saying before, 'They're not like you and me are. They choose to live in their own shit, you know. They don't mind the filth, the Taigs, they grow up with it.'

Dunn looked down at his boots and saw a small wet drop on the toecap of his left boot, widening. The boy's eyes were screwed up, his mouth open.

Three or four officers were staggered around a cell door, trying to get Moran and McIlvenny out. Skids was holding a single towel. Shandy was standing aside, hands over his forehead, calling out, 'The fucker's nutted me!'

It seemed that Moran had jumped out from behind the cell door and cracked Shandy across the bridge of the nose. The other officers went quickly down to join him. They tossed the scrawny, academic looking McIlvenny on to the concrete and set about giving him a kicking while Campbell himself held Moran, shaking him, and making him look at McIlvenny.

'See that, that's because of you he's getting that.' He pulled Moran's head close to his. 'You know where I live, do you? You know where I live?'

McIlvenny had his hands over his face, knees up at his chest, while the prison guards booted him in the stomach, the back, and the arse. Moran was held with his arms behind him and Campbell was still shaking him – not entirely of his own will – he was shaking in spite of himself. Dunn saw how their expressions matched, Moran and Campbell, as they looked at the man on the floor being kicked. They were both gripped as if watching a disaster spread, a fire or a flood. The men who'd been doing the kicking stood back from their effort, wiping their noses with their arms, taking a look at each other to see if it was done.

'Let's get the rest of them out of their cells and get this job finished.'

'See who else wants to fuck around.'

'You all right there Shandy?'

McIlvenny's neck stretched and he put a hand out and felt for the towel beside him. He pulled it across his backside.

'This one can go on the boards again,' Campbell offered Moran to Owen. 'Stick him in twenty-six. Some fucking use your OC is to you now.'

There were just two cells that remained. One was occupied by O'Malley and his cellmate, the other had a single prisoner. With an ear each two officers pulled the single prisoner to the table. His hair fell forwards over his shoulders in two pieces. Rabbit put his fingers up the man's anus. The man's body tensed and he moved his head to the side, his entire face clenched.

'Let's just check the mouth,' said Rabbit, moving around the man and forcing the same fingers into the man's mouth. The group of officers standing by, the grille guard too, fell about laughing. Rabbit looked up at Dunn. 'Get the last ones out, Johnno.'

'Aye, give me a break now,' said Campbell.

Frig and Dunn went over to O'Malley's cell. Frig opened up. Dunn went inside with towels. O'Malley's cellmate was standing, blinking in the corner of the room, his hands holding a towel around his waist. His chest was moving. O'Malley was beside him.

'All right,' said Dunn. 'All right, let's go steady, just come with me, come on.'

The younger man refused to squat. One of the officers came forwards. He was forced down in any case and given a cursory check before being taken over to the wall.

O'Malley stood outside the cell with Dunn behind him, surveying the scene. Many of the prisoners against the wall tried to look at him.

'Bend over,' said Rabbit, indicating the table.

'No.'

A few of the prisoners managed to look round.

'Forget it,' said Campbell suddenly, rolling his sleeves back down. 'We've made our point. Take him away; take the lot of them over to D wing. Let's call it a day.'

Afterwards, most of the officers went off for teatime, for a good drink. Dunn went into the TV room to be apart from the others. He could hear the crescendo of opera from the PO's office, at full volume.

He didn't want any company; the noise of the TV was good enough cover. He was watching it without hearing a word that was being said, without seeing at all what was being shown. Skids came in, offered him a cigarette. He shook his head.

'Those wing-shifts aren't easy,' said Skids, shuffling forward his chair to be close to him. 'I think your man Rabbit takes it too far.'

'Need to take a leak.'

Dunn got up and went out into the dark privacy of a toilet cell. He saw in his mind's eye McIlvenny's hand reaching for the towel. He sat for a while with his head in his hands. The letter to his son creaked in his inside pocket.

Foot above pedal, the charging of the gears, feeling the vehicle starting to pull; then foot to pedal and the wheels turn.

His chest surged and he cried out. He wept for a few minutes, his chest on his knees, then he sat up, wiped his eyes with the sharp-edged toilet paper, flushed the toilet, and went back out.

Skids was in the mess now, alone, smoking, his chair pushed away from the table, his legs planted wide.

'I was looking for you.' He greeted Dunn with gratitude, and a touch of real happiness – as if they were friends. 'Wondered what you were about. I don't like the nights in here over much.'

Then he took his cigarette from his lips, and holding it like a pen, pretended to study it. 'I wouldn't let anyone do that to me.'

19

On her way up to the Ballymurphy Credit Union to sort out the loan plan for Christmas, Kathleen stopped in at The Fiddlers at lunchtime and Aine begged to be allowed to stay, as there was no school.

'Bring her back sober,' she said from the door.

Aine was straight up on a stool at the bar with a lemonade and some crisps, treated like a queen, smiling when she couldn't follow the joke. She sat with a pen and a beer mat, doodling, or playing hangman with one of the men, usually Fergal O'Hanlon, who was in there while it was open, going off labouring for the council when it wasn't.

'I see your gorgeous redhead's back, Sean.'

The pub was a kinder place by far than school and a world without women, wives and mothers was a place without guilt or drudgery, drawing on ancient loyalties, brimfull of men with their red eyes sentimentally inclined, tobacco-stained skin, sagging mouths.

After closing, when the doors were shut, and a group of big-handed, slow-eyed men close by, Fergal took out his harmonica and played across the landscape of melancholy.

With his head on the tilt, the old loose skin on his hands falling back, one hand fluttering before the small instrument like a pigeon wing, he addressed himself to Aine. He had an eye closed, an eye open, and the eye that was open looked smeared with the dark but in the centre of it, there was light. The other men fell quiet and looked on; they had become a congregation. Occasionally as well-known chords surfaced, voices would step in with words and then fall away again.

She saw her father stand by Fergal, transported, his eyes closed; finding privacy. He put a hand softly, tenderly around Fergal's back, resting it on his shoulder, and moved his chin to the harmony, marvelling.

Of a sudden, Fergal stopped, both eyes snapped open and he took the harmonica from his mouth and turned his head to look at Sean's hand. 'What?'

'What?' asked Sean. Then following the direction of Fergal's stern look, he saw his own hand, reddened and removed it.

The group of men roared and hearing the sounds of each other encouraged them to hoot and wheeze all the more.

'"*What?*" your man says.'

'"*What?*" says the other.'

And Sean was grinning at himself and Fergal shook his head and put the harmonica to his mouth again.

Sean winked at his girl on the bar stool in the middle of it all, the girl with long red hair, who was beaming at him, more in love with Sean Moran than her mother had ever been.

20

When he got home from work the night of the wing-shift, Angela was smiling her secretive smile that revealed more than it hid. Her boss had lent her the Datsun for the weekend, to try it out. He was offering it at a good price.

'What else is he offering,' said John Dunn, deadpan, pulling on his jeans. He'd had a shower. 'I said, what else is he offering?'

'I heard you.'

'Well?'

'Are you slabbering, John?'

'*No, I'm chewing a brick*,' he mimicked her. He was buttoning his shirt. He pulled it at the collar, took a quick look in the bathroom mirror and smoothed down his hair.

'Will we take it for a spin, then, John?'

'If you want.'

'Jesus, you're home for once, it's Friday night, we've got a brand new car . . .'

'It's not ours.'

'I don't know what's wrong with you, so I don't.'

He lowered his head as he came out of the bathroom and looked her in the eyes. 'When was the last time we slept together?'

Frowning, tawny hair and freckles, she was sweet looking, sober and clean, the real thing. But with just the one drink in her, and people around, her eyes bulged, her mascara smeared and she looked not so much tarty as needy, and he disliked this recollection.

'You know what I mean Angie. You know what I'm talking about. Don't play-act.'

'For Christ's sakes John. Why are we even talking about it? We've never had to talk about it before. You've barely been home!' She put her hand across her middle and held her arm. She was stood in the corner of the stairwell at the top of the stairs.

He looked past her to the small useless frosted-glass window from which the paint was peeling and which he'd been meaning to do something about.

'I've got the money now to make this place better and not the time. What's the point in that? What do you do of an evening now? Work late? Go for a drink with your boss? Go for a drive?'

'I've no secrets from you, John,' she said. She was wearing eye make-up and lipstick that looked as if it had just been put on. For him.

'I'm sorry.'

'I don't know what's wrong with you.' She made her way down the stairs. When she got to the bottom step she looked back. He had his fingertip under a piece of loose paintwork at the window frame. 'Another letter came for you today from England.'

'Let's try out that car then.' He came trotting down the stairs, putting his hands on her hips, guiding her to the front door. 'What about that promise you made me?'

'You'll be lucky.'

'Yup.'

He opened the front door, let the dark in. Angie switched on the porch light.

'Smell it!' she said, the car door open, leaning in, her feet almost out of her slippers, nose to the dash. 'It's got that new car smell, it smells of coconut.'

He went round to the passenger side, got in.

'What does it do to the gallon?' he said dubiously, his finger on the button for the electric windows.

'I've never had electric windows,' she said, swinging her legs inside and closing the door. She started it up. He gave a half-nod of modest approval, closed his own door.

'Go and lock up, Angie, and let's take it for a spin.'

With the radio playing the slow and curious sound of 'Walking on the Moon', they made their way through East Belfast, alternating the windows. One down, one up, one up, one down. After the junction that lay between Castlereagh Road and Ballygowan Road, Angie put her foot down and the silver Datsun flew along. John lowered his seat.

She pulled into a lay-by, flicked off the lights and turned off the engine.

'Right then Mr Dunn. Now for the rest of my test.'

He leant over and kissed her, putting a hand on her breast. Then he took her own hand and put it down between his legs. She unzipped him, and bent forwards.

When he closed his eyes he saw a man with his head forced to the side, his eyes wide – the image had come up on him from behind, like a knife to his neck. He put his hands on her head to stop her.

'What's wrong?' she said, sitting up and putting on the light over the mirror.

'I don't know. It's not you. I don't know. Let's get back home.'

That night, when she was asleep, he crept back downstairs and read the letter she'd left on the table. Mark was going to come over, as soon as the university term was finished. He'd more than likely be staying for Christmas, then. Jesus. That was a bit heavy going. How was he going to cope? Christmas. He'd felt relieved that with the job he wouldn't have to go to Angie's family. What did the boy want?

John took another leaf of paper from her writing block on the shelves in the front room and he sat down, pen in hand. He looked at the carriage clock on the mantelpiece. It was after one. He was on early unlock.

Dear Angela,

    I should have told you this before. When I was nineteen, in Andover, I met a girl. Long and the short of it is she got pregnant. She

said she'd deal with it and not to worry. That was that, I thought.
Then fourteen years on I was back in Tidworth and so was this mate
of mine from the early days. I bumped into him in the Naafi and he
told me how he'd been in Andover and run into that girl and that she
had a teenage kid now. Looked like me, spit image. I thought he was
joking but I was going to go and see for myself except I was sent back
out here the next Monday. In the summer of '75 I went over for a
break and I went by the pub he said she worked in and I got to speak
to her. We had a few drinks and she told me that it was true, her son
was mine. Her dad had more or less raised the boy. Mark Wilson is the
boy's name. We agreed it was best to leave things how they stood for
the time but she told me where I might find the boy, just to see him,
not to talk. She told me he earnt a few bob doing the milk round in
the town. I saw him then. There was something about him that was
like me that was true. Those letters from England are from him. His
mother told him about me and he says he'd like to get to know me.
He's nineteen himself now. I'd like it if he could come and stay. He's in
his first year of University at Bristol. Sorry about it all.

Love, John.

Then he left the folded note at the bottom of the stairs and tiptoed up to
sleep in the spare room. He lay awake, remembered the things he used to
think of to get himself to sleep when he was a kid, how he used to circu-
late the few benevolent images he got from the Saturday Pictures.

21

Her visit with Sean was on the Wednesday. On Monday she got the tobacco, an ounce. On Tuesday she remembered the Clingfilm. She was shocked she'd not thought of it before. She went out to get it and she got another ounce as well, chiding herself in the lashing rain for not getting it all on the Monday. She'd put that morning by to write to Sean and now she was losing the half of it. When she got in, she made herself a cup and started thinking about her son; how the early years of the Troubles had hit him hard.

Just a boy he'd seen the troops come in to take command, he heard the chaos the night they took away the men for internment, heard the stories that came back from interrogations. When his two uncles, Kathleen's brothers William and Peader, were in Long Kesh, he was sent down to his grandmother's every week with bits and pieces for the parcels. Back then, the prisoners wore their own clothes and cooked their own meals. After Kathleen's father died in 1972, Sean's grandmother, Anne Marie got on with it by herself but Sean lent a hand and went to the butcher's for her when he could. 'It's not funny for Granny getting them parcels together,' he said. Everybody was in the same boat, she'd replied, every other house in West Belfast had someone missing from it. The prisoners relied on those parcels. He brought back steak one time and Anne Marie cooked it and put it out on tin foil to cool. The dog ate it so his grandmother went to her purse and took the money out for him to get another steak. 'And that'll be the last.' She'd cooked it again and when it was cooling, the dog got it again. Sean chased the dog out into the road and the old woman sat down on her doorstep. Her neighbour came out, shopping bag in hand, rain hat on, saw the old woman there and asked what the matter was. Then she gave Anne Marie the money from her purse and went back inside. Sean had gone over to thank the woman.

'You tell Anne Marie that whenever I can help her I will and she's only to ask,' said the woman standing, and her husband in his chair, and Sean saw that they were having bread and sugar sandwiches with their tea.

These were the things he kept to tell her when he got home. He was a mimic as well, her Sean, a natural storyteller. It was his grandfather, Paddy Moran, Sean's father who coaxed him, pointing and insisting they all pay attention while Sean was describing the peelers or the Brits, the box-formation movement of the British soldiers with their loud-hailer, and taking off their voices, 'Disperse or we'll shoot!' and the jeering of their neighbours. 'Disperse – or we'll throw stones!'

In late '72, Thomas, Paddy's second-youngest boy, 'Uncle Tommy', was shot in the back by the Brits, climbing over a fence behind the Falls Road.

Sean was twelve at the time of the funeral and he had stood awestruck and full of untravelled emotion as three men, with balaclavas and berets fired off over the coffin with its tricolour flag.

Her husband had gone around asking for headache pills. 'That's five he's got now,' said Mary, eleven at the time.

His grandfather, Paddy, had not shed a tear that day and he criticized the priest for going too fast such that the father turned to him and said out loud, 'So tell me, what part did I leave out, Paddy?'

'That oul' bastard doesn't care about Thomas being gone,' said Sean the father.

Young Sean made his own way up to his grandfather's, coming back with the tales of Republican history. Then one day about two months after Thomas had died, Sean came in and said, 'Granda's hair's dropped out.' The next week he told them Paddy was moving to Dublin and that he'd said for Sean to say his goodbyes for him. And her husband went up The Fiddlers, came home blind-drunk and slept curled up around the small fern tree in the front of their house.

In his early teens, '73, '74, Sean was the quiet patriot. Full of borrowed virtue. He read the history books and Irish writers that he got from the library. Kathleen heard the same songs played over and over. Now, when she put a Christy Moore on in the evenings and she heard that man's tender, careful voice picking through his thoughts and feelings it brought to mind the afternoon she went through her dead mother's things. Sean had been just fourteen then, standing by while she held this and that up to show him, a brooch, an envelope with a baby curl in it, a shopping list, a saying kept from the paper.

Now she put the tray on her lap, straightened out the piece of toilet paper and pressed down with the black biro. The moment before she began was full of him. Sean, clear-eyed and true. Sean with his three-in-the-morning kisses, crouching, smiling . . . then gone. What could she write to him that was true? That would put things right?

Eilish Purcell stumbled in from across the road all worked up because Bernadette Curran had been arrested that morning and taken to Springfield Barracks for questioning. She'd got Bernie's three kids with her and had come over to use the phone.

'Go in, go in, go in,' she was saying as if she'd three dogs with her. 'That's my day ruined.'

She spent the morning talking about the plans for the street party next summer, smoking through her pack and occasionally commenting on what the three little ones were doing.

'Leave that scab alone, Bobby, wait till it falls off. It is all right if they rip the newspaper? Sure they've no toys or nothing and I'm useless with weans now I'm out of the habit.'

The oldest girl played apart, fiddling with her shoes and socks, humming and flashing a smile at the grown-ups. The two little boys were arguing about which of them was bad.

'You're both bad,' judged Mrs Purcell.

'Sure you're all right to leave them with me and go off if you want.'

Mrs Purcell trembled before the temptation. She was always busy with various residents' committees; she was building a youth club for

Ballymurphy, raising money and enlisting help. Now she was waiting to go off with Mrs O'Sullivan to fetch for the co-op from the wholesalers. They'd converted an old Volkswagon camper van into a small shop – you couldn't get anywhere to buy at a cheap price, so they had to bring it in.

'No, I won't go,' she said, reflectively, exploring her back teeth with a finger. 'We can get tinned spaghetti hoops at three pence less than him up there, sure isn't tinned fruit a price but we're getting it a wee bit cheaper than most, then I'm after some tinned rice pudding. It'll be the RUC spoiling many a dinner round here today if that Bernadette doesn't get back sharp.' She was red-faced, fanning herself with her hand. 'I think I'm going through the change.'

'Take off your coat, Eilish.'

'No I won't, just in case.'

By mid-afternoon, Bernadette Curran was round to get her children. She'd got a taxi from outside the hospital and found she had no money on her. 'I went off in my slippers,' she said, showing her feet, 'and without my purse, but the taxi fella was a nice man from Lenadoon and he says till me, you just out of Springfield? and I says, Aye, and he says, No charge.'

Kathleen made her a cup of tea and with her three children hanging on to her she told them the story: she was taken off at seven . . .

'Half-six it was,' said Mrs Purcell, touching the rim of her black-browed glasses.

'So they says to me what's the gun in the back yard for and I says sure yous are the ones as found it, I didn't know it was there and I've complained before to this here barracks about the fences on my back yard always being tore to pieces by the Brits coming in and out, which is why anyone can get through. They ask me is it this and is it that kind of a gun. I says I don't know. Anyway they bring this woman in to sit with us and she's a bit on the large side and we gets to talking about that Unislim exercise programme, well she asks what exercises work for the thighs and I try to tell her what you do and all and then I says to her hang on I'll have to show you, so I get down on the floor and I'm lifting my leg up and down, hold on a minute.' She lay down on her side and dipped a pointed toe before and behind her other leg. 'Like this.'

The children were pleased, and the two boys hung on to her, trying to ride her leg and the girl bent her knees and squatted to watch.

'Och you did not,' said Mrs Purcell, enjoying the joke, gobbling at her tea and dribbling it, laughing.

Bernadette got up, hands on her thighs, leaning forward. 'Aye, I did and your man says to me, that's enough and I want to know about the gun and I says to him again, I don't know about the gun then she asks me, being a Catholic what do we do for our stomachs after the kids so I says well there's sit-ups and then they have my photo taken with two Red Caps and it's the nicest photo of me I've ever seen so I ask if I can have a copy and he says to me, "Just go home."'

She lit a cigarette and gave them a broad smile. 'So that's been my day.'

'Do you want me to give the kids something to eat, give you a chance to get yourself straight?'

'No, thanks for everything, Kathleen and yourself, Mrs Purcell, but we'll be getting home. Are seeing your Sean tomorrow, then?'

'Aye,' said Kathleen, looking at the clock.

'Give him our love,' said Mrs Purcell, rising.

When they had gone Kathleen put the dinner on and it wasn't until the kids were in bed that she got to write her letter, though she'd been thinking of it all day.

'Tell him he's the only brother worth having,' said Aine before she went to bed. There'd been a row over at the McCanns' after school with all the kids over there and Liam'd come in murderous-faced, calling his sister 'an embarrassment'.

'You're an embarrassment,' Aine had cried at him when they got in, uncertain, wild.

It was hard to pick which hurts mattered. Kathleen called Aine back down. 'You're my baby girl.'

'Is Sean still your baby? What about Liam? He's a baby.'

'Come on now.'

'Tell him Liam's a nightmare. Tell him I miss him and wish it was Liam in there.'

'I'll give him your love.'

One day, in '77, a young man came to the door asking for Sean and she'd said to him that she'd not seen him for a day or two and he seemed relieved and said that she'd not see him for another couple of weeks maybe more as Sean had gone down to the Free State. She'd asked him whether it would be too much to ask him something. He'd looked regretful, and said I've a feeling I know what you want to ask me and I don't know whether to tell you. The poor boy, standing on her doorstep.

She'd said, 'Tell me the truth, is our Sean in the 'Ra?'

He said, 'Don't breathe it to nobody, keep it to yourself.'

She went upstairs and cried, she didn't tell her husband. A month or so later he himself heard Sean upstairs opening and closing a gun and came down crowing about his son being in the 'Ra. She'd wanted to punch his lights out.

'And that's all he is to you! He's more than that to me.'

When Sean came back, she was always nervous about the house, biting the skin around her thumbnails, and the house was raided twice and one time her husband went away with the soldiers. She could count on him for that at least. Between them they gave Sean a bit of time he'd maybe not have had otherwise. She had a cry every night in those days. Then one night her son, Sean, had come in and sat with her by the electric fire and seeing her gnawing at her hands he said, 'Is something on your mind, Mummy?'

'You're on my mind.'

He said, 'I'm all right.'

She'd stood up and gone into the kitchen and cried and he'd come in and put his arms round her. 'You know I'm in the 'Ra don't you, Mummy?'

She never told him not to do it. She said to herself he wouldn't listen, and he was old enough to choose for himself. She could remember him aged three sitting by her as she made the tea, making his own version on the floor. And she'd looked at him and thought, Jesus, you're going to die one day and she'd felt winter grasp her by the throat. Why hadn't she told him not to do it? The truth was she was proud of him being it, she thought he'd get away with it, maybe she thought it would make her somebody.

'I'm a stupid cow.' But she wouldn't let herself have the tears. 'It's not too late. You're his mother. He loves you. Write to him now. And when you see him you can tell him.'

When she wrote to him it was like she was speaking to the kernel of herself, the bit from which good things could grow. Darling Sean. The leisure centre was open. Theresa, as was once his girlfriend, was getting married. His brother was always at the rioting, his sister wasn't coming back from England for Christmas, his father was the same as ever. Aine said to say he was the best brother and she missed him. She wondered if he couldn't learn a trade for when he got out. She was going to be putting money by for him as soon as Christmas was done with. She wished it were her in his place so that he could have his life. She ought to have run away with him when he was a baby, they could have gone to the Free State. To America! To Hong Kong! Or Ceylon! It wouldn't have mattered where. Anywhere but Ballybloodymurphy, Belfast, Ireland, the World, the Universe, as he used to write it. She was praying for him. She must close. Tomorrow, she would see his face. Wasn't he always after saying to her, *Mummy will you stop looking at me*? She would be looking at him tomorrow, whether he liked it or not.

22

Bolton stuck his head in the mess. He was wearing headphones, unplugged, the wire hanging at his side.

'Just had a call,' he said. 'Only heard it because the needle got stuck on the second act of *Carmen*. Fluff. Where does fluff come from in here? They've rung through with a Special Visit for Seamus Nugent. It's to go down as a family visit. It can't be good news. Nugent hasn't taken a visit in three years, he won't put on the uniform.'

'The hard man,' Frig said, proffering a roll of fruit pastilles.

Bolton looked sad. 'Always the purple one,' and popped it in his mouth. 'Dunn, will you take him down for it? Shandy's supposed to be visits runner but I expect he's too drunk—'

'Should I run it past SO, Sir?' asked Frig.

'SO is sleeping it off in the stores. Mr Dunn's going to bring the prisoner up.' He stood at the circle a minute rather than going back to his office. 'Wait up, I'll go down with you Dunn, to get Nugent.' He went for his cap and the two of them strode together towards the wing.

'Prisoner 3334 O'Brien and Prisoner 1052 Nugent . . . both called Seamus as it happens. Open the cell, Officer Dunn.'

Dunn fumbled with the keys, opened the door, stepped into the space.

One of the men was squatting in the corner; the other was standing at the window, his back to his cellmate. There was a different smell, an eggy aroma, warm, somehow at once cosy and sickening.

'The prisoner is going to the toilet, Sir.'

He had a recurrent dream; in it he was desperate to open his bowels but could never find a toilet and when at last he found one and was about to unburden himself with the sense of imminent relief that borders on pleasure, he noticed that the walls of the toilet were transparent and he was being watched.

'Don't go in there for a while if you don't mind,' he'd said formally to Angie the night before. She'd been coming up the stairs with two cups of tea as he emerged.

'Prisoner 1052 Nugent,' Bolton had his eyes on the ceiling of the cell. 'You have been called for a Special Visit. I'd hazard a guess that it's important. Family news.'

The prisoner at the window did not turn. The light outside was dim. There were no lights in their cells. The prisoner who'd been squatting sat now on his piece of foam. He put his finger and thumb to his jaw line and stroked it, looked over at his cellmate, waiting.

'Mr Nugent,' said Bolton, dipping his head and venturing inside the cell. 'It could be important news. I don't know what it is. But it might be about your mother or father. Your wife.'

The prisoner remained as he was, looking outside.

'All right, ok.' Bolton stepped backwards, uncertainly, out of the cell.

Dunn was let home early. 'Why don't you go home, Dunn,' Bolton said. 'We don't need more than ten of us to watch locked doors.'

'That poor wee lad got shot on the Clifton Road, waiting for a bus to go to the Crumlin Road prison,' said Angela, when he got home, turning off the TV and watching the image fade to a dot. 'He wasn't even a proper prison officer but they still shot him. Twenty years old. Married for just three months.'

'Hello you,' said John Dunn, standing in the doorway of the front room.

She remained crouching before the television; she closed her eyes for a second. The way he said those two words, in his flat-vowelled Michael Caine voice, it turned her over. It was the caution of the man that thrilled her. How much he kept back.

'Well,' she was in her nightgown, 'you've always been the deep type, so you have John.'

'You've read the letter then.'

'I thought it might be a love letter at first but no such luck. So, now, have you been seeing this boy's mother at all, in the last few years?'

'No.'

'It's only about the lad then?'

'Yes.'

'He looks like you does he?'

'I'd say so.'

'So you've got a child, then.'

'Yes.'

'Lucky you,' she said, touching his cheek. 'That lump on your face is getting worse, you ought to show it to a doctor.' Her finger was extending towards a small growth that had been beneath his chin for some months. He pulled his face away. 'I don't want anything to change, John. Do you think it's going to change?'

He moved away. 'Sorry,' he said and he went up for his shower.

He stood in the bath, his mouth open, cracked but noiseless. He let the water go all over his face. Then he turned off the taps and dried himself, clearing a space on the steamed mirror with a bit of towel, then touching it to his face; cold.

When he came down he showed her his feet that were all blistered and bruised with the standing around in ill-fitting boots. She said she'd run him a foot soak.

'I've just had a shower.'

'It'll do them good, John.'

He picked up the letter on the table. 'Independent little bastard,' he said, looking dispassionately from the note to his bare feet and back again. Angie was cleaning the washing-up bowl at the sink.

Mark Wilson's writing was long-stroked, spidery. He'd written that he'd make the arrangements to come out himself, would probably take the ferry from Liverpool. He was just finishing up his first term of the second year. He'd stay in Bristol, working at the university bar, stocktaking and closing it up then he'd come over on the Saturday and they could play it by ear from there. He needn't stay with them the whole time. He had a friend in Londonderry he could go and see.

'In Londonderry? Tell him he'd best stop here.'

He went on that John needn't have sent the money; he would bring it back with him.

'Trying to make a point. I said, he's trying to make a point.'

She squeezed a good amount of washing-up liquid into the bowl and turned off the tap, moving her hand in the water before bringing over the bowl. 'I don't know. It's hard to tell with only words to go on.'

'What do you mean by that? All we've got as human beings is words.'

'What have you got yourself in a mood for, now?'

'He's going to come over here and have a go at me for what I did. I didn't know she was going to get pregnant did I? She never gave me the chance to do the right thing. Christ Angie. What will we have in common? Nothing. Nothing at all.'

It occurred to him that his son might come over, have a go at him and go home again. Then they could all get back to their real lives. The boy had had a milk round, he knew that much, so he wasn't soft, he worked in a bar, perhaps he liked a drink. He was at university. Between these pieces of information ran a gamut of other possibilities that he couldn't imagine. He was worried that his son wouldn't be like him and that he wouldn't like him. But if he was like him, it would be hard to take.

Angie thought he would be like him. She'd already found what was in it for her. She talked about the food she'd ordered for Christmas, saying more than once, 'If he's anything like you . . .' adding with an eye to his approval, 'we'd better get in plenty of beer.' She was going to tidy up the spare room, put all the stuff they stored there in boxes under the bed.

He raised his toes and saw the soapy water sliding back on to the hairs of his upper feet, bubbles clustering about his ankles like flies. 'I don't know what's wrong with me, Angie. I've barely been in that prison any time at all and already I've had it up to here.'

'Shame you can't wear your own shoes. Pair of tennis shoes or something would be better with all the walking you do. You could all wear the same kind so it's a uniform like. Dunlops do black ones. Why can't you wear them?'

'You're off your rocker.'

'Well it makes sense. You'd do the job the same, better. Probably cost them less to buy. They ought to think about it.'

'It doesn't matter about the shoes, love,' he said, lifting a foot. 'You know, we've got these bloody great uniforms, we're dressed up like a bunch of clowns. We've got the outsized boots, all we need is red noses. Listen to this right, one of the lads told me how he was on front desk at the Visitors' Centre and this woman was giving him grief because the last visit she'd had was cancelled, and she's going crazy giving off f'ing this and f'ing that, you black-coated bastards and so on and so he calls on the phone for Jaws to come out the front and deal with this woman who's got some mouth on her. Well she goes and buggers off to the toilet, doesn't she, so this little old lady, she's got to be in her seventies, comes up to the desk, shows the officer her visiting pass, nice as pie, and out comes Jaws, picks the old lady up and carries her off, puts her outside, tells her to eff off, her visit's cancelled.' He started to laugh, excusing himself saying, 'It's not funny,' and then he laughed some more until his eyes were watering. To see him like that, Angie started as well. 'Jesus,' she said. 'That's awful, John. Is it true?'

'Yup. That's how it is, see. I don't know whether something's funny or whether I need to laugh so I think it's funny. So tell us, Angie, is it funny?'

'I don't know, I don't know.' She sat on his lap, her legs to the side and they laughed with their arms around each other, her head nesting atop of his, her shiny good hair in his face.

'Let's go to bed, love. Together for once. I'll get up quietly, I don't need an alarm. I'll sneak out.'

'Let me clear this lot away.' She got up.

'Stuck up little git. Big head. I wonder if I'll like him?'

She put their tea plates in the sink, turned the tap on them.

'Angie. You've got a nice arse.'

'Thank you.'

'Angie. Would you rather be the fox or the farmer?'

'I'm not with you.'

'Angie, thanks a lot.'

'What for?'

'About Mark.'

She was asleep when he came out of the bathroom. He'd been in there a long time with the day's paper. At least he was regular. He lay down beside her, but he couldn't sleep. The prison was still with him.

Wordless, Bolton had walked ahead of Dunn to the grille and waited there, hands on his waist, looking away. 'Nothing. Not even "shove the visit". After what, four years? When it could be that his mother is dying.'

He needed to get some sleep. He should stop thinking about it all.

It was as if something in Bolton had just given in.

He had to sleep or he'd feel like shit in the morning. Angie was asleep. If he could just follow in the shade of her breathing, trace the outline of her strength . . .

The cell that is built of bone; the promenade along the ramparts of the skull, twin look-outs through eye sockets, now watch your step, don't slip, there are the nose holes. Turn around. Feel your way. There, back in the blackness is the soft something that has no wall, has no end, it is in here but it goes beyond this cell space, drawing strength from what sun, what water, what humus? To produce what? Excrete what? Soft thing, backwards mattress, riddled with crime. Behind reason and before God. Bastard thing. Troubled until it stops, if it stops. If you can ever stop it—

John woke. He had dropped off. If he went in and out like that a few times he'd be fucked, no chance of sleep. There he was perched on the brink, ready to take the helter-skelter into sleep, but held back by the parental authority of his speaking mind. All of life is a war on your own nature.

Scraping a plate of strawberries into the toilet. The woman's face going from concern to understanding, it was all a joke. Goldfish circling. Then in the palm of a hand. Meter of life. Trembling. Tenuous. Dying alive.

Where was it coming from, when he closed his eyes? He was not in control of the images that came, it was as if he was invaded.

He lay there feeling hate and fear, adrenaline-sauced. There was no way he'd sleep with his heart cracking on at the pace it was going. The bloody prison.

A good soldier respects his enemy. You had to learn to hate them to fight them – that happened naturally, when your mate to your left copped a bullet. It doubled the effectiveness of a unit if one of the lads took a bullet. The killer instinct is revenge, that's all. Like before he went on the screening job when one of the young para lads got ambushed down an alleyway, and John came down afterwards and saw him with three bullets in him, blood in the side of his mouth and his trousers wet, his head to the side, his eyes wide. He'd knelt down to check him. He was dying, he looked scared of where he was going. When John stood up, he hated.

You could hate them and respect them. With the screening job, you were taken out of it after four months because you got to respect them. They put you on patrol on the streets for a few weeks before to get you to hate them.

'Screening.' Funny word. Talking it through beforehand, deciding what you were going to do. Either you got something or you didn't. Small fry, the nobodies, gave you something. The big men wouldn't. They were too much a part of it, they didn't know where they stopped and where 'the cause' began.

Things changed though, and they were right to move you quick out of it. He'd shared half a bottle of scotch with a big IRA man, lay into him then they finished off the bottle together.

He was watching the empty theatre of his mind, waiting for the actors to emerge. There was Jaws addressing the new officers, the spittle between his upper lip and lower lip a little white ball, then a white string, then gone, then back again. Laughter, applause. There was Bolton, the music, the soaring harmonies, and men sweating and raging and fighting.

He thought of Nugent staring at a point across the yard. A goldfish in his bowl head.

23

Bernie Curran stopped by the night before, knowing Kathleen would be anxious about the visit and they must have smoked a packet before she left, handing Kathleen a jar of her 'tabs'.

'I've never taken one in my life. Not even after the weans were born, there's a reason for pain.'

'Half the women in West Belfast are on the nerve pills, Kathleen.' She nodded at the tiny packages wrapped in Clingfilm on the table. 'If you're taking that lot in, believe me you'll need them to get through it. The women that search you, they're horrible. I had one ask me to take off my sanitary towel one time. Can you believe that, from one woman till another?'

'Her fingertips curled around the small bottle and she put it in her bag.

That evening, Sean came back from The Fiddlers at about eleven and found Kathleen still up, smoking with the gas fire on low. He took off his boots and crept across the carpet in his threadbare socks. 'Wish I was going with you.'

'You'd be starting a fight for someone else to finish.'

He gave her a series of cordial squeezes, not at all put off. 'We've sat here like this before, waiting for him to come in.'

It was true that her husband had sat up until Sean came through the door, only then would he turn out the lights, lock the doors and come to bed. A few times she found him asleep on the settee, hands in his pockets.

'He used to come out with some quare wee sayings, Kathy. "Be the good listener," he always used to say that to me.' He gave her his self-pitying look. She gave him a kiss.

The next morning she was down outside the Republican Press Centre at half-past eight waiting with others, mostly women, to board the bus going out to the prison. There was a brittle gaiety. The engine was running, grey smoke curling up from underneath. The smell of diesel and adventure. Water in pools on the pavement and on the road, a cigarette butt making its way across one like a miniature raft. The driver chucked his cigarette into the same puddle. They started filling the bus, from the rear down. Girls and women and many in between.

Brendan Coogan called out the block numbers. Hands went up and he doled out the pill-sized Clingfilm-wrapped notes. She was given one herself.

'Tell Sean it's for O'Malley,' he said, adding, 'You look nice, Kathleen.'

Feeling the brush of the nylon seats on the backs of her thighs, she had the reason she needed to raise herself a little, her hands on the steel bar of the seat in front, and look after him as he went back into the building. His shirt was outside his trousers at the back.

All the women were made-up, wearing their best. One by one they waylaid him, each with a petition of some sort. She looked at those that were boarding. Some of them she'd known since they were girls, when they were all teddy bears, autograph albums and eagerness to please. They spent longer getting back into their jeans than they did having sex the first time they did it, but after they'd got them on again, they had all the certainties of their mothers, they were hard-faced, smoking and knowing. No matter what had been said – 'It's all right, we can do it' – the fella was caught. Girls went like lemmings to the life they had. But boys had to be dragged kicking and screaming. She looked about the bus. Kids and the berew, the occasional drink-up. What a life. Margaret Coogan was right about the young men wanting a war.

She looked at Brendan outside, the sunshine flickering on his hair, his face irritable, his hands in his pockets. He could have been a schoolteacher. Some teenager in a short skirt was standing knock-kneed in front of him, shivering.

The women were loaded. The driver, arms folded, was talking to Coogan, they both looked up at the bus, then Coogan patted his elbow and the man moved.

With women and men it was like with football; you knew who was on the other team by their shirts being different and you managed to find enough dislike for them to play because by Christ you needed the game.

The driver hopped into his seat, bounced.

She'd been up since six doing her hair, her make-up and she'd put on a skirt. The girl in the mini-skirt who'd been outside talking to Coogan sat down heavily beside her. She introduced herself as Sally from the New Lodge. She was going to see her fiancé. They both glanced at her bare legs, which were revealed up to her crotch.

'Seat's itchy,' said Kathleen.

'Aye but you've to suffer for beauty,' said the girl. She had short per-oxide hair, pale skin and dark purple rings under her eyes. 'It's practical, so it is.'

Kathleen shifted. She had the wrapped tobacco, some papers and a couple of notes up inside of her.

When the bus passed the Crumlin Road prison, the women jeered.

'Look,' said her travelling companion, pointing out a watch-tower opposite the prison. 'They just put that up this week, after them screws got killed coming out of here. They're calling the Crum "Death Alley", so they are. Makes your heart bleed.'

As they quit the streets of Belfast for the country roads, the bus filled with cigarette smoke. Kathleen took a small tablet out of the zipped purse in her bag and slipped one into her mouth. Sally from the New Lodge saw her.

'You haven't got a spare one?'

'Aye. Here you go love.' The girl took it without looking at it.

'I need it.'

'Aye.'

'I could use all the help I can get, me.'

'Aye.'

'It's not your normal daytrip.'

'No, no it's not.'

'Mind you, when I'm there, I change. I come over all animal.'

Kathleen looked out of the window, they were leaving the motorway, mounting the side-road into the countryside. 'This is my land,' she thought. 'I gave birth here.' Just like the horse, she waited till dark, pushed the child out with a roar into the morning air of this country, took him beside her, the strange fierce newcomer, whoever he was.

'It's worse when you're a mother,' she said quietly.

'No one could love a person like I love him. I'd kill for him.' The girl popped a sweet into her mouth now and handed one to Kathleen. With the large round boiled sweet in one corner of her mouth, drawing in air like a steam engine and unleashing a deep orange smell, the girl went on, describing how he looked, repeating how she'd kill for him and fixing Kathleen with a look. 'I mean it.'

Kathleen unwrapped the sweet, had to rub the wrapper between finger and thumb a few times to unstick it from her and rolled it into a ball then she squeezed it into the filled mouth of the metal ashtray on the back of the seat. Her cheeks hollowed with the effort of sucking to get the sweet going.

'Killing for them? That's the least of it, love.'

Near Lisburn the prison was accessed by a long country lane, the bus charged past farms and agreeable new homes. Kathleen wondered how they could live so close to the prison. Undistinguished apart from watchtowers, Long Kesh was hidden from the eyes of passersby. There was nothing to see. As they approached the visitors' entrance, they saw a military patrol that waved them to a stop before the gate. Two soldiers came on board and went up and down the bus, a couple lay on the ground outside looking underneath. The driver turned round in his seat. 'That's new,' he said. 'All right ladies, we're here.'

Inside a hut, they stood in a queue to present their visiting letters and identification, benefit books and such, and were told to sit down and wait. Kathleen asked her friend if she should get the stuff out yet. Sally put her finger to her lips and shook her head. They sat there for close to an hour. There was a woman struggling with her baby. The tiny ugly thing was crying and fussing and some of the other women were taking turns to make faces at it or walk round, soothing it with humming.

'I have to keep the bottle for the last minute,' the woman was saying. 'I can't take it in with me.'

'Poor kid.'

'It'll live,' said a woman to her left.

'I was talking about the mother.'

They shared a grin.

'I've got five under ten, so I have. And he's been gone two years now. The weans don't miss him, but I've a boy and a girl, nine and ten, and it's always, when's Daddy coming back? Mind you, I've got it all worked out now – we're like an army. There's nothing I can't handle, me, no with me, it's "come on then Lord, throw another problem at me, make it a good one, I can take it."' The phlegm in her chest and throat set to bubbling.

'When will he be out?'

'He got life. They said he confessed. He never did. It's worse for him than me. He cries tears when I'm in there, God love him. He's nicer inside than he was out. I don't bring the weans down because he can't cope. Och they're all right, it's all "my daddy's in prison for the 'Ra". I'll tell you, this British government, what they've done is, made it a fine thing to be in one of their prisons.' Her voice rose. 'It's a badge of honour to be locked up by the Brits in this country.' There was warm agreement.

'Even so, you should make a complaint.'

'Och, what difference does it make?'

'You might have him home.'

'Aye!' she retorted with hilarious intonation, her eyes wide.

The women around them started laughing and it caught on. Kathleen looked at the woman who was still nodding, arms across her chest and laughed again.

Eventually a screw came forward, held the door open and they were told to get in a van to go the visitors' block.

Her mini-skirted friend nudged her as they went through the door of the block: 'You can get it out here or wait till you get to the toilets over there.'

'Which is best?'

'I keep it in till the last minute. Or I get it out during the visit. You can you see with a skirt like this. My arse is frozen to the bone when I get home.'

They went in a small van round to the main entrance of the prison and were told to file into a wooden building there. Kathleen looked up and observed the crown-and-castle gate motif above which was inscribed 'HMP Maze'.

They were taken aside individually at the visitors' block and a woman prison officer searched the women in a little room. The woman was reservedly efficient. She felt up and down Kathleen's body quickly and brusquely and asked her to open her mouth, then she let her go. No eye contact.

Kathleen went to the toilet to take out her contraband. She gave the little parcels a quick rinse under the tap and patted them dry. She noticed in the mirror the prudish little expression on her face. She'd be feeling more nervous if it wasn't for the tablet. She put the tobacco, papers and flints up her sleeve and the three notes behind her upper lip.

'I look like a fucking chimpanzee,' she thought, glancing in the mirror. Other women were in and out of the toilets too and there was much less talking than before in the waiting-room. Finally they were called one by one and she made her way into the long room with its two rows of cubicles, left, middle, right. She was directed to one to the left, made to sit down and after a while, coming past the raised desk at the back of the room, she saw her Sean.

They embraced, he kissed her cheek, and they were reprimanded by a prison officer and instructed to sit down opposite each other without physical contact. As soon as they'd hugged she'd quickly shaken down the two packets she had and put them into his hand. He had his hands beneath the table. She moved the little paper tablets in her mouth so she could speak. The next thing was to try to get them to him. She was keen to get it over with so she could just enjoy being with him, so she put her hand over her mouth and pretended to cough, without making any noise. She stretched both hands across the table to reach for his. He put one out and luckily it coincided with the one of hers that had the notes in and she pushed them both at him. They were visible for a second before his hand receded, as if smarting from the prison officer's command, 'No contact!'

'Eejit.' She gave the screw a filthy look. Then she took the time to have a good look at her son.

His blond hair was mousey, over his ears, dirty and greasy, he had the beginnings of an uneven beard, the shirt he wore was stained and torn, and his skin was pale. He looked much older than his years. He smelt bad.

'You look well.' She gave him a smile.

'Any cigarettes with you, Mummy?'

She placed the packet on the table and lit one for him and then one for her. He took it and puffed away on it with concentration. He laughed and coughed at the same time, shaking his head. 'You look bloody wonderful. All the fellas will be thinking I've got my girl in.'

'How is it love?'

'Not so bad. I've got a good cellmate. He's teaching me Irish and French. He was a schoolteacher. It's a great group of lads we have on our wing. Our block's not the worst. Some of the other blocks are brutal.' He took a deep drag, then made a little jump in the chair, his body leaning at an angle, one side of his arse lifted. He squinted.

'God save us.'

'Tricky business. How's our Liam and Aine?'

'Aye, dead on. I've written in the—' she nodded, looking circumspect.

'Aye, right.'

'Liam misses you though he won't say it,' she said, tears beginning suddenly to well up. When Sean was on the run, on the odd occasion he'd come into the house before dawn and get into bed with Liam, and she'd wake up and hear the low tones of Sean answering Liam's excitable questions. Nothing had given her more pleasure than to hear them together like that, complicit. The last time, she'd not interrupted, even though she wanted to see Sean herself, she'd let them have their time, only grabbing a kiss for herself as he went out through the back garden.

'I miss him too, the big baby.'

'That shirt's bogging. Is it your own?'

'You know we don't wear the clothes.'

'I wish you'd get a trade. You can learn one in here, can't you? You've got to think of your own future a wee bit as well, you know.'

He used his dying cigarette to light another one.

'You know I'm with you, Sean,' she went on. 'I've joined the Relatives Action Committee. I know you're fighting for all of us. But I can't help but wish . . . Well, when you get out you can start a new life. Just do your time. The war's not in here, love. I can't help thinking this is all my fault. Sean I think about you all the time. I think about you and Granny, how good you were to her. I'm so proud of you. You're such a beautiful boy. And all I hear is how you're on the boards, on punishment. Why do you have to be the one to save the world? Just use your head, love, stand a little bit apart from the others, get yourself out of here in one piece.'

He looked aside. When he looked back at her she knew she'd lost him. He looked her straight in the eyes.

'You can't come here if you're going to say those things to me. Listen to me! I won't ask for you to come again. There'll be no trade, no life worth having until we have our own country. They'll always find a way of keeping us down.'

She bowed her head.

'Mother. Mother, are you listening?' Their eyes met. 'You don't understand how it is. There's men going to die here if they have to.'

'Sean.' She wanted to say, come on, come back to me. She wished she could say, come on, let Mummy take you home, put the tea on. 'Sean.'

'We need you to be strong. All of yous. We can't be broken no matter what they do to us. Go back and tell that to everyone.'

Her eyes were swimming suddenly.

He softened, stretched out his hands across the table. The screws passed about beyond the focus of her eyes. Their fingertips were just an inch or so part, aligned, each one tending towards the other's. When he was born, her first child, the first thing she did was to count the fingers and toes. Perfect. She'd lain back with him on her chest for those first five minutes, wondering, bleeding.

'Every night there's singing or telling stories, quizzes. We stand up at our doors and everyone takes his turn. And me being new I had to sing a song my first night and all I could think of to sing was the record you used to put on over and over again.'

'Well we only had the one record back in the early days. It was that *Do you know the way to San José*?'

'Aye, well now my nickname's Dionne. Some of them didn't get to see me until the mass on a Sunday and they're all saying, Oh it's a terrible disappointment to see you in the flesh, Dionne.'

'Why didn't you sing one of the rebel songs?'

'I couldn't remember the words,' he said, rueful, the Sean she knew. 'All them years listening to them! The other night that Christy Moore one came to me though, "As I Roved Out". Will you get me the words to some of the others Mummy? Write them down for me.'

'Aye, I will love.' She lifted her head and gave him the smile she taught him to wear the first day of school or when things were going wrong, that cheek-lifting, bright-eyed look. He'd copied it perfectly, made it his own. With the shape of their brows just the same as each other, he was the mirror image of her now.

'You know, your Auntie Eileen had you down for a singer. She got me drunk the other night, so she did. On the bottle Mary gave you. Your father came in and walked back out, thought he was back in The Fiddlers, the house smelt that strong of drink and fags.'

'How is the oul bastard?'

'Still old, still a bastard, God love him – someone's got to.'

Sean smiled.

The prison officer beside them leant into their table and tapped on his watch. 'Three more minutes.'

The tablet had worn off.

'I had so much I wanted to say. I can't take my eyes off you, Sean; don't be cross.' Her eyes filled.

'There now, lovely,' he said, reaching out and touching her arm.

'No contact, please. Just two more minutes now.'

She put a hand over her lower face.

'Don't speak,' said Sean.

He put his middle fingertips to his lips, kissed them and offered them to her, then he got up and nodded at the screw before he went shuffling off to the back of the room, the prison officer following behind.

She sat paralyzed until another screw came and lifted her by the arm. She shook him off. All the way out, she turned to look, every couple of steps, just in case they brought Sean back in.

24

Dunn had his second beer half gone and he was looking it in the eye, or else it was looking him in the eye. He wouldn't take another. He was on visits proper. He sat alone as Jaws had gone off to talk to another officer. He wondered what Mark Wilson would think of him, a prison officer. He was a turnkey, a man who sold the fact that he could stand up, stand still, hold fast.

A man at the bar fell off the back of his stool and Dunn laughed out loud. In the noise of the bar, no one heard him.

That afternoon he and Jaws were going up to Bolton's block to fetch O'Malley, this time for his monthly visit.

'Watch him, watch O'Malley, when he's on the visit. I've noticed you're a bit sloppy. Don't you forget who your man O'Malley is now. If you stand over him and the conversation turns funny, anything at all, you make sure you stop it. There's no way the IRA can get anything through if we're on top of it.'

Jaws fell against the wall then he righted himself, without saying anything. When he belched, Dunn was treated to a glimpse of his diet. Jaws offered him a Polo mint at various intervals in the day. Each time Dunn refused it seemed to become increasingly important to Jaws that he accept. 'Take one and put it in your pocket.'

Jaws stopped to talk to Shandy in the mess while Skids and Dunn went off to get the man. Skids seemed down, kept blowing out his lips.

'Your man Jaws is full of drink. I wish I was.' He went along hunched, his nose to the floor like an anteater. 'I thought about being a vet you know. I like animals. They're just wee innocent creatures, aren't they, puppies, kittens, calves, ducks and all. Sheep. I was thinking with the money from this, I could get myself a farm.'

'You're married right?'

'Never met the right girl. So I married the missus.' He blew his lips out again in a sigh. 'Joking. The wife's all right, if you like that sort of thing. We've got a wee boy. Jeremy. She chose the name. He doesn't do much, do you know what I mean? I'd prefer to be on my own with some animals, serious. And a bit of female company from time to time. I could go out for that though.'

They stopped before the cell. 'You've been in the prison service a few years, you should have saved up a good amount of money by now.'

'They've only now started paying so well. Because of the protest. To tell you the truth it's been a right waste of time. I should have been in the army like you Johnno. Seen some action. Stayed the free man.' Skids looked up and down the empty corridor, one hand going for his keys. 'I've done this job for eight years. I was a joiner before. My brother's a joiner. When he's done he can stand back and say, look at that roof, I did that. But I'll have my farm one day. Peace and quiet. Nice and lonely. A farm will suit me down to the ground.' He opened up the cell. '2350 O'Malley up for a visit. Do you want it?'

O'Malley stood up. 'Aye.'

They went down to the orderlies' cell, cell twenty-six, where O'Malley stood over the mirror, compliant. He gave a small bend of the knees.

'All right O'Malley, get the clothes on.' They stood outside for a minute while O'Malley selected the trousers.

'Do you ever find anything up their arses?'

'Ach, you'd be amazed. That's how they bring in their letters and so on. Now, this one fella had the parts for a crystal radio, and another had a camera. Back in the spring there was one got a lighter stuck up there. We had to get the doctor to remove it. The mirror-search is a waste of time. Pure and simple. It's always too far up. Sometimes we use a metal detector. That's how they knew about the lighter. They only do all this rigmarole with the ones on protest. Just part of keeping them in their place. I'm glad it's us have got the upper hand, I tell you. Can you imagine what'll happen in this land if this lot ever get it?' He popped his head back in the cell. 'Will you move yourself, O'Malley.'

There was a ripping sound. O'Malley had made a tear in the trousers, in the seat.

'Go steady.'

The man pulled on some boots and said, 'Ready.'

A few cries came up from the cells as the wing grilles were opened.

'*Slán chara*!'

'*Slán cairde*!' O'Malley was walking with wide-legged footsteps; a hard-man swagger, thought Dunn.

'I'll catch you later,' said Skids at the front door. Dunn nodded.

Jaws and Dunn accompanied O'Malley around the cellblocks to the visitors' centre. There was a sleeting rain. O'Malley walked ahead of them a few paces, impatient at the grilles, hands about his forearms as in the exercise yard. He had the ripped jeans, unlaced boots and a short-sleeved, buttonless shirt drawn about him.

'Cold today, don't envy you,' Dunn said to him as they waited to leave the yard of one block. O'Malley looked at him.

On the way around the perimeter Jaws kept up a repetitive monologue for O'Malley's benefit.

'Suits me this dirt protest thing. I hope yous go on with it till kingdom come. I'm getting paid. Going to take a holiday. I'll send yous a postcard.'

O'Malley laughed derisively a couple of times. Dunn walked alongside him and Jaws went ahead. Jaws was still rattling on as they got to the block. He opened the door, let first O'Malley then Dunn go through.

'Going to be keeping an eye on you O'Malley, with your visit. Seeing your man Coogan so y'are. Funny that you're using your once-a-month visit to see a fella, now? Don't you see enough of men O'Malley? Or is it men you like?'

O'Malley turned in the doorway. 'Do I frighten you?'

There was Jaws, the black jacket with the buttons, the big heels, cap askew, and there was O'Malley, bare arms, in someone else's boots. The wind was blowing into the doorway.

'Are you threatening me O'Malley? Is that what you're doing? Because I can pull this visit too, you know.'

'I'll tell you something mister,' said O'Malley to Dunn. 'Apart from yourself, the company I've had for this walk has been downright fucking tedious, but still, it's good to see the sky.' He looked outwards, upwards then went on inside.

Waiting in one of the anterooms to the Visitors' Centre, for O'Malley to be searched, Jaws said to Dunn, 'Cheeky cunt. I'm not afraid of him, Mr big fucking OC.'

Dunn said nothing.

'You're to stand right over him while he's on his visit, do you understand, Dunn? You've been fucking useless to me today so far.'

The prisoner was signed in for his visit with Brendan Coogan.

'Watch them,' said the officer at the front desk. 'Sinn Fein, my fucking arse.'

O'Malley went to a booth where a man with thick dark hair was sitting, elbows on the table. They grasped each other's hands quickly. Dunn looked at his watch. They had thirty minutes. He saw O'Malley's back hunch then straighten and then his hands came up from under the table. Dunn wondered if he'd put something inside of him.

'You haven't brought in a wee picnic for us then,' said O'Malley, hastily accepting a cigarette and taking a light at the same time. Coogan didn't take a cigarette himself, but pushed the pack towards O'Malley. Looking about him Dunn saw that without exception every prisoner was chain-smoking.

'Aye, well I was planning to take you out for a meal. But look at the state of you, fella. For fuck's sake. Make an effort.'

O'Malley moved his head from side to side as if this was fair comment. He indicated Dunn, '*Is e an fear nua – nil aon fadhb bheith ag caint mar ni thuigeann se.*'

'*Nil me in ann gaeilge maith a labhairt.*'

'Spend some time in here, you'll learn it.'

'I'm no use to you in here.'

A young woman was crying as she was led away. A prisoner was standing, watching her go, his hands in his hair.

Jaws was up at the box, laughing with the officer there. Dunn could hear the odd word, 'holiday', 'postcard'. There were explosive, incredulous laughs from the other fellow.

Dunn could see Jaws on holiday. A beach, somewhere like Spain, sitting up with his head burnt, his shirt over his feet, a warm can of beer, then seeing someone a little bit familiar, gathering up his plastic bag, making a runner, feet hurting on the hot sand, the beer can on its side where he'd been, froth melting.

In the corner of his eye he saw a small white pellet come shooting out of O'Malley's nose and Coogan put a finger on it and slipped it into his mouth. O'Malley was rubbing the side of his nose and saying he had a cold coming. Thanks to moving between that powerful heating on the inside and the cold air on the outside.

He didn't know what to do; what was it they'd exchanged? Was it a pill? He cleared his throat, took his cap off for a minute and put it back on, square. The pair went on, speaking in low monotonous voices, partially in Irish.

His mind went to thinking about Angie and whether the boy coming would change things. He would have to do the numbers on the Datsun, too. It would be good to have it when the boy was there. They needed to get some money down for a mortgage, couldn't keep renting. Wouldn't they have to be married, though?

'It's no good talking about concessions, Nails, about half of this and some of that. The lads won't give in for anything less than the five demands.' O'Malley had raised his voice and Coogan was trying to placate him, but O'Malley slapped his hands down on the table.

'Yous do your part on the outside and we'll play our part in here. We're prepared to take it all the way. All the way. We're not fucking about.'

Coogan was at first conciliatory, murmuring, his head down then he said in a harder voice, 'Just sit tight.'

'Listen. On my wing, we've had four men come off the protest; Mickey's got an arm badly burnt; Seamus was off the block after he got a beating, so as they could hide him away till the bruises faded; Sean Moran's on punishment more than he's on the block; McIlvenny's in the hospital. We've all got worms. We're on bread and water half the time and fuck-all of that. The good news is it's too fucking cold for maggots. And I'll tell you something, there's total commitment. One hundred per cent. But we need to bring this thing to a head now.'

'. . . What's going on . . . getting the word out,' was all that Dunn could make out from Coogan. He had his fingers out to start to count off his points but O'Malley looked resolutely indifferent. He spoke out in a louder voice, running a fingertip around his ear, glancing towards Dunn as if he wanted him to hear.

'Don't yous sit on your laurels with Warrenpoint and Mountbatten and one or two screws picked off. Yous'd better keep it coming till the message hits home. I'll bet you something though; they don't give a fuck about the screws. They'll sit and watch them take the bullets.'

O'Malley looked Dunn straight in the eyes, then leant back in his chair and looked over the room, raising a hand of greeting to one cubicle and turning it into a thumbs up.

In the couple of hours sleep he'd got that night, after a repertoire of visions that were absurd and pointless, Dunn had woken abruptly out of a dream; the growing apprehension of a ring of mountains all around him, moving inwards, on a dark march, and the feeling that whichever way he turned he was facing the wrong way, attending to the wrong things.

Jaws was coming forwards noisily from the back of the room to get O'Malley out; he was bottle-faced, calling out over and over again that time was up.

'That's your lot. Come on Dunn let's get things moving.'

He put his hands on O'Malley's shoulders; O'Malley baulked with a shudder of anger and barged into the table.

Coogan sprang up, fingers at his watch face. 'That was thirteen minutes, you thick bastard.'

'This man is threatening me!'

Other officers came running forwards and O'Malley was wrestled into the corridor.

During the altercation, a small white pellet had fallen in front of Dunn's shoes. He bent down and picked it up.

25

Owen McCann had a red sports bag. He swung it up behind his back, one hand at the shoulder. He walked like a tough guy. He'd grown about a foot in six months. Liam was now shorter than him.

'There's fuck-all in that bag,' said Liam, a step or two behind.

His tie was loose, the hood of his jacket on his head and the rest of it behind him like a cape. He had his hands in his pockets, his satchel across his chest. Liam walked home with Owen, and his sister walked back from her school with Una. The McCanns lived a few houses down across the way but it always seemed sunnier where they were and they had orange flowers in a small strip of front garden in the summer. In the long hot summer of '76 the two families had had a barbecue together in the McCanns' back garden. Liam had never tasted anything as good as charred meat, ketchup, fried onions, inside a bap. Sammy McCann had got the hose out and soaked everyone until their clothes were see-through. His older brother, Sean, had been flirting with Mrs McCann, saying, 'What's that,' with his fingertip on her chest bone and when she looked he flicked at her nose. No one had minded on account of the beer they were all drinking. Liam had had a can of Tennants to himself and gone to sleep in a small tent.

Mrs McCann was a socialist. She did a lot for the community. His dad said he wished she'd do more. His mummy was joining in with her and getting involved in the H block protests. Owen's uncle, Sammy, was standing for election on the anti-H block ticket.

'Your uncle's a politician then,' said Liam.

'Aye.'

'Does he not get to drive a big car?'

'Fuck away.'

'How will he do his politics then?'

'He walks from door to door. Are you going to come in for some toast?'

'And your mum does the marching, like mine's going to. Have you got peanut butter?'

'They all follow my mum. "What do we want – *political status*! When do we want it – *now*!'

'I'd bloody love to go on them marches. I might get to go on the next one. Your uncle's going to be the one with the loud-hailer up the front. You might get a turn. You lucky bastard.'

'Your brother's on the blanket, Liam, you can't get better than that, that trumps everything. You'd be up the front, you and your mum.'

'Thank Jesus for him or we'd be nothing us lot.'

As they crossed the road into the Ballymurphy estate, a British soldier came towards them, gun slung across, a hand on the barrel like it was a handbag. Owen unhitched his sports bag. They always stopped boys with sports bags. Liam's mum wouldn't get him a sports bag.

Owen opened it and the soldier put the nose of the rifle inside pushing the few books apart, plunging it into the dirty games kit. Neither of the boys spoke to him.

'No need to be like that,' said the soldier.

Liam contrived a bright smile. 'He's right. We ought to be polite, Owen. Please, soldier, would you be a good man and leave our country and go back to your own?'

'All right clever clogs. There's nothing I'd like better than to leave you lot to sort out your own quarrels. On your way.'

Owen swung his bag up behind his back again and held the straps with two hands. 'That's what they think about us, that we're all stupid micks.'

Liam looked back over his shoulder, saw the soldier was watching them go.

'Uncle Sammy says the Brits are always doing jokes with an Englishman, a Scotsman and an Irishman, and it always turns out that your man, Paddy, is as thick as shite. There's one about three men in the desert come across a convent and want a drink of water but the ugly old nun with a beard and all says you've got to fuck me first.'

'Jesus.'

'When she closes her eyes your man Paddy fucks her with one sausage after another and then he chucks them out the window and he gets for himself a drink of water and the Brit and the Scot are sitting outside and they say, aye you had your drink but we had two lovely sausages.'

'But it was Paddy who was the smart one.'

'Aye, well they have us down for either thick or cunning.'

They ran around the corner, past a mural depicting a beaming sandy-haired young man, Volunteer Collins who'd been shot in Easter 1970. Over the top of it had been daubed 'We Are Not Criminals' in big black letters.

One of their younger friends from the estate was playing Evil Knievel in the road between the Morans' and the McCanns' houses; he'd set up a ramp on some bricks and was pedalling towards it with a serious expression. He flunked it and Liam and Owen cried out. An old man out walking his dog started hollering.

'Do it yourself then, piss pants,' said the boy, picking himself and his bike up. He called over to Liam to go and get his bike.

'After I've said hello to Mrs McCann. You use the time to practise.'

Mrs McCann was standing looking ill by the window, holding a cigarette to her lips.

'I told Una not to pick up the phone.'

'What happened?' said Owen as soon as he came into the room.

'You're never to answer the phone, you know that, right?' she said, pointing her cigarette at him.

Owen went off into the kitchen followed by Liam. He slung his sports bag on the floor; it landed like a flat tyre.

'We get some loopy phone calls, "Hello, Belfast City morgue here, we've got your name down on the list," that kind of thing. Jesus, look at my uncle in there, he's still wearing flares he's got his head that full of politics.'

'Go easy on that toast, we've got to get sandwiches out of it tomorrow,' Mrs McCann called out from the front room.

They had a slice each, listened to Mrs McCann and Sammy talking for a while, until Owen mouthed 'boring' at Liam and got his schoolbook out to do his homework on his lap.

Liam got up to go.

'Bye, Mrs McCann.'

'Bye bye, love. Tell your mother I'll come over so we can do some work on the posters. And tell her I'm going down to the Kesh next week so I can take in a wee note for Sean.'

Liam went in the house with the intention of charging upstairs, changing out of school uniform and racing out the back to get his bike.

His mother and Aine were cuddling on the settee together, talking. His mother's hand was running through Aine's long red hair, undoing it where it had been in plaits. His mother had been crying, he could see from her swollen nose and ringed eyes.

'I saw Sean today, Liam, did you forget?'

'Oh, aye, how was he?'

'All right, he sends you his love. We were just talking about Christmas. No Mary, no Sean. Still we'll make the best of it won't we.'

'Can I have six pence for a bag of crisps?'

'Aye. I've nothing in for tea. In my bag, love. In the green purse.'

He went to the kitchen to get it and came back saying, 'Mrs McCann is going to come by for the posters and she'll take a note into the Kesh for you.'

'She's going down there is she? I'll play that Christy Moore record of his tonight and get down the words of some of the songs for him. I was saying, Liam, I was sitting in this very same place, two years ago at Christmastime, when Sean was on the run, I was having a wee cry when Una comes in and says, why are you crying missus and I says I miss my son, so I do, I'd do anything to have him come through the front door . . .'

Liam stood in front of her and moved from foot to foot, he needed to have a pee.

'And she says, well I've seen him up at the shops and he says he's coming to see you for Christmas, so you stop your crying. Bossy like her mother. Then he walks right through the door—' His mother was smiling but her eyes were weeping. Liam couldn't understand the way that women laughed and cried at the same time. Thick or cunning.

'That was good, then, Mummy.' He ran upstairs for a pee.

'I'm listening,' said Aine.

'Well that was the last Christmas we had with your brother here. I'd better think of something for your tea,' said Kathleen, treading down the backs of her slippers as she went to the kitchen.

Aine followed her. 'Did we have the tin of Quality Street that year?'

'He came in dressed like a priest your brother did,' she said, raising a potato peeler and looking out the window over the back yard, the litter bouncing across in the wind. 'He'd borrowed the clothes off Father Pearse.'

Kathleen looked at the orange marks on a bald potato and then at the rust in the lines of her palm. She put the peeler and her hand under the cold tap. She started to weep, using the backs of her hands to spread her tears.

Aine pressed the side of her face hard against her mother's back. 'Don't cry Mummy, don't cry.'

26

'Where am I off to then, Stew-pot?'

It was cold there, waiting outside by the main gate. Things were going slower than ever in the queue outside the Tally Lodge with Stuttering Stu the duty officer.

'Wer, wer, wer, wer, wer . . .'

Three other officers put their heads alongside Dunn's; they were like a barbershop quartet, urging him on.

'Workshops?'

'Wer, wer, wer . . .'

'Visits? Hospital?'

'Wer, wer, – gate duty.'

Again. For twelve hours a day – bar the break for lunch and tea – Dunn was in a ten-by-ten space between two gates out in front of Bolton's block, a cold and lonely vigil.

He set himself up a golf course. He dug five small holes in a circle formation in the ground, and he kicked a stone around the course to see if he could get round on par.

Every half hour or so, a wagon would come and he'd admit it, lock the gate once more, and open the next, then lock it again behind the departing wagon. He envied the officers coming out in gangs at lunchtime and teatime. He took his alone when the reluctant replacement arrived, warning him not to be late back.

The fellas from the block came back from the canteen full of liquid humour. It was Saturday afternoon.

'Good night, John-boy.'

'G'night Pa.'

'G'night Mr Godsey. Mr Godsey, what the hell are you doin' in there with Elizabeth?'

This was the 'craic' of the day. Dunn had taken a nap in the stores on his hour off the day before, and Frig had poked his head in and quipped, 'Good night John-boy.'

Rabbit was being just about carried by Skids and Shandy. His glasses were off. Frig stopped.

'Ma, Grandma's left her teeth in my underpants...'

'You take a good joke too far. She'd know to take her teeth out before she gave a blow job, at her age.'

They staggered across to the block, Rabbit's feet dragging. As he locked the block gate after them, Dunn glanced at either wing. You couldn't see any faces at the windows. He wondered what they made of it.

He perfected his game of kick-golf that afternoon. The boy would be there this time next week. He had been thinking through where to take the boy on his day off. It would have been better if Dunn could have been the one to make the first visit. He could have taken him out somewhere to eat maybe, then got away scot-free.

A prison officer. A rented house in East Belfast. The fridge smelt funny, the handset over the bath was cracked and leaking.

If he'd have gone to him, he'd have chucked in this job, said he was between things, nice to have some time off, that sort of thing.

Angie had got a warning in the cornershop the day before. The woman at the till told her people there didn't like their own going against them. Angie'd asked her what she meant and she'd said, your fella's no more than a mercenary, love, aye he's getting nicely paid for banging away folk, but it's not right, people don't like it. She'd called him at work but with him not being on a block she hadn't been able to get hold of him. Out on the wall in front of their house that morning was spray-painted 'Maze Screws – their crime is disloyalty.'

He paced up and down, counting in German: *dreizehn, vierzehn, fünf-zehn*.

He'd got that bloody smuggled note at home, in the spare room, in the old soap dish on the chest of drawers. He ought to turn it in. Before the boy got there. Not his business.

It was chilly so he kept on the move. He was swinging the keys on the end of the chain that fell from his leather belt. This was another of his meagre diversions. The keys were on a steel circle; they made a good noise and quite a swoosh as he swung them like a lasso. The chain was long enough to feel the kinetic force build momentum once he'd got a perfect circle going at his side.

Suddenly he heard the noise of metal against metal, and saw the keys pass through the wire mesh of the fence out into the yard beyond.

'Balls.'

He was standing between two gates with no keys.

'I'm the fucking clown now.'

A second or two before he heard his footsteps on the dirt, he saw the suited figure of one of the governor's staff. For all he knew it might be the governor himself.

'Marvellous.'

'Afternoon, Officer.' It was Lingard. His suit was buttoned against the cold, collar turned up so you could see the felt underneath. He was rubbing his hands together, affable, hair swept over and Brylcreemed.

'Afternoon.'

Lingard clapped his hands as if to prompt Dunn to take action.

'Have you got your pass on you, Sir?'

'What's that?' he said, aspirating the words.

'ID, please, Sir.'

The man raised an eyebrow and felt around inside his breast pocket. He produced a handkerchief and then a pass, which he handed to Dunn through the gate. Dunn scrutinized it. Carl Lingard, Assistant Governor. Cunnilingus.

'You are going to let me in now, Officer . . .?'

He handed back the pass.

'Sir, I'm afraid we're asking every visitor today to comply with a security test.'

'You what?'

'Yes, if you wouldn't mind.'

'I've not heard of this!'

'Well, I'm going to give you a few instructions and if you fulfil them we can go on from there. It's standard. Today.'

'This place is getting more preposterous by the minute.'

'If you could turn about and take five paces, Mr Lingard.'

Carl Lingard did so, muttering all the while.

'Now three to your left, Sir.'

'One, two three,'

'Now bend down, Sir, and slightly to your right there you'll find the keys to the gate.'

Lingard picked them up. 'You cheeky bugger. How the devil did they get there?'

Dunn swung the keyring a little.

Lingard broke into a resounding belly laugh. He handed the keys to Dunn who admitted him, thanking him and apologizing.

'What's your name?'

'John Dunn.'

'You're new. You were on Bolton's block last week?'

'Yes.'

'Yes, well, I thought so. New and English. That accounts for it. There's not many of us in here who still have a sense of humour.' He offered Dunn his hand. Dunn noticed the gold signet ring on his little finger. 'Damned good show.'

'Well thank you for that,' he added, as Dunn showed him to the second gate. 'I don't think I've laughed here since 1976.'

'Mr Lingard, last week you mentioned that if we ever needed to speak to you about anything you'd be available?'

Lingard stepped back up to the fence. 'To me?'

'Yes.'

'Really?'

'Yes. Sir.'

'Well, what we'd do in that case – um let me think – is, well, when are you back on the block?'

'Think I'll be back on it tomorrow, Sir.'

'Right well, Monday we'll get personnel to call you up and then you can say you're off to see them and discreetly pop along into my office for a chat. Present yourself at personnel and they'll show you where to go. Just knock.'

'Thank you.'

'I'll make sure I can open my door!' said Lingard, raising his fist in the air in a cheery salute, half Che Guevara, half Terry Thomas.

27

Mrs Mulhern was standing at the door of her own kitchen, holding her hands, her lips moving long before she spoke. 'I said, whatever do you think you're doing now?'

'She's doing your cupboards out, missus.' Aine was barring her entry.

'Whatever for?'

Kathleen was standing on a stool wiping inside Mrs Mulhern's cupboards. She bent at the knees and ducked to see out the back window. She had Liam in the back yard picking up the litter.

On Sunday afternoons, she and the kids more often than not came over to cook Mrs Mulhern her tea, have a clean up and give her some company if her own family weren't about. She'd had fifteen children and now she lived alone and worried about them and anyone in any way connected with them or the idea of them. Watching the news she'd point out a female news reporter and get herself upset about her daughter who was in Armagh, the women's prison. 'She's a girl, you see, like that one you see.'

'There's a load of shite in here from the nineteen-fifties.'

'And it's still good. I don't want you in there.'

There was a tap at the front window and Mrs Mulhern put her hand on her heart. 'Lord save us.'

'It's Father Pearse!' called Aine.

Kathleen got down from the stool to look. She warned Mrs Mulhern as she went past, 'Now you stay out of that kitchen.'

The old woman went over to the packets and jars on the countertop. 'All good!'

'It's you I'm after Kathleen,' said Father Pearse. 'Hello there Mrs Mulhern, all right are you?'

'Aye I'm all right,' came the grumble. The old woman put a hand on Aine's arm. 'I don't like the modern ones. He rushed through my Paul's funeral, rushed it through. I don't care for his sort. And I don't care if he has got a lot to do, my Paul was special to me.'

'Was he the last one?'

'No. No, he was one of the last though.'

Father Pearse had come by with a letter from Sean, seen the note on the door and gone across the road to find them.

'I didn't see you at Clonard this morning, thought you might be up at the Kesh,' Kathleen said.

'Aye I was. Do you want to read it and I'll wait on you. I'm sure you're in a rush to hear his news.'

'No, Father. That's all right. I saw him Wednesday, that's fast to have a letter back from him. No, it'll wait. Father Fitzgerald gave a nice wee talk today. All about how Christmas might as well be no more than a fairytale if it doesn't reveal the God of Love, about seeking the hidden God in everything. So I'm busy looking for him in Mrs Mulhern's kitchen cupboards just the now.'

Receiving communion, the wafer stuck to her tongue and was hard to swallow and the priest said, '*do this in memory of me*', this is the body, this the blood shed for you. They kept the wound open; that was the faith, to stay with it, abide in it, not to deny it or to try to heal it.

'Kathleen, Sean was on what they call the boards again when I went into the block this morning.'

'Again?'

'I'm afraid so.'

'So you didn't see him at mass then?'

'No, not when he's on punishment.' He took her hand in his. 'It was Gerard McIlvenny as gave me the note. He'd left it with him before he went.' He thought of McIlvenny's stooping posture and winced.

'Sit yourself down, Father,' she said, indicating the armchair.

'I don't think you've to worry overly now about Sean. From what I understand he's not hurt. He assaulted a screw again, so they're saying. He's had three days in the punishment block, should be back on the block this evening.'

'He didn't get a beating did he, Father, my Sean?'

The father shook his head. 'I don't know.'

'Would you tell me if he had?'

'Is there bad news, Mummy?' Aine came in.

'No, lovely, no. Well, aye, in a way there is. We just don't know anything. The father here's come to tell us about Sean. He's on punishment again. Go put the kettle on for Mrs Mulhern. Help her make the tea.'

Father Pearse looked tired and dishevelled, the black of his suit was grey and his shirt was grey too. A man without a woman. She saw that his shoes were filthy; they had dirt and rubbish stuck to them as if they'd been tarred and feathered.

'I wonder what I'm doing wasting my time at the church with the praying,' she said. 'Och don't listen to me. There's the violence before and after the service. The church is filled with people. It's not just us, the Proddies go to theirs. You tell me why, then? Are we getting different stories? Are they being told to kick the shit out of their neighbours?'

'From the time of Christ there's been violence Kathleen; St Paul persecuted the Christians until he saw the light didn't he? It's human nature. And the church is just humans. Well, now the church is very contradictory surely, there's a difference in what it says and what it does; the church has been involved in bloodshed, of course.'

'Why is it that Sean always has to be at the front of things? Why can't my boys just hang back like them Purcell boys do? Some people hang back and they don't suffer do they? Is that not a sin, Father?'

Kathleen heard the kettle straining over its own steam and Mrs Mulhern and Aine exchanging orders.

'I wonder myself sometimes what is a sin, Kathleen.'

'Well if it's me you're asking Father we're both in the shite.'

'What I mean is, how do we tell sin from what is breathing and eating and shitting even . . .'

Aine had two mugs of tea. She stopped in her tracks. 'A sin is a thing you know you oughtn't to do because it will harm someone else. That's different to using the toilet, Father. You can't help that.' She placed their mugs of tea beside them and went back out, returning with an ashtray.

'You're a good girl, Aine,' said the father, taking the ashtray in his hands, balancing it on his knees and reaching around his pockets for his tobacco and papers. 'But those boys, you see, they've nothing to gain personally. What we call a sin is something wrong which benefits you in a worldly way, but those boys they're losing everything.'

He put the rolled-up cigarette in his mouth, then took it out again, looking at the mantelpiece.

'You need a wee break yourself, Father, you should go away down to the Free State for a few days, to your family.'

'I can't leave. How can the church ask me not to be involved with what's going on round here? They might as well ask me not to be involved with Him,' he pointed his cigarette at the semi-naked ornamental figure above the fireplace. He looked at Kathleen's sympathetic face in the pale midday light, a lovely looking woman whose eyes were too lined, and felt sorry for himself. He knew it was indulgent, it felt like eating a cream cake. This too was wrong.

'People is people, if He didn't judge them how can I? Do you know the first year I was here there was one Catholic after another shot down round my way. That was '71. I thought I was in hell. I got real fast with the wake masses. It changed my ideas.'

'Only God can see into people's hearts, Father, isn't that the truth, only He can say why a person does what he does and whether it's all right or not.'

'So it's said. But if that's the case I don't know why they ever invented the fecking church. Maybe they shouldn't have. I wonder if it wasn't a sin.' He stowed his rolled cigarette in his top pocket, got up, wiped his hands together and started to move to the door.

'Are you going Father, already, and your tea not drunk?'

'I've just brought to mind a wee favour I said I'd do. The boys up the road asked me if they could use the car this evening. I said they'd more than likely find the keys on the front tyre and I've to go and keep my word.' He stopped at the door. He looked back guiltily over the room as if he'd left a mess behind. 'We have to support them, Kathleen, the boys are risking their lives for all of us.'

'Aye, of course we do, Father. It can't be easy for you,' she said, and her face was so tender that he felt shame overwhelm him.

'Och Jesus, God, Kathleen. You've got to be strong – there's talk of a hunger strike. And it's serious talk. Look now there's nothing any of us can do to change their minds. They're very firm on it. It's the hardest thing in the world to have to tell a mother. The hardest thing in the world.'

'And you've told them it's all right have you?' She felt a rush of anger; be angry or cry! Always the same choice.

'It's not for me to say . . .'

'Well you've got to tell them it's *wrong*. That the taking of your own life is *wrong*.'

'You see, it's not that simple. I can't tell them that when it's not the case. There's the principle of Double Effect. From St Thomas Aquinas. An action can have two consequences, one is intended, the other isn't. Like at the hospital if they give morphine for pain relief, but it has a second effect and it kills the patient, they're not guilty of murder, do you see? The boys are trying to bring about change, political change, none of them is looking to die.'

'Well I know it's a sin! I know it's wrong! Because I raised him, I raised that boy, he's me and I'm him, he's my life, there's nothing left for me without him.'

'Look Kathleen, calm down. Calm down. Isn't Sean old enough to make his own decisions?'

She had nothing to say; she opened the door for him.

'This is a terrible thing, terrible,' Father Pearse was saying and she wasn't listening. 'All of it, it drags you down and tears you apart and then it kicks you when you're down there. Kathleen. Speaking as your friend, not as a priest, nor as anything else, just watch out for young Liam. One son's enough.'

The priest called out a farewell to Mrs Mulhern and received no answer. After the door closed she came out of the kitchen holding her cup in both hands, shuffling in her slippers towards the window.

'The quick and the dead, that's what seeing him brings to my mind. Rushing and dashing about. He moves too fast to do anybody any good. I knew he'd not stay over long. Well, it's a blessing in some ways. He's not what I call a real priest.' Mrs Mulhern lowered herself into her chair. She cast a grim look through the kitchen to the back garden. 'Lovely boy that Liam. It's a name that's popular enough but there's something sloppy about it. Did you never think of Anthony? That's a holy name. Are you going to close that door, Kathleen, there's a terrible draught on my legs.'

28

Lingard had his back to the window in his office. It offered a view of a cluster of administration buildings, felled oblongs that looked like polystyrene. A thin tree, not long planted, with a yellow plastic flag tied round its neck, was rattled by the wind. From time to time a soldier walked past. Not no man's land but a nobody's land.

On the side wall was a theatre poster for a J. M. Synge 'Playboy of the Western World' performance in Belfast. Lingard's desk bore a few gadgets: an address book which one dialled, a set of eight silver balls suspended by fine, almost transparent, threads. He had a leather-edged ink blotter and an ink pen. There was a framed photo of his family arranged by kneeling height; his hands on his wife's shoulders, hers on the first child's and that child's on the next. This was positioned with precise nonchalance, facing the interlocutor as much as the deputy governor. His chair bounced and squeaked and railed at his movements. With hands performing a variety of limbering-up exercises over the terrain of his blotter, Lingard explained to Dunn how significant his visit was and how he hoped it might augur well.

It was like being in with the headmaster. Part of the latest statement issued to the prison officers by the Provisionals came to Dunn's mind, *'The only safe place for them to live will be in jail.'* This took on a new light as he surveyed the yellowing room with its yellowing occupant.

'Perhaps one or two more of your colleagues will see me as a resource and not the enemy itself! I could get you a tea if you like.'

'No thanks.'

'Ah! You're a cut to the chase sort of fellow,' said Lingard, alternating his expressions between humorous indulgence and serious attention. 'Are you a Catholic?'

He rifled in his drawer and produced a tin of boiled sweets with a fine dusting of sugar on them. He offered one to Dunn.

'No. No, thanks.'

Lingard took one, biting on it as if it were a problem. 'Wondered. Motivation, you see. Anyway, you're a man of few words. Why are you here?' He broke through the sweet and his teeth collided. 'Basically.'

'Well, I've probably made a procedures mistake, Sir. When I was on General Duties I was assigned to visits.'

'With our Mr Jaws. Oh yes, I know the nicknames. For all of them. Have you got one yet? You will do. I wonder if they give us lot nicknames? Do you think they do?'

'I don't know, Sir. I'm new here – still the outsider.'

'Yes of course.'

'Anyway a little rolled-up note, it looked like a pill to me, fell from the table and I picked it up and put it in my pocket. The thing is you see, right before it happened I heard the prisoners talking about the prison officer murders and I was a bit taken aback. I wasn't sure what action to take with the note thing.'

'I'm with you,' said Lingard, swallowing the last of the sweet. 'I'm with you. Of course procedure is to hand it immediately to the PO of visits. But that's beside the point now. I could count on one hand the number of occasions we've intercepted notes between the IRA and prisoners. So well done Dunn. No pun intended. First thing I want to ask you,' he lay his hands flat on the blotter, 'who was the prisoner and who was the visitor?'

'O'Malley was the prisoner. Brendan Coogan his visitor.'

'Really? Well, well. Where is the note?'

'Here, in my pocket.'

'Good. Mind if I see it?'

Dunn slipped it on to the table and Lingard felt for his spectacles in his jacket pocket, never taking his eyes off the pill-shaped note. Dunn was reminded of the television programme that Angie enjoyed, *Antiques Roadshow*. He thought that Lingard might offer him an appraisal and a price too. '*Long Kesh 1979, cellular clearly, HMP Maze, that is, been carried orally I'd say . . . Two pounds fifty.*'

'You haven't read it then,' said Lingard, touching it with his sheathed pen.

'No, Sir, I didn't want to.'

'Right.'

'I believe the prisoner is the OC for the block and I've seen his visitor on the local news, you see him giving the Falls Road side of things.'

'Yes, Brendan Coogan, he does all the talking. The public face of the IRA.' Lingard's pleasure was evident. 'I'm amazed that you haven't been tempted to read it, Dunn. What forbearance. You must be a chess player?'

'No, Sir.'

'Good, good.' He gave the tiny white missive one final prod with the pen. 'Well, let's unwrap it, shall we?'

'Well, over to you now, Sir, I'll be off if you've nothing . . .'

'Come on, Dunn,' his fingers were at the Clingfilm. 'I think I can trust you if you can trust me.'

'Actually, I'd rather not be involved in any way, Sir, I'm just handing it in, that's all . . .'

Lingard was already smoothing out the paper with his fingers.

'Don't worry about that. You've done the right thing Dunn. Sorry. I'm on the inside of the Northern Ireland Office, if you know what I mean.' He looked up and gave Dunn a film star smile. 'I'm on the political side of things. Right. Now I've got something on you and you on me. Okay?' He looked over the top of his glasses. '*A Chara*,' Lingard started to read. 'That means dear friend, *In response to comm. of 29/11 got to tell you that hunger strike is number one on our agenda in order to secure our main objective vis a vis the Brits and exposing all aspects of their imperialism in this country, criminalisation, normalisation, Ulsterisation. As this affects us*. He could mean criminalisation da-dee-da *as* this affects us or he could be starting afresh, hard to tell the writing is perishing small. God knows how they write them. It's a piece of that bloody bog paper you know, like wax paper; we don't get much better up here. Doesn't absorb, fingers go through it. *The hunger strike is the most effective method at our disposal and the most credible to rebut the strategy of criminalisation. The Billy McKee hunger strike of 1972 got political status from Whitelaw. Who knows with the Brits but you've got to think they won't let prisoners die, due to international protest. At the least, it will speed up the talks. You wrote that we might pull off the hunger strike before the final days. Think this is a dangerous thought. Have not communicated it. The level of commitment is running high. There would be no half measures. Well, that's about the heap for now, slán. Kevin.*

'Well. That's really something. Hunger strike. Now I need to consider the information. What would you say was key in there, John?'

'I couldn't say, Sir.'

'The *dangerous thought*. Dangerous for them is good for us. I mean, strategically speaking. This letter states that the hunger strike is their last card. He asks Coogan, their public representative, to play it. Now that's important. There's something in this, Dunn. I just need time to think it through. We all have our part in the game, don't we, John? You've played yours. Now over to me. Although I've got orders, they're probably not what you'd think of as orders, I've got a free hand in some ways. But the truth is I'm from over there, and I have a certain way of looking at things. Justice. This is not my war. I'm here to try and stop it, to foul it up if you like. Put the brakes on. Personally, I don't like killing. I believe in putting killers away and hampering those still on the outside. The IRA have been trying to kick up a big bloody fuss over this place. Making heroes. They'll be creating merry hell about a bloody hunger strike. You said you were a chess player?' Lingard's space heater started to buzz and he tapped it gently.

'No, Sir, I am not.'

'Ah, shame. You see if we know that their Achilles heel so to speak is this *dangerous idea*, that they might *not* go through with a hunger strike, that their last card is a bluff, then we might pursue a policy of shall we say . . . brinkmanship.' He looked at the theatre poster. 'Nobody wants a fellow to die which ever way he dresses, but that's not going to happen, not unless there's a major cockup. That's what this letter here is telling us. So Dunn, there will be no dying, no suicide pact. We have a number of options. We can subtly communicate to them that it won't work and that will be an end to it. They'll pull off and no one will die. We might even manage a little popular support to dampen the bravura of the whole thing. Funny how it's only the Catholics seem able to mobilize themselves that way, but maybe we can get the ones who're more for peace coming out and saying "No to dying".'

He seemed roused, failing to register Dunn's growing expression of disbelief.

'Oh, I'm just speculating, John. I'm a visionary in here. The only one. No, they'd never do anything as low as to get any public opinion working for them. Good God no! Not the Northern Ireland Office. No, I'm an outsider on the inside.' He laughed shortly.

Dunn looked at his watch. It was comfortable sitting in that warm room far from the cell block, and he wouldn't have minded staying longer if Lingard hadn't been spouting on. Dunn hated to hear men talk at length that way. It was only pardonable in drink. He had more than likely made a mistake in giving the note to Lingard. He had hoped to clear the decks, to set himself straight. But things were never straight. The noose just tightened. This mess was of his making and he wanted to move away from it, physically, now.

'Sir,'

'Mr Lingard at a push, if you must, but not 'Sir' for gawd's sake.'

'Having just been on those protest blocks for just a few weeks, I'll tell you, I've seen those young lads in there, I'd say they're quite capable of dying on a hunger strike no matter what anyone says.'

Lingard held his pen up at his lips. 'Would you, John, would you? Still this letter is *entre amis*, as they say, between friends. I think we have to take it at face value. I think they'd know their own minds. Won't keep you, but very, very impressed. You did the right thing with this.

Anything else comes your way, you bring it to me. Between us . . . well, if there were more men like you . . .'

Dunn took his cap off the desk. He stood up and his new set of keys, for the block, swung on their chain against the desk. He put them back in his pocket.

'You and those bloody keys, eh? That gave me a laugh I'll tell you. You're not like the others are you? What's your story, I wonder. Listen, the wife and I like to have people round for drinks from time to time, casual you know, Martinis and jazz music, that sort of a thing. Would you and yours care to come for a drink and a bite? I'll have to check the diary, hold tight.' He held the diary open with one hand and ran a finger down the other side. 'All the bloody Christmas piss-ups. Hang on, Wednesday 19th we're free, would that suit?'

'Thank you, I appreciate it but I'm bound to be working.'

'Well, I'll have a word with the duty officer. Can't promise of course.'

He hopped up and gave Dunn a pat on the back as he went to the door. Dunn shrank away and ducked out.

'*The only safe place for them to live will be in jail.*' How much did his own safety matter to him? After half an hour in Lingard's world, it seemed unimportant, nothing worth dying for.

It was the day of Prison Officer William Benbow's funeral; all visits were cancelled, so the mess was charged with bored anxiety. At unlock, the young kid, Moran, had head-butted Rabbit this time. He was making a name for himself. He'd been put in cell twenty-six again while the PO arranged for someone to come down and issue the order for his transfer back to the boards. He'd only just come back to the block.

'He ought to get it into his thick skull that being on the protest is enough of a qualification.' Bolton was standing in shirtsleeves outside his office doo, peeved, when the deputy governor arrived. 'Come in for a moment, Mr Lingard, we'll have a chat while one of the fellas brings the man up.'

Rabbit offered and went off.

In the mess, Dunn had out the AA pocket map of Northern Ireland that Angie had borrowed from her office. He was studying it ostensibly for directions for the day out with the boy, but he'd become quite gripped by the motoring information, especially the mileage chart. He felt like a whole new vista was opening.

'Listen to this. Me and the lads have cooked up a great fucking scam.' Frig was holding the door handle behind him. 'The scam to end them all. My old Ford, the engine's fucked. Can't shift it. Tomorrow we're going to park it round where the army patrol comes haring in the morning, up past Main Gate. Just round the bend, on the wrong side. We're running a book on the compensation. You in? What about a pound on flattened and full comp to the market value of the car? Any takers?'

'A pound says they stop before they get to it.'

'A pound says you can't get it started to get it there,' said Shandy, stirring a mug of Ovaltine.

'You're a bunch of misery gutses. You'll change your tunes when I get that compensation.'

Shandy tuned the radio, '*Simply having a wonderful Christmas time . . .*'

When the disc jockey announced the time, Dunn and Skids adjusted their watches.

'I gave him another kicking.' Rabbit came in, breathless. 'He gave me a fucking headache, that little Fenian cunt, so I gave him balls-ache.'

There was no one in the TV room. It was *Songs of Praise* from Portadown. The door cracked and Skids shuffled in, sat right him, too close again.

'I'm seeing this woman in Lisburn. Did I tell you? She's married, but she's cracking looking. We're meeting in a pub tonight.'

Dunn said nothing.

'I ought to leave my wife. I'd do the right thing and give her money for the wean. I shouldn't be carrying on like this, this'll be the third time I've seen her. The thing is, like if I start thinking about her and her old man in bed, having sex, it makes me feel sick to my stomach so it does. I was thinking of telling her to get him to use a rubber johnny. I don't want to go in where he's been.'

Dunn excused himself and went off to the privacy of his toilet. '*My church*,' he thought, trousers round his ankles.

29

'*Mummy. There's a lot going on and we're all working hard right now to get the five demands out. We'll be counting on all of you to do your part. See I've put at the bottom of the letter what they are, so see if you can't write some letters yourself to politicians telling them what it is we want. We'll see this thing through together whatever we have to face. I know it was hard for you last time so I won't be asking for you to come up next time. It's for the best. God Bless. Your loving son, Sean. Here follows the five demands.*'

The words that followed were etched in capitals, proud and painstaking as a poem. She put a fingernail between her teeth and ripped the side of it off. It came away unevenly, leaving an orange triangle of pain. She folded the piece of paper and put it in a jar in a cupboard. Then she switched off the overhead light in the kitchen and sat in the dark with her arms folded.

Her husband came in early about ten, sent back as no use, no doubt, and he gave her a swaying greeting from underneath the light in the hallway.

'Rioting up over New Barnsley. Good mind to go up myself and give the boys a hand.'

She watched him from the dark as if she was at a cinema. She told him the children were already in their beds and not to make so much noise. He went up swaying and bracing himself, as if he was mounting the stairs in gale-force conditions. When he was abed and snoring she got up and put on her coat and went out.

It was a quiet night; the moon was a slither of a smile up-ended. You could see the light coming from a few of the shops on the Falls Road. A black taxi-cab came past from time to time. There was a Saracen parked on the corner of the street, near the door to the pub. A couple were saying a long goodnight outside the newsagent's, sharing a cigarette. She made her way up the slight incline, passing the hospital and heading towards Clonard Street, thinking of Sean, then thinking of the young soldier, Frank, both of them nineteen.

'I'm losing my mind over you,' Frank had said, on top of her, touching the hair about her face. 'It's your eyes.'

'There are plenty of other older women, she'd told him, the last time she met him at Colin Glen. Her own world – the family, Belfast, the war – was accelerating, about to take over. She'd struggled to come up with a good reason for leaving the kids with Eileen for a day, in the midst of the raging uncertainty in autumn '69. Off she'd gone, passing some neighbours who were carrying their settee down the street.

It was the only time in her life she'd made love outside. They'd been on the ground, with twigs poking at her backside, his knees scuffed, out of breath. She'd put her legs around his back. He had looked into her eyes all the time they made love, his mouth taut, almost fearful, as if he was falling. The sun had been just behind his head. With the circles upon circles in his eyes, and the light between the trees, and the focus of his concentration, she had been suspended in time, just breathing, watching. And then when he was through, he fell across her. She'd lain there, weighed down, with him still inside her and she'd wept.

The time before, they'd been in the house, upstairs, in the afternoon. Mary came home from school early. There'd been nothing for it but for Frank to go down the stairs and walk right by her, with a stupid hello. She'd come down herself and started to make up a story but Mary went off next door, to see her friend. They'd never spoken about it. Nearly ten years later, when Mary was aged eighteen and leaving for England, Kathleen cried she needed her, these were difficult times with Sean just lifted. When Mary seemed indifferent, Kathleen grew angry.

'There's your brother, giving up his young life to defend us and you off to the very country he's fighting.'

'Ah listen to my mother the great Republican!' she'd said. 'Well maybe I fancy a nice young Brit myself.'

She let her husband go with Mary to the ferry. Her oldest daughter had grown up, quietly judging her mother, become the woman herself, delivered her blow and left home. Kathleen put the girl's things away in the attic and was irritable on Sundays. By then, Sean was on remand in the Crum.

Now she stood in the dark outside the Republican Press Centre, belted trench coat, and she banged on the door as if she meant to break it down. She held the door frame on either side, raised her knee, and booted the door with her heel. She heard the sound of the stairs going. Coogan opened the door.

'I thought it was the Brits.'

'Why did you not think to mention the hunger strike to me?'

He ushered her in and closed the door behind her, locking it in two places. He stood in a short hallway, in front of some stairs. There was a door to his left, marked 'Doctor's Surgery'.

'"*Ach the protest marches will change everything for our boys, so they will.*" Will they fuck. I reckon yous are just getting us to do them to make ourselves feel better! The truth is they are going on a hunger strike and it's your lot who's got them indoctrinated to it.'

'Calm down, will you?'

'And they're still being treated like shite, tortured, beaten. My Sean's on the boards again, God knows what for and I've got a note saying he doesn't want me to come again. He's being brainwashed! And you lot, you're getting Father Pearse to get us ready for losing our sons to a hunger strike next. Well it won't be my son!'

'Calm yourself down!'

'No I won't!'

'Yes it's true they've talked about it, they're talking about it. It was always an option, it always has been. Yes, they're saying that if they don't get the five demands they'll go to a hunger strike. Indoctrinated? That's bullshit, Kathleen. We don't want them to die. They're our friends, our brothers, our cousins, our uncles too, you know. But Christ, we're not in there, they are. If they ask us to support them, to make sure it's not for nothing, what are we supposed to say to them? No? Look, Kathleen, you want us to defend you, you want us to get you out of this, but you don't want to pay a price for it. An army is made up of people's sons. I'm not responsible for what your son does. He's a grown man. You know how it is round here. He's been reared here.'

'You've no idea how he's been reared. I love him!'

'I know you love your son. You're not alone. But you should be proud of him too. He wants to do what's right.'

'I don't care about what's right. Not if it means losing him.'

'I know, I know.'

'No you don't know! That's the trouble with you and your kind. It's easy for you. Until you've got kids you've no idea what love is.'

'All right.'

'Someone like you, you just want to win, at any price.'

'Aye, all right. No, you're right, Kathleen. That's true as a matter of fact.'

'Right then!'

'Right. Now come on upstairs. We'll have a drink and a talk. Come on.' He went up, calling behind, 'We're opposed to it, you know. We're going to do everything we can so it doesn't come to that.'

She ought to go home.

Instead she went up into the office space, with its high ceilings and loose window frames; it was cold in there. There were cardboard boxes everywhere. She sat down on a box, her knees together, feet apart.

'We're about to move offices. We're packing up. We'll have a few days at least before the new address is known so we'll be taking a break from the midnight abuse.' He gave her a wary smile. Then he went around the counter and came back with a bottle of Irish whiskey. 'Here have a drink.'

'No. No thanks.'

He stood looking down at her, his tie loose, his shirt hanging outside of his trousers. He took the stopper out of the bottle with his teeth, then spat it over the back of a box behind him.

'Well now you've got to help me drink it.' He handed the bottle to her. 'Go ahead and have a smoke if you want. Kathleen, we've all lived in the same streets. What we've got going for us in this community is the way we pull together. There's no choice, not for any of us. But they won't beat us.'

She took a swig; it burnt, hateful and necessary.

'No they won't beat us, we'll all be dead though.'

'You're not dead yet.'

'I might as well be.'

'I wish I could see you smile.'

She gave him the bottle.

'Do you know the first time I saw you? You came round for that bag for your brother and I was packing it and I kicked myself after that I should have chucked my stuff into a couple of carrier bags and given it to you.' He had deep wrinkles either side of his eyes when he smiled.

'I'm surprised you remember that with what was going on that day.'

'You were wearing a short pale dress that showed your knees.'

'I've never had such a dress.'

'You did have. It was August. Your legs were suntanned.'

'And Bombay Street was burning.'

Outside there was the noise of a man tapping on the door and shouting '*Tiocfaidh ar la*!' as he went past.

'A well-wisher. Makes a nice change.'

'I don't know what to think any more.' She slumped down. 'I love my son.'

He took a draught of the whiskey and sat down on the ground opposite her, passing it across again. 'No one knows where it's going to end. But we're all in it together.'

'God almighty, if he dies, I shan't care about any of it, fuck it all.' She took a swig. 'Slàinte.' She pressed her fingertips to her lips, tears in her eyes.

He took the bottle back from her and set it down on the ground, then he knelt up, put his hands on the sides of her face and, holding her hair tight over her ears, he kissed her. The box gave way and caved in.

30

John Dunn was in his car at the end of his driveway, looking at his home. It was after eight. Mark Wilson would have arrived by now with a bag of things from his own life.

When John put the key in the door, he heard the sound of Angie chattering. Normally it would be on the phone but now he knew she was talking to Mark Wilson. He stood on the threshold. He cleared his throat and Angie piped up, 'Well, this will be your father, Mark.'

She came out of the kitchen and stood in the hallway. 'He's nice.' She mouthed.

A tall thin lad stood in the door of the kitchen, behind her. He had a tight v-neck sweater, thin-legged black trousers, and a long nose. Mousey, straggling hair. His eyes were friendly.

'Well?' said Angie.

John put his bag down. He held out his hand.

'I'm John. Sorry I smell so bad, it's a long story.'

'The protest,' said the boy, shaking his hand. He was about his height. 'It's good to meet you.'

John emitted a wintry laugh. 'Just got to pop up to the bathroom,' he said, and went upstairs.

'Well. Another cup of tea, Mark?'

The young man looked up the stairs after the prison-officer boots.

'He'll be down in a wee minute, he's not very good at meeting strangers. Not that you're a stranger.' She put a hand on his arm.

The boy followed her into the kitchen and looked outside into the dark. 'Have you always lived round here, Angela?'

'In Belfast? No, Belfast isn't my cup of tea. I'm a wee country girl. But I'd sell my soul to live somewhere warm.' She laughed. Then she changed her expression to be more motherly. 'Now what is it you're studying?'

He became quickly involved in explaining his degree, moving his hands on the table as if he had a tennis ball between them and she nodded as he talked but she was wondering whether John was coming back down at all.

When she heard him on the stairs, she jumped up, told them she was going off to do some bits and bobs, tidy around. 'Give you two the chance to get to know each other.'

'Have a cup of tea with us, love,' said John, stricken.

'I've had three waiting on you.'

'Would you like one, Mark?'

'No thanks.'

'Well then it's just me.'

'I'll leave you to it,' said Angie.

'Well, this is strange,' said Mark. 'Meeting you.'

John leant on the kitchen counter, back to the boy. 'Yes, likewise. So you're at university then? I was never much of a one for the books.'

'Angie said you were doing a law degree.'

'That? I didn't finish it. Started it but couldn't finish it.'

'Law's pretty complicated.'

'I'm not stupid or anything, I'm just more of a doer than a thinker. That's why I'm in this job,' he said, reaching for the sugar tin. 'When I was your age I was already in the army.'

'Were you?'

'Yup.' He poured the boiling water shakily.

'Was that over here?'

'All over the place. Cyprus, Aden, Germany. Yes, here too, three times . . .'

'You got to see the world then. That's something I'd really like do when I've finished.'

'No I didn't really see the world, just went where I was sent, follow-ing orders. I was a technical storeman. Joined the REME, the Royal Electrical and Mechanical Engineers that is. I was attached here and there, you see. Blues and Royals was the last one.'

'Really? That's a good one, isn't it?'

'Depends what you mean by good.'

Upstairs he had popped into the spare room where the boy's bag was on the bed. He'd taken a look around, to see what the boy had brought with him, to see what he was like. One anonymous bag, not big enough for more than a few days, as yet not unpacked. He'd spotted the empty half-soap-dish in which he'd stowed the pill-shaped note. Pink plastic, ridged with white detritus like the in-between of teeth. He put it away in the bathroom cabinet.

'This was always going to be difficult,' Mark said now.

John had an aversion to adolescent boys, he always wanted to knock the softness out of them, he couldn't help it; with their doubting looks and school-book way of talking. There was a whole world between them; him and this university student. The boy's features were fine and as he looked aside, John noticed his eyelashes. Maybe he wasn't his son.

'Would you rather we hadn't decided to do this?'

'No, it's not that. Just had a bit of a day. I'm a bit out of sorts.'

'It sounds like it's a hard job. Mind if I smoke?'

John got up to get an ashtray from the kitchen cupboard. He placed it in front of Mark who was leaning to one side, withdrawing a pack of ten from his trouser pocket. John reached for the matches from the stove.

'Thanks. Want one?'

'I'm fine for now, thanks.' He looked at the cigarettes. Marlboro. 'It's not much of a job. Don't know about hard.'

The boy lit up a cigarette, shook out the match with the gesture of a conjuror, squinted through one eye and exhaled. John sat, rolling back and forth a biro that he'd taken from the small bowl on the table that contained keys, saving stamps.

'So did you like being in the army? What's it like? Did you drive a tank?'

John cracked a sardonic laugh. 'Yeah, I did as it happens, once or twice. It was the right thing for me. My old man left when I was six you see. He came back for a summer, but before that and after that I never had a father. My mother remarried but I never really could call it home. Not a sob story but not exactly the days of my life. Anything was an improvement frankly.'

'I didn't have a father either, so we've got that in common.'

John looked at him, poker-faced. 'No, you didn't did you. Did she not marry, your mother?'

'Nope.'

'Would you like a biscuit or some crisps or something? I'll go ask Angie where she keeps them.'

'No thanks.' Mark's arm pivoted at the elbow, a flat wave. His fingernails were bitten. Dunn had never bitten his nails, he cut them squarely and kept them clean. 'I had a bite at the docks.'

'Was Angie late then?'

'No, I was early. Had my first taste of champ.'

'Good on you.'

'Yeah it was great. Really liked it. Got chatting as well. People seem to be pretty friendly here in fact, despite what you hear.'

John nodded absently. 'Mmm. Well, you know, I'm sorry.' He swallowed.

'For what?'

'I'm not much of a find.'

'You could feel the same way about me.' The boy stubbed out the cigarette. 'So you served in the army over here then?'

'Yes, Three tours. '69. '74 and '76.'

'And you stayed on? Bit of an odd thing to do isn't it? Can't be the run of the mill?'

Where had he learnt his manners, his mannerisms? Who did he take after? There was the sound of canned laughter from the living room. Angie had put on the television. The laughter was a spasm of affected delight. John wondered if it was the *Some Mothers Do 'Ave 'Em* repeats. He and Angie liked to watch them and she usually called him as soon as the piccolo music started up.

'Listen, Mark. What are you hoping for? From me, from this?'

'Well, I wanted to see what you looked like, see who you were. See if you were like me or I was like you.'

'What, and then we both go on our separate ways?'

'If that's what we decide to do.'

'That's not very realistic, Mark.' John thought of the bag upstairs still packed. 'Still, you're welcome, Mark, you're welcome here, you know.'

'Thanks.' He tapped his cigarette on the saucer then put it out. 'So why *did* you stay on here rather than come back to England?'

'Met Angie didn't I? You taste her champ and then you'll know why. You hungry?'

John got up, opened the fridge door, glanced inside. It had been cleaned. There was a small corner of cheese in its wrapper. He took it out and bit into it, then corrected himself, showing it briefly to Mark. Mark waived it. John took another bite, swallowed again, passed his tongue over his teeth. More extravagant hilarity from the sitting room.

'Do you like Frank Spencer?'

'Yes, he's pretty good.'

'Very funny. He's very talented that bloke, what's his name, like cheese biscuits.'

'Crawford, Michael Crawford.'

'Yes that's it. No it wasn't for Angie's champ. By the end of all of that I was an old hand here. You know the other blokes were always asking me, What's it all about Johnno? and all I could say was, it's hard to understand and when you think you know, you don't. They'd be coming up to me every day saying, 'Ere mate, is it about the Pope? and I'm saying, no. Then it's, Is it about the marching? and I'm, no, and then they'd be saying, Is it about land? and all the time all I could say was no. No one can put a finger on it. But then, after a bit, you just sort of accept that's the way it is. And before you know it you're part of it.'

Mark nodded his head in staccato, studious, attentive, absorbed.

'It *is* a different country, that's the first thing you have to get straight.

To be honest with you, I've got a lot of time for the Catholics. The decent ones. Not the IRA. Although you see their discipline when you work in the prison. Anyway I like it here, I like that it's a hard place. England's not for me, it's all white bread and keeping the lawn trimmed. I like the people here, for the most part. Some of them are bastards – but you get that everywhere.'

'And then you joined the prison service after the army?'

'Well, I'm someone who takes orders you see. Maybe you'll be someone who gives them.'

'I hope not.'

'Well you've got to be one or the other.'

'Not me. That's not me at all.'

'You're from a different generation, I suppose. Your mother did her best for you, then? Good woman is she?'

'She never told you about me.'

'No. Well, she wouldn't have. We never did speak. After we broke up. If you can call it that.'

There was silence before a lorry changed gear on its way past the house, wracking its engine, then the tail end of the noise and the creaking of Angie's footsteps, making off to bed.

'Did she say nothing about me then, to you? Your mum?'

'She said that it didn't work out. She said you were both young and didn't know anything. That you were just a kid.'

'I was twenty odd. I'd been in the army five years!'

'Her dad, Ronnie, my granddad, he said she could do as she liked about having the baby. He didn't care what people said. She said you were nice looking but, well, not . . . very deep.'

'Deep! What sort of a word's that? Talk about bloody hippy! Deep. That's another word for wearing sandals isn't it, and moaning a lot.'

'She said it wasn't your fault.'

Appeased, John moved his head from side to side. 'Well yeah, that's true. Still, I should have been more careful.'

'Thanks,' said Mark, the lightest of smiles, too weak to persist. There was a citrus ring around the very centre of his eyes, then North Sea grey-blue. In the hollowing of his cheeks, John glimpsed all the thinking he'd done, this kid, all that thinking that had brought him here, to be sat across from some stranger, a table between them, in a linoleum-floored kitchen in a rented house in East Belfast.

'I'm not very good with words Mark; I didn't mean that the way it sounded. I'm coming across like a right prick. I just meant that it was reckless. If I'd known I had a son, I would have been a father. Like when it came to paying for what you needed. And whatever else.'

'We didn't need money. We were all right. My grandfather was like a father to me. Ronnie. He died last year and Mum told me what she knew about you. She said I look like you, or how she remembered you.'

'You poor bloody sod!' John brought the cold tea up to his widening mouth and as he drank it, he started to splutter, laughing. 'Christ who'd have thought it? And yesterday we didn't know each other from Adam. Bloody hell.' John shook his head, got up and poured the remainder of his tea into the sink. 'Well look, Mark, I've got to be out of here just after five in the morning, but Tuesday we'll have the day together. My Angie, she'll look after you. You ask her if you need something. You don't know us but we're all right. Have you got everything you need, for now?'

Mark stood up.

'Skinny great sod, aren't you?'

'Likewise.'

John crossed the room between the table and the fridge, tendering his hand. He shook the boy's hand, then touched his forearm. 'Good man.'

31

The lights were on at Mrs O'Sullivan's and the Dohertys', and her own front door was wide open. Kathleen hesitated and then she ran. There was a group of people on the front step of the O'Sullivans'.

Sheila McCann broke out from among them, angular, angry. 'For fuck's sake! Where the hell have you been?'

'Where are my children?'

'Aine's in with our Una. They've taken Liam away! Sean is in our house with Sammy, making phone calls.'

There was Roisin and her husband Patrick, both in their nightclothes and Mrs O'Sullivan in a tracksuit and Wellington boots.

'Who? Who has taken him away?'

'The Brits, the peelers.'

'Why?'

'He was up over New Barnsley...'

'He was in bed!'

Roisin looked up the road towards the hills, to the New Barnsley estate. 'He must have gone out, Kathleen.'

'I'll take you round the barracks, Kathleen,' said Mrs O'Sullivan. 'I'll get the wee car out just now. You wait over at Sheila's with your husband.'

Sean was sat in the McCanns' front room with a cup of tea watching Sammy talking on the phone.

'There you are.' His mouth was flat, his eyes yellow. 'It was young Owen that came and told me Liam was taken. He came right up the stairs and shook me in my bed. I thought it was you.'

'I can't leave my house half an hour!'

Owen came out of the kitchen. He had dried blood under his nose, and a great red mark on the side of his head.

'What in God's name were you thinking of you, the pair of you?'

'There was a riot up Springfield. The Prods was shouting "Death to the Taigs" and they set fire to Mr Gianelli's ice-cream van. Donny McArdle came round here telling us to get up there and help. So I went and got Liam up . . .'

Sammy McCann put a hand over the receiver, 'He told me he was going to help him with his homework.'

'Liam had some petrol bombs in a box so we took them up with us. By the time we got there the peelers had come in and they're taking their truncheons to all of us lot and the Prods are still shouting and firing stuff. One of the peelers gets out his handgun, like this, and puts it to this wee lads head just to make him cry. So Liam threw one of his petrol bombs. It wasn't even lit.'

There was a small and pretty trill from the carriage clock on the mantelpiece, it was midnight.

'We all ran off then but the peelers must have grabbed Liam.'

'We've rung round the hospitals. He's not at any of them, Kathleen.'

'The wee lad had shat himself. I said to him how he'd better go home but he says he couldn't go home with a mess in his underpants, so I helped him take them off quick and then I went back up there to look for Liam but there was no one there. I went back up for him. Are they going to put him in prison now?'

There were tears in his eyes. Sheila went to him. 'What am I thinking of? Is this any way for children to grow up? We should have moved down south years ago!'

'I'm not going anywhere,' said Owen.

Sammy replaced the receiver. 'They won't give out anything.'

Mrs O'Sullivan arrived with a small business-like rap on the open door. 'Ready?'

Sean stood up. He had his pyjama bottoms on and his cardigan. He put his hand behind Kathleen's back without touching it. 'I'll come with yous.'

'You're better off at home. I can call you then if I need to. It's better if I go.'

She wouldn't look at him so he just stood nodding, nodding, not saying anything. Then, becoming once more aware of the others, he extended his nodding to them, and there he stood as she brushed past him, smiling a smile he didn't want on his face, his hands reaching for pockets he didn't have.

Mrs O'Sullivan threw the passenger door open for Kathleen. 'We'll make a quick tour of the barracks shall we, love?' she said, putting a hand on the gear stick and shaking it.

Going in Mrs O'Sullivan's car was usually like taking a trip in a horse and cart; her driving graced the road, she went along at the pace of country life, merely rolling to a halt. But now her hair was awry and she started the car with her foot pumping on the pedal, shoved the gear stick into first and they careened down the hill on to the Whiterock.

'Right,' she said, taking the incline with determination. 'Right,' she said, changing gear at last when the car had almost reared up on its haunches with too many revs.

The barracks had wire fencing that went from three yards in front and swooped over the top of the building to prevent bombs from landing inside. There was a central desk in a small front room and an old policeman sitting behind it, a pen behind his ear, intent on his newspaper.

'I'm looking for my son. We've rung round the hospitals.'

'He's not here.'

'You haven't asked me anything about him so how do you know?'

A young constable, who had just emerged from a door behind the desk, came round. He had sandy hair and a kind face. He could have been anyone. 'What was your son wearing?'

'A red football shirt, I think, but I don't know for sure. Manchester United. Running shoes. He's fair. He's thirteen. His name is Liam Moran.'

'I told her,' said the policeman at the desk, putting the end of the biro cap inside his ear and turning it. 'We've not got him.'

The constable pointed them towards the row of plastic seats by the door. 'One minute,' he said. 'Sergeant, that was the quiet wee lad that was in here earlier.'

'I said to you, Constable, we haven't got him here.'

The constable came over to them. 'You'll have to go.'

Mrs O'Sullivan went red in the face. 'If yous think you can treat us like . . .'

'Outside,' he whispered.

Standing on the steps, he closed the station door gently behind him and, holding onto the door handle, said, 'They took him down to Castlereagh.'

The women ran to the car. Mrs O'Sullivan caused the car to flood and cut out. They sat in the dark, silent. Kathleen put her hand on Mrs O'Sullivan's.

'Wait a second and it'll be right again.'

'Aye.'

She tried again and the car started up and they were away towards the centre of Belfast, then swooping away from Divis flats and moving along the roads to Castlereagh.

'It's the name, Kathleen. "Castlereagh", it makes me sick to the stomach.'

They arrived at Castlereagh just after one. Yes, they had a Liam Moran. They told the women to sit and wait, they couldn't tell them anything else.

The pair of them sat, scanning the little printed leaflets and letters affixed to the wall by the door. There were three 'Tufty' road safety posters stuck to the front of the desk with a ferrety sort of a creature pointing out how not to get run down by a car.

Across the chequered flooring, towards the far side of the room, there was another family group.

'Is that not the McGahern's as used to live behind St Peter's?' whispered Mrs O'Sullivan. 'Her old mother used to have a lovely little Scottie dog with a wee red bow in his fringe. The boys are always dressed so badly, God love them. Look like tinkers.'

After a while a police officer came over, red haired and reasonable, and they stood up, the pair of them.

'Where's my son? What are you keeping him in for?'

'We've got a lawyer coming down here.'

'Calm down missus. We're going to let him go. He'll end up in the borstal, though, I'll tell you that.'

'Good on him.'

Kathleen hushed her. 'I want my boy back, Patricia.'

'Listen to your friend, missus.'

'Or you'll have me in here is it, an old woman, aye that'd be nothing for the likes of you, torturing old women.' Mrs O'Sullivan's voice rung out.

The man looked sour. 'Do you want me to tell you to get lost? Right, young Moran would have been out before now apart from the fact that he's refused to sign for his personal possessions. Keeps saying he refuses to recognize us. Wants to play the big man. Aye, well we've had enough of the little hoodlum, best you take him home and tell him to play nicely.'

The women sat again.

'I just want to get him home.' They held hands. 'Patricia, I'd never got you down for the Cumann. They're missing a trick not getting you a gun, so they are.'

Mrs O'Sullivan laughed self-consciously, assumed a penitent expression and looked over at the other group.

Liam came out the back room, big kid's eyes, a man's expression playing about his mouth. Kathleen took him in her arms.

'I love you Liam. Are you all right?'

'Aye, I'm fine. Mummy, I really thought they was going to kill the wee lad.'

She held him to her, kissed his smoky, greasy hair then relinquished him.

'Before I go, I was wondering if I could speak to your man in charge here.'

'I'm in charge as far as you're concerned,' said the red-haired policeman, looking up from his desk, placing more of his weight on his fore-arms.

'Well then. Don't think we don't know what yous get up to in here. You with the guns and sticks and buckets and hoods. Torturing people, ordinary decent people. You're a shower of bloody hypocrites! Talking about law and order and then pretending to drop people from heli-copters. How can you live with yourselves?'

Mrs O'Sullivan started to clap and the other family waiting there joined in as well and one of them said, 'You tell 'em, love,' and then three police officers came forward and took the two women and Liam to the doorway, with Mrs O'Sullivan upbraiding them all the way out and calling out, 'Cowards! Hypocrites! The lot of you! I hope you rot in hell.'

Together in the car outside, Kathleen turned to look at Liam in the back seat and gave him a smile.

'Right. Well, we'd best get going, Pat.'

Mrs O'Sullivan failed to start the engine four times.

'I think it's maybe out of petrol.'

The two women looked around, past Liam, through the semi-circle of the back windscreen to the light of the police station.

Liam closed his eyes. 'Right. Will I go back in and ask where we can get some petrol just the now?'

'Jesus. Best if I go,' said Kathleen.

32

'We've got a washing machine you know,' said Angie, throwing her bags on to the kitchen table. She had been over to her sister's for the morning and brought back her share of the food they'd ordered together from the Christmas catalogue. She took a quick look about.

The floor was clean and the cupboards looked like they'd been given a wipe. There was not a cup or a plate out although she'd left the dish rack full that morning. The boy had his sleeves rolled up, was pushing back his hair with his fingers. He was wearing a t-shirt and corduroy trousers, bare feet.

There was a short row of round wet parcels folded on the draining board. 'I didn't think you'd be home till later. I've just got to rinse these and I'm done.'

'You don't have to do your own washing,' she said, taking off her coat. 'Aren't 19-year-old boys supposed to be out chasing girls? Your mother got you well trained, so she did.'

He emptied the plastic bowl and ran cold water around it, sluiced it out. She saw his reflection in the dark of the window over the sink. He was a lot like his father, physically, but where his father was tense, he was languid.

'Did you clean this kitchen?' She stood with her hands on her hips. Her fringe was flat to her head from the rain.

He turned round with a grin.

She took out her cigarettes. 'You cleaned my kitchen and you're a man, you couldn't credit it. So you've been at this all the day, have you?'

'No I got a bus into the city centre, had a walk round then I went out down the Falls Road in one of those black taxis.'

'Oh Jesus,' she sat down. 'Now you really are having a laugh with me.'

He was squeezing out the white underpants and laying them flat on the draining board. She noticed his socks were on the radiator by the back door.

'Do you have anything needs washing?'

'I will do if you go telling me stories like that.'

'It was very interesting, Angie.'

'Mark,' she said, putting her cigarette into the ashtray. 'I should have had a word with you the day you got here. But we're sick to the teeth with it and we don't talk about it much, especially your father and I. But I've got to give you a wee welcome speech, so I have.'

He wiped his wet hands on his trousers.

'Where do I start? Look, when I was a wee girl we played with Catholics. My parents taught me everyone was the same, Catholic or Protestant, but that didn't stop them sending us out to kick the Pope on the 12th of July. We went to different schools. You never really knew them, like you knew your own.'

'Different schools?' He looked doubtful, slipped a cigarette out of his pack on the table, nodded at her lighter. 'May I?'

She nodded and closed her eyes. He saw in the wrinkles of her eyelids the remnants of pearlized eye shadow, the mascara made five or six points out of her lashes.

'The soldiers, well it was the Catholics that brought them over; it was them that wanted them. Of course they turned against each other and changed their minds then. Then there's been a lot of things happen in these past ten years so's most normal people's lost their patience. See the thing with the IRA is that they would kill a hundred of their own to get one Protestant, they've no conscience, be it a teacher, a postman, a police-man. And the people round here said, well every time you kill a Protestant or plant a bomb we're going to come out and shoot you and it doesn't matter if it's someone walking down the street or some fella going to his work we'll get him.'

Mark had never heard an accent like hers. Her mouth moved, scarcely open, across the fabric of her world like a sewing machine, jolting and juddering at speed, with the needle going in and out, up and down, no time to spare and then suddenly she had it all sewn up. 'But that's stupid, Angie. I mean, you must think so, right?'

'Aye. Welcome to hell.'

'But people are people, I mean has no one ever sat the two sides down together to thrash it out?'

She burst out laughing. 'I wonder sometimes if I was ever young! I'm sorry, I don't want to sound patronizing like but you haven't got a clue. There's a lot of fear amongst the Loyalist people that the Catholics will overrun the place. They have six or seven kids, whereas we have the one or two. They don't want to be British but they're not above taking the welfare. They're good at giving to their own, I'll grant them that, better than we are, everyone round here is for himself. But we don't want to live their way, and why should we? People don't want nuns and priests running their lives, teaching their children. Just because a person wants a united Ireland doesn't make him more Irish than me. You see the difference is we're happy with our lot. We've got our own ways here in Ulster. What we have here, and it's not very much, we've worked for, so we have. Why should we give it away? Let them go down south if that's what they're after.'

'And what about you,' he leant forwards, 'couldn't you go to England?'

'And why should I? This is my home. England's different. I couldn't live there. Look, I'm just trying to tell you how it is and why it's dangerous to go walking about on the Falls Road, you with your British accent and all, they'll be after thinking you're a soldier and you'll be dead and it's not a nice way to die. They'll talk about the Shankill Butchers but when you hear what the IRA does, even to its own, it makes your blood curdle. In the news last week there's a man killed because he's the wrong sort of IRA. They kill each other all the time. In West Belfast, where you were today they bomb their own bars! There was this fella last year, they gave him drugs while they tortured him, to stop him from passing out, to keep him conscious. They took out his fingernails, they pulled his arm out of the socket, they cut off his genitals – for three days they kept the poor man alive and did that to him. And all you hear is the Shankill Butchers.'

What was it in her eyes? For a second, she looked proud. Excited. She had to hide her face, so she took out another cigarette and lit it, her face to the side. He had seen though. He had seen and she had to stop her mouth from smiling at the corners.

'Why do you think we all smoke like chimneys? You see, Mark, they'll take you for a soldier under cover. They're always dragging off British soldiers. One they took not long ago, they went to shoot him in the head and he's pleading with them no and the gun misfires three times and the IRA fella says he's only shooting blanks and you know the poor man must have shit himself because when you think you're being shot dead that's what happens and then he must have been relieved that he was alive and then they went and fired again into his head and killed him. He was just a soldier lad who went drinking in one of their bars and he was clever, they say he had picked up a Belfast accent but they still picked him for a soldier because it's a small place, Mark, everyone knows who you are. You keep your mouth shut and you stay among your own.'

'I've never had my own. My grandfather believed in God but I don't even remember whether he was Catholic or Protestant.'

'Well now, he sounds like a wonderful man, love. Thank God he never had to come here, he'd have left his way of thinking before dinnertime.'

'But you were all born here, you all breathe the same air. You need to sit down and talk about it. A big party, free beer.'

'Och Jesus. That'll never happen. Our lot'd get drunk and the Catholics would be moaning how they'd got less beer than the rest. Anyway I'll get the tea on. Your dad will try and get home early tonight but who knows when it will be. He's got the day off on Tuesday and we'll have a nice wee run out. The poor man. He's got a desperate awful job, Mark, so he has.'

But Mark looked puzzled and annoyed, as if he was being hoodwinked. 'Angie, the people on the Falls Road were all right. I mean I've got an English accent. I went into a petrol station and bought a chocolate bar and they were nice enough.'

'Well you were lucky. Don't do it again or I'll, well I don't know what I'll do,' she said with mock severity, standing behind him and squeezing his shoulders. 'Your dad will do his crunch. He won't have you come to Northern Ireland to get shot at, you daft sod. Sausage, beans and chips. Will that do you? So now, stick your undercrackers in the airing cupboard, will you love, at the top of the stairs.'

He looked troubled, still trying to work it out.

'I've seen men's underpants before, Mark,' she said, 'but I've not seen many men who wash their own.'

33

Father Pearse looked for Kathleen after the novena but she was already gone. He'd seen her up the front. He'd seen the look on her face while she was praying; he'd seen it a thousand times before. It was the women that suffered worst, he always said.

'Such good people. On the bus every week, off to the Kesh,' he told Father Fitzgerald as they took a cup of tea together after the service. 'Dragging one wee child or another. All dolled up. Half-an-hour's worth of hope.'

'I know where you're going Brian, I know what comes next.' The elderly man slipped the purple advent chasuble over his head, leaving just the white surplice. 'It's becoming your daily rant.'

'You've a lot of faith, Michael, you're lucky,' said Father Pearse, dipping a pink wafer sandwich into his cup. The older man went out and came back with a letter.

'See this. This is what we're proposing to send up to the Northern Ireland Office. Read it, if you please.'

Father Pearse skipped the niceties and read out loud from where he deemed it important. *'Anyone who has his ear to the ground and who knows how tensions are building up will be aware that the danger of a hunger strike is real. And that there will be consequences outside of the prison.* Well,' he said, looking up. 'They won't appreciate that.'

'Go on.'

'*. . . must take into account the mental and physical strain under which the prisoners have been living. After up to three years for some, the situation has* *deteriorated into a deadlock.* Aye so it has, that's right. *A priest who is close to the situation and can see which way the wind is blowing . . . prison uniform is the crunch issue as it symbolizes "the status of the criminal".* Now, now what does it go on with, aye. *'With greater freedom of dress, a door to a solution would be open . . . after all female prisoners are not obliged to wear uniforms.'* He lay it down. 'Prisoners of war one day, criminals the next. Criminals that need an army of soldiers to catch them; seven thousand is it now? Well, it's a very nice letter, it is,' he said. 'But it doesn't recognize the nature of the beast.'

'It makes the case for talks,' said Father Fitzgerald.

'But no one's looking for talks, for a middle ground, they're all looking for a clear win.'

'Well, no,' said the older priest, rolling a cigarette. 'There's us and those women of whom you spoke looking to save lives, not lose lives. That's something. The women can be awfully powerful, so they can.'

'What about the church? They can be awful passive, so they can,' said Father Pearse. 'Awful preachifying, awful safe.'

Father Fitzgerald sighed. 'It's no sin to err on the side of caution. My guiding principle, Brian,' he said, licking down the side of the roll-up and sitting back into the steel-framed chair one vertebrae at a time, 'will be to safeguard life, one life at a time, by doing nothing. Precipitously. I shall do all I can against the hunger strike.'

'And the women, they'll be with you, you think?'

'They're mothers, Brian, they'll put their boys first.'

'Aren't we told to love God with all our hearts, mind and souls? These women, there's many of them are very religious in themselves. They've trained temptation out of themselves over the years; they've had a lifetime of suffering, of hardship, of loss. Like Abraham with Isaac, they'll make that sacrifice, Father. They love their God and where they think He is, that's where they'll be.'

'Nonsense, Brian! They've yet to find him. The point is the looking. And no living unsainted woman is strong enough to let her son die. They haven't got it in them. Abraham was a man. It's not a criticism, God help me, it's a fact. God appoints us for different things, men and women. He knows what He's about. And will you stop confusing God with a United Ireland,' said Father Fitzgerald crossly, laying down his roll-up. 'Brian, I'm trying to be patient with you, but you're going down the wrong road, blind.'

'I serve the people on His behalf. The church ought to stop condemning the IRA and start understanding why it's come about, why people feel the way they do.'

'That's cart before horse. The people are sinners not saints, no matter what they're suffering. They've yet to walk in the way of the Lord. And the church is there to try to impart His words to help them.'

'Well it's not working.'

'You know Brian, there are two things I'll say to you – first, that you're in the wrong job and second that I'm too old for this.' Father Fitzgerald took some time to raise himself from the chair. He put his weight on his arthritic hands as he did so, levering against the table. His hands were like marooned sun-baked crabs, shells about to crack. 'You bring to mind that fellow, Camillo Torres. He was a priest. Not a very good one. Didn't he say he had to take off his cassock to serve God better. With a shotgun. Some young hoodlum reminded me about him the other day, the cheeky wee git, using the confession to give *me* a sermon. Watch your step, Brian. You've had too much knowledge of the tree of good and evil. You'll have to ask God for guidance.' He stood looking towards the Celtic cross on top of a far shelf. His eyes and mouth were open and dark, the rims around them pale and dry. 'Don't leave Him out of this, Brian. And when you advise those you say you serve, try and remember it's them that stand to lose their children. He didn't ask that mortals should do the same as Him. He sent the Son so they needn't.'

Father Fitzgerald closed his mouth, opened it for a breath of air and, closing it again, felt a terrible ache in lower skull. He tried to let his jaw hang slack. Lately he'd been sleeping with his teeth too tightly clenched.

34

She liked to stand behind him when he shaved and to put her arms around his softening middle. He shaved without a shirt on, the towel around his waist and he moved his face from side to side, pointing his chin, his cheek stretched out like a canvas.

'Are you all right, John?'

'Umm-hmm.'

She saw the pink points where his razor had been on the skin of his neck and the tendons that hoisted them. 'You wouldn't tell me if you weren't. Would you? That's your typical man.'

He dipped his razor in the water and shook it. 'I'm all right.'

'You're not.' She felt the soft fuzz of his belly hair. She shook his belly. He began on the other cheek.

'He's a nice boy.' She put her face alongside his in the frame of the mirror, withdrew her touch.

He reached for her hands with his wet ones and put them back around him.

'He cleaned the kitchen yesterday. We had quite the chat, you know, when I got in. I told him a bit about things here. I had to have a talk with him. He went off into West Belfast on his own. I suppose he's got an enquiring mind like his father.'

He snorted derisively and she went to go and get dressed. He followed her into the room, watching her as she fastened her bra. He put his hands on her waist, kissed her shoulders. They had made love that morning and now they were at peace with each other.

They had the Datsun again. They drove out north on the A2 travelling along the coastline. So quickly Belfast was behind them.

'I've always had a fancy to live on the seashore, so I have.' Angie pointed out the new housing estate at Rathcoole. 'That's a Protestant one, nice homes, you see. But the Catholics have some nice ones too. Like Twinbrooke. Everyone needs houses.'

'Seems like people think a lot about their houses out here,' Mark remarked, between their seats. They passed by several of the new faux-mansions of the well to do, new bricks, ornate details, even pillars and columns.

'You will too when you have a family, I didn't at your age,' said his father, his hands relaxing on the wheel. 'It drives nicely,' he added, nodding at Angie with respect. 'People here aren't any different from anywhere. Yeah there's the Troubles here and that makes life a bit different, a bit difficult, but people are the same the world over.'

'Oh aye.'

'Angie's told you a bit about things here then?'

'I've read about it in the papers, but you don't get to hear much in England.'

'No. I don't suppose young people are very interested in it all.'

'No one ever talks about it.'

When they came to Carrickfergus, Angie pointed out the castle on the water's edge and Mark craned his neck.

'We'll push on and have a bite in Cushendall,' said John. 'You'll see, this is a beautiful country.'

'In a way it makes it worse,' said Angie, a hand on his knee.

'No it doesn't Angela! There's hope out here in the land. Look at me now, out here I feel like a different man,' he said, lifting himself with a small jump, jolting her hand off him. 'And don't say you do too, Angie . . .' he nodded at her. 'I've a tank full of petrol, a posh car, a lovely lady at my side and some fellow in the back. Who is he anyway Angie? There's miles ahead of us, miles behind, green everywhere. What more can a man ask for?' He looked in the driving mirror and smiled, felt his ears lift.

'It's a great day,' said Mark.

'We don't often get sunshine in December,' said Angie. 'It usually pees down, so it does, freezing cold and it goes right through you. It gets in your shoes, down your neck, urgh, terrible.'

'Angie, I would never have had you down as a whiner.' Mark gave her a little poke.

'She bloody is as well! You're right there, mate.'

'Aye well, I suppose it does look better in the sunshine, it's just you have to wait six months for a spell.'

Driving along the narrow road with the steep green hills to their left and the rough grey sea to their right, Mark spied the tiny old dwellings that stood alone, white walls and meek roofs, set in long grass and tumultuous earth. 'It's beautiful,' he said, his eyes caught. 'Now that's somewhere I could live.'

'I didn't have *you* down as a loner, Mark,' said John.

'Well, I'd need a decent pub close by.'

At the little town of Cushendall they went from one place to the next, and it was the third one that John said would do. It had a log fire and a small square bar and they took the window seat and John bought them each a pint of Guinness. Angie handed John a packet of Panatela's and he lit one and the three of them sat underneath the arbour of its smoke and woody smell.

'*Don't leave your rubbish in Cushendall, take it with you and leave it in Cushendun.*' John pointed out the framed sign on the brick wall.

'See that? That's one thing about this country, despite all of it, they've got a sense of humour.'

He asked Mark to tell him about his grandfather and what they'd liked to do together. Ronnie Wilson was headmaster of the local school. He'd been a self-taught architect on a modest scale.

'I still can't believe he's dead. I keep expecting to hear him going on at me – have I been touching his drafting pencils? He died of a brain tumour. He changed his diet, exercised, tried to beat it but he lost a lot of weight and died within six months. One thing he taught me, well actually he taught me lots of things, but they say you get the measure of a man by how he dies and the thing with Grandad was he never felt sorry for himself. He was in good spirits right up to the end.'

'Liked a drink did he?'

'He wasn't much of a drinker, no.'

'Never trust a man who doesn't take a drop,' John said, getting up and going to the bar.

'I think he's a wee bit jealous,' said Angie.

They had a toasted ham and cheese sandwich each, two slices of cucumber and a quarter tomato on the side. 'But it's the Guinness that makes a meal of it,' John said.

When Mark went to the toilet, Angie said to him, 'Relax, love, enjoy the day.'

He took a quick glance at his watch.

'Stop staring at him all the time, as well.'

'I'm not. Am I?'

'Aye you are. People will be thinking you're poofs.'

'Don't talk silly.' He shifted in his seat, glanced towards the toilet door and said in a low voice, 'I keep trying to see myself in him and I can't. He's got more of her, more of her side. Bloody funny looking lot. A bit girlish isn't he? What do you think? He's got a lazy eye. Have you noticed?'

'So have you. Makes you look like a pervert.'

'Christ.'

'It does something to me.'

'I worry about you sometimes Angela.' The toilet door was opening. 'Listen. He is my son, isn't he?'

'He's your son all right, John.'

'You're sure?'

'Aye I'm sure of it, love.'

The road came to an end just beyond Cushendun and John was perplexed. He jumped out of the car and went into a pub to ask for directions. A man came outside with a cigarette hanging from his lip, pointing and shouting against the rising wind. Rain came down suddenly as though the sheet holding it had given way. John lowered his head and ran back to the car, he leapt in, the car shaking at the axis.

'Blowed if I could make out what he meant,' he said, putting the car into reverse, his hand behind Angie's headrest, looking grimly out through the back window.

At Ballycastle they took a turn to Armoy. John put his foot to the floor. At Armoy, having run into a petrol station to ask directions, he said it had been the wrong thing to do and they headed towards Ballymoney.

'The Causeway is a major tourist spot, you'd think they'd give it a signpost.'

'It's great to get to see the countryside,' said his son.

The car bounded up and along the roads that passed now through farming countryside, great deep valleys and then flattened mountain tops, a religious slogan on a barn-side, a raggle-taggle Union Jack on a telephone cable, a woman out walking, arms stiff like pegs.

'I love the way it rises and falls, totally unpredictable. In England it's more even.'

'More reasonable,' said Angie.

'Will you stop all that rubbish.' John gave Angie a look.

'I'm just saying that . . .'

'I know what you're saying. You've said enough. It's all a drama with you all the time. It's always a bloody tragedy.'

'And that's not true about this place? No place for a young person.'

'Oh, just give it a rest, will you. Jesus.'

John put his foot down after a junction and then applied the break abruptly as a herd of sheep appeared in front of them. A long-coated man with a stick nodded at them without raising his head, the rain weighed down on his cap. Two Border collies were doing their work with joy despite the rain.

'Now that's your real Northern Ireland,' said John.

The road came to a crossroads and they were there, at the car-park for the Giant's Causeway. The rain had almost ceased and John was pleased. With his arm firmly around Angie, he strode out down the pathway, the wind snapping at them. Mark fell a little behind, looking over at the sun sinking forlornly between the breasts of two hills. As they went down into the small cove, it became quite dark. John pointed out the Causeway itself and gave Angie a kiss. The kiss went on and Mark saw Angie's fingers at his father's shoulders, saw his father's back round over her.

Then John put an arm around his son's shoulders and said to him, 'Here you go then, fella, here's the Giant's Causeway and there's stories and legends which another man could tell you but not me.'

They stepped forward, John had his right hand buried deep in the pocket of Angela's raincoat. They climbed up some of the short stacks of stone that looked like children's blocks. They mounted them so that they had a view of the whole and John held both of their hands as the wind lashed them. There they were on the slippery rocks, swaying but standing and if one of them faltered John countered. The sea was grey and navy and white and ragged.

'Well?'

Angie's cheeks were red and her hair wet and she was happy and nervous. She leaned into John to hear the boy's answer.

'Well – it's a long walk for a short drink.'

'Did I hear right? You ungrateful little bastard, you wait till I get a hold of you.'

'You'd never catch me, pal.' Mark set off, lankily running up the hill, looking back.

When Angie got there, John's hand was on Mark's shoulder and he was bent at the waist, panting. 'The air's cold. In your lungs. Angie. It's your shout.'

They had a bowl of soup in the hotel at the top of the hill. It was a prim place: a bar like a four-poster bed, dark wood and stately, waitresses with white aprons and an elderly clientele. The three of them were reckless. John ordered up a Guinness each and they sat at the bar, laughing. The barmaid told them they needed to register at reception in order to eat and they would have to wait until someone came to take their order.

'So I can't just say to you, three bowls of soup please, then?'

'No, I'm sorry Sir,' the skinny girl said, looking awkward. 'There's a procedure.'

'Bloody hell, a procedure! You lucky sods. Why haven't we got procedures Angie? I want procedures when I eat from now on.'

The girl looked sympathetic. 'It is a wee bit ridiculous.'

A lady came over and looked at them from over her half-moon glasses.

'Trouble, Ruth?'

'No, Ma'am.'

'No Ma'am,' said John. 'May I kiss your hand?'

'No you may not,' she said, pulling her cardigan closed.

'I'm so sorry but it's his first time with procedures,' said Mark.

'He's from an English university. So he's used to it.'

'He's got a lovely speaking voice,' said the woman, mollified, going off.

'You're in there, son.'

35

Sammy opened the door, took off his glasses, looked sorrowful. Kathleen explained that she needed to try and give the kids a bit of normal life, then Sheila came to the door with a towel round her head, her mostly bald brows slightly red from where she'd been plucking them. Sammy retreated, regretful, saying a low goodbye.

'I'm not coming on the march, Sheila. I'm taking the kids to the football.'

'And what about your Sean?'

'He's not here so I'm taking the kids I've still got.'

After a few minutes' walk, their mother silent, fuming, Aine said, 'That Sheila McCann can be a right bitch.'

They were taking a holiday from the Troubles; they were going to get themselves ready for Christmas instead. The rest of Ballymurphy was long decked-out. Over at Eilish's you couldn't move. The Purcell boys were artistic; they'd got garlands coming out of their arses as Roisin said. Roisin herself had gone and bought a lovely white artificial tree. Kathleen told Sean he'd have to go out and get them a real one.

'The needles everywhere, stuck in the carpet. More to clean up.'

'I know. I know,' he murmured, looking sour.

'So where's the dustpan and brush then if you know so much about it?'

'Under the stairs? Is it? Is it? Well if you've gone and changed where it is . . .'

The three of them stopped to buy a couple of bags of crisps and a bottle of Coke to share on the way back from the football, and Liam had her laughing going on how sharing a drink with Aine was like having Irish stew.

Owen McCann came round just after six the evening after the march. His mother had been at the front, next to naked, wrapped in a blanket, along with other men and women all barefoot. Sammy McCann was a steward and walked along the side in his raincoat with a loud-hailer.

The two boys made tea and snacks and brought them out tentatively, mugs stowed in elbows and plates on their forearms and in their hands. Both of them were new devotees of the self-prepared snack. They took great slugs from orange squash and bites of cream crackers spread with peanut butter.

Aine lay in front of the TV, moving occasionally to turn up the volume. She'd had her tea. She was watching a quiz show, *Ask the Family*. If there was noise outside she'd get closer and closer to the television, adjusting the volume each time she moved.

'You'll not get inside of it that way Aine,' said her father, pulling her back by the shoulders.

'So the peelers started up with their batons,' said Owen. I always see one I know. I saw them two who were round our house last week, telling the soldiers where to look and what to do; the one's sniffing in the kitchen cupboards saying, I can smell marzipan, and the other's saying, There's flour on the floor here, and so Mummy goes and gets out the Christmas cake to show them. I saw them today. I said hello to them but they acted as if they didn't know me.'

'They thought you'd got some gelignite in there that's what it was,' said Sean, looking sage.

'The Brits opened up with rubber bullets and me and my mum, we jumped over a garden wall and we're laying in dog shite, but at least we're safe, then up behind us comes that soldier as checked our bags the other day, Liam, you know the one, "no need to be that way lads", except now he says, "Get the fuck out of here" and aims his gun at us.'

'Where was your uncle?'

'He was still out there. He was trying to get people out of the way, down the alleyways.'

'Were any of the big men there?' asked Kathleen.

'Och, aye they were all there, my uncle and Francis McNamara and—'

'I mean the H block committee people.'

'That fella Coogan was up the front. I think he got a whack or two.'

'Not serious though?'

'No.' Owen looked at Kathleen for a moment.

'Well I suppose they know what they're about by now. Good luck to them too if they manage to make things better for my Sean.'

'We're having a holiday from the war because it's Christmas.' Aine gave Owen a look full of spite.

When Owen went off home, her children stretched out to watch the TV. They had a love-hate relationship with *Blake's 7*, *Star Trek* and *Doctor Who*. A few years back they'd been scared of *Doctor Who* but now they liked to pick holes in the 'space' programmes, laughing at the characters for being 'soft'. Liam was saying over and over again, like the drunk at the bar, 'That could never happen!' and Aine was agreeing in stern deference to him.

Their daddy sat down with them on the carpet. He gave the kids the rest of the midget gems they'd bought that morning. Kathleen was grilling pork chops for their tea.

'I hope you're not giving them those sweets!'

'No!' He jostled the kids with his elbows, put a finger to his lips.

'Jesus Christ,' said Sean when Kathleen brought in the steaming plates. There was a ring of tinned pineapple on each pork chop and baked beans and potatoes. They each took a newspaper or a magazine from the pile by the armchair and ate on their laps. 'This looks magnificent love.'

Kathleen put a forkful of the meat straight in her mouth. It was hard and tough and she opened her mouth to allow air in to cool it down. She was rattled to find Sean looking at her with suffering affection. He got up to sit next to her on the settee.

'I was hoping to worm my way into your good books with flattery.'

'What? About the dinner? You'll have to try harder than that, Sean. I'm not a tuppenny chocolate bar girl any more you know.'

'Well then, you look very nice at the minute if I might say so.'

He hadn't even asked her where she was the other night.

'Eat your dinner,' she said.

'Thought it might be the love light shining . . .'

'It'll get cold.'

'Aye and I'll get old. Kids, your mother and I are going to bed early tonight.'

'Are we shite.'

'I used to make you sing out.'

'Will you give my head peace,' she said, piling beans on the back of her fork.

'I love it you when you use your harsh and proud voice on me.'

'What's wrong with you Sean Moran?'

There was a shout, the noise of running footsteps and then a gunshot.

'What was that?' They put their plates aside.

Liam ran to the front door.

'Don't open the door Liam!' Sean jumped up.

'I don't want to know, I just don't want any of it today. None of it. I don't care what it is.' Kathleen stood.

Aine put her hands over her ears and inched closer to the TV, turning the volume button up to full.

Sean opened the front door, stood in socks on the doorstep. On the road in front of their house a boy was lying face forward, a paper bag in front of him and the rain was pounding his back.

'What the fuck?' he called but the rain cancelled out his words and a soldier waved his gun at him that he should go back inside.

Two soldiers approached the child, hands on guns, walking sideways with glances left and right. One bent down and lifted a wrist. He let it drop. The hand fell on to the wet road.

They retreated, one using his walkie-talkie.

Sean closed the front door.

'A young lad's been shot dead.'

The closing titles for the TV programme came up and the music was loud and melodramatic.

Aine got up. 'Let's finish the Christmas decorations.'

'Not now love.'

'You always say not now. You said that yesterday and the day before. At this rate we're not going to have a Christmas tree. Everyone else in the whole world will have a Christmas tree and not us.'

'Aine, give us a minute to think will you. For God's sake, there's a lad been killed out there, I've got to call an ambulance.'

'I don't care. I'm still alive.'

'Go to bed!' said Sean. 'Just get up to your room!'

Aine burst into tears and went. Liam sprang up and went after his sister.

'She could have a little bloody feeling!' Sean went for his cigarettes on the mantelpiece.

Kathleen got the phone book out. She cracked the front door, dialled the number, then spoke, standing on the doorstep as far as the coiled cord would let her with the rain smelling like cold tar-soap and the smell of stale breath in the cup of the receiver. Her eyes were on the bare skin between the dead boy's trouser legs and his socks and shoes.

When they went upstairs both children had got themselves ready for bed. They were on Aine's bed, talking and looking at old comic books. Liam was pointing out bits and doing voices. Kathleen stood watching, then closed the door.

Later on, Aine crept downstairs and went to the window by the front door. The rain was still falling and the boy was still lying there.

Her father came up behind her and put one hand on her shoulder and turned out the light with the other.

'Why haven't they moved him Daddy? If he was a Proddy he would-n't be lying there still would he?'

'The soldiers chased him down the road. Maybe he'd stolen something. He didn't stop.'

Round the corner came the lights of the ambulance swinging and veering from blue to pale gold, glittering in the rain and in the puddles.

36

Another prison officer had been killed, claimed by the Belfast brigade of the IRA. He had been serving at the Maze. Police found him after some of his fellow officers called them when he failed to show for night shift. At lunchtime, one of the prison officers stood on a chair and gave a tribute.

'He was the sort of man you wanted standing next to you when there was trouble. Once, when we was on riot squad in the compounds, we were all fired up ready to run and your man was a wee bit ahead of himself, thought he heard the order and sets off roaring across the yard, on his own. He comes back, *"Where the fuck were yous?"*'

There was some low laughter. A silence was observed and afterwards conversation barely resumed. Dunn noticed a man shake another's hand and grasp his arm.

'It could be any of us next,' the barman observed, serving a double from the optic, briskly, roughly, like he was loading a gun. 'If they shoot the poor devils from the mail room of the Crum, they're going to shoot the dogs from the Maze.'

In the afternoon Dunn was on gate duty again and Baxter came through the yard on his own, taking laundry in on a wagon.

'How's it going there Bax?'

'Dead on.'

Baxter stood in with him between the gates and offered him a cigarette.

'On the block, same as normal?'

'Aye, it runs smooth when the PO's about. Mr Dunn, can I ask you a question?'

Dunn nodded, exhaling the smoke, moving his weight from foot to foot to stay warm.

'What did you do with that communication you picked up?'

Dunn stopped still.

'The communication, the little message that dropped on the floor when you were on visits. You picked it up.'

'On whose behalf are you asking?'

'I'm just asking.' He had a fine growth of hair on his chin, like an adolescent.

Dunn let his cigarette fall and used his foot to stub it out. 'I don't know what you're talking about.'

Baxter put his palms up. 'If you picked one up, you should get rid of it, you know, Mr Dunn. It won't do you good to keep it, nor to turn it in. Word to the wise.'

Dunn went to the next gate with his keys in his hand, to let Baxter out. 'I mind my own business, Baxter. I've never needed advice from anyone on that score.'

'Take care of yourself now,' Baxter said as Dunn brought the crisscross wire of the gate between them and locked it.

That night, driving home, John Dunn slowed down and pulled in a little to let a car go by that had been behind him since he left the prison.

A number of possibilities presented themselves regarding the note. O'Malley had told Baxter about it. That meant Baxter was working for the IRA on the inside. He doubted if the IRA would trust a Protestant orderly but nothing was impossible. Else, one of the prison officers had seen Dunn pick up the note and Baxter had overheard a discussion about it. But if he'd just overheard prison officers talking about it, then why would Baxter suggest he destroy the note? That didn't make sense. Only the IRA would want the note destroyed because only they knew what was in it.

In Northern Ireland, nothing was what it seemed. It was only those working inside the British 'intelligence' services that thought things were clean cut. He'd done a few months with them. What a waste of time. Snooping and prying, cross-checking phone numbers, addresses and small ads in the Catholic community newspapers. He'd cut out the photos of the Gaelic football teams, and sent them to the Northern Ireland Office for their files. He clipped messages of support from the families of those on the blanket protest.

It started off that all Republicans were terrorists. Then it became that all Catholics were Republican and then policy changed and they said, they're not terrorists, they're criminals.

If there was an ad in one of the papers, no matter what it was – 'bunk-beds wanted,' for instance – he was to check the phone number at the phone exchange, get an address and see who lived there. One time, when it was an old couple, his boss suggested that they had people coming to stay. 'Are they coming up from *Dublin*?' So they'd put a watch on the house. He'd gone round and got chatting to the old lady. He'd complimented her on the dahlias in her window box. 'Getting it nice for the weans. They got burnt out on the Short Strand.'

'Their grandchildren are coming to stay.' Dunn had said, coming back into the command centre at the end of the two week operation, and his boss had sent him off to check the records of a car hire company. 'See who's coming up from *Dublin*.'

It was Angie who had handed him the bookings to look through. She made him a cup of tea and perched on the edge of the desk while he made notes. He'd been looking at who hired what and when and where they went. Then he looked at her looking at him.

They went out together a few times but his radio was always going off and he would have to abandon her and head off for a very pointless evening sitting and waiting for nothing to happen. She seemed to think what he was doing was all very important and would amiably accept his comings and goings, saying, 'I won't ask you any questions because I know you won't answer them.'

He'd laughed out loud at that.

After several Saturday nights crouching in the dark of an empty flat in Divis tower, with night-sight binoculars, watching one of their suspects down below roll home drunk and piss in the kitchen sink, John Dunn was let off the hook.

But things were worse in the prison. One minute they were prisoners, criminals, the next minute it was a war. A man had to know what he was fighting; it had to be told to him clearly, even if it wasn't clear. Soldiers were to follow orders, the clearer the better. It was the officers who were to sort out the other stuff, the moral complexities.

He was right to hand in the note.

He got back on to the motorway and drove, in the slow lane, lights dipped, foot resting on the accelerator, on auto pilot. He shook a cigarette out of the pack, pressed down the cigarette lighter and waited – the wire rings were glowing orange when he pressed it to the end of the cigarette.

He'd got Shandy to cover for him and dodged out of work about six. He was going to take his son to the local for a pint. He wanted to make sure the boy was staying for Christmas.

John Dunn was on good form when they stepped out for the chips for dinner, pub very much in mind. Mark had said he would be there until the day after Boxing Day.

They had a cigarette each, enjoyed the beer, John asking Mark if it tasted better when someone else pulled it.

'Yup,' said Mark. But it was a job, the only bad thing was getting the occasional drunk to behave and stopping fights breaking out. He asked John what it was like working in a prison.

'Same sort of thing by the sound of it.' He drained his pint, put it down and nodded at the door. 'Best not to talk about it in public though,' he said, getting up. He opened the pub door for his son and nodded at the barman.

They walked down to the fish and chip shop, John zipping up his jacket. His son was wearing a denim jacket. 'Haven't you got anything warmer?'

'What were you worried about in there?' asked Mark, half of each hand in his jean pockets. 'It's your local, right?'

'Yeah, that's right. Wouldn't trust anyone in there though.' He opened the door of the chip shop. 'Evening, Ted.' The old man in there looked up and moaned.

'I haven't got the fat hot enough, can't seem to get the bastard thing to go right since I went over to this new machine.' He pushed his white hat back on his head. 'You'll have to wait for the next batch.'

'Not to worry,' said John. 'We'll have a warm shandy and a stale pickled egg while we wait.' He handed Mark a can of Top Deck from the display on the counter. Then he unscrewed the large jar there and using a small wooden fork, passed an egg to his son and took one for himself. Both men chewed while Ted stood back watching a small piece of raw potato go limp in the oil.

'This is my son.'

The man looked at him. 'I didn't know you had a son.'

'From before I met Angie.'

'Well. He's an ugly brute, like you.'

'Ugly? You must be joking. He's a looker, this kid is.'

The oil sizzled. 'Right let's go. Cod and chips three times?'

'And a battered saveloy.'

They fell quiet drinking their shandies, Ted looking out the side window into the night. He went across to it and pulled the blind down, then he was back at the fryer, shaking the wire basket.

'Right you are, gents.'

He smoothed out the newspaper. 'It gets you down. Wrapping up good food in bad news.'

He lay down a square of white paper on top and placed a battered fish and a square ladleful of chips alongside it. He wrapped them carefully, folding this way and that.

'You've to watch yourself in your line,' he said to John.

'So so. We keep a pretty tight lid on things in there.'

'I wasn't talking about inside.' He put one parcel on the counter and went to do the next. 'People round here are talking about Billy McGovern. They say he took a beating from the prison officers. People say it's wrong, screws against their own.'

'What do you say?'

'I could get myself into a wee bit of bother selling you these chips,' he said, not looking up, but ladling more chips, his brow furrowed. He put down the spoon and turned away with his forearm over his face, coughing deeply.

'You all right?'

The man was perspiring. 'Aye,' he said, and still he didn't look John Dunn in the eye, but went to his folding. 'Sure, we're all just trying to get by, make a living . . .'

He put three packets in a carrier bag, pushed it across the steel counter to John and asked him for two-pounds seventy.

'I'm not ashamed of what I do,' said John, offering three pound-notes.

Ted opened the till and pursed his lips; he looked back at the figures that were flagged on the top of the till and went back into the trays, digging about with his fingers.

'Thirty's your change. Good night.'

They walked home in silence, the night was thick and the way home seemed long. With one hand, John carried the plastic bag and the other he put out towards Mark as they went to cross the wide roadway. A low black car sped past.

'I'm not proud of what I do either. What do you think?'

'I don't know. I don't know if people should be proud of what they do. Or of anything.'

'Is that what your granddad would have said? Sounds like a Leftie.'

The boy demurred.

'People should be proud of what they do, I reckon, if they can. You thought a lot of your grandfather, then.'

'He never said I had to be like him. But he was always there for me. When I messed things up.'

Alongside them and across from them there was uniform dilapidation: fences broken down, litter, the telephone line sagging and bouncing gently underneath the streetlights.

'Mum chucked me out and I went to stay with him.'

'Oh yeah? Why'd she chuck you out?'

'Glue sniffing.'

'You what?'

'I was sixteen. I was just looking for something to do. I was bored. I was nicking stuff too. Mum sent me to Ronnie's. When I was unpacking my bag he came in and saw a whole load of stuff in it, cassette tapes, all new and he asked me about it and I lied, then I told him the truth and he went out and bought a whole load of envelopes and we called up the music stores to get their addresses right and then we packaged up the cassettes and put a note inside to apologize. And that was that, you see. Then he said, right that's done with, you're not a thief. Then we had our tea. Egg and chips and brown sauce, as I recall.'

'You don't do glue sniffing now, do you?'

'Christ no, you've got to be bloody desperate to do that.'

'It was good he was there to set you straight.'

'What about you? Your father left you, you said.'

He thought about his own father; sandy-haired, soft spoken, warm hands, a whistler. Or was that someone he'd seen in a film, at the pictures?

'Like I told you, I was only just six when my old man came back from the war. We were staying with my mum's parents then. My dad heard the army was moving out and we went right away, the three of us, down to Mote Park – that's in Maidstone where I came from – and we took a hut, painted and cleaned and moved right in that night. He clapped his hands, my dad, and said this'll do and when the military police came crashing in in the middle of the night my dad told them to fuck off. All of that week when other families came to try to take it, he told them the same thing. It was exciting to have a dad all of a sudden. And one who'd been a soldier and had medals and broke the rules. We cooked outside and he took me wherever he went. I was just a nipper. On his shoulders, across the park and into the town. 'This is my boy John. He's going to be a general.' He got a job at the Post Office, got a great big bike and on Friday nights he put me on the handlebars and took me to fetch the fish and chips for all of us. Christ, I can remember it like yesterday.' He brandished the carrier bag. 'I bloody licked the print off the newspaper afterwards. The smell of vinegar still makes me think of him.'

'He sounds great.'

'Anyone would have been great. I used to wait for him up at the top of the park, by a stile, with this dog I got, a mutt called Rhett. I was there every evening at five to get that ride on the handlebars. Then one day he didn't come along.'

John motioned Mark to go ahead of him into their driveway.

'What happened?'

'Don't know. My grandfather, my mother's father, he was a hard old bastard, he said Dad had gone off with another woman. Later on he told me Dad had joined up again. Then one time he told me my dad had another family in Norfolk, with kids and a wife. I don't know what happened to him, Mark.'

They were outside the house, going up over the broken cement to the orange door with its crescent window and brass door knocker that no one ever had lain a hand on.

John turned and looked up at the sky. 'He showed me the Great Bear and how to find the North Star.'

When they got in, Angie had laid the table and made them proper shandies to drink. She gave them Jamaica sponge and custard for afters and they sat, sated, in the front room, legs out in front of them, Angie with the button on her trousers undone, exclaiming about the size of herself. They watched *The Two Ronnies*, the two men waltzing across the screen in a succession of costumes; as Tyrolean yodellers, bellringers and finally as female opera singers.

'Why does everyone want to dress up like women all the time?' John belched softly, enjoying the fizz and fat.

When the programme finished Mark asked if they wanted a cup of tea.

'Oh aye, I will have a wee cup, thanks, love,' Angie replied.

'You, Dad?'

'Yes thanks.'

John pulled Angie to him. When the door closed he put his nose into her ear. 'He called me Dad.'

'I heard,' she said, patting his full stomach.

'I like him, Angie; he's a nice kid. He's a good-looking lad, too.'

'You said he looked a wee bit like a girl the other day.'

'No! He was just telling me how he went off the rails, but he sorted himself out. You know, when you think about what she did, his mother, what she took away from both of us. I mean what a bloody thing to do. I'm going to make up for it with him. I'm going to take him on holiday next year. To Germany, where I was stationed. And the other thing is I've been thinking I ought to be giving him a hand, money-wise.'

'All right John but what about us, I want us to think about having a family—'

John tapped Angie's knee. Mark was coming back in with the teas.

'Och Jesus, it's got sugar in it,' said Angie, spilling some as she tasted it, then getting up and taking her tea out to the kitchen.

37

In the run up to Christmas no one was buying pork chops so Kathleen was bringing them home for their dinner again. He was going to make sure there was a turkey set aside for her for Christmas Day so she had one less thing to worry about. When she got in, she took a bath, put on a dress, tights and boots. She was going up to the Republican Press Centre for news about Sean.

The sky was low that day and you could scarcely see beyond West Belfast. Red-brick row-house street after red brick row-house street; she knew the names of them so well she could recite them with her eyes closed. After Whiterock came all the 'Rock' streets – Rockmount, Rockmore, Rockville and Rockdale – then came the playing fields and up the hill, round the hospital and the area around Grosvenor Road were all the English names – Violet Street, Crocus Street, Hawthorn Street – and then Odessa, Abyssinia, Kashmir, Bombay, Sevastopol. She'd never been beyond Liverpool for a weekend, but she thought of England as a mixture of prudish and pretty: peaky cheeks, iced gems, bunting, waist-coats, brass plates on the wall. Thousands of men and women struggling against the rebound of steam presses. *Coronation Street*. Not having much to say to each other. Skimmed milk.

Hundreds of years of bloodshed and still the same tune. Republicans, ready to rise, ready to die, to give their lives, hunger strikes, hangings, the names of their forefathers: Robert Emmett, Donovan Rossa, Tom Clarke, MacSwiney, Pearse.

We've all of us got that searching and seeking for something like God within us, she thought, like the father said, and she caught a glimpse of herself in a shop window, all done up to the nines. It's hard to know what's your own need and what's God. What was God had to be what was not your need. So you had to struggle against all the stuff that was in you.

She saw a group standing smoking around a car jacked-up, three tyres on it and the naked steel centre of the back right wheel turning in the air.

Brendan and Sean thought they'd found what they needed. Brendan had no God and Sean had got one in a green outfit. It was all a mess and only her husband free of it in a way. His tall tales had saved him! The survivor; he'd be jawing on when the others were dead and buried, honours or not.

A Saracen pulled over outside Dunlevey Street and she looked at the British soldiers inside, through the half windows, saw that they were talking animatedly, like women going fruit picking. One of them could be Frank; for all she knew he might be back in Belfast. Some of them came back two or three times.

And what did he believe in, that Frank? Nothing more than his mother and father most like. She crossed over Clonard Street. Thank God she was a Catholic and had miracles to believe in.

'Were you having yourself some naughty thoughts there, Katie?'

Her brother William was smoking a cigarette outside the shop on the corner.

'All the time, William, y'know how it is.' They had a quick chat about a twin tub that he'd got at home for her and was working on.

'It'll be with you after Christmas.'

'God bless you.'

Eileen's Jim came out the shop with a couple of baps and the two men waved as they got in Jim's black taxi and went off. When they were gone she went into the press centre.

She was upstairs, at the back of the room, waiting to speak to Coogan and she looked behind her and saw the dented cardboard box.

When it was her turn, she asked quickly if he had news of Sean. He told her he was going out to the Kesh on the Thursday and could take her down with him if she wanted.

'But I've not got a visit.'

'I've got a meeting there. I'll leave you off in a pub I know, and be back within an hour or so and we can have a drink together.'

'All right then.'

'I want to see you.'

When she left the press centre she bumped into Eilish Purcell in front of St Dominic's.

'You look smart, Kathleen. It's all that makeup. Mind you don't get people talking.'

'Fuck you.'

'What's that?'

'Thank you. Thank you for your words.'

Eilish crossed her hands over her bag and went off into the newsagent's. And then Kathleen did something she'd never done, she went into the pub, ordered herself a half'un, lit a cigarette and enjoyed them with all the old men in the place watching her.

That night she slept on her front with three fingertips of one hand between her legs. She dreamt that Sean was having an affair with Sheila McCann and that Sheila was going over to England for an abortion and that he and the kids were going with her. She was running after Sean who was always just slightly ahead of her so she couldn't catch him. Suddenly a revolving door came between them and wouldn't budge. She watched him go, crying.

She woke up from her dream full of sorrow as if she loved her husband.

38

When Dunn went to inspect the duty roster in the Tally Lodge on the Sunday evening the duty officer was pinning up more sheets – shifts that went into the new year and beyond.

'Is there any flexibility in these? Could I maybe swap the next Sunday I've got for Christmas Day?'

'No you could not,' said the officer, licking a pinprick on his thumb. 'Dunn is it?'

'Yes.'

'Count yourself lucky you've got another day off this month, Mr Dunn. I had some fool of a deputy governor come down and try to put the word on me for you to have this Wednesday night off. As it was I had you down for it, but I nearly changed my mind. Don't try using friends in high places again, all right?'

Dunn headed over to the block, feeling the back of his front lower teeth with his tongue. He'd left home with small bits of mince between them. He was on night guard, on a split shift, he'd torn home after lunchtime to have an early dinner with Mark and Angie.

She'd made a lasagne. She'd never made one before, and he'd never eaten one. It had been in the oven over an hour and he'd stood in the kitchen for the last half hour smelling it while he read the paper, with the saliva loose about his gums. What the fuck could it be? When it came out it was layer upon layer of meat and cheese and he couldn't believe how good it tasted. 'I think I got it right,' she'd said, modestly, ladling more on to his plate until he blew out his cheeks and put his hands on his belly. He gave his son a big grin. 'See with you here the grub's got better. You'll have to stay longer.'

The lasagne hit the spot. Dunn had a hangover from the night before. He'd stayed up drinking with Mark, they'd had a bottle of German wine that Angie's boss had given her at the office party on Saturday night. He and Mark had made themselves an 'Ulster Fry' for tea in her absence, then Dunn had gone to pick her up. He'd arrived to find her alone with three or four men.

'I see they didn't invite their wives,' he commented, hand against spring-loaded office door on their way out.

'Och, John, it was just a casual wee thing.'

'Your boss was dressed up like a pox doctor's clerk.'

'His suit was shiny.'

'So will his balls be if he touches you.'

'Och, I couldn't bring myself to sleep with him,' she said, sinking into a little burp in the passenger seat.

'That's a weight off my mind then. Christ you women. You go on about equal jobs and all that, and then you talk about your boss giving you one. I bet you would as well. Him with his big house, flash car, and the rest.'

'Don't be stupid, John.' She tried to sit up; the seat belt was working against her.

He said nothing, squinting at the traffic lights, waiting for green.

'Since Mark got here, you've been murder to live with.'

He kept quiet.

'You can surely be nice to more than one person at a time.'

'It's got nothing to do with Mark.'

They drove in silence. John took their driveway with the car dipping and rising, banging the undercarriage on the concrete. He yanked the handbrake. 'You're home.'

'I've got nothing against Mark, John.'

John knew she had tears on her face so he wouldn't look at her.

'I'm glad you've found each other. I wish your dad had done for you what you're doing for him.' Then she undid her seat belt and got out the car, slamming the door.

He watched her little legs as she went up the steps, each threatening to be the undoing of the other, then she leant against the door, knees sinking, key in hand. She left the door softly ajar.

Sunday night, with Angie in bed, he'd poured out two mugfuls of the sweet bad wine. Mark said, 'How do people drink that stuff?' and drunk it nevertheless.

'Need. The need to obliterate.' John made the words sound like new cement falling. Mark was in jeans and a t-shirt on the armchair opposite. He looked across at the bare mantelpiece. They didn't like ornaments. 'Could you see this as home?' said John.

'What, *Nor'n I'ron*?'

'Well yeah, here I suppose, with us.'

'I don't know.'

'Do you like beer?'

'I prefer it to this.'

'Well let's polish this off and have a beer.'

'All right.'

John went to get them a beer each and they sparked up their ring pulls, one after the other. 'It's not much here is it? I mean it's not nothing to write home about.'

'It's nice enough. I could give you a hand to paint the walls.'

'Don't have the time.'

'Well, when I come back?'

'Someone like you wants more than this. A university graduate and all that.'

'Oh yeah,' he laughed.

'Did you ever think about what your dad would be like?'

'I sort of knew about you, growing up. Mum wouldn't talk about it apart from the fact that you did exist. She said you'd come around looking for me, but then she was pissed off when I said I wanted to meet you. When I was a kid, I suppose I thought you were off doing something really special, James Bond or something.'

'Didn't your mother have other blokes round then?'

'Yeah. A bit.'

'She didn't get married?'

'Nope.'

'Why was that then?'

'There was a bloke when I was little. But I didn't like him. I was just four or five, and I said I'd run off if he came to live with us. I don't know why but I remember she cried. She must have broken off with him because of me.'

John took a sip from his can. 'It can't have been easy.'

'Because she always chose me, every time, without question, I didn't think I could ask her about you. I knew you were alive, and I thought that if we met it would work out, that we'd get on all right. It was just a case of when.'

Nothing was said for a few minutes. John had his head low, hiding himself, head bobbing. Mark took a long draft of his own beer. It tasted of blood and gas. John sniffed. His eyes were red. He pinched the bridge of his nose.

'To tell you the truth, Mark, I'm not in very good bloody shape right now. I don't know what's going on but after twenty-two years of being the man's man, I must be cracking up.'

His expression was at once offhand and hunted. Later, Mark would recall how John Dunn's face held contradictory emotions which were somehow museum-boxed, too long preserved. Until then, he'd really thought that life was an open adventure, offering fair chances, in which a person could be a real agent.

39

'It's called Whitehouse this one,' said Rory O'Connor, one elbow denting the stack of newspapers on the counter, touching his fingertip to his tongue and turning the pages of a magazine.

Kathleen was up at the paper shop on the Upper Springfield, taking a look through the dirty magazines, having a laugh with the fellow who ran the place.

She snatched it from him. 'Rory that's a midwives' instruction book!'

The door went. Kathleen gave the magazine to Rory and he rolled it up, put it under the counter.

It was Aine. 'There y'are. I knew you'd be here.'

'What about ye love.'

'Aine,' said Rory.

She stood in her pale purple anorak, hood up, so that you could just see her nose and the shape of her sulk, lips almost inside out.

Kathleen was disappointed to see her daughter there, where she was having a joke around, being the laugh. And when she recognized her dismay, it cut deeper. Often, her daughter had this brooding, head-down way with her; she was guilt on the move.

'Mummy, I've only got five pence and it's not enough for anything I want.'

'Not a hello, not a kiss, just *I want* . . .'

'Glad mine have left home,' Rory said. 'Couldn't make a living with them in and out of here. Them and all the other kids, in and out, the doorbell going, hands everywhere.'

'You should have a big sign up on the door saying "No kids",' said Aine.

The man looked taken aback. 'There's no need to get yourself worked up, Aine.'

'All of yous are always moaning on about the kids, well we didn't ask to live.'

Kathleen put a hand on her daughter's shoulder. 'You ought to go down to the press centre, they could use you there to write some pamphlets up.'

'We didn't ask for any of this mess, yous're the ones who made it. There you are standing about joking all the while kids are getting shot dead.'

Kathleen took her daughter by the arm, gripped it too tight. A sort of white heat seared through her brain. She could have killed, and yet she managed to say goodbye to Rory, holding, shaking, pushing Aine through the doorway on to the street. She took her round the corner of the newsagent's and shouted at her.

'What the hell have I done for you to be so bloody rude? God help me but I've a good mind to give you a smacked arse.'

Kathleen had been laughing, she'd been happy, it had been a good day, she'd got a lot done. Now it was ruined.

Aine's nose went long and narrow, her teeth bunched on the inside of her lips, her eyes were on the ground.

'I can't wait for the day you leave home, I can't take any more of you and your moods.' How far could she go? Could she destroy something inside of her daughter to leave her submissive? She took her cigarette packet out of her bag and fumbled for a lighter. 'We should think about you going to live elsewhere, with your auntie. For a while.'

Aine's shoulders rounded, and her hood came slowly further forward until Kathleen could not see her face at all. She was just a pale purple anorak, with legs and feet. White socks, grey from the foot up, in the summer's sandals.

Kathleen lit her cigarette, took a drag and sorrow went through her;

a gut-tearing feeling like the first day of her period, a falling away, an irrevocable loss. She put her hand beneath her daughter's chin to lift it to see her face.

'Well?'

'Why do you always smoke in front of me if you say I shouldn't do it? It will kill me you say, so why do you do it, when you know I'll do the same things as you?'

'What the hell are you going on about now?'

'You want me to go away. You and Auntie Eileen say that Granny was all for the boys. Well and so are you. I miss Mary, we used to talk. You don't even see me! I might as well be dead!'

Kathleen sat down on a small mound of dirt by the side of the pavement, feeling the damp land seep through the arse of her jeans. She took another drag and looked down the hill into the estate in which they lived, grey and white, and beyond the red-brick estates in rows that went all the way down to the slug of a river that didn't bother to make its way out to the ocean but lay stagnant in marshes, with the round industrial gas works and warehouses about it.

'Sit down on the anorak; it's me who'll wash it. Sit down.'

The hood dropped back.

'Look Aine, I'm not asking you to respect me, but these are hard times for all of us. We're all busy, we're all worried and you don't know the half of it. You've got to think about what others are going through.'

'And that's what you do?' Aine looked at her mother with her blonde lashed eyes, heavy-lidded, the face that reflected more of her father's side.

'You don't really know enough about me to judge. That's the job of Him up there, Him alone. Yes as a matter of fact, I do try to do that. Else I would have gone off a long time ago.'

'Not with Sean or Mary here. Not with them at home you wouldn't have.'

'I love Sean and Mary, but no more than either of you.'

'That's not true. Sometimes I think you're good and sometimes I think you're a bad person. Let's go home.'

Kathleen was stunned.

'Listen, Aine, maybe I'm not the best mother in the world. But I'm all you've got, so I am.'

Her daughter looked away, considering this. She didn't answer.

'Come on love. Let's be friends.'

'It doesn't matter,' said Aine, getting up and putting her hands back in her pockets, facing the city. She was starting to build the boundaries of her life, choosing the areas of silence.

As they went to cross the road to go into their own street, Kathleen put her own hand in Aine's pocket and felt the cold strength of the girl's fingers, so alien to her.

'I love you so much, Aine,' she said, suddenly in great need of her daughter.

They stopped outside of a house, to look in at the tall white Christmas tree in the window with its blinking fairy lights. The girl's teeth were chattering as she withdrew her hand, crossed her arms and fixed her eyes upon the Christmas scene.

'If there's one thing I could do for you, Aine, what would it be?'

'Love my Daddy,' said Aine, and her eyes and her mouth fell, and Kathleen saw the habit of sadness in her daughter that ought only to have been acquired, not accepted. She had no need to think of breaking something in her daughter. It was already done.

The Christmas scene stirred. The door to the house opened, there was music and an old pinkish-haired lady came out saying her goodbyes, and with the rain abating, it all fell into place. Kathleen saw clearly.

Whether it was Sean Moran or anybody she was married to, she'd be the same, she'd need to be loved by other men. It was her who was wrong. She ought to tell Sean, let him off the hook.

40

The Lingards lived on Malone Road. They both came to the door. Janet Lingard wore a long multi-coloured dress with a gold belt at the waist, and Carl wore pale slacks, an open-necked shirt and a cravat. Their house smelt of cheese.

John was tense. 'I shouldn't have worn jeans,' he said to Angie out of the corner of his mouth, his hand out to shake with Mrs Lingard.

'I told you.' Angie squeezed his bum.

Janet Lingard put a hand on John's right shoulder and kissed him on either cheek. He was baffled and knew that Angie would be too. Turning he saw Angie stiff as a board, while Janet repeated the act.

He hadn't wanted to come. Lingard had caught him in the block the day before and reminded him. Keen not to be seen with him, he'd hastily agreed they'd be there.

He'd asked Angie to find their number in the phone book to call and make an excuse. She was appalled at the idea. What would she say?

'How about saying I'm ill?'

'It would be a lie so it would and he'd see you at work the next day. He's someone important at the prison, John. He won't ask us again.'

He and Mark were on the couch, watching the rugby. 'Tell him I've just found out I've got a kid and we're a bit surprised, we'd been hoping for a girl.'

There was a dining room as you went in that opened out into a book-

shelved front room with a large bay window and a brown leather sofa
that looked old and uncomfortable.

'We've packed the children off to watch telly in the upstairs sitting
room.' Janet was a tall woman with two competitive front teeth and
important breasts. Her hair was piled up high in a grey and blonde
bun.

'Drinkies?' said Carl Lingard, rubbing his hands together.

'I'd love a beer.'

The Lingards looked at each other.

'I told you to get some beer,' she said brightly.

'Sorry John. No beer. Sherry or white or red?'

'What?'

'Wine, you great fool,' said Angie.

'Whatever you're having.'

'Do you have children, Angela?' Janet asked while her husband went
off to get the wine. Before Angela could reply he came back brandishing
a thin dark bottle. 'Piesporter,' he grinned.

'You're a big chap aren't you, John? We're having a fondue tonight.
No kids then? My oldest Thomas is at Campbell College. We like it,
don't we Carl? I would recommend it to anyone, put your name down
the moment the child's born. I suppose all the prison officers are big
men. Or should I say "*screws*". That's what they call you, don't they?' Her
necklace broke away and fell on to her cleavage. 'Oh balls.'

'Can I give you a hand dear?' Carl tapped John on the arm. 'I say, I
used to be a gynaecologist you know . . .'

'Really?'

'Now I just like to keep my hand in!'

'It's a bit early for that, Toggles, give them a chance to warm up . . .'

Angie looked at John. He gave a slight shake of the head, his eyes
stretched wide, his mouth buried in the glass.

When they sat down to eat the fondue, there was some banter over
whose long fork was whose with Carl refusing to have the pink-ended
one, crying out, 'I'm a boy, I'm a boy! I can't help it. I like it.'

The conversation turned to the prison. Angie, red faced from the heat of the fondue and a few glasses of the wine, told them she found the smell hard to take.

Janet let her breasts settle on the tabletop. 'Do you think that subconsciously, Toggs, they're basically children playing up? Tom wouldn't crap in the potty, but Anthea would you see. And he was just testing me, trying to show me who was boss.' On the end of her fork was a large gherkin, laden with stringy cheese.

Toggles was flushed too. Two bottles of wine had already been drunk and he'd placed the empties on the left-hand side of the dining room window-ledge. 'We're going to get that filled tonight,' he said, pointing at the dusty expanse. She's not really interested in my work of course. I don't blame her.'

'I can't be doing with it. I don't watch the TV either. Oh this Afghanistan thing! Africa! I can't bear to see those bloody mothers with all their babies. You'd think they'd stop having them.'

Angie agreed.

'It makes you cross. They blather on about the poverty but it doesn't stop them having seven kids does it? We've never asked for a handout in our lives. Wouldn't dream of it. Pass the little pickled onions, Togs?'

'I'm not kissing you after those.'

'Sounds like a good deal to me. They ought to just get on with it, like the rest of us, instead of moaning. It's the same here. Do you know,' she said, laying a hand either side of her plate. 'The governor's wife, Penny, she's a friend of mine, she said all that Bombay Street stuff was a load of rubbish. Half of them burnt their own houses. For the money.'

'I find that hard to believe,' John said.

'Quite,' said Carl, frowning. 'Quite.'

'Well let's not talk about it. It's depressing. We get too much of it. Especially with his job. I do support Oxfam though. I buy the cards. We must get your address. They do a lot of good in Africa and Asia. Are you going on holiday next year, Angie?'

'We're getting a new car.'

'We *might*.'

'We said we were.'

'I'm a Rover man myself,' said Carl. 'Classic British quality.'

'We were thinking of a Datsun,' said Angie.

Janet laughed abruptly then apologized. 'There's gateau to follow.'

After dessert, Janet took Angie through her holiday brochures, giving general opinions. The overhead lamp swung as Janet's bun tapped it each time she came across a resort with which she was familiar.

Carl and John were in the front room. 'I'm going to talk to Brendan Coogan tomorrow.'

'Toggles, was it Corfu or Crete we went to with the Walkers?'

'Corfu.' He lowered his voice again. 'I called him and asked him to come in and see me on Thursday. He said all he needed to know was that as AG of a protest block I'm clear on the five demands. I said, "Clear as crystal. And what's more I'm willing to talk." You see, everyone needs respect, that's a key motivator. I give this chappie the time of day and already you see we're getting places.'

'Where do you want to go?'

'I want a face-saving compromise for everyone, John. As I said before, I'm a man alone on this.'

Angie's head was bowed over the magazines, legs pressed together, one shoe behind her ankle. She looked back over her shoulder at him, smiling a full and natural smile. He saw her as if for the first time, saw who she was, saw how her tendency was towards the good. She was kind to the woman, in spite of the woman, because she was kind, not for any other reason. He decided he would ask her to marry him. After Christmas.

'What would you say the IRA strategy was, from what you overheard?'

'Carl, I just caught a few words, two men talking.'

'A continuum, right, Warrenpoint, Mountbatten, external pressure and then what?'

'The prison officers.'

'Right and then what?'

'Well I suppose they think they'll get their five demands.'

'And if they don't? Where does the continuum go?'

'The hunger strike.'

'And that is where it stops. It's the last card. Listen, John. I'm after the straw that broke the camel's back. If I can find that tiny straw and,' he put his fingers together in a pincer movement to demonstrate, 'gently extract it, before the back breaks, then I think I will have achieved something small – but very, very significant.'

Angie was looking at him, quizzically. She must have overheard some of their conversation and wondered what they were talking about.

'Are you a chess player, Dunn?'

'No I'm not as it happens.' John couldn't help smiling.

'No? Never mind. My strategy is checkmate. There are two routes across the board as far as I can see. Either way you start with the pawn. That's Coogan. I'm going to push Coogan, and topple the rest. Here's what I mean. Game number one, let's take the first demand and let's concede it, apparently, let's give the minimum to satisfy their notion of a "concession" which is, after all, all they really want, and for the Government nothing substantive has been transacted. Everyone's happy. No one's dead. The main thing is that Coogan looks like he's the big man in his community. Are you with me? After that we can move on to other things. One step at a time.'

'I'm with you Carl. But I don't buy it, to tell you the truth. They spelt it out pretty clearly. They want the full five.'

'So here's my other thought. Game two, we push them to the hunger strike. Push them to play the card they can't play. If we make it known to them, to Coogan, that it's a waste of their time killing prison officers, that they can carry on with that till the cows come home and nothing changes, that like with kidnapping, we can't come through with the goods because it will only encourage that kind of thing, then they will be forced to go along the continuum to hunger strike. Now, we have good reason to believe, from that little note you brought me, that at that point, they'll pull off. Thus we're saving prison officers' lives by forcing their strategy to a conclusion and there's no hunger strike either.'

'Carl, this is way beyond me and to be honest I don't like to talk about it. I was just a soldier, you know.'

'Right. Right, a soldier thinks, who's going to die here, them or us? And in this strategy, worst case scenario is that some IRA prisoners die. Worst case. We should get them to play the card they can't play, won't play. It's just a ploy. Just as with nuclear deterrence. No one would press the button.' He looked composed enough to sign a cheque, a letter, an order, anything at all.

John glanced up at the shelves. 'You've read all these have you? You shouldn't be talking to someone like me about this, Carl, you know.'

Carl looked affronted. 'Well, any man in any situation has to seek for himself what's right, or what will work best for him . . .'

John shook his head. 'Those men aren't interested in appearances, in saving face, in compromises or concessions and I think they're ready to give their lives. Like I said though, I'm just a soldier. Not a general. I'd rather we didn't talk about it at all. If you don't mind.'

Lingard sat, looking askance, one arm extended along the back of the couch, his fingers drumming.

'I've talked Angie into thinking about Madeira for next year,' said Janet.

John nodded, he wanted to get home. They shouldn't have come out, not with Mark staying for just a few days on his first trip.

When he'd left the prison that evening, his empty Tupperware box in his hand, it was night-time but the prison compound was well lit, bright, even dazzling in places, and Frig had said to him in the stark light at the main gate, 'When I get out of here at night, mate, I don't think about it again, that's that.'

'Janet and Carl have got a new porch you know, part of security measures. Courtesy of the Northern Ireland Office.'

'Bullet proof!' trilled Janet. 'It can be whatever they want; I was just pleased to get a new porch. Next stop a bullet-proof conservatory!'

'Oh you can't worry about all of that, can you?' said Lingard, coming to. 'You'd go bonkers. You can't get paranoid. Otherwise you're just caving in to the thugs. I don't bother with checking under the car. Rees, the AG on the other protest block, he does, his bloody suit's always covered in oil. Do you know, he's more likely to get it than I am because he antagonizes the fellas, you see and I don't do that because for me it's not personal. Rees, you see, he's a local. He takes it too far. Actually, I had to have a word with him. We were taking a walk around one of the protest blocks and the prisoners start shouting abuse at us and bloody Rees goes berserk, leaping about giving them the finger!'

'You can't blame the man,' Angie laughed.

'It's personal for a lot of people,' said John gravely.

'What about you, John?' asked Janet, pouting a little.

Everything's personal he wanted to say. It wasn't before. Maybe it was when you had a family that everything became personal. He put his arm around Angie.

'No, not for me. When I leave the place, I leave it, I don't think about it,' he said, borrowing Frig's lie.

He shook hands with Carl Lingard as they left and said to him, again, 'Forget about that note, Carl. Seriously.'

'Funny,' said Angie in the car. 'That Janet hugged me when we left, like we were best friends. Apart from that though weren't they just like something off the telly? You wonder what people like that are like in real life. On their own.'

41

She met him on the far side of Andersonstown and they drove down towards the prison together. He dropped her off in the town of Hillsborough at a very British pub, The Marquis of Downshire.

'Aye well no one we know will see us here,' she said and got out.

She sat at a round table near the paned window, underneath a row of silver paper bells, smoking and drinking a glass of lager. She read the paper. There was a young lad behind the bar and a few people came in for a lunchtime pint and stood talking with him. Coogan hoped to be back just after one.

All the way there she'd had half his face, serious and closed when he spoke about his work, teasing when he talked about what had happened between them the other night, then wholly formal when he turned to her, saying, 'Don't take this the wrong way, Kathleen, but what's going on with us here, I don't know how long it can go on for. I wouldn't want anyone to see us together.'

'I know.'

'So maybe this is the last time. Now that's not something you normally say to a woman you want to have sex with.'

'Well, you're honest at least. Maybe I should just catch the bus back, I'm not sure this is a good idea myself.'

'Well, now, look; I won't be long in the Kesh. I'm to have a talk with some eejit of a Brit from the office side of things. It'll take me no more than a few minutes. With nothing to offer they've always something to say.'

Alone at the round pub table, she turned another page she hadn't read, glanced at the clock. She rolled forward on the seat. She wanted to be with him again. It might be the last time, like he said. There was no way he could have both the IRA and a woman in his life. But a married woman was not really a woman; asked for nothing got nothing. She just wanted to kiss him again.

She sat swilling the sour golden drink around the glass. When he was with her she was keeping him from his war. Wouldn't the world be a better place if women kept the men who ran the wars from getting there? What about if there was some woman assigned to keeping Paisley erect? He couldn't go about ranting and raving with his trousers out front like a tent. He'd have to stop in. That's what the women's movement should be about.

She went up to the bar and asked for change for the cigarette machine. She bought a pack of B&H as it was all they had and she pulled the wrapper off and opened the box and looked at the slim, firm cigarettes, side by side and obedient. Her fingers smelt of tobacco. She could be anybody. She looked over at the bar, bald heads conferring, insistent repetitions, the conformity of their shouts of laughter.

About half-past one he came into the bar, nodded at her, taking a quick look down and around and to the sides. He ordered a pint of Guinness for himself and a half'un for her. The lunchtime crowd went back to work and it was just the two of them with the lad at the bar talking to a girl.

'Did it go off all right your meeting?'

He wiped his mouth. 'Aye, we've got a couple of hours all to ourselves. What do you want to do?'

'Well they'll be closing here soon.'

'Will we finish these and go for a drive?'

Sat in his car, her empty stomach was hovering like a balloon, buoyed with anticipation. Her mind was soft, drugged by the alcohol. She felt as if she could undo herself. There was no need to be anyone at all.

He drove the car down a country lane, pulled into a lay-by, turned off

the engine and started to kiss her. Then he said, 'Wait there.' He got out
and came round to her side of the car, opened the door and knelt down.
He told her to take down her tights and underwear. When they were at
her knees, he pulled them down around her ankles and pushed her knees
apart and leant into her until his dark hair was at her belly.

Her head filled with visions. She went between memories, seeing herself all the times she was beautiful. She was breathing, she was taking
more than her share. She didn't want a god, she wanted a man. She
wanted him inside her. She could feel his arms struggling as he tried to
undo his trousers.

*I could love you, I could kill you. I want this. This is how I make my mark,
this is where I plant my flag, this is how I stake my claim, this is how I deny
you, this is how I claim you, this is what you owe me, this is what I am
taking, this is how I know I'm alive.*

42

Prisoner 1880, Callaghan, was up for a visit, as was Sean Moran. Dunn was visits runner for the day and he took Callaghan down in the morning and Moran in the afternoon. Both submitted to the mirror-search without too much fuss. Skids gave just a cursory glance and said, 'Fair enough.'

Patsy Callaghan was a big man in his thirties with hair sprouting out of his upper arms and neck. The jeans he chose were small for him; when he emerged the crotch was gaping on them where it had been ripped out by a previous wearer. Skids swore under his breath as if he were going out for the night with a friend who dressed badly. It took Dunn close to twenty minutes to get Callaghan round to the visiting block. The prisoner wanted to take his time, enjoy the walk.

He stood by while Callaghan greeted his girlfriend reservedly. She seemed an odd choice. She was an English woman in her early fifties. Dunn noticed she had a shaved upper lip, her hair was tightly permed. She didn't seem the sort of woman to be the lover of a 'rough, tough Provie'. Callaghan had spent three years on the run, one of them in Canada buying weapons, allegedly.

He had little to say and the woman did most of the talking. Dunn could hear snatches of their conversation, news, the campaign and so on. At the end of the half hour she asked him when she'd be seeing him again and Callaghan said he didn't know. When they kissed goodbye, Callaghan was unwilling, like a boy with his auntie.

After asking Moran if he wanted the visit, Dunn took the boy to cell twenty-six to change and Skids assisted again with the mirror-search. Moran braced himself, closed his eyes, but it was soon clear that the search was a mere formality. Bolton was standing out on the circle. He nodded when he saw Moran emerging peaceably from the wing wearing prison-issue trousers and boots and an orderly's dirty sweatshirt.

'Good job, Mr Dunn.'

Moran was walking in a strange way; either the lack of exercise had affected his gait or he had a substantial collection up his arse. It was not Dunn's business. As they made the cold long walk through checkpoints and grilles to the visiting block, Dunn thought about Christmas, about presents for his son, about a good dinner and whether he should ask him about coming to study at Queens.

'See the football?' asked Moran, suddenly.

'No, no chance. I'm in here all the time.'

'Aye. Same here.'

They both laughed.

Moran was a handsome boy, his smile sure. He was different to the boy who had raged in the exercise yard, he had taken some quick lessons. Dunn dropped behind as they entered the visiting block, noticed the slope of Moran's shoulders as yet unmade, like his own son's.

Waiting at a table was a tall young woman who was stretched about the chair, leaning on one elbow on the table, addressing tart remarks to the officers who stood nearby, ogling her. She wore an Afghan-style fringed mauve coat, and at the end of long legs that reached across the corridor, entwined like a mermaid's tail, were high-heeled boots. Her hair was flicked back, a little Farrah Fawcett in style, and her eyes were dark.

When Moran approached, she stood up and put her arms around his neck, pulling his head to hers, giving him a long kiss. Dunn saw the hollows of their cheeks as their heads moved and Moran's hands going inside the coat. Two of the officers were gawping. Jaws rapped the desk at the back of the room and Dunn asked them to break it up. The young woman used the side of her thumb to wipe the lipstick from Moran's mouth.

'Hello Sean Moran. I'm Nancy Costello.'

'Hello Nancy. Everything okay?'

'Everything's just fine,' she said, looking at him and nodding slowly. There was some sort of understanding, more than likely an exchange had taken place. Moran's hands were under the table.

'Nails wants you to tell Kevin it's still a no. Keep the letters on the five demands coming, he says. It'll all work out Sean, so you keep eating your dinners. You've got the Christmas present there you know.'

'I thought I'd just had that. I'm glad I told my mother not to come now.'

Nancy dropped her coat on to the back of the chair, pivoting a little at the waist, her breasts moving from side to side.

'Did you manage to bangle it all right? Is it your first time?'

'I'm getting used to it. I'd like to conceal something in you, Nancy. Now I know why they rip the crotch of the jeans.'

Dunn saw her slip a little in the seat and drop her shoulders, her hands were underneath the table.

'You're very driven by the cause,' he said.

Jaws banged on the desk again and called out.

'It'll all be over if you don't pack that in kids,' Dunn said. 'Five more minutes.'

'I only needed about thirty more seconds,' said Sean.

The girl gave Dunn cat's eyes.

'What's the football scores then?'

'You're the typical bloody man, so y'are, sex and football. I'll bet you're itching to get back to the lads now to tell them you got felt.'

'Two minutes in the act and two hours in the telling.'

'I don't know about the football but I'll make sure I find out for next time. Sean, I don't know you but you seem like a really nice fella. I'll tell you something from me, from Nancy, if you lads go on hunger strike, you'll die. I know it because it's a woman we're talking about. Thatcher, she won't give in, she's a bitch.'

'I know that Nancy.'

Dunn saw Jaws tapping on his wristwatch. He cleared his throat. 'Two minutes and time's up.'

'Will I see you again Nancy? Will you write to me?'

'Aye, on both counts.'

She stood up, and they kissed again with Nancy's hands in his hair.

'Do me a favour Sean, have a shower next time will you?'

Dunn began to lead the boy away to the back. Moran turned around, pointing his finger at her.

'One day I'll have a bath, with you Nancy! I will!'

She was stood, arms crossed, not listening to the prison officer who wanted to get her out. Sean gave her a last wave.

'I think I'm in love with you Sean Moran!' she shouted out.

Sean gave her the thumbs up and was gone.

On the walk back, tired of the sound of gravel, Dunn said, 'How old are you Moran?'

'Nineteen.'

'You ought to be having a normal life, going out with that girl, going down the pub. And here you are, just a kid, mixed up in all of this.'

They went on together in silence. He supposed the boy had been handed this, just as he was handed his life. But the army was a good life. Even in Northern Ireland in the beginning. He thought about the girls who danced with them in their camp at Dundonald in the summer of '69 when they were welcome in Belfast. All those Catholic girls, pale legs and dark voices. Probably he'd danced with someone who knew this boy's family, maybe he'd even danced with the boy's mother. By the end of the summer things had changed. A girl he'd been out with came up to the wire fence of their camp, one day; her arm was in a sling, her hair was cropped off. She told him she couldn't see him again. 'Come away from the fence, Corporal Dunn!'

'I'll ask the orderly to tell you the football score,' he said as they approached the block.

When John Dunn got in that night, the light was on in the spare room and he popped his head in. They sat for a while with John asking Mark about his childhood and about life at the university.

'Are you worried about the IRA getting you?' said Mark, out of the blue. 'Angie worries.'

'It's her I'm afraid of, not the IRA! Come on, pal, let's get downstairs and have a cup of tea down there, before we're in the shit for keeping her awake with our jawing.' He went loopily down the stairs, jumping from one foot to the other with exaggerated 'shushes', turning back to grimace at his son.

Suddenly John saw the image of his father doing the same to him, the clown's face, calling back to John's mother as they made their way down the steps from the hut in Mote Park, creeping off to the pub together. And then the comic false trip, his dad stumbling forwards, and the boy worried, arms out, fooled. *Had you there, son.*

43

Kathleen and her sister were side by side on Saturday night. She was about to show Eileen the Christmas presents. They were remembering the Christmas their mother made each of them a small set of drawers out of cardboard wrapped with printed material. In each drawer she'd put some treasure – be it a whistle, a balloon, marbles, a hair slide or some cigarette cards. When they opened their presents, their father used to take as much interest as they did, lifting them up for admiration, praising his wife to the skies. They were sentimental, the pair of them. Their mother used to egg their father on to tell a story, or sing a sad song:

> 'In the street, he envies all those lucky boys,
> Then wanders home to last year's broken toys.
> I'm so sorry for that laddie;
> He hasn't got a daddy,
> The little boy that Santa Claus forgot.'

When William started up with that song last Christmastime they'd all hushed him.

'Give it a rest, Billy.'

'For the love of Mary . . .'

He kept going though, enjoying himself, doing the part where the lad sent a note to Santa for some soldiers and a gun and '*it broke his little heart when he found Santa hadn't come*', but they shouted him down. There were enough boys who hadn't got their daddies at home not to need to sing about it.

They were a couple of innocents her parents, do-gooders. When she was just seventeen their mother, Anne Marie, heard that a baby boy down the street was being given away and as her parents had just lost an infant son, her father told her, 'Go you down there and bring back the babby, tell them there's a home for it here.' The baby came with a piece of paper upon which was its birth date. In fact the boy, on closer inspection, was revealed to be a girl. 'Och the poor wee lad's got no mickey,' quipped Anne Marie's mother. Anne Marie raised the baby girl. She called her Fay, after Fay Wray. She was seventeen and the talk was that it was her own child.

It was through Fay that she met Kathleen's father. Michael O'Leary was born in Kerry but his parents had moved to Sailortown for the work. He did a bit for the St Vincent's charity and he used to chat with little Fay and bring her sweets now and again. He got talking to Anne Marie, and after a while they got married.

The two of them were buried in Milltown, their mother joining their father two years after him in '74. They all clubbed together for a white stone and an angel to look down over them.

Their parents never had much in life, they never managed to save a penny. They had a lot of faith. Kathleen reminded Eileen how their parents said the rosary together every evening.

'Jim and I pray at nights too. He prays we do and I pray we don't.'

Kathleen showed her the Sindy doll she'd got for Aine with a fur-trimmed leather raincoat hat and boots.

'Look at her tits,' said Eileen, jabbing at the doll with a dirty-nailed finger. 'She's not a breastfeeder.'

Kathleen had a small Panasonic cassette recorder with a microphone for Liam.

'He can go about recording trouble instead of making it,' said Eileen. 'If only we'd had all girls. Maureen McGuigan had seven girls and not a peep out of them, except for the wee second to last one who looks like a boy and beat the crap out of my Ciaran once.'

'This is for Sean.' Kathleen opened a jeweller's box and inside there was a long slim, silver crucifix with a waif-thin Jesus figure wrapped around it. 'They're allowed their crosses you see.'

'It's beautiful. You've done them all proud. The kids'll be made up. You're not letting your man Santa deliver this lot I hope? Who's doing it this year?'

'It's Fergal O'Hanlon's brother, Dominic again. He started off all right last year, he had all the presents, one for each kid, all labelled up by their mummies and daddies, and he was up the top there, about six-ish, making sure the kids got a chance to look at him. Then he takes a wee drink at each home so that by the time he gets down to us, he's mad tore. The pedal was off of Liam's bike where he'd ridden it himself. I told Liam, look Santa's had a few, that's why it's broken like. He wouldn't come round to fix it when I got Sean to go and ask him, giving off about Santa not giving out guarantees.'

'Francie Keogh used to do it so nice.'

'Aye he did that.' Kathleen lit a cigarette for Eileen and one for herself and they sat smoking. Kathleen put her fingertips to one eye, then the other.

'What is it, love? Have you news about Sean?'

'It's all this about a hunger strike. You know how it is round here, the talk builds and builds and you think it'll go on and then suddenly the thing you've all been talking about has happened. I feel sick all day with the worry and then I pray at night that it won't be my Sean, it won't be him as goes on the hunger strike. It's a terrible thing to pray that it be someone else's son.'

Eileen was a hard-looking woman with a soft heart. She overate, swore like a man and surrounded herself with sentimental ornaments, pretty photo frames, mottoes. She put a hand on her sister's.

'I was going to talk to Father Pearse,' said Kathleen, 'but did you know he's coming out for the hunger strike and saying how we've got to support the boys who's going on it.'

'Well, I don't know what he's thinking of, that man. The church is coming out against it. You turn to the church, Kathleen, it's always been there for us before now.'

'And what if I can't?' Kathleen took her hand away.

'Of course you can. Don't talk stupid, Kathleen.' Eileen followed her sister into the kitchen. 'Whatever are you saying that for?'

'Nothing, I'm just tired and worn out with it all. Who isn't?' She shook the tea tin. There was barely any noise to it. 'I've spent a fortune on presents and such. I took out a loan I'll be paying back until after next summer, just before I take out one for the next Christmas. But you say to yourself, I might as well spend all I can lay my hands on because next year who knows whether we'll all still be here.' She looked out over the back yard. 'Fucking Christmas. Coming along every year, to make it all worse.'

44

With Christmas and the killings there were impromptu 'parties' springing up all around the site of Long Kesh. The most debauched were those in the area of temporary housing known as Silver City. The army brought in women from Lisburn, by bus, even by chopper. It wasn't unusual for a prison officer to claim a bed over there, with a woman, and stay overnight. That was how Skids had met this new woman of his. She'd been getting off with a solider, and when the squaddie left to throw up, Skids moved in.

'I wouldn't normally do that of course,' he'd said.

Skids was on split shift and was going down to Lisburn to see his 'lady' again. He hadn't seemed so excited at the prospect this time, confiding in Dunn before he went off that as she liked him to wear his hat he took it along with him in a carrier bag. Dunn saw the bag between his hands and cracked up.

He was in the mess alone, eating his sandwiches. He focused his vision on the single drop of water suspended at the kitchen tap. His nasal breathing sounded like the noise of a winter wind through a disused house; his nose was full from smoking too much.

Rabbit and Shandy came back from lunch very drunk and decided to head down the wings to talk to the streakers. Frig had been into the PO's office to borrow his record player, amplifier and speakers, and he came out carrying them in a large cardboard box. He left the lot by the mess door and sat down fiddling with the speaker wire.

'That'll be a one way conversation,' Frig said to Dunn. 'Last year, Rabbit went down there asking them if they was all right and wishing them a Merry Christmas and when no one said a word back to him he got himself worked up. But they're trained to say nothing them lot, aren't they? Do you think it's wrong, the drinking?'

'How do you mean?' asked Dunn.

'Well, it's not good for you is it, it's a depresser.'

Rabbit and Shandy came back into the mess.

'That's fucking right that is. They're out there fucking laughing at us the bastards,' said Shandy, pointing to the wings. He had a dark half-moon of sweat under his arm.

Rabbit threw his cap on the table. 'Where's Campbell?'

Campbell came in, highly emotional and full of the Officer Willard killing. Willard had been walking from the Crumlin Road jail to his regular lunch place, the Buff's Club, the day before when he was killed with a single shot in the back, from a .38. He had been warned to stop frequenting it; another officer had been killed on his way there three months prior, in a similar attack.

Campbell had been in the bar with a friend who knew Willard well. Now he recounted their conversation painstakingly, with the others shaking their heads, variously sympathetic, slightly bored, careful not to be caught doing something for themselves. Rabbit was wiping off his boots, Skids was buttering a piece of cold toast to his side. Campbell told the story of Willard's life and his own in parallel, mixing up the one with the other. Both of them had been members of the Royal British Legion, having served in the Second World War, and both were members of the Orange Order and the UDA.

Campbell was close to retirement. He had lost most of his friends. He had lost his wife. His phone calls were all bad. He had a son he never saw except for when he was after something. But he had a lot at stake even so; the past, his memories.

Rabbit looked up, eager to speak, but Campbell kept going.

'See back then was, you cover me, and I'll cover you, and that's all gone, you can't buy that.'

'Cannon-fodder's what we are,' said Rabbit. He was cleaning his nails with the end of a teaspoon.

Campbell tried to bring him into focus; he looked old – and heart-broken. 'He wasn't cannon-fodder, Benny Willard wasn't.'

'Lingus had that IRA fucker Coogan in his office yesterday. Ben Bartlett saw him come in, like he owned the place. His men are out there murdering Willard in cold blood and he's in here getting tea and cake.'

'You what?'

'That lot out there, they're full of it. Never so much as say a word then they're chattering on like monkeys about cannon-fodder.'

Campbell stood up.

'They must be loving it,' Rabbit ground on.

'Willard's life was not cheap,' said Campbell. 'No more were the lives of all of our men, men from our streets who've died for all that is good and right.'

There were looks exchanged. Rabbit couldn't help it, excitement cracked through his face. He had to lower his head to hide it.

They marched off at a hysterical pace, Campbell followed by Shandy and Frig, to 'talk to some of the fellas'.

Rabbit said he'd stay back, ostensibly to help Dunn with the tea, but he went off into the Orient Express with one of Frig's magazines.

It wasn't normal procedure, but Dunn, Baxter and a grille guard took the cart round at teatime. When he got to O'Malley's cell, Dunn handed in the yellow square known as 'cake' and something in O'Malley's look made him say,

'I'm a Brit, you know. I was in the army. I served here.' He poured the tin mugs of tea. 'Plenty of us have died here as well. Just like you lot. Just the same as you.' He handed him the tea. 'We're all cannon-fodder, one way or another.'

'You had your choice,' O'Malley replied.

Dunn looked at the man, standing in shit and piss. 'Yeah. Like you did. You should have chosen something else, mate.'

'Likewise.'

Dunn closed the door. They took the cart back up the wing, through the grilles and into the circle.

'You shouldn't have spoken to him,' the grille guard grumbled. 'You're not supposed to talk to them.'

Dunn gave the trolley a shove. 'Get rid of that lot, Baxter.'

Seeing the PO's office door open, Dunn popped across to use the phone. Rules or no rules, he was calling Angie.

'Hello Angie. Yeah never mind going through our bloody phone number, I just rung it, I know what it is. Look I can't speak long. Get the boy what they call a 'Walkman' when you go into town this afternoon will you, Angie? Frig says they're about a hundred quid. Take the money out the bank. Take what you need.'

She told him she'd already got the boy a coat, a parka. And he'd already told her to get the boy a book-voucher for thirty quid for his studies.

'There's a lot of Christmases I'm making up for. Buy some music to go with it. Frig says the one to get is the Pink Floyd album. Just come out. Get that and The Police and Madness, all the top ones. On cassette, right? Cheers.'

When Dunn went to open the mess door he heard Baxter and Rabbit having a heated conversation. Rabbit's voice, always uneven, was now ranging wildly from high to low tones, as if he contained two people, one angry, one afraid.

'Don't tell me I'm going to be all right, Baxter.'

'Every officer gets them threats.'

'He said the name of the street I live on, says my mother goes shopping on the Shankill on a Friday, says my parents drive a blue Cortina.'

'You'll have to speak to PO.'

'Bollocks. I'm asking you to have a word.'

'Look, I'll tell you what they'd say to you themselves, you keep your head down, you play things straight, you box clever and you'll be all right, but if you're doing things you know aren't right the IRA aren't going to forget about it, no chance. They'll get you on the outside because they can't gct you on the inside.'

'We've all done things, every man here . . .' said Rabbit. 'Who hasn't? You don't just sit and take it.'

The medic came out of his office and locked the door. Dunn went in the mess. Rabbit was standing, putting his jacket on.

'It's a waste of breath talking to you. You with your tattoos, your Red Hand! And your Provie pals! What the fuck are you anyway, Baxter?'

Baxter looked him straight in the eyes, merely tilting his head. 'I'm the good Protestant, every man for himself.'

Rabbit gave the chair a shove; it scraped the floor and hit the table and he left the room.

'Troubled times,' said Baxter, taking Rabbit's plate and cup over to the sink. They were alone.

'Where do you stand Baxter? What is your game?'

'Me? I'm nobody. Ordinary decent criminal.'

'You're full of shit.'

Baxter wiped his hands roughly on a tea-towel and ran a hand through his hair, such that it was slightly wet at the front. He sat down at the table and looked up at Dunn from under his brow as if he was about to unfold a special hand of cards.

'Sit down Mr Dunn, I'll give you the benefit of an education. I'm in for attempted murder, twenty years. But I'll be out in half with this here orderly thing. I'll tell you about me. When I was sixteen and Paisley came round stirring us all up with his speeches, I went with my friends to a meeting. Everyone was in something if you remember, back then in the early seventies.'

'I was in the army.'

'Aye, well like I said, everyone was in something. There were more than fifty-thousand men in the UDA. You went down to the meeting, you held a gong, you swore on the Bible and you were in. Peer pressure, the fuck of it. Often you had to do a job to prove yourself. I did a robbery here and there, nothing to lose, bravado, adrenalin, you know the score.'

'That's not how it was in the army.'

'Aye well. They form the UFF, an elite. I like the sound of that. We go down to the meetings and we pick a job out of a hat. Me and my pal we pick "shoot a Catholic", so off we go, over towards the Short Strand and we shoot a man in the back. It was easy; he fell to the ground and we ran off. Next time we go down we pick from the hat "shoot two Catholics". Now the jobs are supposed to be secret. You pick your own and you don't tell anyone what you picked, but I'm thinking how comes it's two now, is this a set up, will I get "shoot three" next time? But it wasn't like that. The meetings were in the local pub so we have a few. And my friend and I, we tell the fellas, hush hush, we're going for a couple of Catholics coming out of mass in Andersonstown the next Sunday. We get there and we're picking off a couple coming out but some soldiers are there waiting for us. It's a set up. So when I got in here I said to myself, fuck it, I'm not going to let them claim me, I'm going to go it alone. You get to thinking, you see. I probably think about that man I shot more than his wife does. Maybe not. Who's to know? So I came here as an ordinary criminal and I jumped at the chance to be an orderly. And it's worked out that there's a job for me to do.' He raised his nose when he said this and he kept it there in the aftermath of his words, like a dog sniffing events on the wind.

Dunn's tongue was dank and dry with the coffee. Outside he heard the loud, concrete-muffled voices of two prison officers exchanging opinions.

'Yous have got orders from higher up to break these men on the protest, but they're not written orders,' Baxter went on. 'Back in the spring, orders came down to get things moving a bit, finish the dirt protest; the screws were to give the prisoners "baths". Bolton wouldn't do it but the other blocks did. Scalding hot water. The screws took them big yard brooms and brushed the men down, chucked detergent, bleach, and disinfectant all over them. Sure there's them as rewrite the way it happened, like Mr Rabbit. I've never met a man who says he hit someone without provocation, have you? No wonder they're scared now, with the killings going on. They know what they've done.'

Baxter gave his cigarette a gentle tap on the ashtray. 'After those baths in the other blocks O'Malley told me to tell PO what he could tell his colleagues. "We can't beat you in the Maze, you're striking at us where we're vulnerable, but outside we'll punish you for what you've done, so when you walk behind the coffins of your colleagues with crocodile tears, you ask yourselves – What did I do to contribute to his death?'"

'So you reckon you're some sort of a double agent do you, Baxter? I tell you, in the last few days I've fucking heard it all.'

'Nothing so grand as that. I'm a go-between. I keep an ear open. See, someone like your man Campbell, he's putting your lives at risk the way he works. He's putting your life at risk, Mr Dunn.'

Baxter got up and stretched, saying, 'Back to work then,' and Dunn saw again the tattoo of the Red Hand emerge from the sleeves of the denim overalls.

45

It was the last Sunday before Christmas and the Clonard was decorated with white, green and gold, and there was a choir of boys and girls who were the Ecumenical Choir of Belfast. They had nice robes; probably they lived on the Antrim Road, thought Kathleen. Funny how people with money were as a rule more for peace. She'd put all the small change she had – and that she'd taken from her husband's trouser pockets – into the Holy Virgin's money box. During the mass she prayed to God to have more love or less love or whatever it was He thought she needed. Coogan came to her mind and she felt guilt like heartburn. She wondered where he was, what he was doing.

Father Pearse stopped her on her way out. He looked haggard.

'You're not up the Kesh this morning then Father?' she asked him tartly. He was going the next Sunday. She told him to tell Sean it didn't matter about the Christmas visit.

'Tell him, och, just tell him I love him. There's nothing else to say.'

'Kathleen. Please forgive me for not being the priest that you deserve.' His eyes were strained. He whispered, 'I love your family. I don't want your son to die.'

'I know.' She put her hand on his arm. 'Look, Father, I'm sure you'll have had much finer offers but we'd be pleased if you'd take your Christmas dinner with us.'

'I'm supposed to have it up at Corpus Christi with the others. Is it a turkey you're having?'

'Aye. And a Christmas pudding.'

'Well, I can't say no. Thank you. I'll bring a few tins of beer. Leave the carving for me if you like.'

Mrs Coogan was talking to Mrs Purcell up at the door.

Kathleen turned back. 'Wait, Father. You are my priest after all and I'm in a bit of a mess, I didn't go to confession yesterday.'

'I can spare you a few minutes, Kathleen. No need for the box, if you'd like.'

'Let me just tell Mrs O'Sullivan I'm staying back.' She made out of the church with her feet saying, Sean, Brendan, Sean, Brendan. What did it mean, the two of them together as if they were part and parcel?

Mrs Coogan touched Kathleen lightly on the arm as she went to pass by. 'Ach Kathleen,' she said, swaying on beleaguered heels, a stout woman with many seasonal accoutrements. 'Could my Brendan help you out?'

'Oh aye, thank you,' said Kathleen, blushing. 'Merry Christmas to you.'

She hurried out. Mrs O'Sullivan was at the car horn.

Clusters of older people in dark coats were turning their yellow and grey faces to look at her car.

'I want to get one like *The Dukes of Hazzard*. Liven this crowd up.'

'I'm staying for a wee chat with the father,' said Kathleen, her hands on the lowered window. Mrs O'Sullivan put a hand across, fingers clean and dry as pastry.

'Sure, you go on love.'

The car screeched on its tyres as it lurched out into the road and there were soft, chiding exclamations from the groups about the front of the church.

'Now what's the matter Kathleen?' Father Pearse said, sitting down in an armchair opposite hers in a small room with one window at the back of the Clonard.

'There's something I didn't speak of in my last confession that I should have done.' She started to weep. He handed her his hanky from his pocket. 'I took communion, Father, and I shouldn't have.'

'There's only one thing that the church says bars you from the sacraments.'

'I know.'

'The second relationship.'

'That's one way of saying it.'

'You're not the first one, Kathleen.'

'I've done a terrible thing. Twice.'

'Oh Jesus, now calm down. Every day there are people doing it. Look, now, what do I always say in these cases? If you can't break it up overnight, endeavour to break it up as soon as you can. Think of your children who're still at home. You're not going to get out of the relationship overnight, you didn't get into it overnight I suppose. Just do your best, think about the children and the stability they need to get them off on their own way, and where you go after that . . .'

'But I know it's wrong, I know it's wrong and yet I've done it all the same.'

'That's not really relevant, Kathleen. You're flesh and blood. You make mistakes. But as I say to all you mothers, think about the good things you do. Think about getting the children up every day, feeding them, clothing them, loving them, all those things.'

The handkerchief was warm, wet. 'I'm outside of God's love.'

'No no, no. The church harks back to Roman times on the matter but the Bible bears me out. You're not bad because nothing can ever come between you and the love of God made visible in Jesus Christ. Nothing. In other words, nothing that I can do or you can do as a human being. So anyone can share in Holy Communion. Who am I, who is anyone to say you cannot? It's not the teaching of Christ. Nothing, nothing – no matter how big your sins are – nothing can come between you and the love of Jesus Christ.'

'Are you sure?'

'Nothing,' he said adamantly, reaching for her hands and taking them in his own.

'What should I do?'

'Try and stop it.' He shook her hands. 'I say to everyone, restitution is the next thing after a sin. When it's someone who's stolen, that's easy, put something in the St Vincent's next time you have a few bob. Most people know, in their heart, what they have to do. You're an intelligent woman; I don't have to tell you. God's love, His grace, it came before, do you see, it was there for you before, nothing you can do can take it away.'

'I don't really know if I can, if I'm strong enough.'

'You're a good mother.'

'I'm not though. I don't know if I can stop it.'

'Yes you are, yes you can. Now, get away with you. I'll see you tomorrow for Christmas dinner.'

She held out the handkerchief.

He looked at it.

'I'll wash it. And give it to you tomorrow.'

When she was gone, the priest sat for a while. He didn't go to God enough for guidance, he knew it. He didn't hear Him speak any more. He heard the phone ringing, the door knocking, the chatter of the women in the office, the clock ticking, the kettle boiling.

He sat praying, trying to force a place of quiet inside himself to allow the Lord to enter in and speak to him. It took a ferocity of effort now that it hadn't before he came to Belfast.

46

'Fellas, I want you all in my office. Right now, if you please.'

Campbell straightened bodily, but his face was misshapen with anguish as he followed Bolton.

Shandy was coming out of the toilets and Dunn gave him a nod.

'PO wants a word. You all right there?'

'Aye, we're all in the same boat.'

The men stood, arms folded. Bolton took off his jacket and perched on the desk. Dunn leant against the wall.

'I've been asked to bring you together to remind you about personal safety precautions and to impress upon you the need for extra vigilance at the present time.' He put on his glasses and picked up a newspaper. 'I don't suppose any of you read the *Irish News* but I'd like to read you the following statement issued by the IRA on the occasion of Officer Willard's murder yesterday: *"Once again we will remind prison officers that the campaign against them will continue until they desist from carrying on the failed policy of criminalisation. The continuation of this policy is the cause of extreme misery for Republican prisoners of war."'*

Campbell made a noise and moved his foot like a horse at the race gates.

'So are we going to get our houses bullet-proofed now, Sir?' asked Shandy.

'There's no bullet-proofing for officer ranks. Only for the senior staff.'

'Them that don't need it like,' said Frig.

There was a tutting and shaking of heads.

'All I said to you was what the policy is. Now there are things you know you can do to protect yourselves without getting too bloody paranoid.'

'Number One Governor, Rimes, has got his own armoured vehicle,' said Rabbit, looking round, stopping at Campbell.

'The great tart,' said Frig.

'First, you alter your patterns. Good, not to drive here the same way every day; better, not to use the same car. Make as much variance as possible, travel with a pal, use the wife's car if she's got one. If you're going to eat off site, don't go to the same place day in day out; better, don't eat outside. Get your wife and family to alter their schedules as well. Take the car, take the bus, walk, but whatever you do, do something different. Are you with me? Be smart about the house. Don't let the missus hang your blue prison-service shirts out on the line, please lads. Check under the car if you want, some do, some don't. Up to you. I know who's who in the car-park where we do our shopping because I see them drop their keys by accident on purpose, to check underneath. Be careful your security doesn't mark you out. By the by, I presume you've all heard the story of the week? I digress but we could use the laugh. Your man Dripper Dawson had his car blown up this morning – something about his tax disc and his plates not matching and it being parked in an unusual place. The army's Christmas joke I expect. Anyway, Dripper got compensation so he's a happy man . . .'

Frig looked across at Dunn and then at Shandy.

'Where was I? Yes, come and go at different times. Make sure your phone is not in the hallway or in line with a door or window—'

Campbell turned round towards the others, his left arm outstretched, a trigger finger up at his eye. 'Hello this is the IR fucking A. Goodbye.'

'Aye well. You and your wife and family, keep to people you know and trust. Don't make new friends. Don't tell people you don't know anything about your life, be wary of questions.'

'It can be people you know,' said Shandy. 'We've moved four times now and we'll be moving again soon, more than likely. I went up the Prison Service Office and I says what about some protection, what about bullet-proof glass? My wife's been threatened, my kids too, we've had the front door shot at, and they told me they couldn't help me.'

They had heard this before.

'Tell your wives to be careful what they tell people, especially with phone calls when then they don't know the caller; they can give away information without knowing it. You know about keeping your mouth shut inside the prison. Don't get friendly with a prisoner, do not say a word.' Bolton looked at Dunn.

'What about handguns?' asked Shandy.

'I was coming to that. You have to apply for one if you want one.'

'I did,' said Campbell. 'I'm still waiting.'

'I've never had one myself. Not one of the officers killed so far had the chance to fire back, did they? But if it makes you feel better you are entitled to a .22 Starr, which you purchase yourself after you've applied to the police for a gun licence, then you do a firearms course with the police, a day-long thing. Let me know who wants to do it.'

'Ach this is a total waste of time—' Campbell began, meaning to take the floor, but Shandy spoke up.

'I'll do it. I've had enough of the shite we live with, so has the missus. If we've got that underneath the mattress we'll feel a whole lot better.'

'Can I ask a question?' said Dunn. 'Are we more likely to be followed out of here or to be staked out at home?'

'Well, the way things have gone, you're more likely to be followed. Of course they could get hold of information about where you live and that's why I say to take care.'

'How would they get our information?'

'Your next-door neighbour would give it to them,' said Skids.

'Ach, shut the fuck up will you, you miserable son of a bitch,' said Campbell. 'Not on Sandy Row they wouldn't.'

'Your records are held securely. I have your phone numbers so that I can give you a good bollocking over the phone when you're late in or pulling a sicky, but I keep my office locked for the most part. Right, lads, that's it, let's get on with it then.'

Behind him the window had darkened, the rain was falling heavily and stray raindrops had saved themselves by clinging to the windowed spaces between the bars. They too succumbed.

'Given what you say about varying our routes and the like, wouldn't it be wise to have variable shifts?' said Skids.

'Your shifts are variable Skids, you're either late or drunk. That's it for now, lads.'

'He likes to vary his women,' Frig was muttering as they filed out. 'Small tits, big arse, blonde hair, dark muff . . .'

Bolton took his glasses off and sat down, rolling his sleeves back, hands on his desk. The small oat-coloured fruit bowl was empty, with a ring around the interior as if the tide had gone out.

'What is it, Officer Dunn?'

'Nothing, Sir.'

Dunn and Shandy were assigned to tidying the stores that afternoon. There were sheets and blankets screwed up in balls, some empty bottles lying around and toilet rolls, towels and prisoner bedding all awry.

'Ah fuck,' said Shandy, holding an empty bottle. 'I remember this one.'

'You all right, Shandy?' asked Dunn, beginning to fold.

'Where we live, we only had one of the Shankill Butchers two doors down from us all the while. He was lifted in February. Our girls used to play with his, still do, and his girls are all the time around our place. They're nice girls, but it makes my skin crawl.'

'Shit.'

'I saw him today. He's on the Loyalist block that my mate Monty runs. I need to speak with him about the new year's do, because I'm doing the chocolate log for it, but there's no way in hell I'm setting foot over there.'

Dunn stopped folding.

'His girls you know, ach they're only six or seven or so. We can't think how to stop them coming across like. You try to give the kids a normal life, you know, whatever the cost. Well he makes them wee toys all the time in the workshops. Their mother's only told them that their daddy's got a job up at the prison. A doll's house he's made, and so my girls are after asking me, if Sarah and Sophie's daddy can make one of them at work, why can't you? I says, because I can't in my line of work, and they say, sure you can if their daddy can, he works where you work. So then I knew he knew I was here. That was last week. We've got a mixed street where we are. There's this fella, a Catholic, and he says to me, Harry, I moved out of Belfast to be safer and here I am living on the same street as a Shankill Butcher. It was my wife saw your man being arrested. She was stood by the window as they took him off and he pointed right at her. She's terrified in case he thinks she's the one that gave him away.'

'Shandy, calm down. What can he do to you in here?'

'Lenny Murphy got Mervyn Connor, didn't he? In '73, in the Crum, by hook or by crook. And they say the prison officers were in on it. If someone in here doesn't like me? Cyanide in my custard, ground glass in my tea, or a simple bullet on my way home.'

'Come on. What is it you normally say when there's bad news? "Deal". Let's get this done, have a game of cards and a drink or two in the bar at teatime.'

Shandy was biting at the lower knuckle of his thumb. 'The thing is, John-boy, I know too much. I know too many people. I could know something that no one wants me to know. I might not be able to help it. I mightn't even know what that thing is. But someone else might take a different view. This place is like a bloody ants' nest, everyone crawling all over each other. And I can't forget the things I do know. I wish I didn't know some of the stuff I know. I know what people can do to each other, and I don't think I could take it, John, I don't think I could take being tortured. A bullet I could take but being tortured . . .'

'Come off it, Shandy.'

'It's the kids you see. You worry.'

'Cut it out, mate.' He tried to sound friendly but he didn't feel it.

'There are some things you hear and you can't forget and they stay with you and you wish like fuck you'd never heard them or never seen them. You were in the army. You must have seen some terrible things.'

'One or two.'

'You can probably take it better than someone like me. Back in the summer of '72, there was this killing, a Catholic, name of Madden was killed by Lenny Murphy, do you remember reading about it?'

'I was in Germany then.'

'He tortured the man for hours and hours, chipping away at his skin with a knife, and a woman on Louisa Street heard a man screaming at four a.m., "Kill me! Kill me!" I think of that whenever I'm happy, like a curse. I can be in bed with the wife, knowing the kids are tucked up and safe and I think of that and it just about ruins everything.'

Dunn went back to folding with effort and speed, first shaking out, then shoving half-folded blankets further back on the shelves.

'To beg to be killed. And what if it's not me screaming? What if it's one of my kids? What if because of what I've done my own kid's screaming out to be killed?'

'There's a reason people don't talk about that shit.'

Dunn threw down the folded blanket and walked out.

47

On Christmas Eve the prisoners were given tea and a digestive biscuit each about seven. The mugs were returned empty and no biscuits with them. Lights were turned out just after midnight, as normal, and with their door slit uncovered, there was some light from the neon strips on the wing corridor ceiling. Before lights out, the prisoners had stood up at their cell doors to talk through the slits.

That night they had two smokes each; they swung the line early on. They were smoking the tobacco that had been passed to them by the orderly. The screw on duty that night was known as 'Béal Mor', or 'Big Mouth'. He was from England, he had a thick Birmingham accent, but he was not one of the worst.

For Christmas '78 an entertainment had been organized that had become legendary, with songs written and performed, and prizes for contestants. It had gone on until sun up. But 1979 had been rough. Another year had passed and the protest was more than three years old. They were much more than a year older. This Christmas the entertainments were barely considered.

When 'Béal Mor' came back on to the wing, a casual warning went up from Hughie Kearney but the lads carried on smoking. Gerard was up, offering just the one entertainment; he and Sean had written a Christmas quiz. He said it was going to be funny. There was some derisory noise-making from down the block, but for the most part apathy.

Suddenly, they heard the screw saying, 'Excuse moy gentlemen.' In his

Birmingham accent, fat with apology, rippling with nerves, he went on,
'I would like to play for you a record that I got in Belfast. It's by Pink
Floyd.'

Gerard stepped back from the door. Sean sat down on his mattress.

48

Kathleen went up The Fiddlers on Christmas Eve while Mrs O'Sullivan watched the kids. She was going to meet Collette Heaney there. It had occurred to her that there was every chance Brendan would be there that night. She'd mascara'd her eyes.

She remembered how they'd ended up laying on the dirt in a small clearing out near Long Kesh, his head on her shoulder, his cock beating inside of her. 'Don't go falling in love with me,' he'd said.

If she felt the beggar when he said these things, it was her fault. She should do the right thing, and finish it with him. He reminded her of who she wasn't.

Nevertheless, she was walking up to the pub with him in mind.

'I'll have to drop you up by Lenadoon and you can get a cab from there,' he'd said, pulling his trousers up as he stood. 'I can't take the chance of being seen . . .'

'That's fine.' Hands trying to make sense of her tights.

Driving back, few words had passed between them. As she went to get out of the car, he'd said, 'Kathleen. It wasn't just about the sex.'

'Now why did you have to go and say that?'

Every time after being with Brendan, she was miserable. There was a reason adultery was forbidden, that it was a mortal sin akin to suicide; it killed you from the inside out. She'd been feeding something that ought not to grow and now she had to smother it.

When she'd stepped out, Mrs O'Sullivan had been reading to the children. If it was her there she'd have had the TV on and be telling them to be quiet, wishing them away.

She walked into The Fiddlers and saw that it was all men at the bar and she stood, a little awkward, and then when the widest man of the group turned round and opened a space at the bar to which he invited her, she smiled formally.

'Me-eeh, ee-eh, and missus, missus Mo-ran . . . We got a thing going on . . .'

'Hey Sean, it's your other red-head,' called out Flinty at the optic.

Sean came across. 'Well hello, young lady,' and his breath was as rich as Christmas itself for he'd been on the brandy.

'Jesus, Mary and Joseph. I'll have a glass of Martini and lemonade.'

There was a chorus of exaggerated approval and some mimicry.

'Oh fuck way with yous,' she said, putting a pack of cigarettes on the bar and causing laughter.

'Mr O'Hanlon here is just after saying goodbye to his dearly departed mother-in-law.'

'God rest her soul, I'm sorry for your sadness,' said Kathleen, raising her glass.

'What a wasted life,' said O'Hanlon.

'Och, shame. Did she suffer long?'

'Did she fuck. It's mine I'm talking about. When I see a fine-looking woman like yourself, I can't help thinking what a waste to have spent my youth and looks on one woman. Wasn't I Paddy the lad when I lived over in New York with my cousin, going with every girl, Italians, Costa Ricans, Jews – you name it, they were all after my Irish eyes . . .' A laugh went up. 'Back in the fifties there, when I was no more than a lad. Though I did have—'

'Ladies present!' shouted Flinty.

'And my fiancée back in Belfast, my Margaret, she wrote me a letter saying, You must come home and we'll get married for my poor mother is dying and it's her dearest wish. And I come back and the old cow's abed, back on Kashmir Street, and we got married and I moved in with them and that, as they say, was the beginning of the end. Last week the old baggage passes on at last, after twenty years in bed giving orders. Oh, but she could hop up to get herself a wee drink when she thought yous weren't there! Teeth in a glass and "Oh I heard the most terrible noises in the night, thought yous were killing each other, what was it yous were after doing?" Seventy-nine. And good riddance! Now I can start living.'

There was a toast. 'To Fergal's new life . . .!'

'Now I never went with an Italian girl myself,' said Sean, leaning on the bar. 'After I met this lady here I had eyes for nobody else—' the men turned to look at Kathleen. 'But I spent some time in Italy.'

Kathleen knew the story that was coming. 'I'll have another drink.'

She looked across at the mirror over the bar. She saw Collette and her husband coming across talking to people. In the corner she saw Brendan Coogan, rising from amidst a group, getting up to come to the bar.

'Is your Dominic all set for doing the Santa then tonight?' she asked Fergal. He nodded.

Her husband cleared his throat exaggeratedly in her direction. 'As I was saying, I says to your man, pointing at the wee wedding day photo, there's me, and he has a good look at it, and he gives me this look.' Sean nodded with his lower lip jutting and his eyes wide. The group laughed. 'Bella, he says, beautiful it means. He's talking about her, there, the wife. And he brings out a gun, a Luger. I says how much, and he says four pound. I says I'll take eight . . .'

Brendan Coogan was standing next to her.

'Hello Mr Moran.'

'Oh Brendan,' Sean smiled. 'What about ye? Bearing up?'

'I am, thank you.'

'And my lad's all right? Keeping in touch with you is he?'

'He's sound, as far as I know.'

'Let me buy you a wee drink there.'

Coogan shook his head, but Sean insisted.

'A whiskey then,' said Coogan. 'Hello Mrs Moran, how are you doing?'

'Not so bad thank you, Brendan.' Kathleen stood down from the stool. 'Excuse me a minute. I'll come and have a word with you about our Sean if you're stopping a while.'

She went off to the Ladies where she looked again in the mirror and wiped the traces of smudged mascara from under her eyes with toilet paper.

When she came out, Brendan was at the side of the young group he was with. His eyes were quiet and dark as he watched her approach and he set down his beer. She took the chair next to him. The group looked at her briefly and went back to their discussion. He bent his head forwards so that it was next to hers.

'I've been thinking about how I could get to see your breasts in the daylight again.' He took a cigarette from his friend's pack and offered it to her. He lit it, then passed it over, exhaling smoke out of the corner of his mouth.

'You were right the other day though. I've been thinking about it, Brendan, we can't go on.'

'One more time.'

'No. I just can't, Brendan.'

'Ah come on now, don't look so sad and so serious.' He nudged her elbow with his own and handed her his pint to sip from. As she drew the foam across the top of the liquid, she caught the eye of one of the crowd he was with, an older man from Andytown, and smiled. 'Aye, that's a nice pint, I've never tasted that before.' Then she leant forwards and said to him, 'Your mother asked me if you'd helped me out you know.'

'Jesus,' he cracked a smile and brushed a hand against her knee under the table.

'It won't be long before people get to know.' She half rose on her seat, gave a curt wave to Sean and Collette and prepared to leave.

'Sit a bit longer,' he said, staying her knee with his hand. 'Are you all right, Kathleen?'

'How do you mean?'

'Look, I'll keep an eye out for your Sean.'

She stubbed out her cigarette, glanced at the man opposite who was speaking to the woman alongside him with his eyes all the while on Kathleen.

'Aye,' she exhaled smoke. 'Well just don't let him die if you can help it. I've got to go now.'

The chair scraped, making a painful sound, and she went across the wooden floor towards the bar where Sean was letting Guinness run over the sides of a pint glass, looking at her.

The bar door burst open and Dominic O'Hanlon fell through, a garland of dirty cotton wool over his eyes and one round his neck, a beer-splashed red jacket, red trousers and a gnomish hat on his head. Two men close to the door moved to hold him up.

'A glass of Guinness for Rudolph! If you'd be so kind there. And a gasper for Bouncer if you've one to spare.'

49

Loud and angry discordant guitar-strokes squashed the quiet verse of the traditional folk music. An impresario singer offered, with sarcasm, 'a show'. Music rolled and broke in waves. There was the sound of a plane plummeting out of control and then silence, followed by the crying of a newborn.

> *'Mama loves her baby,*
> *And Daddy loves you too*
> *And the sea may look warm to you babe*
> *And the sky may look blue'*

The anger of the drum and guitar took the harmony away again, dashing it to the rocks. A new beat, watchful and constant, emerged; a hospital monitor interspersed with a guitar riff glimmering like sudden rays of sunshine. A whispering voice was singing a warning:

> *'Daddy's flown across the ocean*
> *Leaving just a memory*
> *A snapshot in the family album'*

The music took its time, moving at the pace of a heartbeat, creating tension,

> *'All in all it was just a brick in the wall'*

Then came the sound of helicopter blades turning, the roaring of a military man, followed by cymbals being struck like physical blows. The evils of the teacher.

Gerard was shaking his head at Sean, as if at a great distance, shocked. Before he could say anything an anthem struck up like a protest march. It sounded like the modern age. It was the sound of conviction. Sean felt the adrenalin of right and wrong surge within him.

> *'We don't need no education*
> *We don't need no thought control*
> *No dark sarcasm in the classroom'*

The song seemed to be advancing the perfect cause, overturning the wrong laws, and when the children sang in unison they conveyed certainty and loyalty, love and survival. Guitar riffs soared, one after the other.

There were playground sounds. Sean closed his eyes and laid back; a dream was being piped into his head, ready made. He thought of being about five or six at school. Then came to his mind an image of a baby with his mouth at a nipple, resolute and sucking, adhering to its mother. Like baby Liam. Then, out of nowhere, someone took the baby away, shook it, smacked it so that it screamed then handed it back, and the baby stopped its crying gradually and went back to sucking, albeit with occasional shudders. He remembered the water bucket at Castlereagh, held by the neck in the water until his eyes flooded with darkness and then his head was pulled out and each time he was on the brink of unconsciousness.

After the playground came the sound of a shouting-schoolmaster, a man with a voice the sound of failure; thin and hysterical. Then came the ringing of a phone. It stopped. A man exhaled.

> *'Mother do you think they'll drop the bomb*
> *Mother do you think they'll like this song*
> *Mother do you think they'll try to break my balls*
> *Mother should I build the wall'*

The voice was clear, it had a lilt to it. He and Gerard exchanged looks. Gerard grinned.

'Béal Mor's lost his mind. This isn't in the rule book.'

'It's great.'

'The words, Seany! The words!'

> *'Mother will they put me in the firing line?*
> *Is it just a waste of time?'*

The music moved off and away, travelling on a railroad of guitar chords. They were tapping out the beat with the palms of their hands on their thighs.

How was it for the others after years in here, with no sky, no animals, no children, no women, no sounds beyond the banging of doors, to hear suddenly all the sounds of the world articulated with a crazy passion, as if a dying man was struggling for his last best memories?

After a bird-song came the voice of a boy pointing out an airplane and then male voices harmonizing in reverence to the blue sky. It was like a swoon. It touched his heart and he was afraid.

The music was halted by the sound of a hammer on a dull metal surface. He thought of the Belfast shipyards, saw the cranes. A man intoned despair and then the mood was broken again by rock and roll.

Gerard's head nodded fast to it, like a young man at a concert.

> *'Ooooh I need a dirty woman*
> *Ooooh I need a dirty girl'*

Sean burst out laughing. Gerard laughed as well.

'She'd have to be a dirty woman, in here!' he shouted, his hands cupping his mouth.

The phone rang and this time it was answered. It was a movie within a movie, an American woman moving about, an old British film playing in the background. What did it mean? Could he trust the music?

'Day after day, love turns grey
Like the skin on a dying man'

The pure, absurd joy of rock and roll surged forth again and he leapt up, he couldn't help himself, and with his blanket round his waist he jumped about and Gerard with him. There was shouting and smashing in the music and they charged about their cell like hooligans.

When the music changed again, they stood still. It was slowing to almost nothing with just the sounds of breathing, a woman in deep sleep.

'Listen,' said Gerard.

'Did you ever hear *The Dark Side of the Moon*? That's Pink Floyd as well. They're the best band in the world.'

'They are!'

They stood side by side, nodding in the direction of the door from where the sound came. There was the noise of doors and windows being broken in, breaking glass and a reprise of the earlier anthem.

'I don't need no arms around me
And I don't need no drugs to calm me
I have seen the writing on the wall
Don't think I need any thing at all
No, don't think I need anything at all
All in all it was all just the bricks in the wall
All in all you were all just bricks in the wall'

The men started to move, but the music stopped.

Without warning the singer issued his 'Goodbye' and the sound was gone, as if a door had been shut.

Silence like a knife.

'Well, lads, I'll give you part two next time. Goodnight.' And he turned the lights out.

Sean and Gerard sat down in the dark. There was some distant low light from a watch-tower and soon, when their eyes got used to the dark, they could see the shape of each other.

'I've never heard anything like it,' said Gerard. 'Imagine if we were doing stuff like that.'

'We ought to get them in the 'Ra.'

'That's what I should have been doing,' Gerard went on. 'Music. They took me away, a teacher who'd never killed a person, and I'll get back home, one day, and be something else. God knows what.'

'Listen, Gerard, we're prisoners of war. We've got what we believe in and no one can take it away from us.'

O'Malley called out 'Merry Christmas' in Irish, and Sean and Gerard called back.

'They can't make me a criminal, no matter what they do to me, but what will they make of my two boys? You're best off if you can be like your man Seamus there, just having your one life, on the inside. It's easier.'

'Why don't they talk to each other, Seamus and Seamus?'

'It's like a bad marriage. They fell out a year ago, and haven't spoken since.'

'Jesus. If I piss you off, you'll tell me, right?'

'That music was really something. I might have some dreams tonight. My feet are like fucking ice blocks. Goodnight, Seany.'

'Goodnight.'

His mattress was short. He'd ripped off about a quarter of it in the last couple of months to smear the walls with. He had two blankets but the floor was cold and his mattress was damp. After a while you went numb and then you could sleep. He could hear a man here or there talking, and from further along the sounds of snoring.

He thought about how the music travelled so far and wide. He had thought of his mother, his brother, his family, his community and he had felt anger and excitement, melancholy too. How powerful music was. Even though life was so barren there, he sometimes felt as if he was just now waking up to the world. He thought of the little boy seeing the plane, how man had brought things that were once mysterious down to size. A sky might have been infinite, a lake might have been a sea, before. Now you looked at them knowing they had borders. Why do people want to kill the magic, he wondered, and give answers to things that shouldn't be understood. He'd told Father Pearse he was hanging on to his faith.

'Good,' the priest had replied. 'Because in a hellhole created by man, you need God's mystery.'

'Ooooh I need a dirty woman . . .'

The refrain came back to him. He had air to breathe, food to eat and water to drink but there was a fourth hunger. He thought of Nancy Costello and her words as she left. Maybe she was thinking of him that night. He had an erection. He put his hand down between his legs.

He could hear that Gerard was asleep. He thought about Nancy with her sharp eyes and soft lips. He thought of undressing her.

There were footsteps as the screw walked past to push the button on the wall.

He had an image of her with her hands raised, letting him pull her top over her head, the hair caught for a moment then falling on to her naked shoulders. He would move his eyes from her face to her breasts. He would put his hands on them and kiss her neck and then he would lay her down and let her enjoy his need. He lay awake for some time, the music in his mind, wondering what it was like to have sex with a woman.

50

'What lovely children you have. Little treasures. Now you have a good day tomorrow.' She wished a Merry Christmas to Mrs O'Sullivan.

Kathleen was finishing wrapping the last of the presents in the sitting room when her husband came in the door, giving his exaggerated rendition of a sober man. He knocked into the stairs and the coats there fell down to the ground in surrender, one after the other.

'Ah shites,' he said with a hiss.

'There y'are, drunk as ever, even at Christmas. But sure why should it be different from any other day,' she said, tape a forefinger, holding two sides of wrapping paper together.

'Here I am. Father fucking Christmas.'

'Shush.' She glanced up at the ceiling.

'You think that two kids living in West Belfast believe in Santa Claus, do you?'

'Och shut up. Just shut up. Who cares what you think?'

'Aye, who cares what I think. Not you, that's for real. You're being straight with me now for once.'

'Aye, well not everyone can be the honest man that you are.' She stuck the tag on the present, checked there was a message on the back and read it out: 'Dear Liam, Happy Christmas 1979, love Mum and Dad. I love you.' She underlined it twice. 'The presents are done. Can you please put them in your children's room?'

He went to the fridge and emerged with a whole piece of cheese that he gnawed at. He put it down on the mantelpiece. He stood before her, his legs apart, one eye closed, a finger pointing as if he were about to make a great speech.

'Aye,' was all he said, then he picked up the cheese and put it on top of the small stack of presents and went upstairs, barging into the railing with every step. She heard him sit. She knew he'd fall asleep so she ran up after him. He was undressing, sitting down. It took him a long time that way. She stood there looking at him, with his thinning hair, his beer gut and his hopeless hands failing at each task they came to, going twice at each button, three times to one of his socks.

'What?' he said, looking at her. When he was naked he stood up, took the presents in his arms and went into the children's room.

'Mother of fucking God!'

The light went on and as Kathleen ran in she saw her two children, frowning, startled and disgruntled, looking at their father's naked arse as he turned around and bent down to retrieve the presents. He'd stepped on a hairbrush.

'Och, that's wonderful,' said Kathleen. 'That's really magical, Sean.'

'You all right, Dad,' said Liam.

Aine sat up, startled.

'Sorry the pair of you,' said their father, picking up his piece of cheese last of all.

51

It was Christmas Day. Frig, Shandy and Dunn set off to Clean Jim's Christmas party. Shandy had tinsel round his cap and was in high spirits. Frig smelt of aftershave. Dunn was feeling down. It was the last place he wanted to be. The three of them went up to the 'terrapins', the pre-fab huts that housed their lockers, to pick up a bottle of whiskey.

'We could use a sharpener,' said Frig.

They made their way along the corridor between rows of tall grey metal lockers, each with an officer's tally number. Many had been personalized with stickers, graffiti, cuttings from newspapers. Three officers were standing having a drink, smoking and laughing. One of them asked Frig if they'd like to take a half 'un, and produced three short glasses. Inside his locker was a row of optics with four bottles inverted over them.

'Your health,' said the stocky man whose locker bar it was, and they clinked glasses.

'Are you lot on the dirt blocks?' asked another, who was tall and bald.

'Aye,' said Shandy, taking a swallow. 'Ah!'

'Don't envy you. Jesus, I don't know how you fellas stick it. Doesn't it get to you, the smell?'

'He doesn't normally wear it. It's just because it's Christmas.'

'Brut 69, "*Splash it all over*".'

'You're better off on a protest block than on a regular block, mate,' said Frig. 'We have the streakers locked up all day, it's easy street.'

'We're on a Loyalist block,' said the stocky man. He had a lazy eye.

His glass was empty and smeared; he showed it to his friend who refilled it. 'It's fucking nerve-racking, so it is. You never know when they're going to have you.'

The third man was short, his teeth brown and broken looking. He was nervy like a pony. 'Young fellas, tattoos, no brains. You'd feel sorry for them if they weren't such fucking arseholes.'

'We see some things would make your blood run cold,' said the tall baldy.

'I don't doubt it,' said Shandy.

'We got that Shankill Butcher man on our block,' said the short one. 'No one fucks with him.'

Shandy drained his glass.

The tall man raised his glass, his lips shiny. 'That's a good colour. It's a Shirley Bassey isn't it, Ricky?'

The short man showed them the label. Blackbush. They laughed.

'Are we going to this knees up?' asked Dunn.

'Yeah, we should go lads,' said Frig. 'Knees up at Clean Jim's, fancy coming fellas?'

They shrugged. Their glasses were full.

The three from the dirt block thanked the others for the drink and put their glasses one by one, side by side, on top of the locker; bang, bang, bang.

'Never seen such an ugly bunch of bastards in my life,' said Shandy as they went out through the back of the hut into the grey light and across the dead ground. 'Nice drop though.'

Jim was a stickler for cleanliness and served what some said was the best Guinness in Northern Ireland. Dirty Sam's had none of those attributes but like the Naafi, the Army Dog section and some of the soldiers' bars it was open at lunchtime and it served beer so it had a clientele. The sergeants' mess served spirits but Clean Jim's was still the preference for a knees up. Jim was a hard nut who ran a tight ship.

It was packed. There was some good craic going on. Atop the main table, three officers were hamming it up to the Nolan Sisters' 'I'm in the mood for dancing'. They made staccato, pseudo-female movements, edging and jabbing in triple tandem. They had bar-cloths on their heads and balled-up in their top pockets to produce breasts.

Jim's concession to the spirit of Christmas was a few paper chains over the bar, taped up, sagging. Two officers had rolled up their sleeves and piled in behind the bar to help pour beers. One of them had tinsel round his head. There was a long row of Guinness pints waiting for a second filling, going from milk to coal in their own time, the ashtrays were scarred and scuffed but Jim kept at them, banging them down on the rubbish bin behind the bar.

As ever it was Shandy that pushed through to the bar, Dunn and Frig handing him a pound note each.

Frig pointed out a friend of his who was smoking a cigar in a booze haze at the bar, jacket off, being supported by another officer.

'That fella, Morris Minor we call him, we worked on a regular block together last year. He used to be in the army like you did.' Frig's hair was flattened from his cap. He and Dunn went over. 'All right, Morris?'

'Frig, *moite*!'

Frig introduced 'Johnno' as a new boy.

Morris indicated the round grey telephone with its dark receiver. 'I'm waiting for the call from the hospital. Jim's set it up for switchboard to call through here. My hands are sweaty, my mouth's dry.' His ginger-haired friend handed him a drink. 'It's my first kid.'

Shandy came over with a tray of six pints. The three of them touched glasses and offered their congratulations to the two men waiting for the call.

When the phone rang, Jim cut the music and screamed, 'QUI-ET!' He passed the receiver to the man, who applied himself to listening as if following a broadcast.

'Aye, aye. You what? You what? You fucking what?'

'What is it, boy or a girl?'

'It's a little . . . black . . . boy. Black . . .'

Shandy spat a mouthful of beer on to the bar and attempted to convert his reaction to coughing.

'Oy, where's that Sambo?' shouted Jim.

A black officer waved his hand from a booth. 'Hey, don't look at me, pal,' he called out, in a London accent. 'I wasn't even in the place nine months ago! For fuck's sake.'

'Have you got any nig-nog in the family, Morris?' Jim was leaning across the bar.

Morris put the receiver back to his ear. A look of understanding spread to his eyes. 'You bastards. That was Shagger Martin on the switchboard! I knew I'd heard that voice before! Putting on an English voice! Very funny lads, very funny.'

They weren't such a bad crowd, Dunn thought, there was some craic at least, like in the army. It was always low quality when you had a lot of working-class blokes together from all over the shop and all you had in common was your colour and your dick.

He caught the eye of the black officer across the bar and gave him a small smile.

What would his son think if he could see them now? He was going to start putting money into an account for his son from the new year and give the boy something that would help him get himself off the ground. He knew the boy, because he knew himself. What he didn't know about the boy, he cribbed from memories of his own childhood, cobbling together a pastiche of days filled with small things: fixing the broken wireless, polishing shoes, wiping up the dishes, putting conkers in a tobacco tin, daydreams and games, tall tales and outright lies. And then he went beyond what he knew of himself too and imagined how the boy must have gone to his books, with all the virtues in them standing in for an absent father. He decided he would tell the others about his son.

'Look who it is,' said Shandy, elbowing Dunn's arm so that his Guinness lurched over the rim.

'Ho, ho, ho,' said Frig.

Carl Lingard came into the bar, giving short, static salutes of recognition, which were not returned. By now, what he was supposed to have said to Coogan had been greatly exaggerated, and whatever he really said, unimportant.

'What's he come in here for?' Jim said.

Officers moved apart as Lingard walked through, put their backs to him. A couple of men made it deliberately difficult for him to pass, each presenting his back as a rock. Lingard, sallow, salt-and-treacle hair, squeezed through. Dunn wished he wouldn't press on, wished the man would go back. Seeing Dunn's look, Lingard smiled the sweet smile of hope.

'Hello John, quick lunchtime drink is it?'

Dunn nodded, the bar was almost silent.

'Well, that's a bloody good idea. Can't stop but just popped in to wish you and the lads the best. The Willard thing. It's awful isn't it. Man with a family.'

There was a murmur and talk resumed. Jim put on another record.

> *'Everyone considered him the coward of the county*
> *He'd never stood one single time to prove the county wrong*
> *His mama named him Tommy, but folks just called him "yellow"'*

There was derisive laughter. Under the cover of the music, Lingard was up close to Dunn speaking to him in urgent tones, looking scantily about himself.

'My car's been scratched all down the side. I had a tyre let down last night. I'm wondering if it's got out that I saw Coogan. Did you let it slip?'

'No.'

'Well then I can't think—' Lingard put a hand into the solid mat of his hair.

'A fella saw you with him.'

'Oh my giddy aunt.'

'It's pretty much common knowledge what you said. About the prison officers being cannon-fodder. The men think you've sold them out, that you're dealing with the IRA, swapping their lives for points.'

'What rubbish.'

'Well, that's what they've heard.'

'Well there's only me and Coogan who knows what was said. You don't think that Coogan's told his—'

'It was the Provie prisoners on our block who let on what was said, Carl. Look, what with the killings going on right now and you giving the Provies the go-ahead, from the men's point of view, you've cooked your goose.'

'Bugger.' Lingard passed a hand through his hair again and looked around. The prison officers were watching, some discreetly, many blatantly, and some belligerently. 'Bugger. Well, look John, you must just put the word round that it wasn't meant that way. Not at all. I'm trying to stop more men getting killed. It's precisely the reverse. You tell them that!'

Dunn looked at his colleagues. Frig and Shandy were standing by listening, Frig embarrassed to be so close, Shandy with a look of overt hatred.

'They won't buy it. I can't do it.'

'Oh I see, Dunn.' Lingard looked stricken. 'You've gone over! I thought you were a man apart. No, quite. I see, fine.' He raised his voice again. 'I am on your side.' He chanced upon a new recruit. 'I'm on your side.'

The men either side of the new officer started prodding him and laughing.

There was nothing Dunn could say. When he looked at Lingard he saw the gnome inside of both of them, changing hats and fishing rods. He turned his back to him, went for his glass.

As the others closed in around him, Dunn glanced over his shoulder to see Lingard make his way falteringly out of the bar, jostled all the way.

The song drew to its conclusion, the officers shouting the words, drunk with sincerity:

> 'I promised you Dad not to do the things you done
> I'll walk away from trouble when I can
> Now, please don't think I'm weak
> I didn't turn the other cheek
> And Papa I sure hope you understand,
> Sometimes you gotta fight when you're a man!'

52

'The main thing is not to think about Sean today. Or maybe it's to think of him but not talk of him because we'll all be getting ourselves upset.'

'Aye,' said Aine, banging her peeler on the side of the plastic basin, then using it to take her hair away from her mouth.

'Will I go and get Daddy from the pub?' Liam came into the kitchen with his coat on.

Kathleen looked at the clock; it was just after twelve. 'Wait until one, love. We're not eating until two when Father Pearse gets here and I don't want your daddy in the house bothering me when I'm cooking.'

Liam went out and sat on the slope of scrub grass.

'What's with him? Did he not like his presents?'

Aine went to the window and squashed her nose against it. 'He misses Sean and Mary. Like me.'

'Finish these and pop them in that pan there.' Kathleen took her cardigan from the back of the chair, put it round her shoulders and went outside, banging the door two or three times before she saw her cardigan was caught in it. Liam was looking at her.

'He'll not be coming in that way. Not this year, love.'

'I'm not thinking about Sean.'

'Then why have you got a beak like that on you?'

'I'm wondering why we're all bothering with all of this stuff about Christmas. Nobody wants it but nobody'll say as much. We just have to do it. It's stupid so it is.'

'Aye, well I know how you feel.'

'It was always the four of us kids, Christmas was, and Sean and Daddy playing the fool. Remember how I had a loose tooth and they said, let us take your tooth out for you Liam and we'll give you five bob. Then they tied it and slammed the door and it hurt like hell and they said good lad and never gave me the five bob. The bastards.'

Kathleen looked up at the back window. Wee house, little piece of nothing, and everything inside it worth no more than a few quid. She smiled. 'They were a pair of eejits together.'

'Everyone's gone now.' He got up and went off out the side of the garden, heading up towards The Fiddlers.

53

They were going to wait to have their Christmas dinner in the evening when John Dunn got home. He was going to call the boy's mother in the evening, put him on to her. He hoped to hear the boy tell her how happy he was to have his father at last. He wondered what it was about him that made her decide he was no good for Mark. She'd only known him five minutes. He thought of her face again, as he drove off.

He kept his head down in the afternoon, did his time, did what was required. The other officers loafed around the mess with their feet up. Shandy brought out a successful Christmas cake. He offered each of them a small whiskey to go with a slice.

'Six weeks I've been dripping booze into the cake with a needle. You know, first you make the hole, then you pour it in after, wasting a load of it and then this great Charlie here tells me he could have given me a syringe and made the job easier.' He aimed a thumb at the medical officer who was smiling, eating.

Skids came in and waved a no at the cake, unbuttoned his jacket, his face flushed. He put his hands through his hair. He'd just come back from one of the bars.

'You won't fucking believe this. Lingard's had the shit beaten out of him on the Loyalist block. He's been taken off to the hospital.'

Shandy put down his cake and stopped chewing. The medical officer said something or other, no one cared. Campbell came up behind and put his hands on the back of Shandy's chair.

'You're joking me,' he said, his eyes glittering.

'He goes round both the Loyalist and the Provie blocks to say his piece, you know how he is, well the Loyalists were having a wee Christmas do in the recreation room and Lingard goes in and the doors close behind him and all hell breaks loose. When they opened the doors again he was lying on the floor, at the back of the room.'

'Is he bad?' asked Dunn.

'Aye. He was in there a good ten minutes the lads are saying. Broken ribs, and he got a good kicking in the head as well they said. Nearly took his eye out. He was unconscious when they took him off.'

'Well, well, well,' said Campbell. 'It was bound to happen. He was asking for it.'

'I wouldn't have fancied his odds,' said Skids. 'In there with forty cons – and a vicar.'

Shandy was carefully wiping the crumbs off the table with his hand and helping them to drop on to his small white plate. He got up to arrange the cake back in the tin. 'They could get themselves in trouble for shutting him in there like that.'

'You think he was shut in? On purpose?' asked Dunn.

'Catch yourself on, John-boy,' said Campbell. 'We're not going to bend over and take it up the arse.'

'The man didn't stand a chance. Bloody cowards.'

'And what the fuck are they out there?' said Campbell, pointing at the wing.

He was leaving the prison for the first time at five o' clock. He'd left in the dark of the morning, driving as usual with his shoulders hunched, his head forward, foot to the floor. Christmas Day. Now he left in the dark of the night, wipers on. Gravel span as he exited the compound and pulled on to the by-road. He wondered what his son was like at Christmastime as a boy and who it was that took his first bike out into the street and set him on the saddle.

54

When Liam got to The Fiddlers, his father told him to sit at the side of the bar and wait for him. Brian was there helping out so that Sean could get home for his dinner, but he wanted to have a drink with Flinty and the boys first.

Liam was handed a Coke and some crisps and given a wink. His father had his arm around one of the men.

He looked around for his son, then he looked around again as if he had forgotten what he'd seen the first time. He nodded.

'Won't be long, Liam,' and then he went on confidentially to the three men alongside him. 'She's been awful cold with me, och for years now, years, then she was out the other night, God knows where.'

Flinty looked across at the boy and then at the father and put his finger to his lips.

Brian was sipping on a half'un, looking thoughtful. 'Ach that's terrible for you, Sean, to have them dark thoughts and not to know the truth. I'm not married, thank the Lord, but if I was I think I'd have it out with her. You can't go on as y'are in this terrible pain of not knowing.'

Flinty nodded. 'There might not be any truth to it, Sean. Or if there is, it might not be as bad as you think.'

'What do you mean?'

'Well, it might just be harmless fun.'

'With your man Coogan?' said Brian.

'What do you mean?'

The other man, on whom Sean had been leaning, finished his drink and said, 'She wouldn't be the first. Still, when you think of those as have got their fellas inside and wouldn't so much as look at another man . . . Take my advice Sean, have it out with her, but not today.' He looked over at Liam.

'Would you like a wee chocolate bar there?' said Flinty, his pointy teeth showing.

Liam stood up. 'Come on, Dad. We've to be home for our Christmas dinner.'

Sean's lip curled. 'Aye, you're your mother's boy, so you are, come to bring me back like I'm a dog.'

Liam's cheeks burnt. 'Come on, Dad.'

'Go on,' said Brian. 'Go on home Sean.' And the other men joined in with him.

'Go on, Sean, go on.'

55

John Dunn made a deal with himself that he would drop it, bit by bit, on the way home, and he had an image in his head of the motorway behind him strewn with the furniture of the place, a chair or desk upturned, the water boiler, dented and dripping, the metal lockers on their sides, and all the chits and forms in carbon duplicate, blown by the wind on to the windscreens of oncoming cars and then finally, the great bunch of keys, jettisoned. Keys to nothing. By the time he arrived in East Belfast he was a free man.

He turned off the engine. Christmas Day, 1979. Lingard, possibly dead or dying, his wife at home with the turkey over-cooked, calling her friends for a lift to the hospital, doing everything in the wrong order.

He looked out at his two-up, two-down house, hanging on to the neighbours on one side. A semi in East Belfast. They were waiting for him in there. *'Promise me son not to do the things I done.'* What had Lingard said? *'You've gone over.'*

John Dunn had his forefingers at the bridge of his nose, pressing the corners of his eyes, his wrists wet. He was looking at his house, at the light coming from the front room. He wiped his hands on his trousers, dried his face with the backs of his sleeves. 'I hope everything's all right,' he said to himself, a squirrel of fear turning in his stomach as he put his key in the lock.

'Hello Santa, have you brought me something special?' said Angie, giving him a long kiss at the door. She smelt of booze and fags and a heavy perfume. He held her away from him to look at her. Her hair was up in pins. She was red-faced and her eyes were drooping a little at the sides. 'You're on time for once.'

'You've been at the sherry.' He put his hand on her bum and pulled her to him for another kiss.

'Oh aye. I'm feeling a wee bit loose, so I am.'

From the kitchen he could hear the radio and Nat King Cole, chestnuts roasting . . .

His son came out of the kitchen with a glass of beer, watching them dance together, his father with his arse jutting out, his knees bent, gracelessly moving with Angie between the two walls of the hallway.

'Merry Christmas. I get my sense of rhythm from you, clearly.'

His father wheeled Angie round, kept her in the crook of his left arm, stretching out his other arm to touch Mark's shoulder and he guided them both into the kitchen, joining in with Nat King Cole, in a false baritone.

On the table he saw that there were three settings, a small vase with a red rose in it and mismatching, cracked-handled knives and forks. There was a paper table-cloth with hundreds of fat-bottomed Santas capering up the sides.

'*Merry Christmas – to you.*'

Two filled glasses of beer were on the table. There was a gravy boat with gravy oozing out of its beak. On the kitchen counter sat Pyrex dishes covered with upside-down dinner plates.

'Oh my bloody Brussels sprouts,' said Angie, running to the cooker. She turned off the gas and took the steaming saucepan to the sink and drained it. Steam gushed up all around her and a farty vegetable smell filled the room.

'All right Mark,' said John, taking up a beer. 'Good health, son.'

'Cheers. And thanks. To both of you. I can't believe you've bought me a Walkman.'

'Angie, you gave him the coat and tapes . . . ?'

'Aye, John, I did. As per instructions.'

'It was too much.'

'We're glad you like them,' said Angie, popping a small piece of stuffing into her mouth.

She had taken the tin foil off the turkey. John rolled up his sleeves and stepped forward.

'*Now* I'm home.'

Mark went out of the room and came back with two wrapped presents, which he put beside each of their place settings. He sat at his place while Angie ladled and forked and turned this way and that to get the plates filled. She switched off the radio, leaving a shred of turkey meat on the dial.

John was swaying from the waist as he carved, repeating in a comic operatic voice, '*Merr-rry Christmas to – you!*'

Mark had to move the gifts a little as she set the plates down. 'Oh you shouldn't have love,' said Angie, picking hers up. She opened it.

'What did you give her, Dad?'

'She's a lucky woman, got me, doesn't need presents.'

'Tight bastard,' said Angie, fondly. 'Well he's got me the car though.' Taking off the wrapping she saw that there was a pale box with French perfume inside. 'It must have cost a fortune, Mark.'

'Is it all right?'

She got up and leant over to kiss him, trailing the end of her long beads in her gravy.

'Dad,' Mark said, grinning, nodding at the present in front of John.

'I'm not good at presents. You open it.' He handed it to Angie.

'No John. It's for you.'

'Let's eat first.'

'Open it,' insisted Angie, giving him a kick under the table.

He took it in his hands, starting to unwrap it. Inside was a long thin box. It was a jewellery box. He fumbled for a while, trying to click it open, his face lengthening. Angie helped him. He took out of the box a navy blue, leather-strapped watch.

'It was my grandfather's. It's an Omega from just after the war. I had a new strap put on it.'

'I don't wear watches.'

'You do now,' protested Angie. 'It's a lovely present. So special.'

'Right, you'd best keep it though.' He passed it back to the boy.

'It's for you.'

'It's too much.'

They looked at each other, then Mark got up and walked out of the room. They heard the stairs rattle and shiver.

'John, please tell me why you can't say thank you to the lad?'

'Let's just eat.'

'Not without him.'

'Fine.' John pushed his plate aside. 'I'm going to take a walk. It's too stuffy in here.'

Angie stood up, lit a cigarette and stared out of the back window. 'What do I see in him?' she said to herself, cheek at the cold glass.

56

The turkey was sitting steaming, surrounded by roast potatoes, the vegetables were covered. Kathleen had put the small table from the kitchen in the front room, covered it with a cloth and laid out five places with crackers. She was watching the *Top of the Pops* Christmas show. Aine was on the floor and Father Pearse was sat with a small glass of the beer he'd brought with him. When Liam and his father came in, Kathleen asked Aine to turn off the TV. They all sat at the table. Sean was too much on the one side of his chair, arms hanging, chin loose.

Father Pearse carved and Liam served them all a glass of lemonade. Sean asked for a beer.

'It's a fine bird,' said the priest.

'Ach, I've forgotten the gravy,' said Kathleen, getting up. 'Pull the crackers or something.'

'And a beer for your husband while you're out there.'

Aine offered one end of her cracker to Liam and he held it with limp disdain.

The father served the turkey around, starting with Sean.

'Get started,' called Kathleen from the kitchen.

'Go on then,' said the father. 'Do as your mother says,' and he uncovered the vegetables and served the potatoes too. Sean gave him a long stare.

'Shall I serve you, Sean, or will you do it yourself?'

Sean got up with a grunt and went to the kitchen. Father Pearse shrugged, sat down and offered his cracker to Aine.

Kathleen had the kettle on the boil and some gravy granules in a bowl. The kitchen was steamy; her hair was damp and her apron messy.

'I'll be there in a minute.'

He was looking at her. She looked up and saw that he seemed to be moving in and out of himself. His cheeks inflated with a suppressed burp. She shook her head.

'I didn't know the priest was coming to dinner.'

'Well it's a nice surprise then.'

'Are you *having* him, as well?'

Her back stiffened. 'No, just the turkey. Keep your voice down.'

'They're all talking about you down the pub. Do you know that? Are both of those children mine?'

She carried on stirring. 'Voice down.'

'I want to know. How many men have there been?'

'Och get out of my way.' She went to the kettle for more water.

He grabbed her upper arm. 'Is Aine mine?'

'Ah, now you see there's only me who knows that for sure.'

He went to put a hand on her other arm but she pulled away and stood back from him, grabbing a ladle from the counter top and holding it up as if to hit him.

'Dirty whore!'

Suddenly Father Pearse came between them with his hands up, and Sean grabbed him by the lapels of his jacket.

'Come on now, the pair of yous.'

'You two-faced fat fucking cunt of a man.' Sean was swaying back and forth, concentrating on staying still. He pushed past the children at the kitchen door and took to the stairs. Kathleen ran after him.

'The only cunt of a man here is you! You've ruined another Christmas you useless bastard, I hate you!'

'Don't say that Mummy!'

Father Pearse put his hand on Aine's shoulders. 'Let's eat the dinner your mother has made.'

They sat and said a prayer of thanks for the food and then the plates were passed around. After a while, they heard the sounds of Sean snoring. When Kathleen served the pudding, the father clapped his hands with exaggerated bonhomie.

'I've never seen the like of this. What a lucky old fellow.'

'Father, please forgive us for the performance on this day of all days.'

Father Pearse demurred, a ripple passing through the birthmark on his brow. 'None of it is easy.'

She looked at Liam whose spoon was lying on top of the custard-covered mound, balanced like the needle of a compass. 'Eat your pudding love.' She reached towards him with her fingers. He flinched. Aine and the father set to eating, onerously.

Suddenly Liam took his mother's hand and kissed it.

'Bless you love. Thank you for that,' and she looked at him with her eyes pricking, then ate her pudding.

With the bowls in the sink, and the father's glass filled, she left them to *The Sound of Music* and went upstairs.

57

When John Dunn walked into the spare room, his son put something hastily out of sight into the suitcase beside him. 'I'll be down in a minute.'

'Angie. She's waiting for us.'

'Yes. I'll be right down.'

'Right. Thank you for the watch. It's just that, well, like I said, I'm not very good at presents. It's me that should be giving the presents anyway.'

'Right.'

'I'm not used to all that. Angie knows how I am. I told you, I didn't have a family to speak of. When I left I said to myself, well that's that, bollocks to them, that's all done with now. I turned my back on it all. I never saw any of them again, Mark.'

'I don't know what I'm supposed to say to that. I mean, am I supposed to be impressed at how hard you are or something?'

'I can't help who I am, Mark.'

'Maybe I was stupid to think that we'd just get to know each other and that it would be easy. This girl I know, she said to me to be careful, that there was a reason you weren't around.'

'Let's finish our dinner. Have a drink.'

'Mum never knew you at all, did she? It was just a quick . . .'

'It was a long time ago.'

'Yeah but you haven't changed, have you? I mean you said yourself, the other night, that there was something wrong with you. Even Angie says she hardly knows you.'

'What do you mean?'

'You say you'd have been a father to me. But we'd have had to know each other first, wouldn't we? You and me, we're just pretending. Why? What's the point? What are we doing it for?'

John sat down on the bed, pushing the long bag backwards behind him, facing the 1930's dresser with its drawers that would no longer shut, all of them slightly ajar.

'Mark. You and I, we're a world apart. That's not even a question I'd ask myself. Who am I? In the army it wasn't who you were as a person, but what you stood for. All right it was a bit different when you got to be a corporal because you had to make sure the job was done. But I never thought about much at all until I came back over here in '74. That was a hell of a tour for me. When they said I was coming back again in '76, I couldn't believe it. Why? I kept asking myself. But I made it right. It's life that's made me who I am. It's different for you. You probably do know who you are. But I don't know many men who do. Then the other thing is you've got to know what's right, as well, you've got to have a sense of it. If you don't, you can do bloody terrible things.'

'How do you mean?'

John looked in the mirror of the dressing table and saw them both there. His boy's face was an improvement on his. He saw how his right eye was always crooked in a mirror. His own was thin, dropping, and slightly ugly. He hadn't trimmed his nose hair in a while, his eyebrows were overgrown and he had large dark pores over his nose and lower face. His eyes looked tired and useless, there was just a tiny light glowing in the middle of them.

They had been waiting for this. The boy in his room and at his desk, at the bar, on the ferry, thinking, What if there's something about him that afterwards I wish I didn't know? Here was the place they'd been travelling to; they'd arrived.

'Listen, I'll tell you something about me, Mark, that way you can't ever say you didn't know and the rest of it can be your choice. On that second tour, in '74, they put me out on the streets for a few weeks before I went into screening. You don't know who's going to have a pop at you when you're out there. Being REME I was a bit of a Jack of all trades. I knew everything about all of the equipment, I repaired it and I operated it. If I wasn't fixing an APC, I was driving it. This one day there's me driving, six men in the back, me and the sergeant up front, and we drive it round some of the back streets up by the Falls Road, up and down, clearing people out the way and the fellas in the back are ready to jump out and snatch anyone they're told to. We go down one street and there's a protest march in front of us. A priest is leading it, and there's men and women alongside him, walking, arm in arm, up towards us. At the sides a few people on the pavements are shouting this and that and we slow down. A petrol bomb is lobbed in and hits me on the shoulder. It went out when it was chucked but it douses me in petrol and smashes on the floor. I was treading the glass under my feet. From the back I hear the men start shouting; the tyres are on fire. I look ahead and the priest is waving his arms, trying to calm things down, or to tell people to sit down, I don't know what, but I remember his face, like he knew what was going to happen and the boys in the back are banging on the partition and screaming and the sergeant says to me, "Drive on".'

'Christ.'

'I drove on.'

'Did you hurt anyone?'

'Yes.'

'How can you be you sure?'

'I am.'

'Did you stop and see?'

'No. I know because I heard it.'

'How many?'

'I don't know. One, two, three – I don't know.'

'What do you mean? What happened afterwards?'

'I don't know.' He looked at his hands on his knees. 'I just heard the sound of it, felt it underneath the tyres.'

'What about the sergeant? Didn't he tell you, wasn't there a report?'

'No. The sergeant never spoke to me. If he saw me, he looked away.'

'But you killed people?'

'Nobody knows. Not even Angie. I'm sorry. Believe me. I wish I hadn't.'

58

He was lying on his side with his hands out in front of him. He woke with a shock, opening one eye and looking around, as if recovering from a parachute landing into enemy territory. He tried to swallow.

'We need to talk,' she said.

'I shoved the priest.'

'Aye, you did.'

'I wanted to hit you.'

'Aye, I know.'

'I called him all manner of words.' He sat up. 'I get these pictures in my head of you with other men. God almighty, it's true I've gone and fucked up the entire day.'

He rubbed his face.

'It's true, Sean, you know. There have been other men.'

He closed his eyes.

'But those children are ours, yours and mine.'

'If I ask you who and when I'll be angry, and I won't be able to do anything about it, so I'm gathering myself up, Kathleen, not to ask you.'

She saw the wrinkles at either side of his eyes that criss-crossed with the bags underneath his eyes, made a grid. She saw the arable-grey stubble of his cheeks and chin, the large pink landscape of his forehead lined with four or five west-east tracks. His eyes were the same as when they had met, but more diluted; his lower lashes were pale, like Aine's.

Outside a passer-by was whistling as loudly as he could, a rousing, swelling noise. For what reason?

'I'm going to change. I'm going to take the pledge and give up the drink and I'm going to find myself a new line of work. We're going to put some money aside and we'll go for a trip to Donegal or wherever we fancy.'

She sat beside him. 'I've to try and change as well, Sean.'

'No. I love you. I always have, Kathleen. I always will. I don't care.'

She put an arm about him and with her face on his shoulder she looked across at the dressing table with the small white Madonna, the ornaments, photos and bits and bobs that told the story of her married life and she wondered if she didn't love him at all. They had fought together.

When they went downstairs, Father Pearse was asleep in the armchair, paper hat askew, and Liam and Aine were looking guilty. Aine was holding the microphone and Liam switched off the tape recorder.

'Father Pearse farted,' said Aine, her cheeks struggling. 'We're trying to get another one on record.'

Sean gave the priest a nudge with his knuckle, under the chin.

'What the devil is it now?' said the father, opening his eyes.

'Father,' said Sean, stooping over him, his tone thick as the gravy. 'I want to take the pledge.'

'And I'm fecking Julie Andrews,' said the priest, closing his eyes.

59

Angie's beads were in a small heap next to her plate. The kitchen was filled with cigarette smoke, the food was cold. It was close to ten o'clock. Nobody spoke. The Christmas crackers were pristine.

'That was great, Angie, thanks.' Mark put his knife and fork together. 'Would you mind if I called my mum? I'd like to say Happy Christmas to her before she goes to bed.'

'Of course not love, go ahead.'

John carried on eating, using his fork, elbow on the table.

They heard the whining drone of the apparatus after each number, as the dial swung back to its place of rest.

'Did you apologize?'

He looked up, his fork leaving his mouth. 'In a manner.'

'I don't know what got into you, he was giving you a gift, probably it's his most treasured possession. It broke my heart to see him have to get up like that and walk out. You went and undid all the good work you've put in.'

'I know.' He lay down his knife and fork on the plate and wiped his mouth with the Christmas napkin.

'For God's sake no one asks much of you, John, we only ask you to talk to us . . .'

'Don't start. The way you go on at me sometimes, Angie, I swear, you make me feel like running, like getting in the car and sodding off out of here.'

'Oh aye. Run away why don't you? God forbid John Dunn should have to feel anything, should ever have to say he's wrong or he's sorry.'

'I am wrong and I am sorry!' He stood, throwing his chair back. 'Is that what you want you stupid cow!' He took his plate to the sink and threw it in with the rest. Something broke.

'Merry Christmas to you too! Do your own washing up!' she cried out. He heard her footsteps up the stairs.

After a minute, leaning on the sink, he went and fetched all the plates, ran some water, gingerly took out two, sharp-edged plate halves and put them in the bin, then went to the fridge for a beer. He poured it into his glass. It ran into his stomach like cold acid and he pursued it as if it was medicine.

Mark came back in, looking around for Angie. 'She sends you both all the best. My mum.'

'Can't seem to keep three people round this table tonight. Sit and have a drink with me.'

'No, I'm all right, thanks.'

'I don't blame you. You off to bed as well?'

'Angie's gone up?'

'Yup.'

'Oh.'

'Have a drink with me, will you? Please.'

Mark gave him his glass and his father poured what was left of the can into it.

'I've got these things like little cigars. Have one with me.'

'All right.'

He went into the living room, to the booze cupboard. He could hear Angie up above him, the bed creaked. Inside was a packet of Hamlets that she'd obviously bought him for Christmas Day. He thought of Campbell and started to laugh.

Back in the kitchen, he used Angie's lighter and lit one for himself and one for his son. The boy spluttered and choked and wrinkled his brow.

'They're disgusting.'

'You get used to them if you try.'

The boy shifted position a few times, coughed and spluttered. Finally he put the cigarillo out, and felt in his pockets for his own cigarettes.

'John—'

He threw the lighter across. 'Yup?'

'John, I was thinking. I'm glad you told me what you did.'

His father looked at him, pink smoke billowing out of the side of his face. 'Are you?'

'I'd have done the same. You were under orders.'

Rain had started to fall and it made a soft drumming noise on the lean-to shed. 'I don't think you would have done,' he said.

After a while, John rose to do the washing up. Mark took up the dirty tea-towel and stood alongside him.

'The least I can do is give her a clean kitchen,' said John, hands plunging into the lukewarm water.

Angie was lying in bed, awake, when he went up, pretending to sleep but he knew her well. When she was asleep her body was soft and exuded this sweet smell, she breathed irregularly, normally one limb was at a peculiar angle, against the sense of her body. He knew, without seeing, how she was lying, on her side, her knees drawn in slightly, making a curve of her bum, and her hands together under her chin. Many times he'd fallen asleep alongside her like that, leaving her to her troubled thoughts. But she'd never left him to his.

He felt a deep sorrow rising in him like a man trying to sit up in a coffin, and he couldn't rest. Instead he put a hand on her shoulder and felt her almost recoil.

'Angie.'

He heard the hopeless splitter-splatter of the rain on the car roof outside.

'Angie.'

'Yes?'

'I said I was sorry.'

'And you followed it up by calling me a stupid cow.'

A great slab of rain fell with a crash as some guttering gave way.

'What do you see in me, Angie?'

'It's funny you should ask that.'

He reached for the side lamp and switched it on. Then, in his underpants, he climbed over her, so that he was looking directly down at her. Still on her side, she screwed up her eyes and made a face. 'I'm not interested in you at all, not interested in talking to you, nothing.'

He was still. Baffled. He kissed her face. 'I love you, Angie.'

She opened her eyes. 'Are you all right?'

'I've made a mess of everything, Angie.'

She pulled him to her. 'John, it's all right, darling, it's going to be all right.'

John fell upon her like a dead weight, his face in the pillow, and she thought he was weeping so she didn't move at all and all the while the rain was tipping and tapping and she was murmuring, 'It's all right, I'm here, I'll never go away from you, you know I won't.'

When she woke, she rolled him gently off of her and got up to switch off the side lamp. It was hard to find her way back in the dark, she nearly tripped, and she was relieved when she found the shape of her own place, still warm.

60

The next morning, the Jewish lady rang and Kathleen went over to Eileen's to get Jim to give her a lift up the Antrim Road.

'It's Boxing Day,' she said. 'We're half dead round here.'

Jim came out to stand out behind Eileen, in his slippers, the mark of the sheets on his face, a piece of toast in his mouth.

Kathleen explained it to him in the cab. 'My neighbour, Roisin, she said you've got to snap what's left of the Jews up.'

'I'll try and get our Eileen one for next Christmas.'

He waited for her. She was only in there ten minutes and it was all settled, when she'd start, how many mornings and how much. She thought on her way back how Christmas Day was only the day before and since then they'd changed their jobs, the pair of them. Sean would be at the pub, sober, having handed in his notice. He would have to be the housewife until he found new work.

'The housewife? That'll surely get him off his arse and into something new in no time at all,' said Mrs O'Sullivan when she came over to mind the children. She had her hair in curlers and a headscarf over them; she looked like a small thatched house.

'Well now, I'm going to be giving him some moral support to get him through the night, and tomorrow as well. He'll be on the lemonade both nights.'

'It won't be easy.' Mrs O'Sullivan took a plate Kathleen had dried and gave it another going over with a dishcloth. 'You know what useless gobshites men are. I had to get my Hugh to stop buying those magazines from your man up on the Springfield. What do they call them, top shelf is it? Tit magazines. Aye. Fifty pence here, seventy-five there. Going out of my purse! Upstairs 'reading' and the bed shaking the ceiling. He tried talking me into taking my bra off for a photo with his brother's Polaroid camera. I spoke to Father Lanigan about it. He had a word with Hugh on the quiet and he's never troubled with it since. Mind you, we've prayed over it and I think you have to.'

Mrs O'Sullivan carried on drying dishes, shaking her scarf and curlers.

'Masturbation,' she handed the plate to Kathleen, 'that's what they call it. There you go, love. Dry as a bone.'

Going out through Divismore Crescent on to the Springfield Road that afternoon, Kathleen saw the newsagent's and started to laugh, and once she'd started she couldn't stop. She walked into the bar with a real face-splitting grin. The bar was crowded, men mostly, still in a Christmas mood. An old woman had engaged Sean in an altercation and he was looking frustrated and virtuous in turns.

'He's a thief!' She had a crop of hair on her lips and chin and she was red with rage and drink.

'She's been biting the face off him,' said Fergal, a full glass in his hand.

Sean came along to them passing behind the pumps, and the woman followed him. 'I want my money, I want my money, you.'

'What is it love?' Kathleen put a hand on the old woman's shoulder.

'He's got two pound of mine so he has and he won't give it till me.'

Her husband leant across the bar. 'She came in at dinnertime. She says, hold this two pound for me mister, and whatever happens don't let me have it back until Friday or I'll never have enough for the weekend. I says till her, I know you, missus, you'll be up here come seven shouting for it and accusing me of being the worst son of a bitch has ever walked the earth.'

'And that you are!' piped up the woman, pointing at him, a long-dead cigarette in her hand.

Sean leant back, hands on the bar. 'You see what I have to put up with? I'm that glad that tomorrow is my last night, missus, and I'll never have to go through this hell with you again.'

'Last night?' Her face trembled.

Flinty came over and nodded. 'Aye, he's abandoning us sinners to our thirst for ruination.'

Fergal raised his glass. 'You'll have to harass the landlord himself now, missus.'

The old girl started up again. 'I want my two pound. He's going to be off with it himself, I want it now.'

Sean shook his head and walked off. Flinty looked after him and said to the others conspiratorially, 'I'll never find a barman with as hard a heart as he has, God love him. You can't do the job soft. Mind you, he's got no head for business.' He went to the small cream jug on the shelf. 'Here's your two pound love. Now what can I get you?'

'Gin and bitter lemon.'

Kathleen saw Coogan come in and she gave him a small nod of the head. She looked over at her husband; he was working out change. Behind her, a few people back, she could hear two men, drunken, voices raised, and one was saying, 'Anything I want,' and they were laughing. She turned to take a quick look, saw a man with a bulbous nose and curly hair doing the talking.

'She's got the poor wee lad upstairs so we do it on the floor downstairs; quiet, quiet she says and she puts her chin on the settee and covers her face with a cushion, so she does, to keep the noise down like. So as him upstairs doesn't hear. She's what you call a moaner.'

Another man was wiping his eyes, laughing. 'You'd better not have another one.'

'Aye. I'd best away.'

He put his glass down, gave a wave up and down the bar. When he went to leave, Kathleen put her foot out. He fell heavily, his hands out ahead of him, catching a blow to the side of his head off the bar but stopping himself by clinging to a bar stool. He looked around, puzzled, angry, fearful; his happiness gone.

'. . . make me sick,' said Kathleen under her breath.

Brendan Coogan asked Sean for a Guinness. Sean Moran went to fill the glass, looking wretched. He put it down and asked for the money, his hands flat on the counter, his face away.

'Did you tell him about me?' Coogan asked, moving alongside her.

'No, I've not told him about you.'

'It would be stupid, you know. To tell him or anyone. I think in the circumstances it's best that we're bringing all of this to a close.'

'Och don't be so pompous.'

When he was gone, she looked at his half-empty glass, the traces of foam suspended at the sides, slipping slower than time back towards the dark.

Her husband took her glass away.

'I'll fill it for you.'

He came back with it full and said in a whisper, 'I feel sick inside when I see you talking to him, I feel grey with jealousy.'

'It's green with envy.'

'No it's not,' he said, going to serve someone else.

61

John stood in the doorway in Angie's short towelling robe, a smile stirring on his face, toes flexing on the lino. 'I'm not going in.' He looked very pleased with himself.

'Do you want an egg?' said Mark.

'Why not?' He raised his arms, hands on the doorframe.

'Well there's a turn up for the books. I've never known you eat breakfast.' Angie had a cup of tea at her lips.

'Best meal of the day some say.'

'Do they eat it at the prison then?' She gave an emphatic nod towards his bare hairy thighs. He let his hands fall, pulled on the belt.

'Nope,' he said, moving over to the kettle. 'We're not talking about that place today. That's all done with. *So it is*,' he added in her accent.

'How's that then? You're not going to hand in your notice, John?'

He emptied the kettle out through the lid hole, banging its steel arse, watching blue and white eggshell-like matter falling into the sink.

'Today is a new day. Today, I'm going to be a father to my son. I'm taking Mark out for a walk and a pint. We're going to talk about next year, maybe going on a holiday together, maybe me coming over there to visit.' He filled the kettle from the tap, watching the boy cut the toast into pieces. 'Soldiers?'

'Och, well then if yous've got plans, I'll go off in the new car and see Mummy and Daddy for the day.' She padded forwards a couple of steps, stood a moment so she could see him and he, her. 'Do I need to be worried about you John? They won't keep you on you know if you mess them about.'

John came towards her with his hands out and put them on her waist.

> *'With no loving in our souls and no money in our coats*
> *You can't say we're satisfied*
> *But Angie, An-gie, you can't say we never tri-ied'*

'It's you that's very trying.' She put a fingertip on his chest. 'Are you serious about not going in or are you just having me on?'

There was the sound of water dousing the flame at the gas ring.

'Oy, chef! Easy does it.'

As Mark moved the pan towards the sink, two hands on the handle, John followed with his nose over his son's shoulder.

'Looks like he can boil an egg.'

They sat down to eat breakfast, Angie dipping her soldiers in her egg, watching the two of them immersed in their new-found complicity. When the one was looking elsewhere, the other looked at him. Things weren't the same now he'd got Mark. She wondered if John still needed her in the same way he had done before. He was all she wanted.

After breakfast, the father and son walked out into a dim, grey morning. It was just like any other northern town in the United Kingdom – apart from the hills. It was the hills, so green, so dark, so immediately upon you, that told you this was Ireland. Where they walked in East Belfast, the sides of the pavements were painted a block of red, a block of blue, a block of white. Union Jacks hung faded at windows, or struggled, tatty and flapping, from lampposts. The murals bore paintings of men masked, in combats, pointing a gun at the passer-by. There was graffiti everywhere; threats and promises. You knew where you were in Belfast by the signs; you were never in doubt as to what the loyalties were, and the markings were the vital signs of a body whose politics were personal, person by person.

They hurried along, up Castlereagh Road, past Ballymacarrett where he'd once been billeted and on to the Albert Bridge. They stood in the middle, Dunn pointing out the dockyards, explaining that these were once the draw for working men from all over the country. Angie's mother had told him that every man in their family in East Belfast used to have the dockers' button. Angie's grandparents were dockers. 'You'd get a week's wage and a month to eat it,' was what her grandmother said.

'There's history there . . .' said Dunn.

'You wouldn't come back to England then?'

'No. No, mate. I wouldn't. I need to find another job but it will be here in Northern Ireland. Don't ask me why. Everything's stacked against me. Maybe I owe it something. I should never have gone into that job at the prison. Doing the law studies was a mistake as well. It got me thinking too much.'

He'd started thinking about the way it worked, the deal-making, the way the soldier pays the price for it with his life. People died. People got shot. All the time. It was just numbers if you were able to stick to the paperwork. Just numbers unless it was your family, or unless you were the one who pulled the trigger. Either way, you were fucked. And they lied about it, not just what you were doing it for, but what would happen if you did it.

'A couple of years back, at a disco at Glassmullin Camp off the Falls, a trooper over there, with the Blues and Royals, went berserk and shot three men dead. One of the men got him trapped down an alleyway, put his revolver round the wall and fired off ten rounds. Fortunately one got the guy smack in the head. It was covered up. The trooper was a fuck-up. He'd seen some nasty action. We all knew it.'

No one talked about the killing you did. Even someone like Campbell; when he talked about the Second World War, you'd think it was only the Germans that killed anyone. All of them were like that. Because if you faced it, if you looked at what you'd done, you were dead in the water.

His own grandfather told him he'd bayoneted more than ten Germans in the First World War. He said he only wished he'd stuck it to some more.

'Perhaps you'd better give up all this reading,' was what Angie had said to him. 'It's not doing you any good.'

They walked along Donegal Square. 'I didn't find religion, I found the Maze. I wouldn't want to find religion, anyway. It's just another cover. I'm a fully paid-up atheist. But I've got my doubts. Your mum was right about me, Mark, I'm not very deep.' The pigeons scattered.

The rain was falling in modest drops, one on the back of his neck, then one along the side of his nose. He put his hands on Mark's shoulders, steering him down a side street towards the Europa Hotel.

'You see it's the greatest thing in the world, to give your life for something you believe in. And then on the other hand it's bloody pointless. Your body goes in the ground, feeding animals. And killing for what you believe in is pointless as well. You can't change anyone's mind by killing them. And between those two things there are a whole load of accidents that happen. And now we've got it all happening on a bigger scale. You get people going on about peace not war; that's easy talk. We can all say it's wrong, but none of us can help the fact that it's in us. There's something bloody horrible inside us; a monster. We don't like it so we make out it's not in us personally, we make out it's upstairs or outside or living in someone else's house, and once we've got rid of it, we'll be straight.'

They were stood outside of a pub door on Great Victoria Street. The Crown. 'Let's have a beer then. This is safe enough.'

John Dunn pushed the door and they stepped into the last century. The pub was ornate, with gated booths, dark wood and every inch of ceiling detailed. They ordered up a pint of Guinness each and the barman went back to his conversation while it sat.

He began to look about to see if they sold the Panatelas he liked and as he did a face came into focus and he and another man locked eyes. The man had the weather-beaten face of the construction worker and lively eyes. John began the process of racing through names, places, memories; leaping over years and buildings, scouring envelopes and newspapers, bringing to mind teams and clubs so that he might arrive before the other.

The man stepped forward, smiling as the barman put down their pints and Dunn paid.

'John Dunn, so it is! What about you? I knew it was you! You were the nice squaddie who used to get our electrics going down at Harland and Wolff. You'll have got yourself some medals by now.'

'Wrong man.'

'Ach come on. I know who y'are. You're a good man, we saw you every week back there for a while. When my brother told me he'd seen you round the prison, I wondered to myself if we'd run into each other. You always had time for a wee chat. Come on with you now.'

'Cheers.' John looked over at the right side of the bar; behind a wooden pole there hung a curled flypaper with tens of little black combatants adhered to it, left over from summer.

'Well, I've just the now come home from a job in London, so I have. I'm starting a business doing a spot of painting and decorating. I'm living off the Sandy Row, on Blythe Street, if you ever need some work done.'

John looked around the man at his son, and nodded at his glass to indicate that he should drink up.

'Did you hear the Provies killed a *retired* UDA man the other week? Ken something or other. He was selling burgers and chips out of a caravan with his son. But sure, you screws must be shitting yourselves with all the murderings. God help yous. Now would you tell Baxter, Derek Baxter, that his brother Keith said hello? Any kindnesses at all you can give him would be much appreciated. Shall we have a drink together? Will I buy them or will you?'

'No thanks, we're off now. You done there Mark?'

'See, if you could take our Derek in a packet of fags or something, it would be just great. If I could bring round a couple of wee things some time . . .'

'I can't do it.'

'It'd be worth your while.'

'I can't.' John put a hand on Mark's sleeve and nodded towards the door.

'Well we know where you stand, John Dunn. And we know where you live as well.'

'And I know where you live, you bastard.' John turned at the door, pointing at the man.

The pair of them cut up on to Grosvenor Street, with John looking behind him from time to time. As they got to the roundabout, John stopped. 'Stupid bastard.'

'I thought you said that place was all right.'

'There're people like him everywhere.'

'He threatened you.'

'Forget about it.'

They were back on the bridge. It was dusk; two thin men, hands in pockets, heads down.

'Why don't you take my surname, Mark? Mark Dunn. Sounds all right, doesn't it? It's who you are after all. It's up to you of course.'

62

Christmastime doesn't bring a family closer together, no more than sitting in an inch of your own bath water gets you clean. Kathleen couldn't take days and days in front of the TV, people all around eating your food and nothing to do. So she'd lied to her family, told the one lot the other was coming on Boxing Day and told the other the other was coming, and so they were alone in the afternoon when they came back from The Fiddlers.

Liam went out with his dad to play hurley in the street, pretending he needed him to teach him – anything to keep his daddy busy. Her husband had never been the sportsman and it was years ago that Sean taught Liam. Going up the stairs Kathleen heard the pathetic sound of her son saying, 'Is this right, Daddy?'

She waited outside the kids' bedroom; she learnt about her daughter by eavesdropping on her at play. When she opened the door, Aine was lying on her back on the bed.

'I thought you were tidying, miss.'

Aine made a face.

'Shall I tell you a story?'

'No thanks. I'm just thinking.'

'Shall I tell you about Cuchullain?'

'Yous all tell it differently.'

'Daddy tells it to you, does he?'

'And we've had it at school.'

'Och, well I suppose you're too old for it now.'

'The part when he dies, who the bird is and all, yous tell it different.'

'Never mind. I'll get the tea on.'

'I like it, though. If you want.'

'Which way do you like it?'

'Your way.'

Kathleen sat on the bed, her feet crossing automatically so as not to dirty the covers.

'Cuchullain was a beautiful young man and a fierce warrior; the Hound of Ulster they called him, but his real name was Setanta. He said, "I care not whether I die tomorrow or next year, if only my deeds live after me." He had a good heart and when he had to kill his friend Ferdiad in battle, it broke him. It was a terrible fight, for days and days it wore on, and neither would give in. Cuchullain tried to put Ferdiad off the idea of fighting him, telling him to remember how they'd learnt to fight together from Scathach—'

'*We were heart companions, we were companions in the woods, we were fellows of the same bed, where we used to sleep the balmy sleep,*' Aine interrupted.

'Well done Aine, that's great so it is. Well now but Cuchullain won and when Ferdiad was dying, he wept something desperate and carried him to the shore of the loch that they'd been fighting for so at least he could get close to it.'

'And what about when Cuchullain was dying?'

'The goddess of battle, the Morrigan, och, she had many battles with Cuchullain, disguising herself as a cow, or an eel, or a wolf, or an old woman milking a cow, but he fought her off every time. Then she came to him as a beautiful young woman. Cuchullain wavered then, you see, that was his undoing. His heart was his weakness. In the end, though, he refused her love and in a fury she went for him. His enemies, seeing him weak, they moved in for the kill and when he was in a bad way, dying for sure, he strapped himself to a pillar of stone and carried on fighting. Right up until he died. He'd pledged himself to fight to the death! That's why he tied himself to that stone.'

'Go on.'

'Well then the last thing of all, and some say it was the Morrigan, some not, but a black raven perched on his shoulder and pecked him as he died.'

'Was that the woman then?'

'To my mind it was the Morrigan. She pecked him,' Kathleen pinched up and down Aine's arms and side, 'and pecked him and made sure he had a slow, terrible death.' She poked with her fingers at the girl's ribs until the girl was kicking at her and telling her to stop. She broke free, rolled off the bed, then got back on. 'But why would a person kill someone they loved?'

'A person could kill someone they loved for something they loved better.'

'But Cuchullain killed his friend. What for? For the land? For a hero, he was a bit of an eejit, wasn't he? It can't have been all about the land?'

'It's what they call a tragedy. People tell it just to feel the sadness. Don't ask me why. People need to be sad as much as they need to be happy. We're made that way. The Lord knows why. Maybe our sadness isn't sad to God, maybe to Him it's different – something like colours, or music even.'

'And maybe it's nothing to him what we're feeling. Like when the Purcell lads get a wasp or a fly and they pull its legs off. They catch it in a glass, then they dissect it with the side of the glass, against the window.'

'I think He loves us. Like I love you. You see your child doing things that are going to hurt them but you can't stop them. You can only love them.'

'Like with Sean.'

'Or like with you and your black moods.'

They could have been anywhere, they could have been in a house in a forest, or near the sea or they could have been wealthy or they could have been prisoners, they were just lying in a place, a mother and a child. She thought of Aine in the forest, the day just the two of them went off for a spring picnic. Aine with a stick in the soil, watching the undergrowth break apart, mounted in portions on the backs of the ant soldiers, her knees thick with dirt, uneven front teeth, the sunlight in her hair. They'd sat and eaten their sandwiches and she'd thought to herself, 'This is grand. Why haven't I done this before?' She'd never done it again.

'Do you think you can be anyone you like when you grow up, Aine, do whatever you want?'

'What, and go away from here like Mary?'

'I mean you could do anything you like for a job, you could travel.'

Aine's head rolled away, as if weighted; the heaviest part sank back. 'No, I don't. I want to be here when Sean comes home.'

The others she'd had to hunt for, shriek after and drag back to the house, but Aine had always been close by. Her brothers and sister sought the world on a grand scale, adventures and escapades, but Aine liked to bring order to what she knew.

Kathleen rolled on to her side and looked at her youngest child, the one to whom she'd given the least. She was like a flower growing where it had no right to grow, like a solitary daffodil on a motorway siding; a reminder of the absence of others.

'Are you all right, my darling?'

'Aye.'

Kathleen put her lips to Aine's cheek. She whispered through her skin. 'I know how rare you are, Aine, don't think I don't know that.'

They stayed there a while longer, hand in hand, with Kathleen's thoughts wandering over the left half of the ceiling, and her daughter's over the right.

63

When Angie came in, keys in hand, the boy and his father were in the sitting room talking, and she told them she was going to make the tea. She stood in the kitchen with a box of tea-bags in a hand, coat on, and she cried a little and wiped her cheeks with her free hand, traces of mascara, runny and dirty, on the bone of her thumb. Then she went back to the front room and stood in the doorway again.

The two of them still had their coats on as well. Boxing Day in East Belfast was one of those easily forgotten, in-between days when nothing happened. John's shoes had made a mark on the carpet, and with her there he noted it and put his feet back to rest on it, like his own starter's mark.

She moved to draw the curtains, her coat brushing against John's face.

'I had a nice time with Mummy and Daddy. Helen was there with Mick. They're expecting. They were all the talk with it, the both of them. Mummy got out some old knitting patterns.'

They heard her go into the kitchen and then upstairs.

After a while, Mark went up after her. She was sitting on the bed, taking off her shoes, her back to him.

'Angie. We were just chatting. Dad was talking about what he does next. I don't think he's going to go back to the prison.'

'Is he not? Well, now, it's all right. Don't worry about it Mark, we've been through ups and downs like this before.'

'It's not about you, Angie.'

'We know each other pretty damn well, Mark. I know who he is and

I know that he struggles. When you have a girlfriend or a wife of your own, you'll know how it is, that it's the day in day out stuff. You stick by someone and it passes.'

'I'm sorry, I didn't mean to interfere.'

She turned round, felt her feet through her stockings with her hand. He was the boy when he should be the man, just like his father.

'What do you want for your tea?'

'Shall I make it?'

'I can manage.'

'He wants me to stay until the new year, but I can't. Thanks for letting me stay, Angie. You're good for Dad. He'd be lost without you.'

Angie was making small circles with her toes. 'I love him, Mark, I want a life together. I want children.'

'I'm going to make you both something to eat.'

The cup of tea on the dressing table gave up one last twist of steam. The bone-china cup that her grandmother had given her was so thin that the tea was too hot to the touch. She went to her handbag and took out a pattern for a knitted pram-set; hat, coat, leggings and bootees all in white with a peach ribbon trim. She would ask her mother to keep aside the trim until the baby was born, so she could put it in either blue or pink. She lay forwards on the bed, with the picture between her hands. Dipping her nose, she noted that it smelt of her mother's knitting bag. It reminded her of her childhood. She might be pregnant. She was due on in a few days but she might well be pregnant. She threw herself on to her back, her hands moving over her belly, looking at the Styrofoam square-panelled ceiling.

Downstairs, Mark found a can of Homepride sauce and set about making a turkey curry. He chopped onions, wiping his nose on his forearm as he went. He put the onions into sizzling oil, chopped the rest of the turkey meat into pieces and chucked that in, then he poured the sauce on top. The frying pan was so hot the sauce shrunk from it, so he poured in a mugful of cold water, which seemed to put it to rest. Then he slung the whole lot into a saucepan instead. He got the carrots and Brussels sprouts out of the fridge and tossed them in. There wasn't any rice so he put sliced white bread aside, ready for toasting. He got out currants and desiccated coconut and put them in small bowls. He laid the table. He turned down the heat. He had no appetite.

'It'll be ready in about fifteen minutes, Dad.'

'Sound. So, no hope of changing your mind then?'

'I'm booked on the crossing. We'll see each other again soon.'

'Sure enough. I'll come across. What is it, year two for you at the university now? What will you do after? I've never asked.'

'I've no idea. I might go abroad.'

'Why?'

'To see other things.'

'Have you not got a girlfriend?'

'I did have. She was a bit older than me, actually. Twenty-five, with a kid.'

'Christ almighty, you're only nineteen. What was she thinking of?'

'She wasn't a fallen woman, Dad.'

'You've a bit of experience with women then? At your age I was lucky to get a kiss goodnight.'

'You got more than that, Dad.'

They had a lager each, and when Angie came in John was teasing Mark about his older woman. Angie had recovered her good humour.

'That's where he gets his washing skills from then, she must have had him doing the nappies.'

They ate the curry and she told them more about her sister's news, imitating her brother-in-law who, she said, was 'the big I am', all puffed up and swagger. 'You'd think no one had got a woman pregnant before, and my daddy's going along with him, slapping him on the back, giving him a wee drink of this and that, you know Daddy.'

'He's never offered me a drink. Last Christmas we were there an hour and I said to him, "A bit thirsty mate" and he says, well what do you want, what do you want, all annoyed like, what is it, water, lemonade? I said, what are you drinking then and he says brown ale, but you won't like that. I said, try me old fella, and he gives me this little drop of it, no more than an inch, brown and flat.'

'Ach, it was a couple of inches at least. He didn't want you getting drunk.'

'No chance of that at his place.'

'They're not made of money.'

'That big prick of a man, Mick, he always gets a glass,'

'Aye, well he's come through for my daddy, hasn't he. He married our Helen, did the job.'

John started to speak, pointing his knife at her and then stopped himself and ate instead. He was wondering whether this was the moment. Whether he should ask her while Mark was there. Make an occasion of it. But then he thought about the prison. Thought about Angie's parents, and her having to tell them he was out of work at the present.

They forbade the cook from doing the washing up, going about it the pair of them. Mark stood tuning in the radio, his ear to the fizzy rush of empty space between stations. John put in too much washing up-liquid and Angie handed him back four plates in succession. 'Och, there's even more bubbles on this one, you'll have to rinse them under the tap again, John.'

'This is Madness.'

'You're telling me, pal,' said John, taking back all the plates that were lying under soap bubbles on the draining board and rinsing them off as well.

> *My girl's mad at me*
> *I didn't want to see the film tonight*
> *I found it hard to say*
> *She thought I'd had enough of her*
> *Why can't she see*
> *She's lovely to me*
> *But I like to stay in and watch TV on my own*
> *Every now and then*

John left the tap running in the bowl and began to steer Angie around the kitchen, with her exclaiming about the sink going to flow over. Mark

turned off the tap, slipping on the wet floor, then turned up the volume.
Angie was bemoaning John's clumsiness and he was ignoring her, plying
someone else's trade, feigning Old Time expertise, bending her backwards, one hand at her waist, one hand in hers, his chin raised, his big
feet all over the place.

> *My girl's mad at me*
> *We argued just the other night*
> *I thought we'd got it straight*
> *We talked and talked until it was light*
> *I thought we'd agreed*
> *I thought we'd talked it out*
> *Now when I try to speak*
> *She says that I don't care she says I'm unaware and now she says I'm*
> *   weak*

The song ended with five important drum notes and was done. John
gave an affected little clap towards Angie and said, 'The lovely Angie'.
Then he handed her the cloth saying, 'Your tea-towel, madam?' and
they went back to the sink.

64

It was like she had a great cold iron on her ribcage in bed in the evenings. Some nights her husband heard her weeping; mostly he was passed out with the drink.

'What is it?' he'd said once, putting on the lights, trapping her.

'I'm lonely,' she'd said. 'Switch off the light. It's too bright.'

He'd done so, lain back down and said after a minute, 'I'm lonely as well.' Too many nights like that, she couldn't take another.

They walked home just after closing time, after a round of 'for he's a jolly good fellow'. His last night and he'd had just the two lemonades.

'If you can pass up the drink on your last night, you're going to be just fine, Sean.'

She'd had a few herself though and for the first time in years it was he that steadied her on the way home. He was quiet all the way, clutching her arm as the pavement dipped.

'Do you love that man?'

'No.'

'Good.' There was relief in his voice as he let go of her arm and went ahead to open the front door.

'Do you love this man?'

He allowed her to go through into the house, and remained back at the door.

Mrs O'Sullivan was offering him a good night and when Sean said, 'Thanks for everything, Patricia,' she stopped as if surprised and he considered that either he'd never said it to her before, or he'd never used her first name. That and the fact he was sober.

His wife came out with her and they watched her home.

'I know you're a good person, Sean. I can see you're trying to change yourself. It's just that I don't know you very well.'

She'd kept him at bay a long time with a mix of harshness, reprimand, and occasional, austere good humour; a little untoward daytime innuendo and too tired at night.

'But we've been married twenty years.'

'I know. I was a kid and so were you and what I thought you were, you weren't at all and it's just as well more than likely. To be honest I haven't even wanted to know you.'

'Why?'

'Because, well, because there were things that put me off, like, or that made me think it wasn't worth the trouble.'

'What like?'

She sat down on the front doorstep and after a minute he sat beside her.

'You tell lies.'

'So do you! And yours are worse than mine!'

'Aye, well all right. Look, I don't want to stay with you for the kids' sakes, because we have no choice, I want more than that. A friendship at the very least. With Sean going away it's made me think. That poor woman,' she nodded across the road, the light was still on at Collette Heaney's, 'and that one over there,' she pointed to Mrs Mulhern's. 'They've all lost their sons one way or another, and here am I, and I've just about still got mine. I mean, where else does it happen that half of your neighbours' men are away in jail or dead? I live here. I've got to be able to put something straight. And if I can't put *me* straight what else will get better?'

'It's not your fault all this, you can't mend it. All right. I take your point, I hear you.'

'We've got each other. That's what we've got.'

'Even if we don't like it. I mean, well, you know what I'm saying.'

'Aye. Well, we've got to work it out, Sean. We've got to work together. Take the best. What's good is that you're changing. I can respect you for that.'

'Oh.' He took her hand in his and kissed it.

The light went off over at Mrs Lavery's, and then it went on again in the upstairs room that overlooked the front.

'We could go to bed,' he said. She gave him a taut smile. He continued, without looking at her, 'To our mutual satisfaction, without stereotypical gender roles.'

'What in God's name are you going on about?'

'I did have a read of that wee book you brought home. How sex is more than intercourse.' He made his way adroitly through the unfamiliar words. 'How it's showing your appreciation. To someone with nice tits.'

'You sneaky wee devil.'

He went on in an English accent, looking ahead, straight-necked. 'I am quite willing to stimulate your clitoris during coitus interruptus.'

She hit him. 'For Christ's sakes, Sean, they could have you locked up for saying that!'

He put an arm around her and they sat, giggling.

'Well, I suppose we could,' she said, her nose resting on his shoulder.

'You've been drinking. That's why you're saying that.'

'So you could take advantage of me then.'

'I've not had anything to drink, myself.' He stood up and offered her his hand.

65

Last thing, they watched the Morecambe and Wise Christmas special, with the usual finale skit of Morecambe going home in his raincoat, looking back edgily, while Wise does the big number. Angie went up to bed ahead of them, leaving them to finish their beers.

She was reading a paperback her sister had given her for Christmas, a thick, pale purple book with white Indian pavilions on the front cover. She was going between the end and the beginning, checking to see whether she could be bothered with it. John came up and started annoying her, laying next to her saying, 'That's you all over, that is, a flibbertigibbet.'

'I want to see if it's worth getting involved with.' She was looking serious, pillow propped. 'I can't be doing with it if it's not a happy ending. There's nothing worse than when it leaves you feeling like topping yourself.'

'But you're not supposed to know, that's the point.' He was trying to hold the last pages shut.

'I'm going to make a cuppa, Dad, do either of you want one?' Mark was in the doorway.

'Aye. I will, thanks,' said Angie. 'No sugar though, if you don't mind.'

'I'll go,' said John. 'Mark, you tell this woman why she shouldn't be reading the ending before the beginning because she won't listen to me.'

He got up, adjusted his pyjama waistband and pointed back at Angie. 'Tell her.' Then he went off downstairs.

'Well I think with books you can do as you like.'

'Thank you,' said Angie loudly, so that John would hear. 'Thank you! You do as you like, he says,' she called out. 'If only all men were as reasonable!' She gave Mark a little round-shouldered smile, hunched over a laugh, waiting for the smart alec reply to come back.

There was a great cracking noise, like the bough of a tree broken apart by lightning, the sound of smashing glass and at the core of the noise the certainty of a gunshot. On top of it came a thud and the sound of breaking china.

By that time Mark was down the stairs, shouting, 'Dad, Dad, Dad, oh Jesus Christ, Dad.'

In the kitchen, he held the dishcloth against his father's chest, kneeling over him. 'Hold on Dad, hold on.'

His father's head was against the fridge door and his upper back propped up on Mark's thigh. His mouth was open, his eyes keeling. Mark was pushing the cloth harder and harder against his chest, staunching the blood. Broken china was all over the floor, just in front of his feet. The mugs for the tea. He looked up and saw the hole in the window, and beyond, the night closing back in on itself.

'Call the ambulance, Angie! Call the ambulance!'

Angie was standing in the doorway, transfixed.

'Call the ambulance, will you please, Angie, please!'

She moved to the phone and he heard her dial three times and say, 'My husband's been shot,' and then she gave the address and put the phone down.

She came in and knelt down and held John's hand.

Mark was saying, 'Hold on, Dad,' over and over again.

John's eyes came back, they fell into place and his tongue moved across his lips and he swallowed. He opened his mouth and his throat made a noise. Mark tensed his legs to hold the head up and he took his hands from his father's chest and shook his face. 'The ambulance will be here in a minute, just hold on.'

His father's mouth fell into a line. One eyelid struggled like a butterfly in a jar. Mark put his hands about the sides of John's face, saying, 'They'll be here soon, just take it easy.'

His father's head fell a little as the boy's leg shifted. Mark began pounding his chest, then he started giving him mouth to mouth, then he set to shaking his father.

There were loud knocks at the door and Angie went to answer them. A tall woman from across the way was on the doorstep in her nightdress, her face stricken.

'We heard a gunshot,' she said, breathless, looking around Angie, craning her neck to see.

'My John's been shot.'

'Oh God no. No!' the woman screamed out, seeing John's head in the kitchen doorway.

66

After lights out, Gerard lit them both a thin roll-up and they had their smoke. Some of the lads were saying the rosary, but Gerard said he was going to skip it and smoke instead and Sean agreed to do the same. They had a lot on their minds. O'Malley had given them a short talk in Irish that evening and Gerard was explaining to Sean the bits he'd not been able to follow.

There was a spotlight on across the front yard of the block and Gerard was standing by the window with his face partially revealed. He had his blanket about his shoulders and round him like a poncho. His fingertips went in and out of his thin beard as he sucked on the little cigarette.

'One thing's certain, Sean, we can't go on like this for another, what, ten or fifteen years?'

'What was he saying about what's happening on the outside?'

'There's some talks going on, with O'Fiaich in the middle, and there's some other ones as well with an MI5 man the middle man, but it's not looking good and with this goon Reagan all palled up with Thatcher there's little or no chance of negotiations coming off. In short, there's fuck all. Even a mainland bombing's not going to shift things. They're going on with shooting the screws and that's it.'

Sean was on the mattress, knees up by his chin.

'He's asking for names.'

'For the hunger strike?'

'No, for the coach trip down to Bangor. Fancy coming? The screws are going to buy us all a bag of chips each.'

'What are you going to do? You've got a family.'

Gerard closed the end of his smoke between his fingers. 'I'll tell you, I'm scared, Seany. Who isn't though? Everyone who puts their name down is going to be scared.'

'How many's going on it?'

'He said he'd be going on it.'

'Starting when?'

'They'll hold off a wee while. Nails has got something coming. But O'Malley wants us to get started the moment he has word it hasn't worked. What's it going to do to all the mothers and wives?'

They could hear their neighbours talking in quiet tones.

Gerard pulled the blanket up under his nose. 'Sean?'

'Aye.'

'I know this sounds a bit strange, but in a way I'll be sorry when it's all over. One way or another it's going to come to an end. Sooner or later.'

'Thank fuck.'

'But Seany, in some ways it's been a, what d'ye say, a privilege to be with each other.'

'Ach shut up, Gerry. We're not dead yet. Save your best words for then.'

'The sharing. Like with the tobacco. Would anyone think of taking more than his due?'

'You're always more cheerful after you've had your smoke.'

'It makes you wonder whether socialism only works with men who are oppressed.'

'Right.'

Sean was cold right through and found it hard to go to sleep until he was absolutely exhausted. Gerard had the desired effect on him, night after night, and he wouldn't have swapped him. Gerard would thank him for listening in the mornings and Sean would feel guilty about it because he only heard the half of it; after a while his mind hopped up on to the window ledge, took a trip into West Belfast, looked through his mother's kitchen window then headed out to play in the fields below the mountains.

'The thing is Seany, will it ever be like this again . . .'

Sean slipped down, propping himself on one elbow. 'I know what you're saying, Gerry, but I'm not a socialist or a communist. This is a war and I'm a soldier and I can say hand on heart that it's best it be me here, a single fella with no family. You in your position, you've to think about it another way, I can see that. The hardest thing for me up till now has been thinking about my mother. But I've stopped myself doing that and it's like she's dead.' His mouth was dry with the tobacco. 'See, I buy what O'Malley says, that the only way we can ever win this war is by doing something they don't understand. A criminal wouldn't go on hunger strike. I think he's right, so I'll put my name down. But if I were you, with a family, and with only that stuff about socialism to go on, I'm not sure I would. And no one will blame you if you don't.'

'The worst thing in the world for a man, Seany, do you know what it is? I'll tell you. I didn't come in here because I was an IRA boy. I kept out of it but it came for me anyway. The reason I stay on the protest, is because I couldn't face the shame of not being on it. Of sitting with the prison-issue uniform, the criminal's begs, round my ankles while I take a shit on a proper toilet.'

Sean lay curled up like an animal, his heart beating, thinking that it was possibly better being on the boards because his piece of sponge foam was so damp now.

'How many do you think will put their names down?'

'I don't know.'

'Aye. Well, it's just the next step on from this.'

Sean closed his eyes. There was Nancy and there was no Nancy. He saw hands relinquished across a space, after a dance, the feeling of being pulled backwards to his own side of the dance hall. And in the palm of his hand still the feeling of her, the cool skin of her bare arms, without rings or bracelets, just honest, and soft.

Sean was drifting into a dream; his cellmate's small voice came through like the beam of a pocket torch in the dark.

'Seany?'

'Aye?'

'I'll be putting my name down for it.' He sounded as if he was making an admission, nervous as if what he said would ruin things between them.

Sean felt for Gerard's hand, grasped it and shook it, then he let it go, and his head fell back further even than the ground it lay on, way, way back.

67

Two days after Christmas, there were RUC men on the doorstep over at the Laverys'. When Kathleen opened her front door, she saw Roisin with her hand over her mouth and Eilish across the way the same. Mrs Lavery was down on her knees. They had to drag her inside, like hauling a dead body.

Her son, Eammon, had been trying to bomb a police station in East Belfast. He had thrown the bomb up at the fence but it had come back at him and exploded. He was eighteen. A council dustman had been seriously injured as well, trying to stop the boy.

They sat in with Mrs Lavery for the morning, making the phone calls to her family for her. Sheila called round the next day to say that the wake would be on the Monday.

'Where the heart lies, the feet wander,' Mrs Lavery liked to say, and so she asked that the funeral be held at the church where they lived before, when the children were all young. But the priest there refused to give funerals to IRA volunteers, would not allow the tricolour flag into the church. Father Pearse agreed to perform the necessaries at her own house before the procession to Milltown Cemetery, on the last day of the year, on the Monday.

Father Pearse and the neighbours came in through the front door. Sean Moran was overseeing those that were to come in by the rear. Men came singly or in twos down the alleyway between the houses, hopped over the short fence into the Laverys' back garden. Sean shook hands with them, using both of his hands, his hair slicked back, a cigarette on low burn. He wore a black armband. He, Sammy McCann, and the oldest Lavery boy were the stewards.

Liam and Owen had been sent down to the Whiterock to keep an eye on RUC and army movements, and one or the other came back from time to time to report. It was normal for funerals to be postponed a few times due to the RUC stopping the procession, splitting up the mourners, arresting attendees. Two of Mrs Lavery's grandsons were covering the Upper Springfield entry to the street. Mrs Lavery's family were in the front room.

The women came in through the front door bringing with them tea or coffee or biscuits or a bottle of drink. They had a word with Mrs Lavery then made to find a task in the kitchen, elbowing themselves in, fiddling about, glancing at the clock.

Sheila and Kathleen got there at nine and Mrs Lavery was in the kitchen with them for an hour or more going back over the boy's life, like a prosecuting barrister, bringing out, piece by piece, the evidence for herself being responsible for Eammon's death.

'When I think I used to let him play at it when he was a wean – the Brits and the 'Ra, the Brits and the 'Ra. And going and getting upset in front of him. We wasn't able to get ourselves a home at the time, you see.'

Whenever they went to interrupt her, to comfort her, she pushed aside their gestures, starting up with a fresher, angrier memory.

'We always talked about the Prods this and that. Och I knew there was something going on. Him and your Sean all the chat until you walked in. And then that fella Mickey, friend of yours, Sheila, up in Eammon's room with him, the door closed. And him going away down south for a couple of weeks and me just praying they didn't get caught. Well and I got what I wanted. He didn't get caught.'

'We have to defend ourselves round here,' said Sheila. 'Your Eammon—'

'I wish he'd been caught.'

There was nothing they could offer Mrs Lavery; their children were still alive. Sheila sat with her weak coffee, stirring it, her face discontented. Kathleen carried on spreading margarine on to baps, making each surface yellow and even with her knife, saying nothing.

'You can't expect anyone else to love your sons like you do,' said Mrs Lavery. 'You've got to do it yourself.'

One of her grandsons put his head round the door. 'Seems like it's fine to go ahead, Granny, if you want.'

'Aye,' she said, and she took up her apron and hid her face in it.

The boy came over to her. 'Come on then,' he said. He put his arms around her until she said she was fine and he asked her if she was sure and she nodded and they went out into the front room.

Sheila put the coffee mugs in the sink. 'If mothers hadn't always sacrificed their sons for what was right, things would never have stood a chance of getting better.'

'Wasn't it you that night my Liam was taken off that said you should have moved away for the sake of the kids?'

'We all get our weak moments.'

The front room was dark, the curtains were closed and had been that way since the body was brought home the day before. The grandfather clock in the corner had been stayed and covered with a cloth; a mirror had been turned to face the wall. The young man was in an open white coffin on a put-up table near to the front windows. There was a candlestick at each end. At the bottom of the coffin was the tricolour flag with a black beret and black gloves neatly folded on top. Mrs Lavery stood by the coffin a while, one hand on it, like a mother at a cradle, looking out towards the mountains through a crack between the curtains.

Martin Lavery, the father, went around with a bottle of whiskey, pressing people to take one; kindly eyed, worried that everyone had a drink. He fussed over those that had to take their drop from a mug, apologizing and saying, 'It ought to have been a glass, if we'd had a moment to get ourselves together you'd have had a glass.'

Sean went into the front room and drew the curtains closer together. Mrs Lavery started to sob and her hand was taken by one of her daughters and kissed. Her oldest son stood behind her with his hands on her shoulders. Father Pearse asked whether he should begin.

Liam and Owen were taking occasional glimpses behind the curtains. The grandsons chose to go and stand at the back door, watching. When one of them came and tapped Sean Moran on the shoulder, Sean stepped back out of the room, finger to his lips, ostentatious in his apparent desire to go unnoticed, and was heard to give hearty greetings.

Four men entered wearing black sweaters, trousers, berets and dark glasses. They took their places, two at either side of the coffin. Father Pearse began the mass, a hand on Mrs Lavery's shoulder.

Kathleen saw Liam looking at the volunteers. Three more men entered, dressed in combat fatigues and balaclavas. Her husband was standing close to them, and thinking his son was looking at him, he gave him a dignified nod.

Mrs Lavery's elderly mother had a hearing aid that went off with a buzz and a whirr occasionally, and the group was trying its best to ignore both its noise and her loving chiding of the equipment. It was likely that she'd soon be coming to live with her daughter and son-in-law, going into Eammon's room that was.

As the father gave the mass, Kathleen looked over at Liam, his eyes moving between the window and the volunteers, almost oblivious to the corpse.

She looked at the coffin, the pale, serene face of Eammon, his slim body in a suit that he'd never worn in his life. She looked at her neighbours and friends. She looked at her husband and then she looked back at Liam. She thought, 'Who can I trust to love you like I do?' No amount of death, no church, nothing could breach the gap between love for one's own son and love for another's. She looked down at the mother, whose hand was inside the coffin, fingertips on his collarbone.

The mass ended abruptly. Sean looked at his watch. Father Pearse smiled with relief and went to bless Mrs Lavery who was on her knees crying with abandon.

People moved apart and spoke in low voices. Mr Lavery asked everyone to help themselves to the food in the kitchen and then he went to find the whiskey for refills.

The cortège would stop where the Whiterock met the Falls, Sean explained to the three men in fatigues. The coffin would be placed on a wooden stand on the roadway and on his signal they should appear from behind the shop at the corner and fire the volley.

'You'll see Bernie Curran's sister, Gràinne, waiting where you come. The guns will be in her pram. She's gone down ahead. The father will get the bullets to her now and she'll load them up.'

Pushing past him to go out to the kitchen and bring in some food, Kathleen bumped into Brendan Coogan in the hallway. He was wearing a brown leather jacket, zipped up, and his face was unshaven.

'Hello Kathleen.'

'It's terrible, terrible for her, she's broken up, her life's over. How can any of it be worth it.'

His face hardened as it had when she'd used the wrong word for the executions of the prison officers.

She was forced towards him a little as someone passed behind her. She put a hand on one of his and moved her fingertips between the hard knuckles. She didn't know why, afterwards. Then Eilish Purcell was upon them, a hand on each of their backs, asking if they would come to a meeting the next week.

'We've got to press on with the youth centre. Young people need something besides the war. It's occasions like these that make it all the more required,' she was saying, and Kathleen saw Mr Lavery, who'd been making in their direction with his bottle, hunch his shoulders, wheel around and move off in another direction. Mrs Lavery was being steered through to the kitchen. Coogan excused himself.

'I've got to be away now. I'm sorry for your loss, Mrs Lavery.'

In the front room someone stood on the cat's tail and a screech rang out, causing a frisson of silence and a little relieved, tremorous, laughter and chit chat.

Kathleen's husband touched her lightly on the arm, asking her for a word. His breathing was laboured and he looked stressed. She wondered if it wasn't that he badly wanted a drink. She followed him towards the back door and he stood in front of her, his hands at his sides.

'I am not my father,' he said. 'I was always wanting to be the big man. Like my brothers. But now I don't care about him or any of them at all.'

'All right.'

'Aye, that's how it is.'

'You've just to be yourself, Sean.'

'That's right, Kathleen, aye,' he agreed, then asked her, 'What do you want me to be?'

Father Pearse came back into the hallway, shaking out his raincoat and trying to find the armhole in it, with Collette behind him trying to help him get it straight, the pair of them apparently at odds.

'Thank you, thank you,' he was saying irritably. 'We need to be getting a move on, Sean, I've to press ahead now.'

'The bullets!' said Sean to Kathleen, suddenly panicked. 'I meant for the father to take them down with him. Oh Jesus, where did I put the bloody things? They're in the fucking biscuit tin!'

He leapt into the kitchen with Kathleen following. 'What shall I put them in?'

'Here,' said Kathleen, picking up a carrier bag on the counter top. 'I'll stick a bap in it as well.' Sean threw his handful of bullets in on top.

'I'll see you out, Father!' called Kathleen, going quickly after him with the bag. 'I've got your dinner here!'

There were two RUC constables on the doorstep, looking nervous. Father Pearse assumed an expression that was both supercilious and exasperated. 'We must do the holy mass where we can these days.'

'Would there be any paramilitary trappings in there?' the older of the two asked, apple cheeked.

'Ach, no, for God's sake, no,' the father protested roughly.

'Now just you wait a minute there,' said the younger one, hand out.

'Excuse me.' Kathleen was propelled forwards by those behind her.

The four men in uniform emerged first, each in gloves, sunglasses and berets. The first of them had the tricolour folded over his forearm. The three men in combats and balaclavas followed. Sean Moran was behind, saying blindly, 'All clear, lads, all clear.'

The RUC men stood back, surprised, speechless, short on ideas.

With a hand making a small wave, Father Pearse made his way down the street at a smart pace; in the other hand he held a carrier bag in which there was an egg bap and some bullets.

68

The press was there waiting for them when they came out of the hospital in the early hours. It was a shock, flashes going off and questions being asked. The footage was replayed on the evening news, with a young reporter saying, 'The latest prison officer to be killed . . .'

And although they were quiet people with not many friends, throughout the weekend there were people coming and going, and the body was brought home on the Saturday and given the proper Irish wake.

Her mother and father came and stayed, so she slept on the couch in the front room, with him. She couldn't sleep and kept thinking of things to slip into the coffin with him – a couple of Panatelas, a wee note. She knew she wouldn't have him for long.

At the wake, there were a couple of old army friends who came by, men that she had only met the once or twice. Mark had got their numbers from John's pocket address-book.

Some of the prison officers came too. Hardy and Higgins? Foster? She was confused. Then they said, you'll have maybe heard of Frig and Shandy, Skids? In the kitchen, Shandy, a big tussle-headed man in his too-tight suit, came out to help her but he had something on his mind, it was clear. She offered to make him something to eat.

'We do the job and we bury our dead.'

'It's terrible.' She handed him a sandwich.

'It is,' he agreed, taking it, absorbed suddenly by the two white slices and the ham between them.

'Mustard?' she said. He shook his head.

The senior officer from the block, Mr Campbell, came by and took a whiskey, choking up with anguish as he looked into the coffin.

'He was a quiet fellow, didn't know him long, but you knew where he stood. He was a decent man.'

Later, he stood in the front garden a while on his own, and after most of the others had gone he was still there so Angie went out to him. They exchanged the usual niceties, knowing they'd never see each other again, then as they went to shake hands he took her in his arms, and she felt him shaking and he started to weep, saying, to explain himself, 'I lost my wife myself not long ago.'

'I'm sorry. Do you have children?'

'A son.'

'That's something.' Then she said, 'I might be pregnant. I hope I am. It would be something of him to keep.'

There was a wreath from the governor, with his apologies for events that precluded his being there that day. Janet Lingard sent a note saying that her husband had been badly beaten and was in hospital recovering, and as she was up there most days she couldn't come to the funeral, but she was very sorry for the news and would come by and visit if that was all right next week. Neighbours came in too and brought cakes and drink.

A group of four Catholic women came up from the Falls Road and gave her some flowers, saying they were sorry. They wouldn't stop for a drink. She stood watching them go, not knowing what to think.

And the last night, before the funeral, when she was alone with him, whispering and smoking, from eleven to six in the morning, she told him about it all.

'Your friend Roger came by, lives in Donaghadee now with his wife and a kid. Lovely man. Said, John did call me from time to time for news and that, he was never was meant for the army you know, he was a thinker, a loner. He said he'd lived with you in a small caravan in the hills in Cyprus. Then, just as he got his coat on to go, he tells me how when you were in Cyprus, one of the married men out there had a baby, and just a week old or so the poor wee thing died. His wife fell apart and they couldn't get themselves to the funeral, so her husband asked you if you'd do it for them. He said you drove the coffin down through the hills and it was just you and the priest and the coffin. He said you told him how, when you were driving down there, you told that dead baby the story of the three bears. Jesus, John, I can see you now. Your funny flat voice and your eyes on the road.'

Around six o'clock, Mark brought her in a cup of tea. 'I'll go and get washed,' she said.

She paused at the door on the way out to look at him by the coffin. He had picked up one of John's hands, slipped the watch over it, and fastened it around his father's wrist.

She was losing the pair of them.

New Year's Day, 1980, Donegal

New Year's Day 1990, Prague

69

They didn't stop till they were at Letterkenny, the first town in the Republic, and there they went into a small tea shop and had two teas and a lemonade and a Coke, and he had a chocolate bar and shared it round, looking at the wrapping critically and saying, 'There's not much to that. Bloody English, Cadbury's. I bet they're mean with it when it goes overseas. I bet they say, don't put so much in there, that lot'll not know the difference.'

Then they were back in the car, bumping over the topsy-turvy land on a narrow roadway, until they came across a two-pump petrol station and Kathleen got out and asked which way was Bunbeg. There was a stand inside the small room with a few loaves of bread on it and some buns, so she brought six iced buns back with her. It was a brittle winter day, but the car was warm with the four of them and they were happy going between grassy hills, following a single road that was inexorable, stupid, lovely. To the sides, set at disinterested angles, heedless of the road, there were single-room dwellings, some disused, some with smoke coming out of the chimney.

An elderly woman out walking stopped in her tracks as she saw them coming, looked at the car as if it were romance itself and waved hard at them.

When they came to a small village – a few homes and a lone pub – they were obliged to come to a standstill. There was an old man standing in the middle of the road, using his stick to indicate that they should slow down.

'Would you be going in that direction?' he asked at the driver's window, pointing forwards. 'I'm a wee bit out of sorts and I could use the lift.'

Liam got out to let him in and once inside, the man sat bolt upright in the middle, between the seats, two hands about his walking stick, holding it proud, flagless.

'And this is your car!' he said, impressed by the Ford Escort. His tweed jacket was tied together with a piece of string. Liam got back in and slammed the door. The man winced.

'We were lent it by our priest,' said Kathleen.

'You must be very holy,' he said, smiling, steadying himself as they took off. He craned his neck to watch Sean at the gear stick and leant forward to watch his foot on the clutch. 'Lovely gear change,' he said happily, and nearly fell forward between the front seats.

'You have a beautiful countryside out here.'

'Aye we do that.' He was squinting, one eye closed, his tongue drying on to his lip. 'Just pull over some time on the right, down there, in your own time, Sir.'

Sean pulled the stick into second, slowed to a stop.

''Tis a fine driver you are, Sir, may the Lord give you all you need in life.'

He put a hand on either of the front seats both to congratulate them again and to lever himself up and out. Liam was standing outside, waiting. In a minute, he was back inside and the door was closed. The man was on the road behind them. On their knees, looking out the back window, the children watched him wave his stick, then head towards a little house on a ridge.

'He was full,' said Liam, fingers squeezing his nose. Kathleen cracked her window and Sean followed suit.

There were small, white bungalows with thatched roofs dotted here and there on the peaty hillsides towards Bunbeg. Skirting the ocean for a while, they went up and down hill and came to the village itself with its couple of pubs, some guest houses, a post office, a general store and a single, rather maudlin, hotel, no lights on.

'I feel comfortable here. In Ireland proper,' he said to his wife.

'It's all Ireland proper. No one can say it's not, the land is the land.'

When they got to the sandy beach, Sean stopped the car, and they sighed at the glistening flat sand and the sea that lapped and spread circles of glitter drops. Then he started up the car and drove it forwards on to the sand, with Kathleen exclaiming and the children drawing in great happy breaths of excitement.

'Now it's our beach,' he said, stopping the car just at the water's edge.

"*Tis a fine driver y'are, Sir*,' said Kathleen, in their passenger's voice. She opened the bag she had and handed round baps and then, steadying a bottle between her thighs and getting Sean to hold two mugs at a time, she poured lemonade. The children leant forwards to see what their parents had inside their sandwiches, looked at each other's, put their own mugs between their feet and then they ate, the four of them, looking at the view up ahead and all around them, and at the marooned sailing-boat that had been abandoned in the harbour. The wind shook the car.

'It's like we're in the boat ourselves. It makes me feel cosy.' Aine shivered.

'Didn't we always say it was the bad weather outside made it good to be inside? I can't imagine living in a warm climate. I wouldn't need a family if I did. I'd be off down the road.'

'And we'd all be right after you,' said Sean, giving her his heavy romantic look, the one she used to dread, full of misplaced admiration, booze-heavy. But he was sober. It was New Year's Day. It was nice that he bothered.

The kids got out and went running, they took their shoes off and paddled.

'Only Irish kids could find fun in that, socks off in the freezing cold,' said Sean, watching them, proud. They had the doors open and smoked together.

'I was thinking of Genoa on the way here,' he went on. 'No, I'm not going to tell the story again. But I'd forgotten the bit about how I missed you when I was away. Jesus Christ, Kathleen, you'd have loved it there in Italy, just dripping with pure beauty, so it was. We got a lift round the coast to this wee town called Portofino. A gem of a place. I thought of you all the time, walking about with a plastic bag, thinking how I'd like to get you this and that from the shops they had there. And I brought you back a wee tea-towel with a ship on it, didn't I, along with that stupid damned ashtray. Ach Jesus. Sorry about that. You know, every foot of the place was flowers, and it was all old and fine and these wee lizards went racing about the hill pathways and there was this big mandarin-coloured church on the hill, sitting in the sun like it owned the place. I'd have liked to have been with you there, to have taken you back to a hotel, to be with you in nobody's bed and to say, she's mine and I'm the luckiest man in the world. And here we are in Bunbeg and it's fifteen years gone by since then, and I'm glad to have you here with me. I'm grateful, Kathleen.'

Aine was peering into the water, sat on a rock, and Liam was alongside of her looking into the same place. He said something and he splashed her.

'Sean, I was thinking that maybe I should love our Sean less or others more. Other people I mean. But I can't love Sean less. So I've got to love the others more.'

'You think too much.'

'You talk too much. It's with you talking, I get to thinking.'

On the way there he'd been telling her a story about his time in Australia. She'd been bored and not heard him and then tried to listen and felt guilty that her thoughts were elsewhere and that her inclination was to look for the lie, to put him down.

'I'm not a good person, Sean, I don't know why you think I am.'

'Because I believe you are.'

'That just makes me feel worse, so it does. I was thinking about you on the way here. About how baby Sean came along and I loved him so much it took me over. Well, I want to say that I'm proud of you for giving up the drink the way you have. Honest to God it's a miracle.'

'It's only been a few days.'

'A *wee* miracle then.'

He took her hand in his.

'They're getting soaked,' he said, nodding at the children in the pale light as they ran into the brisk waves, grabbing what they could for themselves. She bristled with the cold and closed her door. He did the same.

'Sean's away,' he said, and his voice sounded different without the noise of the sea and the wind taking from it. 'He's away, love. We don't know when he's coming back or even if he is.' He squeezed her hand. 'He's my son too.'

The children had been writing in the wet sand. Liam was putting down 'IRA' and Aine had written with her big toe, 'The Police'. Her brother was standing, hands on hips, abusing her.

'Death comes unasked. That's what they say. Any time, any place, anywhere – like with your Martini drink. Well so does life, Kathleen, and so does love. The best thing of all is when we don't do the thinking for ourselves, we just get on with what we're given.' He tucked his chin into his coat.

'Do we have to go back to the Murph? Can't we just take off? On a boat, like you used to, with some handsome strangers?'

'And there's me on my hammock while you're off with the captain in first class.'

And she saw the old Sean and she saw the new Sean and she saw the humour in the both of them.

'Are you ever going to take me on a honeymoon or is this it? Is this all I've got to look forward to?'

'This is it, Kathleen.'

'All right then. So long as I know.'

His eyes were pale and loose with a tiny core of granite, and she felt that she loved him and doubted him, and she was glad she knew both things even though they were hard to take together, and she decided to try not to hurt him any more, even though she would. She couldn't trust him, he couldn't trust her, but it was warm there with him and it didn't matter. She lay her head on his chest. This was just one moment, not the best one, not the last one, nor the beginning of something else; in the next minute they might be quarrelling again. He put an arm about her and kissed her head, his lips moving in her hair. With his hand he stroked her, kept her close.

The kids' faces came up at their father's side window; they were squashing their noses and pressing their tongues into their chins to make monsters of themselves.

'That's our lot then,' said Sean, pulling away. 'Time to break open them iced buns, missus.'

Afterword

In 1981, in the Maze Prison/Long Kesh, ten Irish Republican prisoners died on hunger strike in pursuit of their demand to be treated as political prisoners. During the fast one of the prisoners, Bobby Sands, was elected a Member of the Westminster Parliament. The fast was eventually discontinued, largely due to the medical intervention of the men's families, against their wishes.

The Northern Ireland cease-fires and subsequent peace talks leading to the signing of the Good Friday Agreement were supported by members of the Republican movement and Loyalist paramilitary groups as politicians, activists, lobbyists, aides, social workers, voluntary workers, committee members, writers etc., many of whom had passed through Long Kesh/Maze Prison.

Acknowledgements

This novel abides by certain elements of many real incidents as related to the author, and even though the specific placing of events and dates and much of the 'real news' might suggest 'real people', I wish to emphasize that no real living person figures in this fiction.

Due to the nature of this book many of those who contributed their recollections of the era wish to go unacknowledged. I thank them for what they shared with me.

For those who have agreed to be acknowledged, I am obliged to simply note the names. Suffice it to say here that every story came with hospitality, and became, in the telling, indelible in this writer's mind. Thank you.

Connie Comerford, Mr & Mrs Comerford, Mickey and Monica Culbert, Margaret Collins and her wonderful family, Kate and Gerard Clarke, Derek Crawford, Del, Philomena Duffy, Derek Frape, Mick Hamlin, Richard Hilton, Eileen Loughran, Dr Laurence McKeown, Jackie McMullen, Danny Morrison, Eilish Norton, Sean Paul O'Hare, Sandra Peacock, Eilish Reilly, Sadie Rice, Kathleen Rooney, Nick Rose, Fra Stone, Marie Ann Stone, Father Matt Wallace, John Walker, Des Waterworth, Fr. Des Wilson. Thanks to the man with the view, the man with the farm and to WC and JM.

For their gentle assistance, I am much obliged to Lt-Col. Grossman, Claire Hackett, Jim McGivern, Finlay Spratt, Michele Devlin, Mark McCaffrey, Kris Brown and Yvonne Murphy at Linenhall, Martin Melaugh of the CAIN website, Mike Ritchie at Coiste na n-Iarchimi, Kieran McEvoy and particularly Duncan McLaughlan.

Thanks to Dominic Hayhoe at Forces Reunited; I had the chance to get acquainted with 125 of their 125,000 former British soldiers.

With every courtesy, the Northern Ireland Office made it possible for me to take a long look round the now disused 'H' blocks.

Sue Martin, Maureen Martin, Margaret Purcell, Cliodhna and Gordy Purcell Smyth are the great friends who helped me in my travels and travails, responding sympathetically to my questions. Sue converted a hangover into a performance on a rainy day in August in the South of France. Sue, you are the best.

With thanks to my family and close friends for listening. Janet Bass, Jim Body, Fiona Burles, Leslie and Vera Dean, Marie Doig, Denise Dunbar Dean, Rob Dunbar, Sophie Harman, Eric and Carol Houseknecht, Babar Javed, Jason and Mirian Lamberth, Catherine and Paul Lyons, Claire Potter, Iris Soan, Bette Waller.

Mes chers amis, Nicole Vilhem, Raymond Guisano et Brigitte Dutouquet, je vous remercie pour votre gentillesse surtout envers les gosses, aussi que leurs parents.

My love and thanks to Beryl and Tim for kissing the Blarney stone together before I was born. You know it's always for you.

With thanks to Gill Coleridge and Lucy Luck and the rest of the team at RCW.

Simon & Schuster/Scribner have given me their dedicated support; Nigel Stoneman and Rochelle Venables in particular. Thanks for everything.

I need to specifically acknowledge the enormous contribution of my editor Ben Ball to the writing of this. His judgement moves ahead of mine, and is of stunning exactitude and insight. I am so grateful.

John, this book has wrought change in our lives. Thank you for hanging on in there, and for the world's finest support system; the kettle on the go, bangers on the barbie, the pop of the cork at six. I love you.

I have been absent from my home and from my beloved children, Jules, Cassien and Elsa Rose and I'm sorry for it. This writing, this book, none of it is without cost. In here is our story, too.

I hope that you will all find in here a kind of proof of love.

Lorgues, February 2005

Copyright permissions for reproduced lyrics:

Scribner

Becoming Strangers
Louise Dean

'I didn't know whether to laugh or cry. In the end, I
was so uplifted, I did both'
Julie Myerson, *Guardian*

Jan and Annemieke are going on their last holiday
together. Thirty years their senior, Dorothy and
George are on one of their first.

When these four people meet on an island in the
Caribbean, they find more than an escape from their
daily existence. They discover that it's not too late to
save the rest of their lives.

'Both page turning and heartbreaking . . . one of
the books of the year'
Independent

ISBN 0-7432-4000-6
PRICE £6.99